NOTES FROM
A BLACK
WOMAN'S
DIARY

NOTES FROM A BLACK WOMAN'S DIARY

SELECTED WORKS OF KATHLEEN COLLINS

KATHLEEN COLLINS

An Imprint of HarperCollinsPublishers

FIRST EDITION

Designed by Suet Yee Chong

Library of Congress Cataloging-in-Publication Data has been applied for.

ISBN 978-0-06-280095-4

19 20 21 22 23 LSC 10 9 8 7 6 5 4 3 2 1

CONTENTS

FOREWORD

It is tempting to get out of the way and let a voice like Kathleen Collins's introduce itself: start at the opening line "She came in while I was recording and asked to listen to every Nina Simone album in the house," and it will likely be a very long time before you are willing to part with this book or be pulled away from the richness and sense of forward motion Collins puts on the page. Readers coming to this work familiar with Collins's films or previously published work will already be aware of her many singular gifts; readers who are new to her work are lucky to begin discovering them here. This collection includes previously unpublished fiction, nonfiction, plays, and screenplays, including the screenplay for Collins's important and celebrated film *Losing Ground*. It is an important text for scholars, artists, and any reader seeking the pleasure of discovering a distinct and profoundly important writer.

I came to Collins's work as a fiction writer preoccupied with interiority, namely the gulf between the public self and the private self that creates the narrative tension in every kind of story we might tell. Like Collins, I am specifically interested in the ways that this gulf is fraught or policed for black women, given the particular ways in which we are often silenced or misheard, the particular structural forces that may compel us to perform or acquiesce. To my mind then, the greatest marvel of Collins's writing is that she is a magician in her use of interiority: she can slip just underneath a moment of tension barely noticed by those in the world of the story and give us a character's entire interior life, but she is also a master of the moments when the interior becomes exterior, when all pretense drops away and the unsayable is given words and said out loud.

It is a privilege to see this tremendous gift at work across multiple forms and genres. The distinct eye that audiences have for some time been able to see in her work as a director carries over into her work as a prose writer—she has a filmmaker's instinct for when to pause the narrative, when to linger in a moment. The pleasure of seeing this sensibility at play in fiction is that readers can watch Collins inhabit the same moment from multiple perspectives and be dazzled, not only by her ability to know when to back up and show the scene again, but also by the sharp clarity of the voices she puts on the page and the way they layer a scene to make it feel new and more complete when revisited. It is rare for an artist to be so talented in forms that ask such different things, but it is a wonder to see them all in action.

"One never talks out loud without wishing for an audience," a character in one of Collins's plays says, but this work understands how fraught and complicated the wish for an audience can be, how much ground can immediately be lost in the space between speaking and being heard. The question of what it means to have, to want, or to acknowledge an audience is explored with nuance throughout this text. Collins deftly portrays many of the ways in which black women can be at once watched and unseen, as well as the possibility of spaces to render a woman invisible and the hurt that engenders. Her exploration of the differences among being unabashedly yourself, performing a self, and reaching those alarming moments when the distinction is no longer quite so clear is sophisticated and provocative and as relevant today as it was when these stories were written.

Collins understands acutely the forces that pressure African American characters toward what we now call "respectability politics," and she renders with sympathy and gentle satire those characters who would enforce them, while freeing herself to let her own work ignore any constraints such politics would place upon it. "Colored people don't talk about sex . . . you ever notice that . . . they are so exposed in this life they are unwilling to admit to further undressing . . ." one of Collins's characters says, but the tender truth of this observation for some of her characters can coexist with frank discussion of sex from others. Collins isn't afraid to put sex on the page, to let her characters be sensual, bawdy, and vulgar when they need to be. That willingness to let the characters she writes be exposed in all of their truths and desires, even as she understands the ways concealment can be a necessary survival strategy, is at the center of this work's complexity and timelessness. These are the protagonists I wanted to be reading all my life: black women who are artists and intellectuals, both struggling and not; black families fumbling through the private truths of public grief; black women who chafe at the ways their proscribed paths would confine them, but are sometimes lonely in the alternative spaces they build, or daunted by the possibility of imagining them; black women willing to risk exposure, but still in search of those who are equally willing to really look at them. Collins is a writer who never flinches from the difficult things or from the most difficult version of the self.

It is a marvel, too, to have access to not only Collins's created worlds, but to some of her notes and letters, which give insight to her process and preoccupations. In "Notes from a Black Woman's Diary," after a candid and complicated note attempting to locate her project as an artist, Collins concludes, "Instead of dealing with race I went in search of love . . . and what I found was a very hungry colored lady." That hunger to be loved—to be loved even while seeing clearly the ways in which love might be flimsy, or fleeting, or deceitful, or simply not, in the end, enough—is just beneath the surface of so much of this work. The love of not just romantic partners, but parents, stepparents, strangers who seem to see each other with a momentary clarity— these loves are illuminated here in writing willing to bring the reader to the center of the moments of connection and disconnection, of disappointment and wonder, that mark people and make them who they are.

Later in her notes, Collins writes of a conversation after a friend's husband's suicide: "Death marks the end of living in the future." It is hard to read her words about facing the loss of future possibilities without thinking about all the possibilities lost to her early death to cancer: what other work there might have been, what her longer presence with us as an artist and teacher would have meant to another generation of artists and readers. Mercifully, because we have so much of Collins's previously unpublished work left to explore, it isn't true in her case that death has kept her work from having a future or kept new readers from discovering its continuing possibilities. It is a joy to see this work brought into the growing canon of women's voices we might have lost, and an honor to introduce it to a new audience.

—Danielle Evans

EDITOR'S NOTE

My mother employed a few stylistic quirks that I was not comfortable editing out, which you will notice throughout your reading: she loved the ellipsis and was also fond of using boldface and underlining for certain words or phrases, presumably for emphasis.

—Nina Lorez Collins

I

STORIES

"SCAPEGOAT CHILD"

1

In the crucible of our family my sister burned like molten steel. Once I saw her arms outspread her legs hanging limp and useless wet saliva dripping from her tongue. I screamed they surrounded her lifted her onto the sheets where she convulsed for hours traces of stain and guilt shattering her face my sister my sister cunning participant spectator victim inside the ugly family circle.

Her name was Josephine. No shortening to a rounder, softer sound like Josie or Jo was ever allowed her name was Josephine. Wide eyes alert for trouble a mouth that protruded too far lips too full for comfort. A skinny knock-kneed girl who stared so hard one day her eyes crossed locked and the full lips took on a slight tremor.

Her room was on the top floor a tiny place with a wooden ceiling that stared down at her. Yellow roses on her bedspread. A shiny dark floor at her feet. In the mornings she came to life early pounced awake before us ran to perch outside our door.

Her thin little legs hop out of bed eyes crossed alert she slips down the stairs in the morning stillness. We are all asleep while she listens and waits. Who will greet her when the door opens who will smile give up the first of their morning love? Our father trips over her thin body on his way to the bathroom. Through the crack in the door she watches our slow momma fall on her knees to pray.

She sits and waits. No one comes to lift her in their arms. The day is over. But tomorrow she will begin again, early early even earlier.

At breakfast she will not eat. Her head falls back eyes disappear deep inside their sockets while we watch. An angry mob of three we watch and wait. Then she comes back slowly her head comes forward eyes slip back into place she giggles a silly burble that pushes her lips out too far. Then our father sends her reeling a hard slap with all his might until the burble is gone she sits staring cross-eyed at the three of us a twisted smile pushing out her lips.

The day my father married my mother my sister was three years old. She trotted to the ceremony on skinny wings a beaky little bird pinned down by other memories, an earlier womb ancient kisses that sent her to bed and woke her up. Perched high on ancient shoulders she watched our father join himself to the pretty woman with the long old maid's eyes the stiff cheeks and black hair piled high high high on her head. A balmy September day bright blue with trees and sky and little Josephine sitting atop her perch like a beaky bird sniffing the air for an old melody a plumper rounder mommy once a plumper rounder mommy who sat by a window and died just sat by a window and died.

They lift her down she squeezes her skinny legs between our father's tall unbending frame climbing frantically to reach his face seek one last embrace before this balmy day tramples her to death. I had a mommy once didn't I have a mommy once. Nobody answers. The pretty lady with the black hair smiles a mute and frozen smile the skinny child is handed back to ancient arms that fold her one last time.

There is a room that lives in her memory large and blue where someone comes in at night to read to her. There is a cozy chair thick with cushions beside an open window and a glass for her to fetch water for the woman in the cozy chair. There is someone who says her name Jo . . . se . . . phine it has a laugh in it warm eyes a lap rocking back and forth. There is . . . she sits up, spitefully awake a tiny hawk quivering on the edge of memory, where death confusion a host of uneasy comings and goings plague her, whispering women who stroked her hair a father with a shamed broken face a flight of steps she climbed on all fours nimbly up and down up and down she would not be still slipping in and out where grief reigned her shrill little arms hopping up and down.

The lady with the black hair puts her to bed. Are you my new mommy she asks are you my new mommy while a wooden ceiling stares down at her yellow roses drift in and out the window she stares at the lady with the pretty cheeks are you my new mommy she asks and the lady frowns a scolding look comes into her eyes I'm your mommy she answers her cheeks are tight the eyes too round. The child will not be still she squirms in the cold bed you're my new mommy she asks my new new mommy holding tight to the silent blue room the face that asks for a glass of water you're my new mommy she squirms her shrill little body will not be still.

2

Over against this tale is another: about the pretty lady with the high cheekbones about the shamefaced man with the tall unbending frame about love and the acting out of only the rituals of love about loss and grief and the old maid's eyes in the pretty woman's face and the sense of shame in the tall man's eyes. A family tale stretching its wiry elusive fingers backward and forward until it finally reaches out to the skinny little girl in her top-floor room.

The pretty lady's name is Letitia. She was thirty-eight when she came to mother the squirming child. Lace collars framed her round face with the too-round eyes her dresses were dark things that grated as she walked she had the bearing of a Sunday school teacher a rigidity that fluttered beneath the bright gracious smile the sweet voice that trilled up and down something stone-faced, an old maid's current already fixed immutable behind the well-meaning smile.

Letitia's mother's name was Sadie a big-boned woman with thick plaits hanging down her back silent eyes like an Indian's. Her father's name was Hood he drank too much spent years beside his spitoon chewing tobacco and shrinking further further inside a drunken shell. She had one sister, Lavinia, a tiny slice brittle to look at frail hysterical attached to Letitia like an ant to an oak tree.

The tall unbending man is Roland. He was thirty-two to her thirty-eight. Six years balanced by grief a squirming child a newborn infant. Six years a distance held in check by his persuasive manner. He presented himself well handsome, strict in his bearing a strong argumentative tone in his voice. Beneath the smooth-riding surface was chaos pure unaccountable chaos a swarming beehive of fury and grief.

His father's name was Jeremy a nearsighted madman raging against his five sons storms that demolished the house scattered the children left a hollow wailing at the center of each of them. His mother, Ella, was a large woman with thick mahogany hair scooped tight in a bun. Stern, implacable, an immovable object at the center of Jeremy's myopic lashings.

All these folk are Negroes what dark brooding what hopeless feelings underpin the already cruel family landscape who can say but all these folk are Negroes.

Death fits in the picture a handsome woman with no trace of sternness a cool smile on her lips and brow death fits in the picture the abrupt cessation of a sweet potent struggle with life death fits in the picture and a momma a momma God in Heaven bless the seamless connection of a momma.

3

It's Josephine we chose to carry our wounds grow cross-eyed burbled confused pins sticking out from all sides it's Josephine we chose with her shrill cries and gestures her convulsive goings-on it's Josephine we chose.

Wound tighter than a drum beating the air with her fists she screams for our father Daddy she screams I don't want to take a nap don't make me take a nap a hollow flapping of wings to beat away his absence beat away the round eyes that stare and wait I don't want to take a nap she screams her little wings convulse out of one crossed eye she watches I don't want to take a nap she screams the round eyes turn to stone only pain is left she wishes she could be still only pain is left she wishes she could be still.

Instead she yelps flaps her wings ceremonies dance in her head Letitia becomes the injured party.

The house is quiet sunlight wanders in and out the baby sleeps. Josephine climbs out of bed to watch it this tiny thing silent and still she takes its hand its little fingers move back and forth she touches its face the little eyes do not open she climbs into the crib nestles her squirming body beside the still flesh free of memory and sleeps.

Who watches over a new lady in stiff dresses pretty red lips round eyes dim and lackluster she moves from room to room up and down the corridors of a new house broken off from the past. A new lady watches over unaccustomed to children to our father's boisterous presence to strange rooms free of Sadie and Hood. A new lady watches over a thin grating when she walks a sweetened whisper when she talks a new lady watches over dull patina for our glossy hysteria.

The house is quiet. Josephine sleeps beside the still baby, Letitia sits crocheting in the afternoon sun. The front door opens before he can cross the threshold Josephine comes to life slips screaming down the stairs into his arms. Roland looks. Letitia comes to the doorway. The child begins to do things her eyes begin to roll her head bobs back and forth the child begins to do things. Roland looks. Letitia stands in the doorway. The child keeps doing things sticks out her tongue shrieks and quivers like a useless monkey the child keeps doing things. Roland looks. Letitia stands in the doorway. The child keeps doing things sticks out her tongue shrieks and quivers like a useless monkey the child keeps doing things. Roland looks. Letitia stands in the doorway. The child keeps doing things a tiny cauldron growing bright before their eyes Roland reaches out lifts her in his arms carries her up to her room. The baby is awake he shuts the door sits down on the yellow roses begins to speak a mother was needed a mother his face crumples guilt and grief control him a mother was needed a mother he begins to cry. The room is still Josephine stops her squirming, at ease at last behind the closed door, drifting inside his familiar smell of grief and misunderstanding at ease at last in this petrified place where just the three of them may go only the three of them may go.

4

Wounded in her body she carried our pain wars were fought a bloody field emerged wounded in her body she carried our pain darting in and out of the shadows like a small soldier.

Nothing grew between Letitia and Roland. Walls went up the house locked from the inside nothing moved. All motion came from Josephine. Thumb stuck to her lips her body twitching all motion came from Josephine.

She was always underfoot turning herself into a smoke screen of nervous faults and failings, a weeding ground that we could rake and pull.

She was always underfoot in the heat of battle she would fight on both sides help the terrified Letitia to her feet pummel Roland's advancing body with her tight little fists.

She was always underfoot a squirming reminder of dead memories and dreams.

Then one day she burst. Her little legs flew apart her stubborn little arms took to the sky her head rattled and shook her overworked eyes fled from their sockets a sudden restless wind was blowing her apart too many wars had been fought on her soil too many wars had been fought on her soil she would not be still. Together they must pin her down. The pretty lady with the stiff eyes the warm daddy connected backward in time. Together they must pin her down their uneasy union will jell in her body.

"NINA SIMONE"

She came in while I was recording and asked to listen to every Nina Simone album in the house. I was just about to introduce the next side: "How 'bout a little Herbie Hancock now, with George Coleman on tenor sax, Ron Carter on bass, Tony Williams on drums, and, of course, Herbie on piano . . . that's right: 'Maiden Voyage' . . ."

Which puts us around 1965. And puts her in a pageboy with bangs. Light-skinned. Nice eyes.

I took her to lunch at Frank's. Found out she was a Pisces, too. Nice eyes. Nice teeth. She was writing an article on Nina so we talked a lot about that, how much she dug her and all. Then she walked me back to the studio and I told her I'd put together all the albums we had.

The next time she came I picked up something childish about her and I knew she was married white. Something too wide-eyed. She helped me put together the albums for my show and we joked around a lot. She had good legs.

She sat through my whole show laughing at the way I signal the record start, so I almost missed a lot of cues. She had a heavy laugh almost out of character with that naive face. We had a good time.

She drove me home and I asked her to come in.

My husband and I had been together almost a year and a half when I decided to become a writer. I thought I should start with essays and articles because that would be the best way to develop a style. I was a real Nina Simone fan so I thought, Why not do an article on Nina Simone? I'll go up to Harlem to the big jazz station and do my research and try to sell it to one of the music magazines. I was very excited and went up to the station the next day.

I ended up in one of the recording studios by accident. And he grinned at me. It was such a broad grin, while all the time he was reading from the back of a record cover—". . . and, of course, Herbie on piano . . . that's right: 'Maiden Voyage' . . ."—and his finger seemed to glide through the air to signal the man in the other booth to start the record.

"What can I do for you, young lady?" he asked in that same smooth voice.

I told him that I was doing a story on Nina Simone and that I wanted to listen to every Nina Simone album in the house. He grinned. And soon after we were walking up 125th Street to lunch. I was starving. He asked when my birthday was and we found out we were born a week apart. His voice was so smooth. I told him I was married. But I didn't tell him my husband was white.

He told me to come back on Saturday and I could listen to the records.

It was raining the next time I came. He was busy selecting the albums for his show, so I helped him. He teased me a lot.

I was wearing a yellow mini with new sandals and I felt very free. Until I thought about my husband; then I felt uncomfortable.

I sat through all of his show and teased him so much that several times he almost said the wrong thing or almost forgot to make an announcement on time. It was fun.

When I drove him home he asked me to come in.

I didn't like being married but I was happy with her. Color never had much part in it, I don't think. She was very fair anyway and very middle class in her attitudes. But there wasn't anything pretentious about her. She radiated a beautiful kind of enthusiasm for life.

She had this great idea to do a piece on Nina Simone. I'd always encouraged her to write and I thought it was great she was beginning to start projects on her own. I suggested she go up to Harlem to the jazz station and get hold of all Nina's records.

When she came back she was so excited and described in great detail how she watched this smooth dude run his show, how he took her to lunch and promised to dig out all Nina's albums for her.

We'd been together about a year and I don't think the idea of another man had ever entered her head. She was very idealistic and believed in love as something exclusive. I know I was like a god for her.

But this little encounter had awakened a kind of friskiness I'd never seen before. You could almost see her wagging her tail. It was very cute and appealing, and I fell even more in love with her.

Then one night she came home looking odd and jumpy.

I was sharing a friend's apartment at the time. My wife and I had just split up. My friend was watching the ball game in the living room, so the only place for us to talk was in the bedroom.

I looked through a stack of records I had in the corner, trying to find some more old Nina Simone albums, while she sat on the bed and watched. She had on a cute mini. She kept looking at me. We kept looking at each other, really. I started teasing her about how all Pisces can read each other's mind because we're the most far-out people in the zodiac. She smiled.

I looked at her . . . And I wanted her so bad. It came down on me like that.

I told her that the best person for a Pisces was probably another Pisces, because we are impossible people to understand, being that we are basically mystics and know more about life than most people. She smiled.

I knew she could feel it. I could tell. Her eyes got too wide and she couldn't stop smiling.

A big fat man was watching television when we came in. He was stripped to the waist and his stomach was hanging out.

We went into the bedroom where there was a white bedspread. He started looking through his album collection to see if he had any more of Nina's old albums. I sat down on the bed.

He told me that I had Pisces eyes. Even off the air his voice was still this wonderful smooth thing.

He found one of her early albums and handed it to me. I looked at him. And then this feeling took over my vagina. I couldn't believe it! I *couldn't* be feeling this for someone else. I wanted him really badly. My insides hurt.

———

I wanted to know if they'd made love. That's all I wanted to know. It was killing me. She looked so lost and uncertain. I just wanted her to tell me if they had or not. I reassured her that it wouldn't change anything, that I wouldn't love her any less, but would she just please tell me what happened.

Finally she did. And it was nothing, really. She admitted wanting to and how that had really surprised her that she could want anybody besides me. She was still pretty shook up over it. But she ran before anything could happen.

I know that's when I began to love her less. I'd wanted her to have him. I'd wanted her to come back all frisky and playful and let me take her after him. But she ran before anything could happen.

Pretty soon after that it was over for me.

"RASCHIDA"

She was tall and thin. Her face reminded you of violet orchids on a thin gauze party dress. Her eyes never moved and her lips barely parted. She lived on the first floor of a Brooklyn brownstone near Prospect Park. Alone. Making quilts and cooking Brunswick stew.

You came into a roomy sit-down kitchen with windows overlooking a backyard. Trees. Sunlight in the afternoon. A hardwood floor. Oval windows facing a Brooklyn street. A corduroy couch. Two wicker chairs. A floor-to-ceiling three-way light fixture. A rubber plant. A Princess telephone.

The chicken was melting. The tomatoes were peeled. Hot peppercorns floated in the cool potatoes and the okra sputtered its seeds into the hot oil. Twelve ears of corn waited to be shaved. She made good Brunswick stew. She had just finished a black-blue-maroon quilt. She was nineteen.

"Raschida, there's this new boy here from Kenya. He wants to fuck me. Can we use your bed? Leave some ice cream. He likes to eat ice cream after he fucks."

She shaved the corn and thought about Domilie. She

would beg him to be gentle, saying she had a soft womb. Then she inserted it herself. Carefully. And instructed him how to move . . . come in low . . . keep coming . . . there . . . don't move. Then she would lift her legs and pull him in farther. Don't move. Her legs made circles in the air. Push. Her legs were like scissors cutting the air. Push. Push. Her legs and arms began to flail. Beating his back. Push. Straight ahead. PUSH. PUSH. PUSH. A hail of screams shook the air. Her legs collapsed. Pushing him out.

She finished shaving the corn. Deposited the mass of wilted tomatoes, wilted potatoes, sputtered okra, and peppercorns into the boneless flesh of the chicken.

She had an 11:30 appointment at Les Joy Coiffures. They were going to cut her hair short with long bangs down to her eyes . . .

On the way home she passed Norma Jean's Outlet and bought a pair of maroon shorts and a lavender silk blouse. She came in looking furtive. And expectant. Her eyes peeping out from under the bangs.

"Raschida, you cut your hair! You don't look the same. This is Gerard. The stew is very good and the quilt is beautiful. We just used it," she said. Giggling.

"Gerard just arrived today, from Kenya. Do you want some ice cream? We just had ours," she said. Giggling.

"Where did you get that blouse and those shorts? I didn't know you liked clothes. We ate two quarts of banana marshmallow. There's another quart in the refrigerator. Maybe Gerard will eat some more," she said. Giggling.

Raschida took out the ice cream. Gerard smiled. Raschida began to eat. Gerard smiled. He was angular and bony.

"Your hair looks good. Who did it? Caroline? She cut it well. And whose idea was it to give you those bangs? I think Gerard wants some more ice cream," she said. Laughing.

Raschida served him and they finished off the last quart of banana marshmallow.

"Gerard liked your Brunswick stew. He said it tastes like Kenyan food. He ate two bowls. Before . . ." she said. Laughing.

"How many quilts have you made? I told Gerard this was your tenth quilt in a year. You've been here a year, right? And I've used every one of them," she said. Laughing.

"Show them to Gerard. Come on. They're all stacked up in the closet. Take them down. Look, Gerard, look at that one all covered with roses. Oh, that goes back a long time. I remember that one, and the old one covered with daisies. Like you were doing it in the grass. Where's the winter one, Raschida? With all the snow and the little fireplaces in velvet. And where's the summer one, with the little pools of water all over it? All blue. Can't she make quilts, Gerard?"

"Lie down on this one, Raschida. See how it matches your blouses. Lie down next to Raschida, Gerard. What was that noise? Did I fart again? I farted? I'm sorry. It must be all the Brunswick stew on top of the ice cream on top of . . ."

Why don't you make a love quilt, Raschida? Show her how to make a love quilt, Gerard. Take your thing out and show her how to make a love quilt. No, Raschida. He'll take off your pants. Let him take off your pants. And your blouse. Doesn't she look cute with those bangs, Gerard? Oh, Raschida, you're tiny! I didn't know you were so tiny! Look at those little nubs on you. Little rosebuds, Gerard. Aren't they like rosebuds? How do they feel, Gerard? Like little rosebuds? Oh, Raschida, I'm shivering. What was that noise? Did I fart again? I'm sorry. Isn't he big, Raschida? Look how big he is. Oh, Raschida. I'm shivering. He's so big. How did he ever get inside me, Raschida? Did I put you inside me? How is anything that big going to get inside you, Raschida?

Oh, Gerard, I'm shivering. Don't touch her like that. She's wet, isn't she? Oh, Raschida, your hair looks so cute with these bangs coming down to your eyes. She's wet, isn't she, Gerard? And her little nipples just fit between your lips. Oh, Gerard, I'm shivering.

He wants to see if you're moist enough, Raschida. Relax. He's very big. You have to be moist or else it will hurt. Oh, Gerard, are you going to put it in now? Take it in your hands, Raschida. Make him take his time. Hold it. Put it in yourself. Make him take his time. Put the tip in, baby. Feel the tip? Just put the tip inside a little bit. Oh yes, Raschida. Isn't that nice? I'm shivering. Relax your hands, Raschida. Let him move in now. Don't push, Gerard. Oh, please don't push. Oh, Gerard, look at your ass moving into her. Open your legs, Raschida. Open them. He's coming in now. Oh, Gerard, your ass is tightening up. Let him move in now. Let him move in now, Raschida. Don't try to stop him, Raschida. I'm shivering. Don't try to stop him. Don't stop him. His ass is tightening up. Push, Gerard. Don't stop, Raschida. Take him. Oh God, I'm farting. Excuse me. I'm farting. Raschida, take him. Raschida, he's moving fast now. Raschida, take him, take him, take him. Oh God, take him, woman. Oh God, I'm farting. Excuse me. I'm farting. He's there, isn't he? Look at your legs, Raschida. He's in so far you can't control your legs. Oh God. Oh God, Jesus. Let him have you. Let him have you. Oh, Gerard. Oh, Gerard. Oh Jesus, Gerard, I'm coming with you. Coming with you. Oh Jesus, Gerard.

II

NOVEL EXCERPT: "LOLLIE"

EXCERPT FROM AN UNFINISHED NOVEL: "LOLLIE: A SUBURBAN TALE"

ANDREW BEGINS

I met Lollie on a clear day when you could see forever. R brought her to the house. She was his chosen demo queen. The best, he bragged. She could make a good song suck pussy and a bad one piss gold, he boasted with extravagant noises, a lot of finger-popping and strutting around the room (behavior, by the way, that he exhibited only around us). If you met R in the street you'd swear he was the last of a long line of bourgeois Negroes, a tightfisted little brown man out to prove himself to the world. He even dressed the part: spiffy bow tie clipped nattily in place, oxford shoes polished to a highfalutin shine, hair slicked down via the old stocking cap, of course glasses—thick-framed myopic lenses that only the nearsighted can't live without. They take me for a scholar, he would boast, speaking of the world in general, his public, a ghostly army of folk he felt he should impress for no precise reason other than that it was the colored thing to do: impress folk whoever wherever whatever they may be. This unwritten code of black living he obeyed like a soldier trained to salute.

Lollie shook everybody's hand, a formal gesture that was one of her signatures. She reached out, held your hand firmly, just long enough to communicate that she lived on unflinching ground. Then she smiled. Let her eyes light up the rest of her face. And waited for someone to make the next move. Which Marsha did, or Emma, or Janice. I can't recall. I just remember that she was swooped away in a minute, led out of my sight faster than I could bear. That I hung back on the steps indecisively. It was not my policy to mingle openhandedly in the racket and noise of family goings-on. I stuck pretty much to my study until around dinnertime, when the call of gossip and intrigue got the better of me.

Just as I was climbing the steps she came back for her pocketbook. I need a cigarette, she said (out loud, though not especially to me). Music makes me want to smoke, she added. Then smiled. And walked sloppily out of my sight with an awkward gait that I recognized as one of her signatures—a zigzagging through space as if she were avoiding bumping into things . . . felt things that crowded the air and kept her from walking a straight line. It was then that I knew she could sing. Not because of R's boastful prelude, not because I knew shit about music, but because of the way she walked, treading a line that said life can get out of hand, go haywire and blow up in your face. I could read in that precarious zigzagging across space the uneasy notes that would make her voice something distinct. It was just a feeling. A writer backing an artistic hunch. I went upstairs and shut the door.

Few sounds reach as far as my tower in the sky, where I alone preside over one eccentric room. Books lie about in stacked piles, a gray metal desk sits in the middle looking broad and ugly. Cardboard boxes abound. It's a dumb room. I apologize for describing it—descriptive writing is not my cup of tea. But that room was a source of much family contention: Janice especially mocked it for its lack of atmosphere. She wanted it lined with wall-to-wall bookcases, mahogany furniture, paintings—all of which would add a musty odor of authorship to the place. The room angered her, much as I anger her with my flabby stance. Oh God, she's likely to exclaim, don't get me started on his muddled way of doing things, it makes my blood boil and spurt. For instance, take his homebody thing. He thinks that staying put is wisdom. It's one of his serious but confused notions that one gets to the same place by not moving at all! Oh God, it makes me want to send a swift one flying up his ass. All this driveling he does about home and hearth! His whole artistic stance is built on failures, characters who never evolve, a host of shlimazl-like types who never get anywhere. In his menagerie, there are failed writers, failed blacks, failed husbands, failed lovers, failed TV producers. Failure reeks from every page! And then he turns these specimen into heroes as if failure were a kind of hip Sony Walkman that the loser takes out while he strolls aimlessly along, making fun of those who play faster, coarser games with life. At least they play! The wimp! How can I stand up to life and admit I married a wimp! And she'd collapse in a fit of laughter, struck down by my inertia hovering and laying claim to her energy.

By the time I came down Lollie was gone. To rave reviews. To all of them oohing and aahing on her behalf. You should have heard her, Janice said, poking me in the arm, you should have come down for once from that dumb tower of yours. It's not often that a voice like that comes knocking at our door, and where were you but hiding up there dissecting words. She's the best.

Andrew, R threw in for good measure, she makes my

songs shine, and he speared another lamb chop, greedy and high on his tunes.

Don't you love the sound of her name? Emma mused. It rolls around the tongue like music. There should be shrines built to such a voice, Saint Lollie of the Golden Tones. Poppa, why are there no saintly distinctions for those who feed life with beauty? Are they not also the Saint Teresas of the world? When Lollie sings, I feel reverent, my heart cries aloud! Don't laugh at your dear rational Em, I mean what I say. I swear to you that when Lollie was singing a biblical understanding gripped me in the center of my chest, I felt the world as a deep abiding place, myself as someone alive forever! Stop laughing, all of you, stop that indecent guffawing at my expense! And don't make any of your boastful comments, R, about how black people carry around life's soul, while white people feed off the crumbs. This is no ordinary white family you've dropped in on, and you've already stayed long enough to cut out the racial con games. Lollie can sing, whether or not her skin is a true part of the equation. She's got a voice that grips the soul, a voice that makes me chilly and confused. I can feel it in my chest like the colors of the rainbow. And she laughed with a husky defiance that surprised all of us.

I don't like to hear you talk like that, Marsha said slowly, you never talk like that, you talk about law and order and justice, you talk about aiding and abetting the poor, about changing the system to include the defenseless and the weak. You never talk about God or rainbows. That woman hypnotized you, took away your concrete mind. Only Momma can talk that way and be full of truth. Lollie. I never heard of anybody called Lollie. It's a suspicious-sounding name. I won't be fooled by anyone called Lollie. Lollie. It scares me. Then she looked around as if she didn't recognize us anymore. What's happened? The spell is broken! What we had is gone gone gone! And she began to weep uncontrollably.

Janice got up quickly to comfort her, folded her in her arms while we looked on, bewildered.

Marsha saw the whole thing the moment Lollie stepped through the door. Saw it the way a child confronts danger and begs God to make it disappear, saw it the way Janice would have seen it if she'd spread out her cards, done a Celtic Cross on me. She would have seen the Tower cross my King of Swords, the World reversed, the Ten of Cups reversed, betrayal and disruption screaming out at us, while one earth-bound spirit who could only be me retrenched deeper and deeper inside himself.

ANDREW LETS JANICE SPEAK

What is this, my chance to harangue? The rejected wife gets to have her say? You are too generous, with the kind and overbearing manners of a schmuck. You remember everything. No detail escapes that prurient mind of yours (I've picked up a few literary turns of the screw in all our years of cohabitational exile). It's just like you to give me my say in this seemingly open gesture, like the good boy that you are, holding out your hands for a slap on the wrists.

All right, let's say I agree to play by the rules and make it a good story. After all, you've stolen many a tale from me, straight from the horse's mouth. Most of it, of course, I'd sworn never to reveal, a psychiatrist's brain being a store-house of tales. But you had an uncanny way of wangling scraps and pieces, just enough to rebuild your always sinking dam of tales. I used to warn our friends, our enemies, who-ever stopped at our table for an hour's affectionate stroking. Watch out for Andrew, he's all ears and antennae, don't let slip any hint of private times or he'll turn you into a story, an unexpected tale that mirrors all your flaws. I gave this warning indiscriminately to the thin and helpless, the sleek and well-fed, even to those disarming little waifs who straggled in behind the children. No stray soul was exempt from your literary designs, and ours was, as you surely remember, a house full of strays. The merest hint of distress, and we opened our doors wide, played Mother and Father Superior to the poor assembled. I wish to speak of only one such creature (knowing your just and generous spirit, you would, I'm sure, allow me to drift down any anecdotal stream, but I'm playing by the rules, a strict unflabby tale is my goal, as it has been yours every day of that horizontal life). R I feel compelled to speak about. R who arrived just as the seams in our well-knit little drama were about to come undone. Up until then I have to admit we were having a pretty good time, kept up a lively chorus, between ourselves and the children, that had all the markings of a good jazz combo. You played the inveterate straight man, a perfect foil for our foolishness, our comic bits. And I . . . I do feel the need to describe myself. After all, this piece is not a solo sung for you alone. I'm in it up to my ears, and this is how I see myself . . . a trim little piece with an edgy voice and a loud laugh—my outstanding trait. It was forever embarrassing you with its raucous overtones—too sexual, especially for a woman who did not give it up easily and who would have preferred not to have to give it up at all. The juicy needs of sex, all that slipping and sliding, fell on a deaf body and sent you tripping over your own stiff needs, until they fell into a kind of literary stupor, where food, wine, a crowded dialogue with children and other interesting strays, dulled your true desire to *get some*. Not that you didn't eventually do that. That is, after all, what we're coming to. The whole point of this leaden tale is all about your finally getting some and ripping apart the seams of that easy rhythm we were dancing to.

But don't rush me. It was, as I was saying, a cozy little scene with ample room for each of our insanities: your sullen need to stroke out the perfect tale, my vulgar foraging around in other people's insides, our children's happy coddling of themselves and others inside that soft, indulgent atmosphere. To say that we were *sacredly vulgar,* not only with each other but with the strangers who crossed our doorstep, is a truly fine way of putting it. It characterizes to perfection that careless mix of lazy but welcoming vibes that attracted so many odd souls to our door.

Something like that. Some vibrant metaphor. I leave it in your hands to shape and polish. I do the rough draft, you do the polishing. It was the basis of our whole act, a kind of sloppy teamwork we settled on early in the game. Whenever your mother came (speaking of sloppy souls), I used to play advance man for your act. I'd meet her at the train station (you didn't drive, which was also your excuse for not accompanying me). Just as I'd flung my arms wide, begun the role of exuberant daughter-in-law, she'd brush past me, fasten herself to the nearest porter. I'm looking for someone they call my daughter-in-law, I'd hear her say. I have no memory for faces, all I've been told is hearsay, my son says she's Jewish, I have no idea what Jews look like. Can you point her out to me? Gritting my teeth, I'd advance upon her. Momma, what a pleasure to have found you! Who is this woman? she'd ask the porter. She acts as if she knows me, yet nowhere in my pictures have I ever snapped that face. I've cut my hair! I'd shout. It must be difficult to recognize a daughter-in-law who's changed her style, but wait, I'll show you my picture, taken last month when Roberto turned six! Then I'd slip out the photograph, move her surreptitiously forward under the porter's watchful gaze. Look at Roberto, Momma, look how he's grown! Surely your grandson remains a visual speck on that otherwise blurred landscape! And I'd shove her in the car and take off in a flash.

The children would come flying out to greet her. Momma Em, our grandma, flesh of Poppa's flesh, spirit of his spirit! They were smart little elves, always reaching out to touch the core of our lives—insinuating their way down to the bottoms of our souls. In Heaven they must have made the connection that landed us together. Who are these people? your mother would shout. Where am I? You're at my house, Momma, you'd say, and laugh with exasperation, and try to move her memory forward beyond the day you left home. Only on occasion did she relent, agree to recognize you as her son. Then she'd gather the children about her, beginning some bewildering saga that took up most of the day. What a shiksa she was with her tales—flitting from one story to the next like a schizophrenic queen! All your stories come straight from your mother's breast, she weaned you forever on her queer imagination.

Enough already. I sound just like her, her Yiddish confusion has settled on my tongue. I no longer know who I am. It's your hovering that's done me in. *When it's time to say good-bye it's time to say good-bye,* crooned R in one of his many tributes to our lost vulgarity and joy. Oh, he could croon! Flatten himself to the keys, his fingers flying up and down! He had the bold flamboyance of a good emcee, the cool silver voice of Billy Eckstine, the homeless behavior of a rejected child. Perfect grist for my psychological mill is precisely how you put it (and as you well know, I did apply my very considerable skill on his behalf).

In truth, I was the family magician. Past present future wove a full and easy tapestry before my eyes. I could see (as you well know the gift has diminished, the trauma of your roaming shut down my sight). The children were quite proud of this and brought me many clients, poor diminished souls without a future or a past. Ask my momma what's in store, Marsha would say, she'll tell you everything. Speak to them. Momma, pass your hand across their faces and tell them what you see. Then she'd imitate me, lift her childish hands and make a circle. Oh, Momma, one day she shouted, I can see, too! There's nothing good ahead for him, he'll be dead before winter! Oh my God, Momma, I see his stiff body blowing in the breeze! And she screamed with all her might, ran from the room in a fit of terror, promised with all her heart and soul never again to imitate me. Roberto ignored my powers until late in the game (he's truly your son, a skeptical soul, gullible to a fault only when his own needs are involved). Enough already that you sniff around daily in people's insides, he'd say, why add insult to injury with psychic vibrations! But when he reached the age of macho charisma, and pretty young women camped outside our door, he'd slip into our bed in the middle of the night. Tell me, Momma, which one really loves me, which one only wants this stiff thing between my legs. I'm confused, Momma, love and romance are too much a mystery, open my eyes, Momma, so I can see.

Emma, of course, found all this amusing. Her wry sense of humor thrived on that sort of thing. As the least whimsical sibling, she'd made a definite decision to be contrary, as contrary as contrary can be. Never agree with whatever conclusion. Face life with defiance, an improbable stance. Everything must add up, Momma, she'd reproach me, your psychic contortions are pure energy flow. It's all math and science, don't think you're a priestess. From any point on a circle life is always the same. Remember that, Momma, don't let all these predictions go to your head, I won't have you thinking you stand out in a crowd. Emma, our Emma, the great leveler of the clan. Only she rebuked you and your sedentary ways. Why doesn't Poppa go out like other fathers, why this silly obsession with words on a page? And she'd give you the finger (a vulgar gesture, I agree, but who counted symbols when love was falling from trees?).

One day I said to you, You're about to get some! I see you riding some female body like a stallion in heat! And a vision of you romping and frolicking in bed danced before my eyes! You shrugged, grinned with slight indulgence as if the whole thing were really no concern of yours. *That's* your reaction when I tell you your future! You don't deserve to have a *thing* happen to you! And what about me? I wondered. Where will I be while you're screwing around? I turned on the camera in search of some picture that would show me myself. Nothing. A fog. Oh God, I've got no future. I'll be left alone, discarded and blurred!

Just then R arrives and the melody moves forward. He's been to an audition. How did it go, R? we ask. Do not ask needless questions, he says, and sighs, no one recognized me. I wish I could get R's way of speaking right (there I could use a little of your literary assistance, your writer's penchant for faking the truth). R talks like a musical grammarian, as if before there were words there were semicolons and commas, a whole army of punctuation that is more important. He's always looking for pauses, the brief hiatus where words hang. It's not surprising that what strikes you is not what he says. It all has a similar picky phraseology that doesn't ring true. What you watch in order to get at R is his expression, the appalling look of dismay that lives on his face.

For R *is* a black man (technically speaking he's a medium shade of brown). Cultural information of a more specific nature (whether he grew up on the block or in some elite suburb) is hard to come by. Where he'd been, what he'd been doing up until the day he knocked on our door, remains one of those mysteries time has refused to help solve. He referred to no one. No hardworking mother, no devoted aunt, no father. When questioned acutely as Emma was wont to do, he'd retreat into one chosen line, I'm without hindrance, and shut his mouth. That's ridiculous, Emma would counter, no one alive is unobstructed, the past is a shackle always pulling one down (she was in her "psychological" phase, toying on and off with the idea of following in her mother's magical footsteps)!

Even I have difficulties with R's seeming amnesia. From a psychiatric perspective it's an untenable position, not to mention the literary dead end it creates. What's a character without a past? Even if you were convinced that in those months and months of unorthodox analysis I unearthed a gold mine of family secrets that I kept to myself. Often at the dinner table you'd put out your customary feelers: How was Madame X? Was Señor Y feeling potent again? I'd throw out my usual tidbits, an evasive line about a new client's virginity, some bit of hilarity to get you off the track. But you kept right on sniffing, just as if you could smell R directly under my skin. One time I tried to fool you, made up a whole history for him on the spot: he grew up in Newark, New Jersey, in the Clinton Street Projects, a rough neighborhood knee-deep in poverty and dope. Then he went to some school of music and art, where his talents were refined, his sensibility appreciated, and he left Newark behind biting the proverbial dust. There was some disruption in his family. Murder. Suicide. Both are events he witnessed before the age of nine. There's a sister, too, the connection is incestuous, but I haven't pinned that down yet, it's just a guess.

Then I sat back on my laurels. You took a few puffs on

your pipe. You think that half-baked tale can slip by me? That's the kind of shit colored people repeat, they know full well whites want a rags-to-riches saga, or some rags-to-riches bullshit full of incest and dope. Stop this coy narrative bullshit (you have the foulest mouth in the whole of the Jewish kingdom) and hand over the real story!

Boy, did that make me giddy! I had you eating out of my hands for a few measly words! Look at your father, children, I shouted, the dope would kill for a brand-new tale! I was all but collapsed in a fit of weeping laughter.

All right already, since this is my final resting place in your memory it's not fair to withhold all the goodies from you. And I agree, the tête-à-têtes between R and myself are full of juicy tidbits that would make a ripe addition to your storehouse of tales. So I'll give you a sample hour between R and myself . . . I'M SITTING BEHIND MY DESK AT THE END OF THE DAY (the capitals are like stage directions—it's not so different, the analytical hour from a one-act play). R ARRIVES IN TRENCH COAT AND FRENCH BERET (he is full of symbolic clothing—vests, hats, baggy trousers—affirmations of another era, where he felt he belonged). HE TAKES OFF HIS FRENCH BERET, SMOOTHES HIS HAIR DOWN TO EXAGGERATED SLEEKNESS. HE IS NOT EXACTLY HANDSOME. HIS FACE IS TOO ANXIOUS. THERE IS A CAREFUL, ALMOST TOO-MANNERED QUALITY ABOUT HIM. HE IS CAUTIOUS TO A FAULT. AND THIS DETRACTS FROM HIS MASCULINITY. HE REFUSES THE CHAIR MOST PATIENTS READILY GOBBLE UP; WHEN I OFFER HIM A FULL-BLOWN COUCH HE LAUGHS WITH DERISION (that is too much a cliché for his intelligent despair). INSTEAD HE PACES RHYTHMICALLY, TO AND FRO, TO SOME MELODY HE'S REHEARS-

ING THAT SOOTHES HIS NERVOUS PAIN. JANICE (that's me): Sit down, R, there's no need for all this pacing. (Forgive the sterile lines, psychiatrists have no flair for words.) R: You ask me to do what everybody else does, come in here and sit like a lump on a log? HE SHAKES HIS HEAD DOGGEDLY, KEEPS MOVING BACK AND FORTH WITH RHYTHMIC UNEASE. JANICE: All right, have it your way. But today I insist you talk about your past. Anything. However insignificant. Why don't we begin with your mother? (Oh God, the banalities of the psychiatric trade!) R CRACKS UP. SLAPS HIS THIGH LIKE A DRUMMER HITTING THE CYMBALS. MAKES A LONG WRY FACE, HIS EYES DROOPING LIKE A DOG'S. JANICE: Stop it, R, who taught you to make such a down face? R PULLS AT HIS EYES. MAKES THEM DROOP EVEN FARTHER. JANICE ERUPTS WITH LAUGHTER. JANICE (CONVULSING): Stop it, R. I'm splitting a gasket, that's a nasty trick to make me lose control! R SHOVES OUT HIS LOWER LIP. BEGINS SCRATCHING AND BARKING LIKE HE'S CLIMBING A TREE.

JANICE HOWLS AND RISES FROM HER SEAT. JANICE (JOINING IN THE MERRIMENT): Let me show you my duck walk, R. SHE BEGINS TO WADDLE AND CLUCK. JANICE (WADDLING): Can you do the Stubby? R (STILL CLIMBING): What's that? JANICE (CLUCKING): I never met a black person who hadn't heard about the Stubby! R (GROWING WARY): You're looking for a soft spot, some Negro place of entry. JANICE (IGNORING HIS WARINESS): This is how it begins, *snap,* two-three-four, and *snap,* two-three-four, and *snap snap,* three-four, and *snap snap,* three-four. SHE BEGINS TO SLIP AND SLIDE AROUND THE ROOM. AN INFECTIOUS FLOW THAT GRABS R BY THE BALLS. JAN-

ICE (ENGULFED): Sweet! Oh, how sweet! If only we could remember to live by the beat! R (CRACKING UP): No ideas, please, don't make it heavy with ideas. HE SHIFTS INTO HIS OWN FINGER-POPPING SLIDE. R: Let's break out of this fey four/four shit, kick the beat back to a sweeter place. Ba ba-ba, ba-ba ba! Ba ba-ba, ba-ba ba! Kick that beat back! AND HE DRIFTS THEM FORWARD, ADDING SWEETER SYNCOPATION TO THE WAY THEY MOVE. THEY ARE BOTH CAUGHT UP IN THE RISE AND FALL. (I know by now you are writhing in your writer's grave. I hear every objection: What? No words? No soiled confessions? You mean all that transpired was this hippie vibes-and-rhythm shit? Fuck!)

The truth is it took R a long time to warm up. Walking into my office was no easy sit-down-and-get-on-with-it affair. R played it like a good musician, insisted on a careful warm-up, a prelude, if you will. By this time we both might be high as kites. R had the capacity to make me truly giddy, I'd break out in raucous giggles, begin to spill the beans, until my own freaky childhood got played on the strings. Generally, I keep a tight lid on my past (unwilling to wind up in one of your cerebral stories). But R and I made a pact to spill everything. He confessed he lived only to screw, the fleshy contact being his only source of relief. R placed in his dick his only hope of salvation, kept it active, stroked it daily, allowed women to lead it directly to the source. Once there he drank deeply until he cried aloud and drowned all his tears. Everything else was pure anxiety, he was scared out of his wits. I understood how he felt. My own childhood memories pulled bitter strings. I confessed my craving for a lively song and dance. Not sex. God forbid I should ever be nibbled on like a piece of meat! But I had to have action, things spinning around me, people clowning for attention with me at the center (I'm the one who kept our house in an uproar, you merely profited from the multitudes I drew). I gave him my one and only home movie: me in bed with my brother, who alone, I confessed, was allowed a real nibbling. I let him eat away at my flesh to stifle my sobs. It was by no means your orthodox fifty-minute hour.

Then we'd come home for dinner, walk through the door all giggles. I've brought R home for dinner! The children would come squealing forward. Marsha would coax him straight to the piano and, while he played, begin a rakish dance. Emma would drift in playing her recorder, with Roberto swift on her heels, banging away on his newest percussive device—drums, cymbals, congas, tom-toms (since the dawn of his childhood Roberto grooved on tapping out his thoughts). Even you had no strenuous objection to R's hovering presence. His enigmatic posture was almost a story in itself. Ah! I confess a longing for those simple-minded days, when life seemed an endless *mechaieh*! R played and sang. Marsha danced. Roberto tapped and hummed along. Emma sat lotus-like, drawing on the vibes. With you on the couch smoking your pipe, while I applauded from beginning to end (there is no appropriate moment to show appreciation). Then R would drift into some clairvoyant melody . . .

> *Sometimes when it's sunny*
> *You can watch heat rise*
> *Cast a perfect shadow*
> *Over our demise*
>
> *Colors of a rainbow*
> *In a gloomy sky*
> *Keep the day from falling*
> *Into sad disguise*

Winter chill remembered
On a hot spring day
Causes one to shiver
Tremble with dismay

Who can call us strangers
Who saw our joy
Only nonbelievers
Speak of broken toys

Sweet, sweet R. Strange that he should be the one to bring Lollie into our house. The pied piper called the tune, and in she walked.

III

NOTES FROM A BLACK WOMAN'S DIARY

December 27, 1975

I often wonder if keeping a notebook, a diary of what transpired yesterday and the day before yesterday, isn't a very vain activity, a bad habit I picked up from some indolent soul with time to spare. Yet I am not an indolent soul. And I do not have much time to spare. But I keep a diary. Going back, back, back. And when I re-read parts of it, a feeling of solidity takes hold of me. If it is also well written and manages to go to the heart of the moment as I lived it, leaving me free, now, to recall it with all its contours intact, then I feel great satisfaction. As if I had accomplished something significant. Here, for example, is an entry written when my son was born . . .

November 17, 1972

For just a few minutes, there, in the delivery room, the doctor and I came face-to-face with each other. All our strengths and weaknesses hanging in the balance, suspended between this new life that stubbornly resisted an easy birthing. I, howling like a bull, feared I had come to the limit of my strength before I could suck this creature out into the open. The doctor, cursing my weakness, refused to listen to my pain, a pain that is like none other on the face of the earth. I swear it: it is as if your whole body were being ripped inside out hour after agonizing hour. And then it was all obliterated in a second, as I leaned forward to see the head and the shoulders and the bowled-up legs come out of me. From somewhere, somehow, beyond me came one last push, lasting and lasting until my child had cleared the light of day.

That child is now three years old. But sometimes, on a winter night, when no other reading material satisfies me, I find myself going back over entries like that, as if the writing had given the experience an autonomous existence. It is still my experience and yet abstracted, separated, existing in a place that has a larger meaning.

Where did this note-keeping habit come from? I have always liked to read memoirs, autobiographies, biographies; always been interested in the inner life. It is true that with age this habit is diminishing—as if, with age, my life is sufficient material unto itself and doesn't require any further comparison with other lives. But this is very recent. When I was younger I devoured them—indiscriminately—concerned, at first, only with the person's love life: the great love of their existence . . . how it turned out, what joy and sorrow it brought . . . I think I was preparing myself for a great love, storing up information on how to behave when it finally came along . . . But then, one spring, I find this entry . . .

April 10
These past few months, I have stopped thinking of my life in terms of a man, stopped holding up in front of me some secret myth of union. And accepted head-on my capacity to live well on my own.

When I go back to that entry and the others that surround it, I can pick up the flavor of a new beginning. I recall when I first realized that I might have inside me the capacity to reap a great deal on my own.

So when the "love interest" subsided, I turned to memoirs for strength, just as if I were asking someone to show me, show me how to fight loneliness and anxiety and

fear and insecurity. Show me how to come to terms with
my life. And last year I find this entry . . .

January 23

I have made my way clear of loneliness and guilt
by simply being. By simply refusing to accede to self-
pity. I have made my way clear to a certain plateau
that has nothing to do with happiness or even peace,
simply with a kind of mute taking stock and holding
myself to the present moment.

Re-reading that, I recall the winter when I decided to
live. Regardless.

It is worth examining the reasons why anyone keeps
a diary. The most general reason probably has something
to do with making the moments count, giving them
some weight and substance, so that they do not slip by
unattended. Often, when I have gone back to an entry,
I have been very glad I wrote it down, knowing that
otherwise I might have lost it. For example, a short one-
liner I ran across the other day . . .

October 11

Death marks the end of living in the future.

A note that reminds me of long talks with a very close
friend whose husband committed suicide. When she tried to
explain to me what was the hardest thing for her to face, she
came to see that it was the absence of any future possibilities.
With separation, divorce, or a long absence, there is still
hope that the future will bring a reconciliation or a return.
But death marks the end of living in the future. And this,
for her, was almost unbearable.

There are random notes that still intrigue me, giving as they do the impression of a moment or the playful exploration of a feeling or an idea. Notes like . . .

September 9
They're selling an old medieval house on Mason's Road, where the rooms go on endlessly, like a labyrinth. We went there on Saturday and bought five red chairs for the kitchen.

September 16
A lovely conversation with B. I was describing how the emptiness of the house, the absence of furniture and furnishings, is depressing me. He replied: "Oh, we'll find a dream for that, too! I'll come over in my trench coat; we're somewhere in Russia, along the Black Sea in winter. With only our candles and a fire . . . do you have a fireplace? Good . . . that's all we need . . . We'll turn the emptiness into a bleak Russian night for the soul . . . how's that, baby?"

December 12
It is our disappointments that mold us the most.

October 26
B made a bright red swing for the kids, which he hung from a pine tree.

November 17
The difference between the white men I have known intimately and the black men I have known intimately: their emotional accessibility. In white

men (I think this is true of the women, too), it is
an immense struggle to make contact with their
emotional center, to feel them out and touch some
kind of base. With black men, while the behavior
may be complex, contradictory, often inexplicable,
the emotional core is extremely accessible,
wonderfully readable, radiating an incredible warmth.
I think of B . . . , of H . . . , of N . . . , of G . . .
Whereas with D . . . or JW . . . or C . . . there is
an inaccessibility that exercises an entirely different
fascination. It is precisely their unreadableness that
is provocative. Still, all the men I have cared deeply
about seem to share one thing in common, regardless
of race: a remarkable masculine self-possession before
which I do nothing but yield.

October 26

I am stern with my children. Sometimes my
sternness surprises me.

March 5

Making love one night last week, for the first
time I became conscious of my warmth as a woman.
The feeling that there were wonderful secrets inside
me . . . there . . . for whoever wanted to listen, really
listen . . .

November 19

It rained hard today. After lunch I sat in the
kitchen sipping a can of beer. The beer made me very
sleepy, so I came in to take a nap. It was one of those
deep naps, where the wind and the rain conspire to
take you into a deep, secure slumber. Every muscle

goes limp. You awaken, as you awaken sometimes after really good lovemaking: spent, but incredibly rested and content.

February 8

Riding in the car, the day was suddenly dreary, bleak. And life seemed monotonous and sad. I wanted to cry. It seems that I have watched enough winters come in, turned the clocks back enough times, watched the rain turn the world black too many days. Only my children really hold me to life. They give me the patience to wait it out for a new day.

January 13

On my desk sits a photograph taken in the '30s of several young women gathered for some festive occasion. They are all in their twenties, all the daughters of prominent black families. They are smiling, some holding hands. One of them is to become my mother. Another is to become the mother of my first lover . . .

January 23

The extremism, the tenacity in me. I will hold on. I *will* to hold on. Until all the cards have been played.

February 24

On the phone with B . . . over an hour, about men and women. In the end I am close to tears, recognizing that all the things we take so personally, all the things we suffer over so dreadfully, have so little to do with us. I try to describe to him the terror

I feel in the face of a man's freedom, the boundless arbitrariness of it. How ruthless it can be in pursuit of itself. Men become themselves out of a refusal of certain kinds of limitations, women out of an acceptance of them. Women *are* bound. They must come to terms with a whole centrifugal force of taboos that they cannot violate without doing severe violence to themselves. We *are* in bondage to life. A woman's life is a terrible thing. Make no mistake about it. And I believe in liberation, but I don't believe it is at all the thing we think it is.

March 18

We can't fight time. We can't get over anything faster than we're supposed to. Whatever we have to live through we have to live through until its time is up. I'm saying all this to say that I think my present sense of clarity is not my victory, but time's.

And so it goes. As if the words could weight down the fleetingness and force it to exist in some more physical, more irrevocable way.

But I don't think that explains it all. If it *is* only vanity that makes me write, it is a more full-fledged, more encompassing vanity than those entries would betray. Because the diary is also an effort to justify the choices I've made, the ??? of life I've chosen. As if I am explaining myself against some later moment when I am to be judged . . .

April 11

I could have occupied myself with race all these years. The climate was certainly ripe for me to have done so. I could have explored myself within the context of a young black life groping its way into maturity across the rising tide of racial affirmation. I could have done that. After all, I'm a colored lady. My father died a somewhat broken colored death. My mother ended it all at my birth. And my second mother practiced a far too studied gentility. But I didn't do that. No, I turned far inside, where there was only me and love to deal with. I turned far inside till I could measure every beat of love—love living on sex, love emptied of sex, love scratching and screaming in jealousy, love neglected until it turned itself into a life so solitary there was almost no way out. Instead of dealing with race I went in search of love . . . and what I found was a very hungry colored lady.

July 19

There is no such thing as a helpless black woman (even M . . . , who plays the helpless creature, plays it to D's whiteness, plays it to his white ideas about women . . .). There is no cultural conditioning, no unspoken expectation *anywhere,* that would allow me to believe I could afford to be helpless. The attitude of helplessness, of dependence, is foreign to me, based on assumptions that are alien to my upbringing. There was only one dominant theme in my childhood: holding on, no matter what . . . shifting and turning and choreographing and juggling and manipulating life to stay inside it! To live! And perhaps even grow! If a man came along . . . all right, so much the nicer . . . But the game goes on, the necessity to be a self goes on. I don't know how to be helpless. I don't know how *not* to make things work.

October 12

It is all about an urge, a powerful and overwhelming urge, to fulfill myself, to fulfill this life that is inside me, to fulfill it in every way, leaving nothing untapped. That is what it is all about: the excesses, the anxiety, the restlessness, the pain, carrying around in me this irrepressible need to fulfill myself in every way possible.

Sometimes I know I go places in the diary that take my breath away. As if there were someone else living inside me with her own determined will to see and speak clearly. Because I don't write to protect myself or to say things I don't dare say to others. I don't cater to any pampered image of myself as a too sensitive soul for whom the world is too much and the diary her only friend. I am neither too fragile nor too sensitive. I have many true friends, and the betrayals I have known I have asked for. I don't write to hide from the world.

If I write because of some illusion, it is not *that* illusion. But I think there is another one. Once on the phone with a friend, she made a comment about me that caused me to pick up my notebook as soon as I hung up . . .

January 17

On the phone with S . . . her perception about how a thing is true in my head long before it has any concrete reality. True! I live way ahead of myself in some ways, seeing things long before it is their time to come into being. It even makes me lie, caught in a wave that takes me beyond myself, inside another moment not yet fully conceived. That is the basis of all my lies, all my really fantastic lies. But there is more to it than that. There is also a reluctance to bore, to be found dull and sad; so I spin my little webs to hold others at arm's length. I *know* the moment when another's pain becomes tedious. I *know* the tolerance level of compassion, how thin it is, how rapidly it dissolves. We *must* dignify our sadness. We must wrap ourselves in some thread, some magical spell that allows others to see us as we'd like to be! I know it isn't *true*! But it has a pale, incomplete, and somewhat fragile virtue: it distracts! And look how much better everyone breathes with a little distraction, a little appearance for fantasy's sake. But oh, dear God, don't punish me for my lies, don't punish me for putting the cart before the horse. Because if it turns out that no one will ever love me for what I am, at least people will have loved me for what they thought I was . . . And it may be, finally, that I was the most terrible kind of realist.

I begin to think I write to keep control of the present. And when I'm not interested in the present, when I'm waiting for something to happen, then I don't write so regularly, the notes become sporadic avoidances. The most voluminous volumes are when I am living very much inside the present, waiting for a child to be born, living out of the city to write, and so on. Then I make endless observations about the most trivial, fleeting impressions, moments, thoughts, feelings. Entries like . . .

February 15
Something is happening to me. A kind of clarity. A cementing of my life to the here and now. Every day is wonderful through here. It has a kind of

affirmation to it. A force. Even in its most tedious moments.

March 23

Bright and sunny. And a real ordinary Sunday. Went with B . . . for a walk. Drank wine and sat in the sun. Nina and Miwo came in about six—dirty and wet from playing outdoors all day. Dinner, then a bath for both of them.

March 16

2:00 A.M. Nothing is ever as it seems. It is an absolute requirement that we come to terms with the abstract notion we have painted of things and distinguish it from the real . . . All this prompted by a dog named Juno whom I agreed to keep for a few days. But he arrived tonight and left tonight after a ferocious whining and banging scene in my kitchen. My agreeing to keep him, of course, came out of some abstract notion I had about all dogs being friendly, easygoing, and wise, so that I refused to zero in on Juno's peculiarities, which make him difficult, obnoxious, and stupid. The same mistake pins down my difficulties with ML . . . I had in my head some abstract notion about a friendly, cheerful, devoted housekeeper, good with the children, making cookies and doing things with them and altogether lifting somewhat the burdens of Motherhood. But again I tripped over an abstract notion only to stumble on ML . . . mute, wizened, self-righteous, incapable of communicating with the kids, and altogether *increasing* the burdens of Motherhood. If it were not two o'clock in the morning I could probably get a lot more mileage out of this discovery. I am sure it covers a wide expanse of territory, affecting many of the decisions I have made and many of the roads I have traveled. Perhaps it is all we are ever doing in life: constantly sorting out what is real from some abstract notion we've taken a fancy to. What a relief to have Juno out of the house.

July 11

From my 5:30 A.M. vantage point I have watched the day come alive. Watched the river go from a cloudy mist to a soft, bright sunny fogginess. Listened to some mournful, repetitive bird humming a sad refrain and the boat bells hitting the wind. And now my room is full of sunlight and it is 7:30 and I am alive.

When I look back over those days I see how centered I was in the present, connecting myself to the life in hand. Even now it is a period that makes me nostalgic. All those periods in my life when I have been very alone—waiting for a child, in the midst of a play or a film script or a story— those are the periods when growth seems to come in bursts. I am still. I listen. I learn. I'm not very concerned about tomorrow.

But at other times, life takes over and the diary recedes. Then I feel in me a kind of determination to soak up life. Then I run away from these notes and make only cursory remarks.

September 21

I would like to catch up on some days left discarded . . .

September 24

I seem to avoid these notes like the plague. As
if I don't dare take off, don't dare say anything, so
tentative is everything.

September 27

I really cannot write much these days. What is
clear to me I am unwilling to pin down too quickly. I
want it loose, like I feel it.

September 28

I don't write often these days—not here, not in
these pages. I am abstracted, in limbo, hanging on by
threads. But it is difficult to speak about this limbo,
to describe it. The journey is too personal to write
about . . .

The most that can be said is that I trust these shallow
periods, when I have left the solid ground of the present.
When I leave that ground, it is because I am healed and
the danger is past and a more risky life is manageable. One
day toward the end of one of those times I wrote these
notes . . .

Sunday, August 24

Rain. Alone in the house. I've just finished a
book about the psychic experiences of a woman
named Jan Bartell. While I have never known any
paranormal events, I know I lead my life psychically,
not only the larger moments of it, but the very
smallest. I am always listening, knowing that if I
listen I will be guided correctly, even if it means
pain or discomfort. I cannot ever recall being

without this "listening." It is almost a feeling of
being watched over and protected. I remember at a
very difficult time last spring my car kept breaking
down and draining away the little bit of money I
was budgeting so carefully. I was standing in the
kitchen thinking, This is just one thing too many,
I can't cope with these car problems . . . when the
phone rang and the bank had cleared my very shaky
credit for a new car. When I hung up, I found myself
saying thank you to the space around me . . . thank
you . . . you knew that was too much for me, didn't
you, that I'm just hanging on by so little . . . I don't
know who I am talking to at times like that, but
the "listening" dictates everything I do—when I
go shopping, when I stay home, when I put myself
to making money, when I decide to live broke and
write, when I have children . . . always I am listening
for the right moment, always I am trying to make
a complete circle and come back where I belong. I
don't know why this is so, why I try to stay in touch
with what can take me further, make me stronger,
give me greater self-containment . . . I don't know
why this is so. But I know it is at the source, that all
my electricity, all my running power, comes from
this field around me with which I must remain in
tune. And when I come to a dead end, when things
get muddy and my mind races overboard into a fog, I
have to go somewhere and sit. Then help will come,
a direction will be made clear.

IV

LETTERS

Note: My mother left hundreds of letters, and I've included here just a small sampling and offered a bit of context preceding each one. —Nina Lorez Collins

Written at age nineteen to her conservative parents, who are not happy about her activism at Skidmore College.

January 5, 1962

Hello My Daddy and My Mommy,

I have first re-read your letter of late November—I send it back to you for re-reading—for there I feel we reached such a good, good peace together. And there we <u>felt</u>—each other—and the understanding was implicit—perhaps never to be explicit.

I have felt good in the last few days—quietly preparing for my exams, reading and thinking—desperately trying to ask the right questions and find the right answers. It has been good and peaceful to be here for the first time in so very long—I should finish. I know that now, because I want to, first of all for <u>myself</u>—and I am glad about that. I should work, study hard to pass the biology, but if not I shall take it next semester and pass it then. But I shall finish, and I shall finish in June—and this itself gives me a sense of contentment.

It has been a quiet weekend, but I have enjoyed the rest and the sleep. I have spent most of it in my room, reading and writing—taking naps when I felt tired—and generally putting myself in good physical shape for exams. Hank called Saturday night and in his gentlé, strong way made things even nicer and that made me very happy.

The turmoil and discovery of Christmas are past and perhaps, too, the brutality of a rebellious daughter—who cannot apologize for rebelling—but who wishes she had had the wisdom to do it with less pain. Your letter sees this all; this is why I send it back.

I shall stay away for a while, methinks, no, not because I feel I must—but because my coming would not be peaceful for you at this stage. And when next I come, that is how I want it to be—peaceful and right—my respecting the way life makes you happy rather than <u>demanding</u> that <u>you</u> follow my path. But through all of this perhaps I am learning some good things about what love <u>really</u> means. And I know that I love you both very much—and I know that I write now <u>because</u> I love you, <u>not</u> because I feel responsible or feel you need me—for you don't and I know this—not in the sense that I have felt.

Nor do I feel deserted—for it is the strength and understanding you have given me that gives me the faith to know that I can find a healthy and full life.

Yes, Daddy—you are right. You have a daughter who is perhaps in some ways still a child—but you have wisely rejected the child and in your own way demanded the daughter. And this is so much helping me to grow.

Thank you, Mommy. Thank you, Daddy. Please let me hear from you.

Much love,
Kathleen

Written at age twenty in Albany, Georgia (where she worked with the Student Nonviolent Coordinating Committee [SNCC]), to her only sister, Francine, the inspiration for the character Josephine in the story "Scapegoat Child."

August 3, 1962
Dear Frannie,

It was awfully good to talk with all of you last night, especially Daddy, as I had felt great apprehension during those days in jail after your letter was received.

Sometimes I felt you were cynical toward me, feeling I was being unfair to Daddy, but I feel that this was your natural concern in what I'm sure was a very tense situation. I knew when I decided to come south that it meant distress to Mother and Daddy, and though I was sorry I had to and have to worry them, this could not be the determining factor. For one must move upon the things that one is committed to.

There's a biblical quote that goes: "He to whom much is given, much is asked in return." The suffering and pain I have witnessed reinforce the truth of this statement. I ask over and over again: Why—why was I so blessed? There must be a reason—and that is to give to others. Otherwise life is a total absurdity of injustice.

But I do not feel I am the sacrificial lamb—because I do not believe there is such a thing as sacrifice. Nor do I feel I should be held in admiration or pride. For truly I believe we all do the things we want to do. And I wanted with all my soul to go south and I wanted to go to jail—because I wanted to pray that right would triumph. I wanted to pray on the steps of city hall in Albany. To confront all of those policemen and city officials with the moral issue—the fact that they have made us dogs—but I wanted to force them to see me and others as human beings who feel pain and frustration, who, too, can cry and be hurt.

And if I could not pray, then I wanted to go to jail for what I believed. But do not feel proud of me, Frannie. I don't deserve it.

All I want is to live my life as honestly as possible, giving what I can to other human beings—all kinds, black, white, or yellow—because this is the way I want to live—never selling other people cheap—because we are all in this crazy game, or play, called life together. And I want always to live simply—perhaps wandering for many years—finding my joy and peace in a sunrise, in a rainstorm—finding my happiness in seeing another smile.

Perhaps I make no sense; maybe I'm some kind of nut. But I have to respond to these things inside me—perhaps most of all because I must always try and be true to Kathleen.

Forgive my rambling, Frannie—these weeks here have been so full of the brutal, the painful, and the beautiful that sometimes I feel suffocated. But I guess I am rambling most of all because I am begging to be understood by you. Because I want to be able to cry on your shoulder maybe, sometimes when the road is rough. But more than this because I want you to cry on my shoulder, maybe, when things don't look too rosy.

And maybe I'm rambling on because I want to tear down forever those unconscious and sometimes conscious walls of hostility that have kept us from a truly deep and genuine relationship.

And maybe I'm rambling because I want to release all the guilt I have inside me because I've been a lousy, cold, selfish sister so much of the time.

But mostly I'm rambling because I have you. And I

think finally we are really becoming sisters. And this fills me with such happiness that the tears are beginning.

Love,
Kathleen

Written at age thirty to her mother, now a widow. My mother was married at this time to my father, but the union was rocky and full of separations.

Dec. 30th 1972
Dear Momma,

Happy New Year. Though I do not imagine having to face another year without Daddy can ever be too happy a time. I can only think of what I would feel without Douglas. That is the curse as well as the joy of really loving someone: you know in the end you must suffer more for it.

Also, as I said on the phone, I may be a little farther away than before and have one more child to travel with, but I am still mobile and strong and being with you at any crisis point would and _is_ just a fact of my life.

Nina had a nice, though quiet Christmas. Emilio is doing fine. They're both well over the flu, having not been outside at all since we came back from your house. But this morning Douglas took Nina out for the first time. He came up last night and this morning took her into town with him. She was delighted.

Here is a check. I'm sorry I had to call upon you again. I hope '73 puts us on some more solid foundation. I have a feeling it will. There are good signs that Douglas's business is going to make it.

Love,
Kathleen

Written to Bluette, one of her closest girlfriends and the inspiration for the character Liliane in A Summer Diary.

September 14, 1973
Dear Bluette,

My man has finally understood what it means to harm someone else. We had a scene, which will leave a very long-lasting impression: I was hysterical, like an animal, frustrated because he didn't seem to understand what was going on with me. Suddenly, an innocent remark of his plunged me into a fit of rage. I think I must have blacked out for a moment, because I rushed toward the open window and climbed onto the ledge with a speed that was almost superhuman. Douglas tore me away from there. I was one second away from hurling myself out the window. There, in his arms, I envisioned myself already dead, on the ground, because during those few seconds I had been overcome by something, I no longer knew the person that was acting that way. All that I knew with absolute clarity was that at that very moment I had been capable of killing myself. Afterward I shook for several hours; I was completely out of it . . . I imagined Nina's terrible suffering, Emilio's instinctive loss (they were not there when it happened). Douglas was next to me, crying like a baby. The most rational of everyone: he led me to understand how my moving to Woodstock had left him feeling abandoned . . . There was nothing but a little boy talking . . . He told me about that terrible night not long after our move when he had felt this abandonment . . . All the contradictions. Rationally he understood . . . he saw me as being capable of total acceptance . . . and the shattering of this image with such violence. I can't find the words for it.

It's an experience, which will fill us up for a lifetime.

Oh, Bluette, suddenly, in a second, I would have transformed the lives of several people, by an act . . . but you know in the depths of your being what I am talking about. But what I'm trying to touch is the inner violence, as if the soul has limits, which the heart knows nothing about. As if it were my soul that were controlling me, which could no longer tolerate the injustice of existence . . . that perhaps a suicide is not necessarily selfish but rather required by the force of the soul . . . When I try and capture these few seconds, all that I can grasp is a force which suddenly came to life in me and which dominated everything.

That's the story. This morning is thick with fog.

Kathy

Written to Peggy, another dear friend (and the inspiration for the girlfriend character in the story "The Happy Family" from Whatever Happened to Interracial Love?), *whom she met when they were both teenagers working for SNCC.*

1974, a Sunday morning
Dear Peggy,

Your call was long awaited, with patience, like a place remaining open that only you could reach. Now it is quiet. God! The revolutions we live! And yet every day unfolds with all the safety of habit and repetition, the outer shell goes on about its tasks and the world, for the most part, is none the wiser. Yet inside! Inside! What revolutions are possible! So many people are born inside us while others are sent away, often to their death . . . where is the Kathy of 18 and Peggy of 18 whose lives first touched . . . where have they gone? Do we hold, even, still, a passing acquaintance with them? I wonder . . . Stayed awake much of last night in the aftermath of your call, the clean places I can finally see I am reaching, the hands–off places that will not allow sneaky compromises.

Much love,
Kathy

Another to Peggy. My mother, now thirty-eight, is long divorced and living and raising us in Rockland County. I am eleven, my brother, Emilio, eight. She has a married lover named Henry Roth and is deep in the throes of her writing career.

February 16, 1980
Dear Peggy,

A winter entirely without snow until this morning—only to awaken to a nice sleek coating. The river whitish gray in the distance. I come downstairs. Throw a few more logs on my brand-new woodstove that sits in the living room fireplace now and heats the entire house! (Have not burned a <u>drop</u> of oil all winter!) Now I have the full pleasure of my living room in the mornings—it used to be the "cold" room, the "avoided" room somehow throwing the gravity of the house off-balance. Now we use it constantly. For the past several months I have been reading intensely, volumes of classic novels: all of Henry James, all of Ford Madox Ford, all of Thomas Mann, all of Anthony Powell, and some odd writers Henry discovers for me. It has been a long period of wonderful withdrawal. The kids came home day after day to find me curled up in the living room by the stove reading to my soul's content. It has been the fullest, the most pleasing of times. Have not written a word in months. Henry and I went for weeks barely seeing each other—he in a kind of terrible sadness, yet there,

with me, bringing me books—me in a kind of incredible
lassitude, empty and quiet, wanting only more and more
and more quiet. Long phone calls with each other. Quiet
lunches. Held intact. Never a question of not being held
intact. Then, a new phase . . . I can feel it starting. Just this
week we got our first perfectly color-corrected print of the
movie. Already it has been snatched up by one important
film festival! Screenings now begin—promotion, lectures—
the New York State Council on the Arts just awarded us
a Post-Production Grant! I can feel it starting . . . a busy
time. And I am ready for it. Fully rested, content within
myself again. Have been buying myself pretty clothes—a
pleasure I have not indulged in over three years. Have a
yearning for silk blouses, loose-fitting slacks, "my lingerie
dresses," as Henry calls them. The center of my life is very
involved in Henry, Nina, and Emilio these days. Nina and I
have come through grandly, "in the grand manner," as she
laughingly describes it. Faced each other with such honesty
from which neither of us flinched. She saw clear through
to my impossibly troubled childhood, I to my terrific fright
at her growing up. Layers upon layers fell away and the
most uplifting kind of pleasure returned, her face and body
in the last few months have become again so loose and
lovely, so happy with herself and her home. I cannot tell
you how light the air is, simple, direct, without games or
subterfuge. Emilio is still fine and easy, direct, macho in the
most absurdly funny ways . . . to Henry I am attached these
days as if suddenly I took on some new tone. It is hard to
describe: like breathing for two, sensing whatever is going
on with him immediately, sometimes it is uncanny. The
other day, around dinnertime, I was suddenly in a terrible
state, nervous, anxious . . . when he called, about an hour
later, I blurted out, "For the last hour you have been in

the most intense pain, suddenly discouraged beyond belief, the hurt has been awful . . ." There was only silence. It is like the texture of my skin has changed, become porous to everything connected to him, open, breathing in some new way. This is the time in my life when loving a man has caught up with me.

What else to say . . . Nina is cleaning the house around me, and laughing, her looseness a delight to watch. My last play, IN THE MIDNIGHT HOUR, has just been accepted for publication for a book of seven plays by women of the '70s. That pleases me. It is a play I am very fond of.

We now have two dogs (a fat, old black-and-white springer with long droopy eyes and ears) and a cat who is the wiliest little adventurous guy. First cat I've ever liked.

I hug you with all my best love and thoughts.

Kathleen

To me, her sixteen-year-old daughter, after an argument.

April, 1985

Nina,

Here's where the false note may still be—that somehow because I understand what's happening to you that I expect something in return. When I left you this morning, I had the feeling of something dishonest in me, even when I said what I felt, know to be true, about your feeling different about yourself, about your beauty, and so on—what I said, I meant, honestly. But the note that's false is my using it to soothe things, or to make sure you're not too alienated from me. The point is: just as I have no right to use my supporting you financially against you, I also have no right to make my ability to understand a form of possession, or of keeping you beholden to me. That's it. That's the trap, that some part of me would try to hold on BECAUSE I UNDERSTAND. My understanding must be ruthlessly excluded from the thing. In fact, it may be crippling. It may be that you can find out more about yourself from Douglas now than from me (and even my sensing this would explain the degree of anger that overtook me). And that really what happened on Saturday was the irony of that embittered me—that one person could give a great deal, the other very little, and yet neither has much to do with ANYTHING. That ultimately everything connected with love must be stripped away until it is entirely free.

Mom

A letter to seventeen-year-old me. She's recently fallen in love with Alfred Prettyman, the man who would become her second husband, and she's getting ready to move from the house she raised us in, in Piermont, to a house she bought with him in Upper Nyack. I'm living in Manhattan, having just finished my freshman year at Barnard College.

July 30, 1987
Nina,

Your letter made me see again that childhood picture of you I kept getting and it reflected all the things we talked about on the phone. I was so happy to have that call with you, it was full and touched on so many places that have caused such deep wounds. In a way it has been good for me to be here this summer, because while I have terrible scars I would not like to leave here without knowing I have made peace with them. There have been angry, dead days that have hung as heavy as you well know a day in

Piermont can hang. I don't like to think how it would have been if my own life had not shifted and Alfred entered it. I suspect I would have had the good sense not to stay here and live both loneliness and stifling deadness. And while even with Alfred I could have put together enough money to be elsewhere, it has mattered to our relationship that I be near. Also it has given me time to look at our life here from a different perspective. I am grateful to this house, it gave all of us a haven for many years and it provided a kind of continuity that may also have steadied both you and Emilio when I was on such rocky ground. Many people have come to us and been support when we needed them—Ronald, Radar, Asa, Kathie R, Jane—and while we have also given them asylum, their presence was valuable, especially to you children, in allowing you someone else to relate to when I was here but not here in spirit or heart. And for my own loneliness it was good. It has wonderful personal energy, this house, and I drew on it often when I felt such horrifying loneliness. I could fix it different ways, paint, paper, make it pretty. There is the river and the strange sustenance I know I have drawn from its presence. And being single it was easier not to be in a city and face the competitive social stress of weekends alone. I think our lives and some of the strength you talk about comes from the stability and beauty that held us here and that did not fall away until 1983.

Often while raising you alone, when I would look at both of you—and this refers again to your remark about strength—I was positive both of you had just that: strength. I think in your case I counted on it early and because it was only <u>my</u> strength that was holding me together, I blindly ignored what a crippling, empty thing strength is without vulnerability, softness, giving in to love. As I could give in to none of them for fear of being utterly devastated by my

own loneliness and hurt, I couldn't possibly allow myself
to love you children except by being a good caretaker and
a good provider. I, literally, put my love into that and kept
my heart closed. It was all the love I could handle, all I
could provide. I was going through my own life keeping up,
coping, holding on, trying not to fall apart.

But there was value in those years. The emptiness made
me free of fear. It helped me to become free in many ways
that most women, particularly, never achieve. I got over
many insecurities and especially any fear of being alone. I
think, a few months before I met Alfred—we were driving,
and I said to you I felt, finally, that my life was on course. It
was. Through illness, solitude, finding my way clear to love
you children, forgiving Momma and Pop Pop, finding a
confident voice as a writer—all these little things, these little
victories, so to speak, took place in this house, bit by bit,
year by year, until I found myself, saw clear into my own
heart and knew not only that I could love but that I could
love because I was whole: the past forgiven, the present an
alive, vital process I was willing to live fully every single
moment without needing to cheat or hide or play games
either with myself or others. It was at that point that Alfred
walked in the door. And I am grateful it was not a moment
sooner. I needed all that time, all that loneliness, all that
fear and sadness, grief, shock, what have you. I needed it all
because it was through it all, by taking off each layer, and
then going down to take off another, that I reached me and
found there a very nice woman . . .

Nor was it until I found her that I could offer her to
you children, for I could not offer what I did not know was
there.

When it comes to Daddy, I think in many ways my
own anger at him is just beginning to surface. Oh, he can

make me furious, and I could allow myself to fight with him, but I think it is only now that I really see that for me he wreaked tremendous havoc, humiliation, loss. For me, there is something evil in his presence. But I speak of that ONLY FOR ME. IT IS SOMETHING I FEEL AS THE WOMAN HE MARRIED—in no way do I wish to inflict it on your feelings or your relationship to him. I think that is precisely what I am trying to do now. Separate what he did to me from what I tried to get him to do for you children. Because over the past several years, most of my fighting and quarreling with him has been in order to try to get him to be some semblance of a father to you children. It is only now that I feel you both are grown enough to handle that yourselves—and also probably because of Alfred that I am forced, finally, to look at what he denied me both as his wife and as the mother of his children. The horror of that denial is monumental. To me. There are no amends possible. No forgiveness, really. The toll was too tremendous, the insensitivity too extreme, my inability to stop it too fragile. And the too-muchness of it led to a strange death between us that I feel now must be honored.

That paragraph came out without my hardly knowing I had written it. Ignore it, please, insofar as it concerns you, for it doesn't concern you and I'm confident you know that.

There is a saying that goes, "A woman scorned is a terrible thing . . ." I always felt there was something negative in that quote, that it meant that women were somehow vengeful or more spiteful than men, but I begin to see it doesn't mean that at all. When women give, truly, it is with all of them, particularly with emotional centers that once tampered with are hell to repair. The terribleness is not vengeance but the irreparable damage to that well-spring that I sense to be peculiarly feminine, a well-spring that, quite literally, at its best, rises up and floods life with love and light and a capacity to give that is shimmering. Forgive the rush forward into poetry but it is the only image that fits. The terribleness is the drying up of that well-spring, which then cuts off the entire emotional center, which in my case should have been connected to you children but couldn't be . . .

Just as in many ways Grandma couldn't love Aunt Francine and myself as her real children because Pop Pop didn't allow her ever to forget that there had been a real mother, a real wife, and that she was a substitute, second best, a necessity out of another woman's death. It is that pain that I know shaped both Grandma's life and the lives of Aunt Francine and myself. It locked us all in so tight that no authentic mothering could reach us from the woman who truly was our mother regardless of birth or not. Nor do I kid myself that much of that denial did not form the mothering I gave you two. It couldn't have been otherwise. Darkness is what I call it. The soul's inability to claim its rightful portion of love and in return to give back in full measure an abundant loving of its own.

Now when I experience myself it is as if the center of me had light cascading constantly through it. I draw those I love close to me simply by breathing and when I breathe fully, those I love—you, Emilio, Alfred—pass through me full of light. We bless each other. We ask and receive forgiveness. We go on with our separate lives but they are changed, shaped, sustained, supported by this love that is as light and free as fine-spun gold. Be well, my child . . .

Love, Mom . . .

A letter to me, age eighteen, while I am doing a study abroad program in Vienna. She's dying of breast cancer and keeping it a secret. She died on September 18, 1988, and called me home two weeks before.

February 9, 1988
Dear Nin,

That was a good phone call. The best. Always the best when we get to the TRUTH. It is changing of course. This Mother thing. And just as I, in my unreasonableness, wanted you home every weekend last year—around me—you cling, too, to some custodial definition of CARE-package mothering. It is the years, the habits, it is everything. It is refreshing to me to feel every now and then, toward you and Emilio, that the caretaking is finished, and I am free again! Hard to digest, I'm sure. But true. Every step away is both sad and liberating. For you. For me. We will change our relationship a million times as the years move. And that is because we are committed to change and not to static energy. It is our way, not many people want growth the way we do. Most people want to settle, find a place of comfort and cling to it. But in all our years of living that is not how we structured things. We lived together, yes, but it was always understood that as some new interest emerged, some new adventure presented itself, it was to be taken advantage of, and if it brought change in its wake, so be it. In that sense I have always loved your and Emilio's separateness from me, always cherished that I was in fact simply your custodian, so to speak, for a period of time until you had your own wings. I still feel that way. That your flying through life on your own pleasure, your own wits, your own steam, is the true excitement, your true living. And my own flying an equally important thing. And that ultimately it is only delight in another that holds one, that is captivating, all else must be a respect for their freedom. Don't worry, though, as all requests are honored if possible. You have only to say when you need me, momentarily, to give pure mothering. It is, after all, and after all those years, quite deeply ingrained in me and has given me such intense pleasure that it continues to live.

Love on top of love,
MOM

V

PLAYS

THE BROTHERS: A TRAGEDY IN THREE ACTS

THE CHARACTERS*

MR. NORRELL, an undertaker; around forty-seven.

MARIETTA WINSTON, a woman in her late fifties.

LILLIE EDWARDS, a woman of thirty; Marietta's sister-in-law.

ROSIE GOULD, a woman around fifty-five; mother.

LETITIA EDWARDS, a woman in her late sixties; Marietta's sister-in-law.

DANIELLE EDWARDS, a woman in her early thirties; Marietta's sister-in-law.

CAROLINE EDWARDS, a woman in her late fifties; Marietta's sister-in-law.

THE ORDERLY, should be played by Mr. Norrell.

* *All the characters are Negro.*

THE PLACE

A series of suggested rooms in which these women live.

THE TIME

Sometimes the present, sometimes the past.

PROLOGUE: MR. NORRELL

[Mr. Norrell's office. Large desk with a gold nameplate reading: MR. NORRELL, FUNERAL DIRECTOR. The rest of the office is solemnly but correctly furnished with a few comfortable chairs facing the desk, dark curtains at the window, thick carpet underfoot, a somber hushed feeling pervading the atmosphere. Stage left and barely visible is the edge of a casket with a large spray of chrysanthemums on top of it, so that one has the feeling of being right next door to the viewing room. Organ music comes intermittently from that room with renderings of several different hymns: "Amazing Grace! (How Sweet the

Sound)," "Must Jesus Bear the Cross Alone?," "When I've
Done the Best I Can."

*MR. NORRELL sits at his desk. He is a distinguished-
looking man, light-skinned, shiny black hair touched with gray,
dressed in a dark suit that is well tailored.*

*When the play opens, he is busy at his desk, which is cluttered
with funeral advertisements for caskets, layouts, embalming
fluids, etc. A light shines on all the papers, heightening the air
of preoccupation about him. MRS. WINSTON enters. She is
an attractive, well-dressed woman with a fast-moving, abrupt,
yet deliberate manner. She alternates between a certain feisty
comic humor, like an actress playing a variety of parts, and a
sad, almost maudlin melancholia. The minute she reaches the
doorway she begins speaking.]*

MRS. WINSTON. *[aggressive]* Mr. Norrell . . . you are
Mr. Norrell. No one else buries any of the Edwards but you.

[Mr. Norrell looks up.]

MRS. WINSTON. My husband just died. He is not an
Edwards, though to his dying day he got confused. I kept
him confused. I and my four brothers, all of whom have
passed through these very walls on their way God knows
where.

[SHE steps into the room.]

MRS. WINSTON. I'm Marietta Winston, the only sister of
four stern imaginative brothers. Franklin was my favorite,
followed in quick succession by Nelson the baby, Lawrence
the eldest and most dangerous, and Jeremy the nervous one.
They were all nervous but Jeremy twitched . . . twitched
and stuttered . . . *[She begins to speak like Jeremy, her body*

begins to twitch, her eyes blink incessantly.] 'N . . . n . . . n . . . ow . . . M . . . M . . . Mar . . . ietta, y . . . you g . . . **g** . . . g . . . go r . . . r . . . ight do . . . wn t . . . t . . . o Mi . . . Mi . . . Mis . . . ter Nor . . . Norrell's . . .' *[relaxing]* 'All right, Jeremy,' I'd say, and pat him on the arm. Can you imagine, at the end he'd lost one of his legs from painting houses. All his life he painted houses, climbed up and down ladders with his bucket of paint, paint on his belts, paint on his shirts, went to his son's wedding with paint on his Sunday trousers. Lived in Detroit in the heart of the automobile industry painting houses . . . *[again speaking like him]* 'N . . . n . . . a . . . ow, M . . . M . . . Mar . . . ietta, y . . . you c . . . coo co . . . me a . . . nd st . . . st . . . stay w . . . w . . . ith us a . . . fe . . . fe . . . w da . . . days . . .' *[relaxing]* 'Oh, Jeremy,' I'd say, 'I can't do that! Why there are so **many** of you!' And there were! The children never left home! The girl just mooned around with a couple of babies, the boys were in and out at all hours, you'd never know they had wives and children . . . *[imitating the sons]* 'Daaaa-dy . . . where are you, Daaaa-dy . . .' *[amused]* Then they'd go look in the refrigerator, leave . . . come another hour they'd be back again! *[imitating the sons]* 'Daaaa-dy, what you doin', Daaaa-dy . . .' He'd sit there with his leg gone . . . 'Wh . . . wh . . . wh . . . at y . . . y . . . you . . . w . . . w . . . want, b . . . b . . . boys . . .' 'Just want to make sure you're all right, Daaaa-dy . . .' *[relaxing]* And he'd chuckle . . . *[She chuckles just like him, grows visibly sadder.]* Jeremy . . .

[MR. NORRELL, getting impatient, gets up.
MRS. WINSTON moves briskly forward.]

MRS. WINSTON. No need for you to rise. None of my brothers ever rose for me. *[speaking like them]* 'Marietta, come sit with us so we can talk . . .'

[SHE sits down, begins talking to her boys. Mr. Norrell is visibly irritated.]

MRS. WINSTON. Oh, Nelson, you don't mean to say you're thinking of never leaving your bed . . . Lawrence, you can't have done anything that mean . . . How can you stand it, Franklin, how is it you can stand one more minute of it? *[She looks up at Mr. Norrell.]* What a merry-go-round! Round and round they went, round **and** round. They couldn't stop . . . not one of them knew how to stop . . . Nelson pouted his way to an early grave, just couldn't seem to get back up and live . . . *[whining like Nelson]* 'I don't want to, Marietta, I just don't want to . . .' *[seeing him]* Then he'd stretch out on his back and play dead . . . *[She pauses, then dramatically shifts her tone.]* And Lawrence, our smoothie! Riverview's first colored lawyer, our natural smoothie . . . hair black and shiny as coal, the waters <u>parted</u> for Lawrence. You ever know evil, evil is the hardest thing to see when it's staring at you through the eyes of your very own brother . . . *[She shifts again.]* But it's Richard I've come to bury . . .

[MR. NORRELL, relieved, sits down.]

MRS. WINSTON. My easygoing Richard who smoked himself to death. 'You're the last of my boys,' I'd say to him, 'when you're gone I've got no more boys to look after me.' *[She looks at Mr. Norrell.]* Who's gonna tell a little old thing like me what to do . . .

[Pause. SHE takes out a cigarette, offers him one, which he accepts. HE takes a big black lighter from his desk, lights both of them. MRS. WINSTON sits back, smokes, slips eerily into one of her brothers' voices.]

MRS. WINSTON. *[with a deep chuckle]* '**You** tell Mr. Norrell you want a brass casket for Richard, brass does not rot . . .'

[MR. NORRELL smokes, more and more ill at ease.]

MRS. WINSTON. *[with the same deep chuckle]* 'Now when I'm gone, Marietta, you tell Mr. Norrell I want a quiet, dignified service. A late-evening wake that begins around nine and an early-morning service. Let those who knew me well rise to the occasion and have their say. No flowers. I've seen my fill of chrysanthemums, roses, gardenias—there's not a funeral spray in the world I want near my grave. No, sir . . . you be sure Mr. Norrell remembers that . . .' *[Now her voice takes on a harsh, aggressive edge.]* 'Now, Marietta, you tell Mr. Norrell it's the best all the way, he's to spare no cash on the funeral trimmings. Lay me out in my Brooks Brothers special, heap the place with flowers, every fancy spray you can find for your beloved Lawrence . . .' *[an evil chuckle follows]* 'Make sure there's no open casket unless I'm done up fine, look just like myself. It's to be a midnight service, Marietta, with the burial at dawn. That'll show 'em, Lawrence Edwards goes out in style . . .' *[Again the evil chuckle. Now she begins to pout and whine.]* 'Mr. Norrell knows best, Marietta, you tell him it was a dumb life, all I did was lay around waitin' for him anyway. You tell him not to bother with much, I don't want nobody peerin' down at me, Marietta, so keep the casket closed. Just music at the service, no eulogy, what would they say about me anyway . . . that he lay still for years waitin' for death to take him away.

You leave it to Mr. Norrell, Marietta . . .' *[Now she begins to twitch.]* 'N . . . n . . . ow, M . . . Mar . . . ietta, d . . . d . . . don't y . . . y . . . you m . . . ma . . . ke a fu . . . fu . . . ss, I . . . I'm g . . . gone th . . . th . . . that's all . . . I . . . I . . . wa . . . was h . . . here an . . . and . . . I . . . 'm g . . . gone. Th . . . th . . . l . . . l . . . ast o . . . of th . . . the Edwards bo . . . boys t . . . t . . . to fi . . . nd him . . . self so . . . so . . . me peace . . .'

[SHE gets up, snapping herself out of it.]

MRS. WINSTON. Can you imagine the life I've led! Pushed around by four big stubborn boys churning and dancing inside me! *[She is beside herself.]* Now just who is Marietta Winston . . . she has money . . . *[She gets a kick out of that.]* could pick myself up some nice young thing . . . You do the dancing, sweetie, I'll pay the tune. I've kept up appearances. I am snappy and fresh . . . *[All of a sudden she becomes maudlin, almost screams out.]* But my boys, my boys, look what happened to all my boys . . .

[She breaks down completely. Mr. Norrell is beside himself.]

MRS. WINSTON. I remember everything! Just like it was a movie! I can tell you who stood where, what they said, what they were wearing when they said it . . . I can tell you who cried, who smiled, who lay still and pouted. Everything. Exactly . . .

[She goes back to the beginning.]

MRS. WINSTON. Pop was so full of fire, the need to be different . . . first colored to get a job with the post office, first colored to own property in Riverview, he was like an explosion . . . handsome, funny, nearsighted, mean . . . kept the whole house bristling at the seams . . . *[She becomes* *her father.]* 'Now, Lawrence, you come down with me next week and take that post office exam. I want one of my boys to put in a good show there . . .' *[She chuckles meanly.]* 'Ella . . . you stop fussing over these boys, I know what each and every one of them better turn out to be . . . I will not tolerate from my boys any scrawny colored lives . . .' *[His violence overwhelms her.]* 'That fool of a man, did he forget it was Josh Edwards he was talking to . . . I may be too skin deep, locked forever behind this stone wall, but may no fool ever forget it's still Josh Edwards he's dealing with . . .'

> *[The last thrust seems to release her, she sits rocking back and forth.]*

MRS. WINSTON. We loved him . . . we thought he was just the greatest . . . every mood, every moment in that house came from him . . . he pumped us full to overflowing, not one of us could breathe for all his fire inside us . . . *[She is suddenly exhausted.]* Jeremy fled . . . took his nervous stuttering self off to the navy, put the length and breadth of the automobile industry in Pop's way. Nelson had one searing burst of glory, flew through the air two Olympics in a row, glittered with medals, broke one world record after another, came home at the ripe age of twenty-seven, took to his bed, began rehearsing his death. *[It becomes harder and harder for her to breathe.]* Lawrence stomped his way to the top, became the first of the first of the coloreds . . . *[She tries to laugh but has difficulty breathing.]* . . . stepped on everybody to get where he was going, left a trail of mangled bodies in his wake, crushed me, crushed my Franklin . . . *[She can hardly breathe. Lawrence's voice takes over.]* 'Now, Marietta . . . don't you go on about that . . . I didn't know Franklin had it in

him. Old boy knew every crafty politician in the state . . .
valuable connections, especially when they're coming at
me fast and furious from my own flesh and blood . . .'

[She chuckles meanly, begins to choke. MR. NORRELL gets
up quickly, brings her a glass of water, which she sips slowly.]

MRS. WINSTON. *[breathing more easily]* You are too kind
with the cool manners of my Franklin . . .

[MR. NORRELL sits down.]

MRS. WINSTON. . . . a mortician himself later turned state
senator, far surpassing Lawrence the eldest as the first of
the first of the first of the coloreds . . . *[Now she laughs in*
her own inimitable way.] He was a fool, my Franklin . . . of
all my boys he was the only one I did not expect to turn
out a fool . . . he hated the undertaking business . . . *[She*
looks at Mr. Norrell.] . . . as I suspect you must, who wants
to spend his life keeping the dead? *[assuming Franklin's*
voice] 'Undertakers don't age, Marietta, they stick a little
embalming fluid up the old veins . . . a touch of death that
adds to the overall distinction . . .'

[She chuckles like Franklin. MR. NORRELL lights a
cigarette.]

MRS. WINSTON. *[still in Franklin's voice]* 'A dead body tells a
lot of secrets, Marietta . . .'

[She sits forward as if Mr. Norrell were Franklin.]

MRS. WINSTON. What **do** you mean, Franklin, now you
just tell me what you mean . . .

[She begins to carry on a two-way conversation.
MR. NORRELL smokes relentlessly.]

MRS. WINSTON. 'The other day they brought me Old
Man Wilson . . .' 'You mean Slade Wilson, who used to live
in Riverview? . . .' 'The same, Marietta, the same . . .' 'He
was a handsome man, Franklin. I remember him strutting
down Penn Street with his ebony caries.' 'The Sport, we
boys **used** to call him the Sport . . .' '**How** did he look in
death, Franklin? Did he keep his spiffy looks . . .' 'That
he did, Marietta, but if the truth be told he had almost no
genitals . . .' 'No <u>genitals</u> . . . oh, Franklin, you can't mean
to be telling me that.' *[And she bursts out laughing, sits staring
at Mr. Norrell.]* Oh, Franklin, there's nobody but nobody I
ever laughed with like you . . .

[SHE gets up gaily.]

MRS. WINSTON. 'Tell me what I'm to wear, Franklin,
Richard's taking me to the Links' **Dance** . . .' 'Now,
Marietta, you wear that blue silk dress I picked out for you
with those beige satin pumps, long gloves, your hair back
in a chignon, and just a little makeup, you are not a woman
who should wear much makeup . . .'

[SHE spins slowly around.]

MRS. WINSTON. '. . . it was a lovely dance, Franklin, I
looked just fine, you would have been proud of me . . .
Lawrence came with that sleek little Fieldsboro girl who
looks so much like him. I think they're going to get
married, Franklin . . . two sleekly polished souls, oh,
everyone you can imagine was there, the Hurleys, the
Atkins . . . missed you of course . . . Lillie would have
made quite a splash, is she better, Franklin . . . will she
ever be better for her Frankie Boy . . .' *[That makes her
really laugh.]* That is such a truly embarrassing name, only
Lillie could think of such a thing . . . out of her wide-

ranging memory for the coy romantic touch she calls you her Frankie Boy . . . *[She imitates Lillie.]* 'Oh, Frankie Boy, why are you so mean to me, he can be so mean to me, Marietta . . .'

[SHE sits down, becoming delirious.]

MRS. WINSTON. Oh boy oh boy . . . Lillie didn't last long **enough** to smile at . . . Franklin began to shrivel, grief, guilt, children, the hoity-toity Gould in-laws, oh boy oh boy . . . thought he could save his life with a brand-new wife, prim, precious, with none of Lillie's saving romantic touches, oh boy oh boy . . . *[She begins to rock.]* . . . did they ever dry each other out . . . *[She imitates the prim wife.]* 'That doesn't seem like a wise course to me, Franklin, we have very few frivolous dollars . . .' *[Now she takes Franklin's part.]* 'Frivolous your <u>soul</u> . . . there's enough there for the theater, a classy dinner afterward, and I'll be damned if you'll spend one cent of that money for anything else . . .' *[She rocks sadly.]* . . . boy oh boy . . . two pinched nerves drying each other out . . . *[Her body begins to twitch.]* Still, he moved forward . . . finished school, laid the embalming business to rest, took up politics . . . inched **his way** forward in spite of everything . . . like some awful soldier, enemies on every side, an ever-growing body of enemies on every side . . .

[By now she is really delirious. MR. NORRELL gets up to get her another glass of water.]

MRS. WINSTON. *[delirious]* Why did you make me one of them, Franklin . . . I was never your enemy, the things Lawrence said should never have come between us . . .

[MR. NORRELL hands her the water, which SHE knocks over as she rises, rushes toward the coffin in the viewing room.]

MRS. WINSTON. *[beside herself]* You took all the answers, each and every one of you, slipped out from under long before it was time, long before it was time you slipped away . . . ran headlong into silence, left me to walk around in your shoes, your unfinished lives, the woes of your wives and children hanging on my heart . . .

[MR. NORRELL tries to restrain her. SHE pushes him away.]

MRS. WINSTON. *[screaming at him]* I'd bring them back . . . take away your flowers, the chill trappings of your precious ceremony that no one can touch. I'd bring them back, shovel them out from under, tell them to answer their beloved Marietta for all the unfinished tales left burning in my lap . . .

[SHE kneels before the coffin weeping.]

MRS. WINSTON. No stately rest for me . . . no stately rest for me . . .

[MR. NORRELL gently pulls her away from the coffin.]

MRS. WINSTON. *[growing meek]* Now I commend my Richard unto your care . . .

[SHE sits down. MR. NORRELL sits down. They begin to make the funeral arrangements. As she talks, the stage will grow progressively darker.]

MRS. WINSTON. *[businesslike]* He would like to be buried in his navy-blue serge suit with his careful polka-dot tie, a white shirt starched as crisp and stiff as his soul. A midday service, the sun high overhead brightening the memory of one who lived in the shadows . . .

[Lights go out quickly.]

END OF PROLOGUE

ACT I: FRANKIE BOY
SCENE 1

[LILLIE EDWARDS emerges from darkness, rushes quietly downstage. She is an elegant-looking woman, extremely fair, with long black hair pulled severely away from her face. She is a little on the plump side, giving an impression of robust physical and mental health, when in fact she is far too delicate, almost fragile. She is wearing a nightgown, robe, and slippers.

As she begins to talk, lights come up on an empty chaise lounge by an open window. Chintz curtains blow back and forth. LILLIE talks as if she were stretched out in that chaise lounge writing a letter.]

LILLIE. *[looking over toward the lounge]* Frankie Boy, I'm sitting by the window on one of those cool spring days. There is not the least suspicion of rain nor of too much sunshine. You might think it was fall if you were not, as I am, attentive to the fact that Momma's magnolia tree is about to burst into bloom. No, it is not fall, for me it may never be fall again. Oh, I say that, then five minutes later I feel so strong, so very strong, all my love for you comes racing through my mind and I can't imagine why or how I could have such a morbid thought. I am better, really I am. Every day I grow better and better. Our little Rowena takes excellent care of me, brings me a glass of water—all she can comfortably carry at her age—whenever I ask. I can watch her play from this window. She has a favorite game of sitting securely on her haunches on the gravel beneath my window with her spinning top. She manages, without losing her balance, to pump the thing full of air, so that it spins an amazingly long time while she sways back and forth on her haunches. She is an eager child, there is such a bright readiness in her face as if already she was much too alert . . . is that the kind of thing mothers say about their young ones . . . I don't know, but sometimes her alertness feels like a presentiment . . . *[She turns aside.]* What can I say to you on such a nice cool day beside these up-and-down fragments . . . that I am still with you as if it were only this morning that you were last here, not five long days and nights ago, that tomorrow begins another **week**end—this one without you, and I am not looking forward to it at all . . .

[Lights go out, leaving the stage in darkness.]

[Lights come up on ROSIE GOULD sitting in her garden. She is a handsome woman, also very fair, her black hair tinged with silver. She has an utterly charming manner, yet inside it one senses a frightening aloofness.]

ROSIE. *[to herself]* Every color in the rainbow abounds in my garden . . . fuchsia and petal **pink,** deep rose and crimson blue, golden yellow and bright flamingo, soon to come out of hiding, all of them, to bloom right here in my very own garden . . .

[She claps her hands softly.]

[Offstage we hear LILLIE's voice.]

LILLIE. Momma . . .

ROSIE. *[in a proud, yet forbidding tone]* I am in my garden, soon to become a thing of beauty. I am picturing to myself where things will appear and when . . . my forsythia have already come and gone . . . my magnolia will soon appear along with the bright ivory petals of my dogwood . . . then my daffodils, my pale white and yellow jonquils . . . then slowly a feast of colors will follow, surprising me at every turn . . .

[Offstage we hear LILLIE's voice.]

LILLIE. It's almost my death, Momma . . . what flowers will you grow on my grave . . .

[Lights go out.]

[Lights come up on LILLIE, again emerging out of darkness. As she begins to speak lights come up on an empty four-poster bed propped high with lace pillows, covered with soft sheets and an elegant lace coverlet. The bed is turned down. LILLIE talks as if she were lying in bed writing a letter.]

LILLIE. *[looking toward the bed]* Frankie Boy, tonight I can't sleep at all. If you were here I could. If your arms were around me and I knew we had touched each other dearly, then I could fall asleep. Without that my nice big bed is a torment. Everything has become a torment. The little baby above my head I scarcely recognize as my own. She is so tiny, so silent, as if already not two months in this world she knew that nothing but silence will do. She never cries. Rowena refuses to believe she is really alive, her silence offends Rowena's eager alertness. I have two children from my Frankie Boy! And my strength is gone, not my loving strength and faith in you, but a little weakness I can't seem to define. Where does it come from when I am so eager for there to be no obstacles in our way. If only you could see how I toss and turn on Momma's delicate sheets, when she brought me here for the ease and comfort of her surroundings. They are easy . . . I have only to lie still and get well, while you spend those awful nights guarding that warehouse, come home in the morning to see who may have died, try to catch some sleep before your classes . . . all of a sudden the phone rings, someone really is dead, and whoopee! We have a case! Perhaps the first in weeks, so many weeks you scarcely remember how to embalm them! *[that makes her laugh]* Oh, Frankie Boy . . . sometimes at night when you're off at your watchman's job, I think to myself, what a strange life we lead, waiting for death to knock at our door. And when it comes, why, we're rich! For a **minute** all our bills are paid, we meet the Hurleys for lunch, join Marietta and Richard at the theater. Momma takes me shopping for a fine silk or two. I do up my hair, pretend to a grandeur death has loaned me for an hour . . . only an hour . . . *[She seems to collapse.]* Oh, Frankie Boy, the little girl from Cape May is tired . . .

[ROSIE enters, goes over to the bed.]

ROSIE. You're not asleep.

LILLIE. *[from the other side of the room]* No, Momma . . .

[ROSIE pats the bed, smoothes down the covers.]

ROSIE. My nice soft silks and lavender, who can't find sleep in such a fragrant bed . . .

[She fluffs the pillows.]

ROSIE. . . . only a child that death is seeking, my only child that death is seeking.

[*She sits down on the bed. Lights go out.*]

[*Lights come up on ROSIE and LILLIE sitting in Rosie's garden.*]

LILLIE. And where is my Frankie Boy you say . . .

ROSIE. I don't say, that I never say, nor ask, nor remember.

LILLIE. He can't come this weekend, Momma, he's busy embalming our dead. We have two of them . . .

ROSIE. [*clapping her hands*] No details, please.

LILLIE. [*with strange pride*] An old man of seventy, a girl of fifteen. One died of old age, the other only God knows why . . . a welfare death. Payment is an assured thing with a welfare death.

ROSIE. [*rising*] And then she speaks of money, on a day like today, when everything I own is in bloom . . . and you with your own car, a post at the normal school, pretty suits and sweaters to hang on that handsome frame . . .

LILLIE. [*sighing*] Before my Frankie Boy . . .

[*ROSIE turns angrily. Lights go down quickly.*]

[*Lights come up on ROSIE.*]

ROSIE. A dead daughter, that's a fine thing to talk about. I never speak of a dead daughter. Oh, there are letters, photographs taken up to the age of thirty, a little child who screams from the top of the stairs . . . Where's my mommie . . . [*haughtily*] How many times do I have to tell you, child, your mother has gone to Heaven, where all dead mothers go . . . to Heaven, where it is fragrant, sweet smelling, and white lilacs are in bloom the year round . . .

[She claps her hands. Feverishly. Lights go out.]

[Lights come up quickly on LILLIE emerging from darkness. As she begins to speak, lights come up on the empty chaise lounge beside the open window.]

LILLIE. *[looking over at the chaise lounge]* Bring me some water, my little Rowena, I'm thirsty, God, I'm thirsty, and my back feels broken in two, I could scream forever from the pain, as if the center of me were cracking, **splintering** in all directions. The thought of my children makes me bleed. They watch and wait for me to disappear. I will disappear so completely . . . leave scarcely a trace. Momma will shut her eyes, carry me to the furthest corner of her mind, a little garden no one can enter. Frankie Boy will hold on to my letters, all the words I've written, the little notes left on our bed whenever I went out, the long epistles from my sleepless nights. I have written my heart out to Frankie Boy . . . *[She giggles.]* Frankie Boy . . . I'm sitting by this window, the first soft breeze of spring blowing in my face. Right now you must be in one of your classes . . . Embalming Fluids 2, The Anatomy of Dead and Living Corpses . . . *[She giggles.]* . . . while I spend my days on this cozy lounge thinking of well-turned phrases to send your way, all my fine thoughts racing lazily across the page. You struggle, while I remain demure, stretched out on my chair, a pretty afghan thrown across my knees . . . *[defiantly]* I love it when thoughts are well said. It is my way of keeping up, keeping my little weakness at bay . . . *[as if writing in a diary]* Today I watched Momma's magnolias open their eyes. First they stiffen, then their blossoms pout forth in an unexpected burst of glory. I sip my water. The light **changes** a million times a minute. Sometimes it glares at me as if for the last time, and I try to imagine <u>exactly</u> what my life has been . . . *[She grips herself, screams.]* Momma! Don't forget me . . .

[Lights go out.]

[Lights come up on ROSIE, walking toward the four-poster bed. It is empty, the covers delicately turned down like before. ROSIE smoothes the sheets and pillows.]

ROSIE. You can't sleep.

[LILLIE answers from a darkened corner.]

LILLIE. No, Momma.

ROSIE. Then we'll have tea with honey in my best porcelain cups.

LILLIE. A ceremony to hold back our tears.

[ROSIE sits down on the bed, begins to cry.]

LILLIE. This is how it will happen . . . alone, away from everyone, my momma will lay out her tears . . . There will be no public mourning, no outward display of grief. On the last day she will put on her black crepe de chine, walk dry-eyed behind my coffin. The ceremonies by which she lives permit no sentimental conclusions.

[Lights go out.]

[Lights come up on LILLIE. She dances as if Frankie Boy were dancing with her. She is beautifully dressed in a silk print, dark pumps, a flower in her hair.]

LILLIE. *[gaily]* It's my name that covers me . . . without it they'd call me a **hussy**. They would! Consider it shameless the way I pursue you. No sooner have I dismissed my class than I race to my car, barrel nineteen miles down the road, wake you from your watchman's slumber . . . your grandmother turns away when I race up the steps . . . 'Shameless hussy,' she says . . . still, she is kind to me, she doesn't tell your folks how the Gould's eccentric daughter pursues you . . . oh, I'm eccentric . . . I come from the queerest Negro stock in all of Burlington County . . . too fancy, hushed and elegant . . . don't hold it against me, with you I'm beyond all that . . . just hold me . . . *[She dances with vehemence.]* Is it possible ever for me to be held enough . . . I don't think so . . . if death were coming in one hour all I'd **ask** is that you hold me . . . I get cold fast, my one and only weakness is a terrible chill that starts at the base of my spine . . . *[Her legs seem to give way.]* Oh, for one minute to know why I am . . .

   [Lights go out.]

   [Lights come up quickly on ROSIE, sitting in a rocking chair.]

LILLIE. *[offstage]* Momma!

   [SHE comes running in, still in her silk dress.]

LILLIE. It was a lovely dance!

   [ROSIE doesn't answer.]

LILLIE. I danced every dance with Franklin Edwards from Riverview, a handsome man who will be magnificent one of these days. Not now . . . he's only a mortician, a watchman at night to make ends meet. But he's in school, an education major like I was, he'll be a teacher one day, then a principal, he is determined, it's written all over his face, this intention to succeed . . . he is brown, not very, but a little browner than any of us . . .

[She waits. ROSIE doesn't say a thing.]

LILLIE. *[laughing]* I call him my Frankie Boy . . .

[Lights go out.]

[Lights come up on LILLIE, standing on a staircase. Same silk dress. She leans over the railing as if speaking to someone below.]

LILLIE. Is he asleep, Grandma Edwards . . . he must be. It's foolish of me to come, don't scold me. I can't help it. I can hardly teach my class for thinking of him. I call him my ghostly lover, he is everywhere I turn but I don't for one minute believe he's real unless I can touch him, see him with my own eyes . . . it's foolish, it must be foolish . . . I can stop and say that because he is only seconds away and you don't mind, I can see it in your eyes that you don't really mind . . .

[SHE rushes up the steps. Lights go out.]

[Lights come up on ROSIE in her rocking chair. She is reading a letter. We hear Lillie's voice offstage.]

LILLIE'S VOICE. Dear Momma, I think of you so much at night when Frankie Boy's gone to his warehouse, and I'm alone in this queer house in this awful town for the sake of better and better dead bodies . . . *[She giggles.]* How can I write such things . . . when one day, you'll see, my Frankie Boy will make it up to me. I have such confidence in him, it's just the present that is hard and sometimes ugly, when I have in me all your spoiled love of beauty. You think I'm wrong, don't you . . . from the beginning you washed your elegant hands of me, clapped softly three times, and *whoosh!* I'm gone . . . *[She begins to recite.]*

> My Rosie is a fair, fair thing
> with nerves of molten steel
> She only likes the softest things
> that she alone can feel
> She never looks for ugliness
> the crack inside the wall
> But turns to stare at lilacs
> and the bursting joy of fall
> My Rosie is like springtime
> her gleeful hands rejoice
> She has a way of living life
> outside the least remorse
> She is so pale and lovely
> surrounds herself with things
> The beauty of the moment is
> all she cares to sing
> What's done is done
> my Rosie says
> and never looks behind
> When I am dead and in my grave
> she'll never weep nor pine . . .

[Lights go out.]

[Lights come up on ROSIE in her garden. LILLIE enters in her robe and slippers.]

LILLIE. I can't sleep.

ROSIE. Would you like some tea?

LILLIE. No thank you, Momma. Why are you up so late?

ROSIE. It's so silent . . . I can feel it in my fingers . . .

[She claps her hands softly, begins to sing.]

ROSIE. *[singing]*

> What a fellowship,
> What a joy to be,
> Leaning on the everlasting Lord . . .
> Leaning . . . leaning . . .
> Leaning on the everlasting Lord . . .

[She hums, continues to clap softly.]

LILLIE. *[amused]* You never go to church, Momma.

ROSIE. *[still clapping softly]* I have my own little service right here in my garden. It is as fine an altar as one could make . . . the Lord Himself often comes here to take His rest . . . *[amused]* We speak of many things . . . the vivid purple tint of my anemones . . . that cluster of pale blue roses, an unheard of achievement **in** the breeding of roses. He tells me His sorrows. Trouble is always a step away, I remind Him . . . one must be <u>careful</u> to keep it at that distance, then I serve tea, the best of all rituals, a quiet communion without blood or sacrifice . . . *[She claps her hands softly.]*

> Leaning . . . **leaning** . . .
> Leaning on the everlasting Lord . . .

[Lights go out.]

[LILLIE emerges from darkness. As she begins to talk, lights come up on the four-poster bed, empty, the covers delicately pulled back like before. She speaks as if she were lying in bed writing a letter.]

LILLIE. *[looking toward the bed]* Frankie Boy, one last
and final letter before you come for me, it is almost
time for you to come . . . or will you have to send that
pompous Mr. Norrell, who will be the final one to lay his
obsequious hands on me. I wish it were you . . . that must
sound awfully morbid . . . the dying lady requests that
her husband embalm her . . . think of it . . . your proud
and dazzling Lillie embalmed . . . *[that breaks her down]*
They don't want you here . . . they will never forgive you
when I'm gone . . . they're queer diluted stock, they take
no Negro measure of themselves . . . you remind them of
that and they will not forgive you for it . . . they wish to
remain simply and everlastingly Goulds . . . *[drifting]* I've
thought of a name for myself. When I'm gone my children
should call me Dead Lillie . . . show us Dead Lillie's letters,
Poppa . . . is that her photograph, how old was Dead Lillie
when this picture was taken . . . is Dead Lillie really our
mother . . . *[crying out in shame]* How can <u>anyone</u> be so
weak as to die . . .

[Lights go out.]

*[Come up on LILLIE in the four-poster bed. Morning sunlight
streams through the windows.]*

LILLIE. *[awakening]* Bring me flowers, Momma . . .
jonquils and lilies but no gladiolas. My Frankie Boy's
coming and he hates gladiolas . . . *[She screams.]* Don't
put them on my grave . . . nothing that reminds him of
death and all its trimmings . . . *[She lies back, exhausted.]*
He's had his fill, my Frankie Boy . . . *[drifting, delirious]* Oh,
Frankie Boy, you can be so mean, all of a sudden those
gray eyes change . . . it can't be you looking at me, so
eager to lash out and hurt as if you held Pop Edwards's

cane in your hand . . . is it Pop Edwards I'm seeing . . .
[sitting up] . . . hacking away at Ella with his cane . . .
what he wants from life is just outside his skin, so he hacks
away, his mustache bristles, his glasses fall from his face,
he sweeps all of you away on his angry tide . . . *[realizing]*
He's dead! Frankie Boy . . . not five minutes in his coffin,
and I'm to follow in his footsteps . . . that mean, angry
man hacking away at life . . . while I give up . . . who
wants to live off of anger . . . you Edwardses can . . . it's
your anger that pushes you along, all that terrible nervous
anger . . . you'll amount to something because of your
anger . . . not me . . . the drab passages are too much
for me . . . even my children can't hold me in the face
of all the drab passages . . . *[exhausted, drifting]* Where's
Rowena, that little alert child who screams already before
I'm gone . . . can I have you one more time, Frankie Boy,
feel your strange eccentric body inside mine one more
time . . . the last time it was awful, you looked at me with
such distaste as if already I was dead . . . Rosie's the match
for you . . . her elegant mystery pitted against your nervous
anger, there's a battle I'll miss . . .

[She moves restlessly in the bed. ROSIE comes in.]

ROSIE. *[coldly]* Franklin is here.

LILLIE. Where's the sun, Momma . . . it was warm on my
face just a few minutes ago . . .

[Lights go out.]

END OF SCENE 1

SCENE 2

[*When the scene begins the stage is in darkness. A phone is ringing. Lights come up slowly on the second or third ring. We're in a living room that is strictly middle class, not elegant, but in which every effort has been made to make things comfortable. There are a few fine pieces: a grandfather clock in one corner, a handsome upright piano in another, a couple of very expensive lamps.*

LETITIA EDWARDS rushes forward to an alcove off the living room. She is around sixty-five, of medium-brown complexion, dressed in a simple print dress. Her gray hair is cut short and severely styled. Her manner is prim, like an old maid's. Her eyes are large and sad, and her voice is a singsong kind of thing that she mistakes for elegance. She picks up the phone.]

LETITIA. Hello . . . Yes, Marietta, I've already called Mr. Norrell, yes . . . he'll be here any minute . . . he went very fast, Marietta, no, he did not linger nor speak aloud . . . that is to say, there were no final words. I know how you Edwardses like final words, the last summation, but in the end Franklin simply died . . . I'll begin that tomorrow . . . it's all written down, Marietta, I just have to read it to Mr. Norrell . . . no flowers, you know that, he hated every funeral spray that ever lived, the instructions say no funeral sprays in any shape, form, or arrangement, that is an adamant request . . . he wishes to be buried in the morning, any time before noon . . . [*his death suddenly hits her*] . . . here . . . oh, I don't think we have to worry about that, Marietta, it will be in all the papers, he died a state senator, remember . . . he was on his way . . . I said he was on his way . . . the girls, of course, right away I called

the girls. Rowena was hysterical, as always, Richmond
will have to calm her down, Lillian was her usual practical
self. They're on their way. Then I called Rosie, he would
want Rosie to know immediately . . . oh, she won't do
that, she's old, just as haughty as ever, and doesn't believe
in funerals . . . oh, the girls will help me with that, and
Mrs. Anderson will take care of the food . . . don't bother,
Marietta, there'll be plenty . . . no, he left the very minute
Franklin died . . . *[She snaps her fingers in a prim, funny way.]*
Just like that! And he was gone . . . looked at me like I
should have made Franklin deed him his senate seat. It's
absurd the way that man thinks, couldn't see enough of
Franklin these past few years, was always meeting him at
the capitol for lunch, sending us **invitations** to his splashy
parties . . . no, he never saw it that way, Marietta, he was
pleased, ever so pleased, to have his older brother pay
attention to him at last . . . no, Marietta, he didn't . . . what's
the point of rehashing all that now . . . I know . . . *[firmly]*
No, he never saw it that way . . . *[Pause.]* Oh, Marietta,
don't get yourself all worked up, that's the way it was . . .
[She sighs to herself.] . . . every moment in an Edwards life
is a production . . . I'm here . . . don't go on like that,
Marietta, **Franklin** loved you, you know that . . . look at
all the misunderstandings I've lived with from the moment
I stepped into dead mademoiselle's shoes . . . *[Silence.]* That
always does finish things, doesn't it . . . I can hear you all
now . . . 'at last **Franklin's** free to join Dead Lillie' . . .
'who's Letitia, whoever heard of Letitia' . . . *[She gets up.]* I
should go, Marietta, Mr. Norrell will be here soon, the girls
will be coming . . . all right . . . that's fine.

*[She hangs up, comes into the living room talking thoroughly to
herself.]*

LETITIA. *[to herself]* Oh, there's a lot more to say, nobody wants to hear it but there's a lot more to say . . . even Franklin didn't want to listen . . . shut his ears, turned away . . . like he could never bring himself to *see me* . . . *[She sits down.]* What was it about *me*, Franklin . . . did you think I was a puzzle . . . a sphinx . . . a little brown nun sniffing at you behind my tears . . . one time Lillian said to me . . . 'Mother, in that dress you look just like **a nun** . . .' 'Maybe I am,' I answered, 'behind this brown veil maybe there lives a nun . . .'

[She makes a funny, prim sound that is not quite a laugh. The phone rings again, but she does not move.]

LETITIA. Now who will that be . . . could be Marietta again, she has a penchant for details and I omit so many . . . or Lawrence, His Sleekness, eager to add some theatrical detail to Franklin's burial.

[The phone keeps ringing.]

LETITIA. Thank God it will not be Nelson, bawling away in despair, his face doubled up like some awful child Franklin must save again and again . . .

[SHE gets up, answers the phone.]

LETITIA. Hello . . . yes, Rosie . . . I have the deed, yes, Mt. Olive Cemetery . . . he goes in the same plot as Dead Lillie, yes . . . I've always known that, Rosie, he made it clear from the beginning that he promised her that, yes . . . I hold it against no one, Rosie, I am not nor have I ever been that kind of wife, what would have been the point, I was thirty-eight when Franklin married me, too old to bang my head against stone walls . . . yes . . . well, he tried, Rosie, always to do right by you, and you certainly have done well by the girls . . . that's not like you to bring up water under the bridge, Rosie . . . oh, he wouldn't expect you to do that, he used to say, 'Rosie does not like funerals, in the end she chose not to go even to Dead Lillie's' . . . yes . . . *[Silence.]* The girls are on their way, I'm sure they'll call you . . . certainly Rowena will when she gets here . . . no, Richmond's driving her . . . who knows how Lillian will get here . . . *[Her voice takes on a note of pride.]* She's secretive, always full of surprises, but once she's here she'll think of everything I would overlook. She is Franklin's daughter to the letter . . . *[Pause.]* . . . I expect several of them will attend, Rosie, including the governor, so I've been told . . . he died an important man . . . I said he died an important man . . . *[Silence.]* Just think of it, in the end he did you proud, became a son-in-law you could be proud of, didn't he . . . yes . . . *[softly]* He would have done **anything** to hear you say that, Rosie . . . *[Silence.]* . . . no, there is no point going over all that now . . . yes, the children will call . . . all right, Rosie . . .

[She hangs up, but continues to sit there, as if still talking to Rosie.]

LETITIA. *[inwardly to Rosie]* My **conversation** was never with you . . . Franklin's was . . . all his remarks were addressed to you . . . his clothes, his house, his children, his ambition, all his remarks were addressed to you . . .

[SHE gets up, comes into the living room, and sits down. She sits very rigid and still.]

LETITIA. *[to herself]* That's why they call **me** the Buddha, the Rock of Gibraltar . . . the immovable object between Franklin and Dead Lillie . . . *[She leans slightly forward.]* . . . propelling Franklin forward into upward

mobility. I did that . . . the years were long and lean, but
I did that . . . *[with pride]* I did not leave . . . *[She moves a
little in her seat.]* I think that is my great accomplishment,
that I did not leave . . . *[Almost a laugh escapes, she moves a
little more.]* Occasionally I took an extra pair of shoes, fled
momentarily to quieter parts, but that I only did three
times. The third time I said to myself, 'You're going to see
this thing through, if for no other reason than for the sake
of the girls, Lillian especially . . . hiding away in your closet
counting your shoes . . .' *[Her voice breaks, she grows very still
indeed.]* There's no point . . . hurricanes have gone by, great
tidal waves have swept under the bridge, there's no point . . .
[She taps her foot to keep from crying.] Just the other day
Franklin said to me . . . 'Letitia, you've really been good for
me, your common sense, your stubbornness, I don't think
I'd have made it without you . . .' *[Her foot taps a little more
insistently.]* Those were his words exactly. I have an excellent
memory for detail . . .

> *[She begins to cry. When the phone rings, she gets up quickly to
> answer it.]*

LETITIA. Hello . . . oh, Danielle, I didn't expect to hear
your voice . . . I don't know, I thought it was Rowena or
Lillian telling me when they might arrive . . . yes . . . well,
he didn't last long after Nelson, did he . . . no, very fast,
the Edwardses don't linger, that much we ought to have
been prepared for, yes . . . *[Silence.]* And how are you . . .
you've got a better sense of humor than most, that's why . . .
yes . . . I spoke to Marietta just a little while ago . . . no,
Jeremy hasn't called, but Marietta spoke to him, they've got
to come all the way from Detroit, I'm sure that takes a little
organizing, yes . . . *[She chuckles.]* The gathering of the clan,
as you say . . . but the volatile ones are gone. Lawrence is

left to bluster to himself . . . it's better this way, Danielle,
I don't think Nelson could have stood it, no, he depended
too much on Franklin . . . yes . . . you're right about that,
as I say you really do have a sense of humor, yes . . . *[She
is becoming impatient.]* That's **funny,** yes . . . that has all
the earmarks of what Franklin would call the Danielle
touch . . . *[She is growing more impatient and irritable.]* You're
right, we certainly have, I . . . all right, Danielle, that's fine,
yes . . .

[She hangs up quickly, impatient, irritated.]

LETITIA. *[to herself]* All that sly good humor is wasted on
me . . . the fast repartee, the quick draw, they all think
they're masters at the quick draw . . .

*[SHE starts to move away when the phone rings again. Irritated,
she answers it quickly.]*

LETITIA. *[with muted anger]* Hello . . . Lawrence . . . well,
I was talking to Danielle and before that Rosie . . . she
called, yes . . . what's that got to do with it . . . no, I've
already made arrangements with Mrs. Anderson . . . who
said anything about gourmet cuisine . . . oh, Lawrence . . .
[She becomes edgy.] . . . he's on his way . . . Whitman . . . why
Franklin would have a fit . . . but you're talking about white
politicians, Lawrence . . . oh, Lawrence . . . *[She becomes more
edgy.]* . . . no, not yet . . . well it takes a while, I'm sure . . .
you mean the funeral . . . I'll see that they leave space . . .
fine . . . <u>you'll</u> lead them in . . . why it's got nothing to
do with you, Mr. Norrell can seat them just fine . . . what
hearse . . . who said anything about a horse-drawn hearse!
My God, Lawrence . . . *[She is beside herself.]* . . . he's not
Kennedy . . . *[She begins to tap her foot.]* I'm here . . . I'll leave
that to Lillian, she's the literary one . . . Reverend Grant . . .

it's all written down, Lawrence, Franklin left precise
instructions about everything . . . I'm sure one of them will
want to speak on behalf of his colleagues . . . about what . . .
what are you talking about . . . I never heard of such a
thing, you're not supposed to speak at your brother's funeral,
it's not a rally . . . *[trying to placate him]* He wouldn't want
anything showy, Lawrence, you know that . . . well, maybe
that's where you differ . . . I said maybe that's where you
differ . . . liquor, for what . . . I'm not serving any drinks
to any politicians, Lawrence . . . *[She tightens suddenly.]* That
may be, but I know what Franklin would expect . . . *[She
goes even tighter.]* I'm still his wife . . . after I've put him in
the ground you can think what you like . . . *[She tries to
keep from crying.]* I put in twenty-six years . . . somewhere,
in somebody's eyes, that's got to have some performance
value . . . *[She shifts ground violently to keep from crying.]* I
think someone's at the door, Lawrence . . . most likely
Mr. Norrell . . . yes . . .

[She hangs up quickly, a bit flustered and feeling guilty for lying.]

LETITIA. *[nervous]* Even in the face of mockery are white
lies allowed . . .

[SHE paces uncertainly, flustered and a bit out of control.]

LETITIA. *[to herself, with prim, nervous guilt]* I have no
performance value . . . I know that . . . in his crueler
moments Franklin would say I'm one of those women
whose dresses are always getting caught between their
buttocks. I see myself still in the early days of our marriage,
when I struggled in and out of silks and gabardine only to
provoke again and again his sharp rebuke that my dress had
slipped somewhere between my buttocks . . .

[She gestures self-consciously, almost as if to feel behind her.]

LETITIA. *[seeking an audience]* When I was first introduced as the replacement for Dead Lillie, mouths fell, heads turned away, Lawrence had the awful dramatic gall to call me a Negro **nun,** all of them flared and snorted like racehorses at the gate . . . **Franklin** could see, then and forever after, that I had no performance value . . .

[SHE moves farther downstage, as if in her mind she has created a real audience.]

LETITIA. *[directly to the audience]* The Edwardses are all fine performers . . . even the in-laws must measure up. Marietta's Richard is a quiet, withdrawn man, but with a sense of humor so dry and funny it crackles . . . Danielle has always held her own with a kind of sly, slow wit that baffled and amused Nelson . . . Lawrence met his match in Caroline, they goad each other in a violent tit for tat. Nobody speaks of Aurora. But then, nobody speaks of Jeremy . . . who dares not speak for himself because he stutters too badly. Aurora and Jeremy are the poor relations in the clan. That leaves me and Dead Lillie . . . who was without question the star in-law performer, holding her own against all of them with her superior grace and style. She even had the good sense to die early, while she could still dazzle them . . .

[SHE steps forward, literally and figuratively into the spotlight. The room fades.]

LETITIA. That leaves me . . . I was thirty-eight when Franklin married me. Up until then I lived at home and worked as the medical assistant to a prestigious New York doctor . . . only once before had I ever considered marriage . . . Richard was his name, but when I found out

he had a violent temper I got out of that pretty quick . . .
little did I know that ten years later I would land in the
lion's den with a man who would roar and scream at me
until I knew no rest . . . *[that amuses her]* I don't often
appreciate jokes, but that is a pretty good one that got played
on me . . .

[She steps slightly forward, more confidentially.]

LETITIA. I was most certainly untouched, no man had
ever laid a finger on me . . . when it came Franklin's time
I lay exceedingly still . . . he was very handsome, Franklin,
sable-colored with piercing light eyes and fine crinkly
hair. I think I was flattered . . . *[She turns aside, somewhat
embarrassed.]* . . . why else would a woman of thirty-eight
marry a man with two daughters. Rowena had just turned
six, Lillian was less than two . . . a shy child with a face like
a cherub . . . I don't think she understood a thing so she
fastened herself to me, became my shadow . . . whenever I
moved so did she . . . even when I went to the bathroom
she would wait nervously outside the door . . . the *few times*
I decided to leave I came home to find her counting my
shoes . . . *[that makes her sad]* Rowena was wily, too full
of memory . . . it was 'Dead Lillie this' and 'Dead Lillie
that' and 'Where, where, oh, where could Dead Lillie be
now' . . . there was no end to her whining and stomping
about. Franklin would come home, the child would start to
flail and scream . . . he'd swear I'd been beating her, come
after me fists raised, eyes burning . . . call me every name in
the book, send plates glasses ashtrays flying past my head . . .
he had the worst, the very worst, temper I ever witnessed in
my life . . . I'm told his father was the same . . . a terrifying
kind of anger that came at you in violent doses, all of them

have it . . . Marietta goes shrill the moment she enters a
room, Lawrence would kill if he could just go unpunished,
Nelson turned his inward and beat himself to death, poor
Jeremy hides it all behind a stutter and a twitch . . . mad
souls . . . every one of them, with the in-laws bringing
up the rear . . . didn't I say I landed in the lion's den?
[She straightens suddenly.] But it took me unawares . . . I
barely had time to turn into a sphinx . . . *[She grows rigid,
immovable]* . . . that's what I did . . . grew dumb and silent
just as fast as I could . . .

*[She folds her hands, distancing her voice and body from the
scenes she remembers.]*

LETITIA. *[coldly]* I could not rant and rave . . . had **none** of
Dead Lillie's **charm** . . . no dry mocking humor to carry
me through. There they all were . . . time and time again
leaping at the slightest spark to set themselves on fire . . .
[She backs away from the memory.] . . . went still as a mouse,
did **not** move a muscle . . . they named me the Sphinx . . .
'Where's the Sphinx,' Lawrence would shout as soon as he
hit the door, 'Franklin's Negro nun who keeps watch at the
gate . . .'

[Her hands remain folded, she grows very still indeed.]

LETITIA. *[with cold amusement]* It got on their nerves that I
wouldn't enter into the spirit of things . . . 'You need a sense
of humor, Letitia,' Danielle would say, 'you can't gather ye
among the clan without a sense of humor . . .' and she'd
puff on her cigarette . . . *[Pause.]* . . . but it drove Franklin
to distraction . . . 'You can hold a grudge longer than any
woman on earth,' he'd scream, 'damn house feels like a
tomb every time you get your feathers ruffled, don't think

you fool me with that act, either . . . pouting is your best performance, your one and <u>only</u> performance . . .'

[She becomes a little more animated.]

LETITIA. *[seeing him]* Then he'd slam the door, or throw something . . . or get into his car and ride around until he had an accident. He was an accident-prone man . . . dishes broke under his fingertips, lamps and furniture got polished to death . . . floors squeaked when he scrubbed them, the girls jumped at his touch . . . 'you pout, get that silly dumb look like candy wouldn't melt in your mouth, it'll melt all right, you can swallow a whole lot, but you never let on a thing . . . that's your secret weapon, you never let on a thing . . .' *[Imitating him gets her charged up.]* Then he'd go off and scrub the bathroom floor . . . braid the girls' hair before they went to bed, fuss over what I was going to wear to church, march from room to room like a general on tour . . .

[She begins to breathe a little heavily.]

LETITIA. *[feeling him]* He was everywhere . . . inside the size of the bra the girls wore, checking my girdle to be sure it was tight . . . 'Letitia . . . that dress looks like the Salvation Army turned it down . . . now don't you dare wear those shoes, between the dress and those Red Cross stockings you already look like a refugee . . .'

[She tugs at her dress. Franklin's voice takes over.]

LETITIA. *[becoming him]* 'And don't go all numb and rigid because I called you a refugee . . . can't you laugh, is there a whiff of humor anywhere . . . underneath that brown somber mask . . . damn, Letitia . . .'

[SHE backs away as he hits her, falls awkwardly to the floor.]

LETITIA. *[drifting]* I used to think of Dead Lillie then, asleep and laughing in some rose garden of time . . . see her sharp eyes that stared at me from Franklin's dresser, the vague hint of a smile that played around her mouth. There's nothing she could tell me . . . no . . . if she were here it's I who would talk volumes in her ear . . . but in the eyes that smile I sometimes think it's me she sees, not Franklin . . . the cloak she wore is wrapped around my arms. She is no more . . . her time is all my music, and when I'm gone the best she wrote is dead . . .

[The spotlight on Letitia begins to fade. Lights come up in the living room as the phone begins to ring insistently.]

END OF ACT I

ACT II: NELSON THE BABY

[Lights come up on DANIELLE EDWARDS standing at the bottom of the staircase in a suburban home. To her left is the living room, while the dining room and kitchen are straight ahead. The dining room has a huge mahogany table that takes up the center of the room with a sideboard behind it and a china closet at the opposite end. An old lace tablecloth covers the table, there are papers and dishes strewn on top of it. Beyond the dining room we can glimpse the kitchen. These two rooms are well lit, they are the focus of most of the activity; the living room is in shadows, as if lit only by the morning sun. It has photographs in gold frames, a brocade couch and armchairs, coffee table, rug, etc.—the somewhat unimaginative accoutrements of a suburban living room.

*We see DANIELLE, who is shouting upstairs. She is a
beautiful woman in her early thirties with skin as white as any
white woman's, jet-black hair worn loosely away from her face, a
deeply rouged complexion, and a raspy voice like some old-time
vaudeville actress. Style is her dominant note, a kind of raunchy
elegance heightened by her stunning looks.]*

DANIELLE. *[shouting upstairs]* I told you they didn't have any
Ralston . . . *[She mumbles to herself.]* Ralston, Ralston . . .
he's always got to have the damn Ralston . . . *[She shouts
upstairs.]* I got Wheatena, it's as good as Ralston any
day. I can fix it the same way and you won't know the
difference . . .

[She waits for an answer. None is forthcoming.]

DANIELLE. *[to herself]* This is going to be one of his silent
days.

[SHE starts toward the kitchen when the phone rings.]

DANIELLE. Hello . . . how you doin' . . . I was just fixing
breakfast for His Highness . . . oh, he's awake, he's up there
crying because I couldn't get any Ralston . . . there are days
when all he remembers is your mother at the breakfast table
eating her Ralston with her teeth out and her mahogany
hair falling into the bowl . . . that's the scene exactly,
straight from the horse's mouth . . . on any one of those
days that start with the Ralston scenario I know I'm in for
a biggie . . . *[She laughs, coughs in a throaty way.]* . . . I don't
remember . . . oh, he goes to the bathroom again, that much
we got squared away, but you're talking about a giant step,
like descending the staircase to the lower depths . . . he
hasn't managed that in months . . .

[SHE grabs a cigarette and lights it.]

DANIELLE. No, the old boy is up there in his element . . . weeping and gnashing away . . . *[Again the throaty laugh.]* How are you . . . good . . . oh, I don't know, Marietta, these Sundays do him in . . . **Franklin** gets to screaming, Lawrence tries to throw him out of bed . . . he's a basket case for three days after you all leave . . . just this **morning** he asked if you were coming and I could see he was getting all worked up . . .

[Just then she hears a loud thump from upstairs.]

DANIELLE. *[to herself]* Oh Lord, it's one of those **mornings** when he won't even call my name . . . what . . . no, His Highness just called . . . hold on a minute.

[SHE goes to the bottom of the stairs.]

DANIELLE. *[shouting up]* I've got the damn cereal cooking away . . . give me five minutes and you'll have it piping hot with raisins and brown sugar . . .

[She waits for an answer. None is forthcoming. She goes back to the phone.]

DANIELLE. His Highness is in rare form today . . . what . . . why don't you try coming one at a time . . . individual attacks, rather than 'the collective assault' . . . *[that amuses her]* . . . I don't know, Marietta, he takes pills when I'm sleeping, pills when I go to the store, even slips in a few every time I go pee . . . if I hid them in Hell he'd find them, he likes the idea of taking pills, makes him feel like a real invalid. The true joke is that the things are supposed to keep the depressions from going below a certain par . . . not with him . . . every time he takes one he hits rock bottom . . . *[that amuses her]* . . . starts crawling around on all fours . . . for despair and despair and despair, Nelson has no equal . . .

[The thump-thump from upstairs begins again.]

DANIELLE. I gotta go, Marietta . . . why don't you just come alone, he doesn't mind you so much . . . all right.

[She hangs up, yells upstairs from where she is.]

DANIELLE. *[shouting]* I'm on my way . . .

[SHE goes into the kitchen, mumbling out loud as she fixes his breakfast, passing in and out of our sight.]

DANIELLE. *[amused]* I got my tray, a dainty napkin for His Highness, the raisins and brown sugar, a little fresh cream . . .

[SHE comes out with her tray, crosses to the staircase and goes up, mumbling all the way.]

DANIELLE. Now I ask you . . . is this the life for a woman of my quality . . . I was supposed to <u>glitter</u> . . . powder my face, rouge my cheeks, and <u>glitter</u> . . . with a name like Danielle Winters silks and satins were the order of the day . . . have I fallen . . . have I fallen . . .

[SHE disappears at the top of the steps. We hear her talking to Nelson.]

DANIELLE. *[offstage]* You keep telling yourself it's Ralston, it's got raisins and brown sugar and it's **crunchy** and creamy sweet just like Ralston . . . with all her teeth out and her hair falling into the bowl your mother could have eaten it . . . it's the same . . . where are my cigarettes . . . eat the Ralston, Nelson . . . taste it for God's sake . . . *[getting mad]* Taste it, you baby . . . *[getting madder and louder]* Did **anyone** ever tell you you're a baby baby baby . . . I'm getting out of here . . .

[SHE comes marching down the steps, still yelling up to him.]

DANIELLE. *[yelling]* And the clan's coming, too, any hour now they'll be gathering to say the Edwards Requiem over you . . . *[She turns and screams up the steps.]* Lawrence will get you out of that bed . . . if he were here now the damn Ralston would be **burning** your insides . . .

[She waits for an answer. None is forthcoming. She sits down on the steps, exhausted.]

DANIELLE. It's not even nine o'clock and we're off to a **running** start . . . *[that amuses her]* The gears are **churning,** we've **gone** from low to high **in** a matter of seconds . . . *[She coughs the true smoker's cough, gets up.]* Where are my cigarettes . . .

[SHE crosses to the dining room, lights up.]

DANIELLE. Oh boy oh boy . . . another <u>famous</u> Sunday is in the making . . .

[SHE goes into the kitchen, comes back with a cup of coffee, sits down at the table.]

DANIELLE. Oh boy oh boy . . .

[She sits there smoking and drinking her coffee. After a while, there's a thump-thump from overhead. Not moving, she yells up.]

DANIELLE. *[yelling]* Does that mean you ate your Ralston . . . one thump if you did, two if you didn't . . .

[After a while: one sullen thump is returned.]

DANIELLE. *[yelling, laughing]* Bravo! Then I'll stay . . .

[SHE comes to the foot of the stairs.]

DANIELLE. *[yelling]* I'll stage-manage one more Sunday for **you** before I take off for the big time, you can't hold a star down . . . I have a career waiting on the other side of your despair . . . don't you forget that . . .

[In a good mood now, SHE goes into the living room and puts on a record. It should be Carmen McRae or Anita O'Day singing "Taking a Chance on Love." She two-steps lightly around the room singing along with the tune.]

DANIELLE. *[talking loud enough for him to hear her]* I'm thinking about the glitter and the glamour . . . Germany, London, the New York track scene, when it was all the way with Nelson . . . *[Again that throaty intermittent chuckle that, along with her heavy smoker's cough, serves as frequent punctuation to whatever she is saying.]* Cruising down the stretch, legs flying, light-years ahead of whoever took second, catching your trophies from princes and queens . . . *[She bows inside her dance.]* When I met you it was at the beginning of the fast hot-stepping life, the taste of medals was in your mouth. There were whiskey . . . and women in every room you entered. One day you strolled in with me . . . the Negro Marlon Brando arm in arm with the Negro Elizabeth Taylor . . . heads turned, eyes flew out their sockets, the women squirmed in their seats . . . *[yelling loudly]* We were flying then, weren't we . . . jet-settin' it Negro style across the **continent**. Breakfast at the Carleton at two in the **afternoon,** lavish old parties we dropped in on at dawn . . .

[She sings.]

Here I go again, I hear the trumpets blow again . . .

[She coughs.]

Whiskey . . . women . . . a taste of glory when you flew down that track . . . *[She coughs harder.]* . . . what more could any young man ask . . . *[She collapses in a fit of coughing.]* . . . if he wasn't an Edwards, had no memory for the fatal Edwards touch. *[She lights a cigarette, laughs, yells up at him.]* Goddamn it, Nelson, you were supposed to take me straight to the big time, it was supposed to be all <u>glitter</u> . . . is this the big time . . . is this what you meant by the big time . . .

[SHE goes to the bottom of the steps and listens.]

DANIELLE. *[to herself]* What am I waitin' for . . . the Boddhisattva to leave his throne . . . does God give up the keys to the kingdom . . . *[She sits down on the steps with her cigarette.]* . . . does the devil split from Hell . . . *[now laughing]* . . . do the archangels drop their wings . . . and God said, 'Let there be despair,' and Nelson dropped from the sky . . . *[She gets a kick out of that.]* Oh boy oh boy . . .

[She collapses in a fit of coughing, the phone rings, she gets up languidly to answer it.]

DANIELLE. Hello . . . yes, Franklin . . . no, I'm just gathered round the old familial hearth with my morning coffee . . . no, he just finished his breakfast . . . I'll ask . . .

[SHE goes to the bottom of the stairs.]

DANIELLE. *[yelling up]* It's Franklin . . . second-in-command and most beloved of your brothers, will you speak to him . . .

[She waits. There is no answer forthcoming.]

DANIELLE. Pick up the phone, Nelson . . . Sunday salutations are the order of the day . . .

[No answer. She goes back to the phone.]

DANIELLE. Sorry, Franklin, I can't even get a thump . . .
I know, it's Sunday . . . did you talk to Marietta . . .
I suggested maybe you should come one at a time, he
gets awfully worn out after 'the grand assembly' . . . he
performed after last week . . . kept me awake three nights
in a row . . . oh, he cried and cried over the way Lawrence
beat him, says you didn't defend him enough . . . I can't
stand to see him whipped like that, Franklin, he's not a
baby . . . well, beatings are not gonna get him out of that
bed . . . no, the man calls at least once a month, he's got that
job whenever he wants it . . . says Nelson can run the whole
athletic program, they'll make him regional director . . . he
tells the man that it's pointless . . . Negro existence . . .

[They both laugh.]

DANIELLE. He keeps him on the phone for hours, with
all his theories, about the futility of Negro existence . . .
[She begins to imitate Nelson.] 'Now, Marshall,' he says . . .
[She caricatures to perfection his Marlon Brando drawl.] '. . . you
and I both know that the Negro athlete, once he falls from
grace, has nowhere to run . . . the track and field were his
last defense . . . once these fall . . .' *[She's got Franklin really
laughing by now]* '. . . he returns to the void . . . Negro life is
a void, Marshall, you and I both know that . . .'

[They are both laughing.]

DANIELLE. I'm up there waving to him to shut up . . . the
man's offering him a classy job, and he's rambling on about
'the Negro void' . . . *[She is really amused.]* He does have his
moments . . .

[A thump-thump from overhead.]

DANIELLE. Hold it a second, Franklin . . .

[SHE goes to the bottom of the stairs.]

DANIELLE. *[yelling up]* What do you want . . .

[There is no answer.]

DANIELLE. *[to herself]* Now how am I supposed to Morse code this one . . . *[She yells up.]* One thump if you want something, two if you're just mad that I'm on the phone . . .

[Two clear thumps are returned.]

DANIELLE. *[amused]* I'm telling Franklin about your famous conversations with Mr. Marshall . . .

[She waits for an answer. There is none.]

DANIELLE. Why don't you pick up the phone, Nelson . . . maybe if you speak to him they won't come . . .

[She listens, then goes back to the phone.]

DANIELLE. Did he pick up . . . I thought maybe . . . well, if you can't persuade Lawrence then you should all come . . . I can't handle the 'Charger' by myself . . . all right.

[She hangs up, comes toward the steps.]

DANIELLE. *[yelling up]* They're coming, the whole damn circus is gathering . . .

[SHE disappears up the steps.]

DANIELLE. *[talking to Nelson]* How was your Ralston . . . you ate every drop . . . good for you . . . you think you should change your pajamas, those are getting bedridden . . . get up for a minute so I can straighten the bed . . . get out the bed, Nelson, or I'll sic Lawrence on you the minute he

hits that door, I'll turn you in for bad behavior . . . do you
have to pee . . . then go pee while I'm making the bed . . .
[her tone changes] Honestly, Nelson, you're never gonna get
out of here . . . *[realizing something]* . . . you're already half
buried, I can't touch this bed without feeling it . . . *[It sounds
like she's crying.]* . . . you look the same, just as you always
did . . . you don't age a bit, even when you cry and your face
gets bloated, it always goes back to looking the same . . .
[We hear her walking around.] Honestly, Nelson, I won't have
a child at this rate . . . what would I tell the kid . . . he'd
see all your scrapbooks and trophies . . . it just wouldn't
make any sense . . . what am I supposed to do, wait around
until you cry yourself to death . . . I'm gonna get old . . .
the Elizabeth Taylor scenario can't last forever . . . wait, let
me fix your pillows, what are you crying about . . . *[beside
herself]* . . . what are you always crying about . . .

*[SHE comes quickly down the steps, heads for the sideboard,
pours herself a drink, which she downs quickly.]*

DANIELLE. *[yelling up]* Who the hell do you think you
are . . . Job . . . the whole damn race is Job, what makes you
so special . . . you think you're the prophet . . . Nelson the
Prophet, leading his people through the Valley of Tears . . .
seven goddamn years . . . my God, Nelson, how can you find
so much to cry about . . . *[moving toward the stairs, yelling]* . . .
just get up and go to work! We'll have a few kids, a few
drinks, then you can die, why does it have to be such a
big production . . . always the damn tears . . . *[She is almost
crying herself.]* . . . for all you Edwardses life is the biggest,
fattest tearjerker I ever sat through in my life, you can't just
get up, get dressed, eat, sleep, pee, like normal Negroes . . .
no, every second has got to be momentous! Filled to
overflowing! *[She is beside herself.]* . . . Franklin broods, you

weep, Lawrence rages . . . poor Jeremy couldn't compete with that act so he worked out his own little twitch-and-dance routine . . . *[She yells, almost screams.]* . . . there have been <u>Negroes</u> before you, there will be <u>Negroes</u> when you are all long gone and the earth has dried up your tears . . . God in Heaven tell me why you all need to be so special . . .

[Exhausted, on the verge of crying, she goes for another drink, lights a cigarette, paces—rapidly smoking and drinking. She is silent for a while. When she finally begins to talk again, the tone is quiet . . . ominous, yet comic.]

DANIELLE. In a little while that bell will ring . . . another <u>famous</u> Sunday will begin . . . for openers there'll be Franklin and Letitia, always the first on the scene . . . Franklin likes to set the right ministerial tone for the event . . . *[She is getting a little drunk, begins to gesture theatrically.]* . . . his stern eyes will pass benevolently over me, look quickly toward the upper room where Nelson waits for his blessing . . . Letitia will stare, she wants nothing to do with all these unholy communions, she'll find a chair in the farthest corner of that room . . . sit, fold her hands, smile . . . not at me, not at the unholy scene before her eyes, but at some blank memory as disconnected as possible from this mad ritual . . .

[SHE jumps suddenly, as if startled already by the bell ringing.]

DANIELLE. Marietta will ring that bell an inordinate number of times, forever fearful of being left out when her brothers are in the heat of things, she'll come in all breathless . . . 'Where's Franklin, where's Franklin . . .' Rush up the steps after him. Richard will tip his hat, give out the quick dry laugh . . . 'All set for another biggie . . .' He'll wink and glide over to where Letitia sits, try and amuse her for a while, but when the fifth joke falls flat he'll slip on the TV and call it a day . . . *[Her nerves are getting more and more jangled, her voice takes on a different edge.]* . . . the Charger never rings, knocks, or announces his presence . . . all of a sudden it's hot . . . two snakes just slid in . . . I take Caroline's mink, offer them both a drink . . . *[She takes on Lawrence's diabolical tone.]* 'You got anything decent . . . a little brandy, I'll have a little brandy . . . none of that lower-class stuff you and Nelson guzzle to perfection . . .' *[Now she takes on Caroline's nasty repartee.]* 'Serve him anything, Danielle, the damn ball buster'll slop gin if he's nervous enough, wait till he gets all worked up, then hand him the lowest low-down drink you can think of . . . and turn on some music, will you . . . when he gets going I gotta have something to drown the misery . . .'

[DANIELLE drifts forward Caroline-style—puts on Lou Rawls singing "Stormy Monday" and with her hands on her hips greets the others in the room.]

DANIELLE. *[playing Caroline]* 'La-di-da, Letitia . . .' *[She bows.]* 'What's the good word, Richard my boy . . .' *[She turns around suddenly, as if Lawrence were staring at her.]* 'Don't you stare at me like that, I'll scratch your eyes out . . . you lay one finger on sweet Caroline and you won't have enough strength to get up those steps . . . Nelson's the target, today's Sunday, remember . . . Nelson's the target . . .' *[She watches him go up the steps.]* 'There he goes . . . *plonk plonk plonk* . . . like the damn executioner . . .'

[All of a sudden the phone rings, jarring Danielle, who is caught inside the drama, and can't move.]

DANIELLE. *[sure of it]* It's the Charger . . .

[SHE rushes to the bottom of the steps, yells up.]

DANIELLE. *[in a panic]* It's the Charger . . . and I'm not gonna answer it . . .

[The phone keeps ringing.]

DANIELLE. *[yelling over it]* I bet you anything Marietta told him I didn't want him to come, and he's hopping mad . . . the damn line's on fire . . . he's gonna blast through that door like a tornado . . . *[She is beside herself.]* And you expect me to stage-manage that act, answer the phone, Nelson . . . *[She screams, totally out of control.]* Answer the damn phone!!

[The phone rings and rings. Lou Rawls sings on and on. Lights go out.]

END OF ACT II

ACT III: LAWRENCE THE ELDEST

[When the lights come up, the room in which CAROLINE EDWARDS sits contains the following: a hospital-type bed with a washstand beside it, two chairs—one a straight hard-backed affair, the other slightly more comfortable looking. It is a room in a mental institution—abstract, indifferent, belonging to no one.

CAROLINE sits in the more comfortable of the two chairs, dressed in a hospital nightgown and slippers. She is a woman in her late fifties, light-skinned with extremely black hair, now starting to gray. She was once a very striking woman and the sharp outlines of this remain. But even at her best there was always something severe about her looks. Her eyes are too large and defiant, her mouth is a bit cruel. There is a drawn, waxed look about her cheeks, which were once rouged a too-bright red. She has a harsh, astringent voice that makes one uneasy.

An orderly, dressed in white, enters the room a few seconds after the lights come up.]

CAROLINE. *[hearing someone at the door]* Is that you, Mr. Norrell . . .

[The orderly enters the room, stands near the door waiting.]

CAROLINE. *[relieved]* I thought you were Mr. Norrell . . . then I thought, well, you can't be Mr. Norrell, I'm not dead yet, am I . . .

[The orderly just stands there.]

CAROLINE. *[with scorn]* You're as stupid as Mr. Norrell, standing there with your mouth gaping open like some deaf-mute . . . he's an obsequious man, I hate obsequious men. What'd you come in here for anyway . . . I ate, I've been to the bathroom, I've had my walk . . . every day you come in around this time . . . I don't ask for you, I never ring that bell for anyone . . . it's my loneliness that defines me . . . when I can feel the full pressure and the weight of it, **then** I know I am still alive . . . that Lawrence has not extinguished me . . . *[that amuses her]* . . . he used to threaten me with <u>extinction</u> . . . not death, not murder . . . total extinction . . . as if I were a rat, some incredible scurrying thing forever getting in his way . . . *[She looks at the orderly.]* Sit down . . .

[He does. There is silence for a while.]

CAROLINE. *[after a while]* It's not yet night, is it . . . nor is it any longer day. Without a window or a watch I could tell this hour any day, it always feels the same . . . restless, uneasy, the taste of death on your tongue . . . Lawrence would finish off an easy three drinks around this time, while I stood on the balcony and watched . . . *[Pause.]* . . . it was an ordinary house we lived in, cluttered with Lawrence's fancy taste, but above the living room was a balcony . . . it didn't belong in that house . . . it was the kind of balcony you might find in a dance hall . . .

[Music, some '40s dance piece, is heard in the distance, disembodied, like a memory.]

CAROLINE. *[swaying slightly]* I was **standing** on just such a balcony, in a floral gown, when Lawrence first walked in . . . glided across that floor like a panther, his skin shining, his hair glistening, his eyes almost leaping out at you, he took up the whole floor . . . I watched him from above . . . he looked up, saw me, suggested I come down and dance. I could dance as well as he could. It was tit for tat . . . he was all sleekness and ease, so was I . . . we looked like twins . . . same olive skin, same shiny black hair, even our eyes were the same hazel green . . . it was tit for tat . . .

[The music stops. She looks at the orderly.]

CAROLINE. *[with absolute clarity]* You've heard the whole story before . . . don't think I don't know that, nor should you flatter yourself that I repeat it for your benefit. I'm not a seductive woman. There's not a flirtatious bone in my body. I'm hollow, all burned out, and this is the only story I know. If once a day you allow me to retell it, I take advantage of that for one reason: I like to recall that balcony . . . *[Her voice takes on a softer tone.]* From it I can see everything, it was the first house we looked at soon after our wedding. It stood on a corner on a little street in Riverview. When you opened the door, the light struck the balcony, like a chapel in some ornate cathedral . . . I went straight up to it, stood looking down at Lawrence, who paced back and forth . . . 'What do you think, what do you think . . .' 'I like this balcony,' I said, 'it gives the house airs . . .' 'That's no reason, that's no reason,' he said. 'It's enough reason for me,' I answered, and we took it. *[She laughs suddenly.]* You don't know Lawrence . . . you can't appreciate that balcony unless you know Lawrence . . . for a colored man he took up a tremendous amount of space . . . he was full of schemes, complicated plots and maneuvers, he lived at a feverish pitch, always on the go, working out his maneuvers in advance. I used to like to be on that balcony when he came home . . . he didn't enter a room like normal people, he charged in . . . the door <u>flew</u> open and there he was, standing on the threshold like in some third-rate detective movie. He'd look around, then look up at me . . . 'What you doing, what you doing . . .' 'I'm watchin' you,' I'd say. 'Nothing special about me, nothing special about me . . .' Then he'd take inventory, move from room to room admiring the best pieces, a Chippendale chair he'd just bought, a velvet Empire couch, a new set of silverware, a Persian rug . . . all the Edwardses had a fine eye for things, a perfect smell for the best, a disdain for cheapness . . . they should all have been born white, they spent their lives trying to jump out their skin . . . 'We're going to the theater, to the theater,' he'd say, 'look sleek, look sleek, I don't want to be seen with you unless you look sleek,' and he'd pace up and down while I got dressed . . .

[SHE gets up dramatically.]

CAROLINE. I'd come to the balcony . . . 'How do I look . . .' He'd look up . . . I used to wear a lot of rouge, bright lipstick, somber elegant colors like burgundy and

chiffon black, pile my hair high on top of my head . . . 'I
look gorgeous,' I'd shout, 'I know I do, now you say it or
you'll never get me down those steps . . .' 'The theater can't
wait, the theater can't wait,' he'd answer, and stand there
watching me . . . it was tit for tat, two unyielding souls . . .
making the rounds of all the chic Philadelphia parties
and dances . . . Lawrence was still with the post office
then, he didn't even have his degree, but they accepted
us everywhere . . . we were fair, **stunning** to look at, the
money . . .

[She stops suddenly, turns toward the orderly.]

CAROLINE. . . . you always ask me where the money came
from . . . I worked . . . you always want to know what I
did . . . *[boldly]* I scrubbed people's floors . . . rich people,
white people, elegant people . . . I may have looked like
Hedy Lamarr after seven, but up until then . . . oh, not
forever, I didn't do that forever, it was, in fact, a well-kept
secret, not even the clan knew it . . . Lawrence hated it . . .
I was stylish, I was chic, but I had no schooling, I couldn't
type, do bookkeeping . . . Lawrence wanted to finish
school, get the great all-American degree . . . my family
had worked for the Lippincotts for years . . . I was like a
daughter to them . . . they got Lawrence off when he was
caught . . .

[She stops, holds her breath, laughing.]

CAROLINE. *[excited]* Now there's a juicy scandal that would
have broken up the clan, sent Pop Edwards to an early grave,
lost Lawrence the mantle of most favored and honorable
son . . . it happened on a bright Saturday **morning,** two
marshals pulled up before our door . . . I was **standing** on
the balcony, Lawrence let them in, they held a warrant for

his arrest . . . systematic opening of the mail, fleecing it for checks and cash . . . a clumsy story, they'd been watching him for weeks . . . they put the handcuffs on, he looked up at me . . . 'See to it, see to it . . .' and he was gone. Spent one night behind bars before Mr. Lippincott could pull the right strings . . .

[SHE sits down.]

CAROLINE. *[coldly]* There was no trial, no *fuss,* no one in the clan knew a thing . . . when he came back to the house we had our first full-scale fight . . . we used to skirmish over what dress I'd wear, over the awful meal I just cooked—I was never great in the kitchen—over whether or not to go to so-and-so's party . . . silly things, screaming at each other over silly things, a kind of feverish, childish **fighting** like two spoiled brats . . . we were spoiled brats . . . I was the youngest of five, he was the oldest of five, it amounted to the same thing . . . everything between us amounted to the same thing . . . I stood on that balcony and preened, he stood below me pacing and scheming . . . the **rhythm** was lovely, a kind of evenly matched greediness . . . *[Her voice grows softer.]* . . . in bed he was as quick and hurried as ever, but it was a fast even draw for both of us . . .

[She sits still for a moment, then laughs, like letting out a breath.]

CAROLINE. *[in a strange voice]* Colored people don't talk about sex . . . you ever notice that . . . they are so exposed in this life they are unwilling to admit to any further undressing . . . I never had a good intimate conversation with any of my sisters-in-law . . . I'd have liked to, I would have enjoyed a few bawdy talks about the brothers . . . Franklin, for instance, with his two wives, or Nelson, who lived in bed anyway . . . *[that makes her laugh]* . . . but we never talked, at all those gatherings **none** of us ever pulled away to speak to each other . . . we stood on the sidelines in **anticipation** of the main event: a bloody skirmish between Lawrence and Franklin, Marietta spouting morbid tales to excite her brothers' fancy, one of Nelson's brooding sermons on the Negro void, a sudden flogging administered by Lawrence when Nelson got out of hand . . .

[She recalls it all with great amusement.]

CAROLINE. *[seeing it]* We were like stagehands . . . running here and there to pick up a lamp that fell, sweep up a broken glass, bring someone a drink or a bandage . . . the action was so high-pitched, the Edwardses' control of center stage so complete, it reduced us to a bunch of bleeding stagehands . . . oh, we did bleed, there was blood all over the place . . .

[She shakes her head, sits silently for a while.]

CAROLINE. *[sadly]* . . . but I wish they'd come see me . . . Danielle or Letitia, even Marietta with her masculine abruptness . . . sometimes I get lonely for their recollections, wish to hear, between us, the repetition of some mad Sunday we lived through together . . . but they never liked me . . . I was too brittle with an acid tongue, and I liked to flaunt my clothes . . . *[She chuckles.]* Soon after that post office business, I began to let the Lippincotts give me things . . . hand-me-down sealskins and minks, silk dresses and scarves . . . I <u>dressed</u> for those Sundays . . . by then Lawrence and I were at each other anyway, we became famous for our volatile displays, could lash each other in public with deadly speed, it was a nasty performance . . . it's hard to remember when it became nasty . . . not long after

that business . . . he began to go to school full-time, I took
a second job with another family who were friends of the
Lippincotts . . . on those days I had to wear a uniform—
crisp black silk with a white cap . . . drove Lawrence clear
out of his skull, the veins on his forehead popped out
when he saw me in that . . . *[She begins to drift.]* . . . it got
uneven . . . the something between us got uneven, it was
no longer tit for tat . . . was it me or Lawrence who drove
the two of us so hard . . . he devoured school, couldn't get
his degrees fast enough, became a shrewd real estate lawyer
before I could blink . . . we had a daughter, Laura . . . a
queer child who never spoke . . . later . . . much later I
understood that she wasn't ill or maimed or retarded, she
just knew she couldn't be heard above the din . . .

[She puts her hands over her ears.]

CAROLINE. *[loudly]* We were noisy, all right . . . Lawrence
got more and more churned up . . . he had women by then,
money . . . ugly things started to spill out . . . *[Her tone
changes.]* He began to call me the maid . . . 'Where's the
maid, where's the maid,' he'd shout as soon as he hit that
door . . . I'd come to the balcony . . . 'Who are you talking
to . . .' 'I'm talking to the maid,' and he'd fling his hat up at
me. I'd fling it back along with an ashtray or anything else
I could get my hands on . . . 'Don't call me that,' I'd say,
'that's how you got through all those schools, in case you've
forgotten . . .' 'Listen to the maid, listen to the maid, got
five cents' worth of education and she's putting herself on a
pedestal . . .' *[with feeling]* He was cocky as all get-out in his
flannels and gabardines . . . his hair was so black it shone,
and his skin was as smooth and sleek as a baby's . . . *[growing
agitated]* . . . he was all churned up and boiling . . . I wish I
could have talked to someone about how alive he was . . .

[SHE gets up, in a growing state of agitation. Her tone becomes harder.]

CAROLINE. *[seeing it]* He kept it up . . . it became his opening salutation when he reached the door . . . 'Is the maid about, where's the maid . . .' Then he'd look up, see me on the balcony . . . 'There she is, there she is, **standing** on her pedestal . . . she should be down here **when** I come in, ready to take my hat . . .' 'This is my last line of defense,' I'd shout, 'I don't move from here . . .' *[Her voice takes on more of an edge.]* And I didn't . . . I made sure he never came through that door that he didn't find me **standing** there . . .

[She looks around desperately for a mirror, tries to see her reflection in the walls.]

CAROLINE. *[growing shrill]* One time I decided to dress up before he came home . . . **I put on** a nice silk print, powdered and rouged my cheeks, piled my hair high on my head, waited **on** the balcony . . . he came through the door, looked up . . . 'I see the maid's been robbing the wardrobe . . .' such a dead cold in his voice it snapped me in two . . . I threw a marble statue straight at his face . . . pitched it with deadly accuracy so it wouldn't go astray . . .

[She stops suddenly, looks confused, then laughs in a kind of lowlife conspiratorial way.]

CAROLINE. *[snapped]* Hedy Lamarr was gone, a Negro maid stood in her place . . . dowdy, unkempt, wearing somebody else's hand-me-downs . . .

[Lights come down quickly.]

END OF ACT III

EPILOGUE: MY BOYS, MY BOYS

[Lights come up on a bare stage. MR. NORRELL, dimly lit so that he is mostly in shadows, stands in a corner surrounded by huge funeral sprays. He is dressed in black.

MARIETTA comes in, rushing as always. She, too, is dressed in black, a veil half covering her face. She carries a huge bouquet of gladioli. She rushes forward, consumed by a kind of frantic, nervous energy.]

MARIETTA. *[breathless]* I promised Franklin I would not be late . . . these flowers must go on the coffin, Lawrence wanted the biggest, the grandest, the most splendid of bouquets and I have assembled these in his honor . . . *[She looks over at Mr. Norrell.]* . . . don't look at me like that, Mr. Norrell, you act as if I don't know who I'm burying . . . it's Jeremy's turn at last, I know that . . . he called me the night before . . . 'Marietta . . . I . . . I' . . . m g . . . g . . . going . . . it . . . it . . . it . . . 's a . . . a . . . about ti . . . ti . . . me d . . . d . . . don't you th . . . th . . . think . . .' *[She drops her flowers, cries out.]* No, Jeremy . . . we hardly had a minute, there was always Aurora sitting in the middle between us with her pickles and her fat pregnant eyes, and the boys keeping watch over you, and that silly girl-child who could do nothing but breed . . . where did you go, Jeremy . . . my fine-looking sailor in your navy-blue suit looking at life between a stutter and a smile, it can't be time for you to leave . . . *[She begins to cry, seems to see him dead, stretched out in his coffin.]* Our quiet one . . . no fights, no quarrels . . . early early on you took your leave, placed a firm but gentle distance between us, left the four of us behind to rant and rave . . .

[SHE bends over to touch him. MR. NORRELL moves slightly forward as if flicking a switch. Organ music comes on followed by a deep contralto voice singing "When I've Done the Best I Can." Marietta grows more agitated.]

MARIETTA. *[calling out]* Franklin . . . is that you . . . is that your stern demanding face I see once more . . . look at you, you've been crying . . . as always life has turned out wrong for your too-fine, upstanding soul . . . how much you needed Lawrence's mockery, a little nasty edge against your righteous thrusts . . . *[She seems to touch his coffin.]* . . . there, there . . . lie still . . . you fought so many battles, made mountains out of small demeaning hills . . . you never slept, your soul was much too watchful, even to death you bring a nervous grief . . . *[She seems to touch him gently, growing ever more sad.]* Look at me . . . I'm still your same unbending sister, full of whispering thoughts for you and you alone, I have no one . . . my life is just a memory . . . caskets and grief and floral-covered graves . . .

[She cries, she cries. MR. NORRELL steps forward to comfort her, causing a violent reaction.]

MARIETTA. *[screaming at him]* My boys, my boys . . . tell me what you did with all my boys . . . where's my Nelson, his puffy cheeks and Marlon Brando jowl, the sad sly smile of one who died defeated, breathing his last in pillows soaked with grief . . . *[She seems to touch Nelson's face.]* Speak to me . . . open those frowning eyes and live . . . *[getting angry]* . . . get up when Lawrence beats you . . . send him flailing through some new space and time . . .

[SHE lunges at Mr. Norrell, seeing only Lawrence.]

MARIETTA. . . . you went too quickly . . . there should have been time to see you squirm with guilt and grief . . .

[SHE pulls violently at Mr. Norrell.]

MARIETTA. . . . you went too fast, I never got my answers . . . from all of you I'm left suspended . . . jerking at life betrayed and dangling still . . .

[She looks around, lost, confused. Mr. Norrell begins to subdue her.]

MARIETTA. I know no peace . . . my dreams are all a fury . . . *[Suddenly she pulls away, screams at the top of her lungs.]* Show me who's dead! What male soul needs my mourning!!

[SHE falls to the ground, begins to gather up her flowers.]

MARIETTA. I'll strew his grave with wilted female things!

[Lights go out quickly.]

END OF EPILOGUE

REMEMBRANCE: A PLAY IN ONE ACT

for
SERET

THE CHARACTERS

A black woman in her late thirties.

THE PLACE

An apartment.

THE TIME

The present.

[The WOMAN is already onstage when the play opens. One is struck immediately by a fragile quality about her, as of one who finds daily life difficult, almost unbearable. There should be no hint of madness. She is not mad, nor should the role be played in a distracted fashion. But she is preoccupied, and her preoccupations, since they render her out of synch with everyday life, should give a disjointed feeling to the way we experience her.

*It is suggested that she be dressed in a light, summery dress.
She's pretty, but again in a disconnected way without makeup
or guile.*

*When the lights first come up, all we see is a dresser of the
kind commonly found in bedrooms. On it there is a candle, a
glass of water, a silver cross. Later on, as the lights come up,
we will discover a bed in the room. And as the play progresses,
the WOMAN will move through several spaces that suggest an
apartment. Every effort should be made, however, to keep the
environment as abstract as possible.*

*The WOMAN holds a bouquet of hand-picked flowers,
which, after some hesitation, she places on the dresser somewhat
ceremoniously, as if it were an offering. She's somewhat self-
conscious doing this, and as she turns around, she becomes aware
of a whole audience watching her.]*

THE WOMAN. *[self-conscious]* I know this is a poor excuse
for an altar. I've never made one before and I don't have
much spiritual imagination, it seems . . . Besides, there's no
room for it on a dresser cluttered with Joe's and my things.
This is a shared room . . .

[Lights come up on an unmade double bed.]

THE WOMAN. Both our shoes, socks, underwear clutter up
the place. It's a mess. A shared mess. And because I share it, I
have no right to make an altar meant for me and God alone,
particularly since I have no desire to justify my need for
such an altar, and Joe, patient though he is with a wife who
stumbles through wifeliness, maternity, domesticity, like a
feeble onlooker, would probably draw the line at spiritual
replenishment . . . *[She laughs somewhat giddily.]* After all,

he'd say, there are four of us in only five rooms. The boys are forced to share a bedroom . . .

[Lights come up on a space suggesting a boys' bedroom, cluttered with five- and three-year-old paraphernalia.]

[SHE walks away.]

THE WOMAN. The kitchen is no more than a box . . .

[Lights come up on a space suggesting a tiny kitchen.]

THE WOMAN. And the bathroom is, as mothers the world over will agree, the most sought-after retreat. The taboo of the toilet works against husbands and children alike . . .

[Lights pop up quickly on a toilet seat, then just as quickly pop out.]

THE WOMAN. And the living room belongs to all of us, regardless of size or sex . . . the TV, stereo, books, plants, paintings, piano, drums, trumpet assemble themselves here and wait . . .

[As she enumerates, lights come up on a space suggesting all the above.]

THE WOMAN. It's cozy. Joe does wonders with plants, even though we're in the back and the light is poor . . . *[switching]* And I make excellent French toast . . . *[proudly]* Robbie, my eldest, always pats me on the back after he's made a glutton of himself over my French toast. 'Very good, Mommie,' he says, and pats me all over . . . Immediately, I sense he's seen clear through me and knows that I am too disconnected to be his momma, mother, mommie, and that this house, kitchen, car, plant, bicycle, street, TV are all out there in some reality that's got nothing to do with me . . . *[embarrassed but feeling silly]* Though I see to it that I behave . . .

[SHE *runs into the bedroom, mimes tucking the boys in, straightening up their things, etc. Then, exhausted, she goes into the bedroom and lies down, then mimes touching her husband, Joe.]*

THE WOMAN. Joe makes the real meals. Steaks and rice, spinach and Caesar salads, hovering over them like he does his plants, until they come out tender and delicious. The boys know that Joe is a hundred percent all here . . . He takes long strides from room to room, and each step confirms his hundred percent presence among us . . .

[SHE *mimes touching Joe gently, then rolls over, away from him.]*

THE WOMAN. It's not easy to pin down the exact moment when I went looking for God . . .

[SHE *gets out of bed carefully, so as not to wake Joe.]*

THE WOMAN. I know it happened in the bathroom, which is where I often go in the middle of the night, or the middle of the day, for that matter, if there's a three-year-old–five-year-old ambush under way, or if Joe's been around too long banging on his drums like in another incarnation he must have been Max Roach, or if the rooms close down, just shut down all of a sudden . . . And I want to pee on the living room rug, flaked as it is with fake Oriental gold colors that will not be distinguishable from my fake Oriental gold urine . . . I lock myself in the bathroom faster than you can say 'spit on me!!' *[growing shy, like a young girl]* The truth is, I've been locking myself in bathrooms since I was around three, which is about when I knew that I would never develop along real lines . . . My own mom, dad, sis, house, garden, street were like so many trees in a forest, I had to sit long hours in the bathroom just to <u>keep</u> track . . . *[getting a little defensive]* For a while, I got in the habit of numbering things, or repeating out loud ad infinitum name, address, phone number, address, phone number, name . . . *[giggling uncontrollably]* But I no longer try and fool myself that this <u>means</u> something . . . *[more matter-of-factly]* Now I simply try, during those sojourns in the bathroom, to locate myself, apart from other things . . . *[trying for precision]* To do this, I first have to separate myself . . . from kitchen, house, garden, street, Robbie, Sammy, Joe, the everyday zombie me . . . *[giggling]* Flagrant arm movements help . . .

[SHE flicks her wrists, then slowly makes bolder flicking motions with her arms, neck, shoulders, until eventually her whole body begins to flick and tremble with such complete abandon that it's comic.]

THE WOMAN. I try to get them out of me! <u>Feel</u> them leave . . . until I'm no longer knotted up with Joe's building contracts, Robbie's bedwetting, my dad's pathetic illness, my own dysfunctioning psyche standing around observing all of them like a dumb reporter . . . I have <u>to drop</u> all of them, which requires my flailing about . . . *[One final shudder, then laughter, relief.]* I admit, the bathroom is pretty tiny for all this, I can only move between the toilet bowl and the sink . . . *[giggling]* But it's good discipline for a dancer, which is what I do professionally, I dance . . . *[growing silly]* Others wait on tables or go on welfare, I dance . . .

[SHE executes an astonishing little number, then bows dismissively.]

THE WOMAN. But that's beside the point . . .

[SHE shudders again, to release the "dancer" in her.]

THE WOMAN. Dancer, mamie, mom, wife, kitchen, daughter, sister, car, piano . . .

[SHE flicks them all away, sits down on the toilet seat and is silent a good while. When finally she speaks, it's to herself: the self she comes there to find.]

THE WOMAN. Hi. How are you . . . *[self-conscious]* I never know what to call you. I know that you're me, but I don't want to get you confused with the everyday <u>zombie</u> me. I come in here to discard her and find you, who listens to God . . . *[She begins to cry, gently.]* You've been crying again. It's God who makes you cry. He's so silent, and His silence is such a lovely thing . . . *[She cries freely, without despair.]* Last night, I dreamt I danced in the image of God. There was no ground, the air was my ground. The air was everything, the music came from the air, it was silent but I could feel it sing . . . *[growing annoyed at herself]* Listen to me, I can't stop talking! My mouth is full of words! Who needs my words, not God, not the you in me who yearns for His silence to surround me . . .

[She sits very still inside a prolonged silence, which is so pleasing to her that sometimes she cries. After a while, the awareness that there is an audience watching her creeps in, and she reluctantly gets to her feet.]

THE WOMAN. I was trying to give you an impression of my séance, meditation, withdrawal . . . whatever you choose to call what happens during my bathroom retreats . . . *[feeling ordinary reality intruding]* The point is that while everybody else plays Apache or trot the dog and/or especially when they've all gone to sleep, I wander into the bathroom to find God . . . *[feeling silly]* God . . . Who the hell is God, when Robbie's kicking Sammy in the teeth . . . and Sammy's chucking his food out the window . . . and Joe's patting me on the head, while I'm down on my knees trying to mop up my tears . . . how can I, in my <u>feeble</u> condition as a mummy/mommie . . . *[growing giddy with silliness]* . . . have the nerve to go looking for God . . . *[She collapses with laughter.]* And what God . . . Jehovah, Jesus, Baba, the Old Rugged Cross, the Fountain Filled with Blood, like you could open the Christian language and find God . . . *[scornfully]*

> Must Jesus bear the cross alone and all the world go
> free,
> No there's a cross for everyone and there's a cross for
> me . . .

[She gestures in amusement at all such language.] Though I go to a lot of colored churches. You can <u>cry</u> in a colored church . . .

[We become slowly aware of a deep gospel voice singing "Just a Closer Walk with Thee." The WOMAN is deeply moved.]

THE WOMAN. Colored people remember something from somewhere, sometime, someplace, and cry because they know it and recognize it at the same time . . .

[She's crying freely now, overwhelmed by the singing. Lights grow tight around her as if she were in a church.]

THE WOMAN. God, Father, Holy Spirit. I want Your light and love around me. I reach out to You. I ask to locate myself in You, extend my body, mind, and soul, my yearnings . . . for which I have no words. No voice. Held back as I am by time. Only inside do I dance to Your music that repeats and repeats itself, a silent echo that will not be still . . . I wait. The memory of your love returns to me. I clasp my hands. The pain in my heart frightens me . . . *[more passionate]* I dare myself to say out loud: God. And repeat: God. Like an echo it returns to me: God. I place myself inside the echo. I grow weak with remembrance. Cause me to remember that I may locate myself forever inside Your silence and be still . . .

[By the time she finishes, the hymn has faded away. Released, but growing suddenly uneasy, the WOMAN runs into the bedroom to check on Joe, then into the boys' room, where she mimes tucking them in tight. Unable to stop moving, she drifts from room to room in a daze.]

THE WOMAN. Somewhere around the time I started crying in colored churches, I lost my bearings. At the best of times it was difficult for me to keep track . . . take the boys to nursery school, to the park . . . cook, clean, make love, get to rehearsals on time if I was doing a show . . . *[with physical revolt]* <u>Movement</u> became more difficult for me . . . I wanted to sit still, I thought if I could just sit still long enough, I could figure out everything . . . Robbie, Sammy, Joe, drums, dancing, parks, shopping malls, bicycles, toys, sinks . . .

[SHE collapses on the floor.]

THE WOMAN. I needed something, some ritual that would bring God here, where I breathe. So I lit a candle . . .

[Lights grow dim around her.]

THE WOMAN. I put it on the dresser in our bedroom, in the midst of Joe's cuff links and ties, my perfumes, his aftershave cream . . .

[Lights come up on a candle burning on the dresser in the bedroom. The WOMAN gets up and goes into the bedroom, sits down at the foot of the bed facing the candle. She sits there for a long time before finally she speaks.]

THE WOMAN. I light this candle for You. I don't know why, but it slows things down. And the light's soft, it doesn't glare at me. I should stop speaking, I know, but I need to greet You, welcome You, right now Your silence is too much for me . . . It won't move, sometimes it moves and the power of it lifts me . . . But sometimes it's too **silent,** I feel I have to speak . . . *[growing suddenly bold]* Call on You . . . out of my own holiness . . . <u>provoke</u> You . . .

[Awed by her own boldness, she waits. The waiting should be prolonged, until something happens inside her, a confirmation of some sort to which she responds.]

THE WOMAN. Out of my own holiness, I provoke You . . . with my breath I draw You from me . . . *[suddenly overjoyed, remembering everything]* I forget You, then remember, forget, then remember . . . it's a dance, my dance . . . to forget You in order that I might remember You, it goes on forever, this dance . . . I forget in order that I might remember . . .

[Relieved, SHE begins to cry. She remains in this state until a door slams, suddenly startling her. She gets up quickly, frantically mimes straightening up the room as if it would give off telltale signs. She looks at the altar, hesitates, then with sudden decisiveness blows out the candle, swoops the flowers, candle, and cross into the top drawer and rearranges the surface with neckties, cuff links, perfume, and things.]

THE WOMAN. That's Joe. The first time I lit a candle he came home unexpectedly. The boys were still in school. I couldn't have looked more guilty if there'd been a man in bed with me. 'Are you all right?' he said. 'I'm just fine, what are you doing home at this time of day?' 'I was thinking about you more than usual,' he said. 'Why? I'm fine, just fine.' He looked around the room. *[more vehemently]* 'I'm fine, just fine, do you want lunch, the boys will be home soon.' He reached for me . . . I screamed . . . *[with violence]* Which world will it be . . .

BLACKOUT

THE READING: A PLAY IN ONE ACT

for
BILLIE

THE CHARACTERS

MARGUERITE SIMPSON, a black woman in her late forties.
HELEN MILLS, a white woman in her early forties.
The WOMAN, an older black woman—the psychic's assistant.

THE PLACE

The waiting room of a psychic's office.

THE TIME

The present.

[The play opens in a waiting room of the kind almost familiar to us . . . a few innocuous chairs, a scattering of Redbook, Mademoiselle, Good Housekeeping *magazines, the usual coffee table routine. Other touches render the room more bizarre:*

lit candles of different shapes and sizes; statues and other occult-looking objects; floor pillows that are scattered about; one stately white armchair that is too imposing for the room. And facing the audience, an inner door concealed behind a curtain or drape.

MARGUERITE SIMPSON, a black woman in her late forties, sits in the armchair. She is impeccably groomed: expensive clothes, shoes, handbag—everything is in place and stylishly so. She is a woman who takes nothing lightly but has worked hard to organize a careful life.

A few minutes after the play begins, a candle goes out. MARGUERITE stares at it, annoyed by the sudden lack of symmetry. Finally, unable to stand it, she takes out a book of matches, gets up, and relights it. Satisfied, she returns to her seat. Within seconds it goes out again. Determined to let it be, she shifts her gaze.]

MARGUERITE. This must be a trick she plays. In all occult tales, shutters fly open, doors squeak, candles sputter and die out. I refuse to play.

[But the unlit candle annoys her too much. SHE takes out her matches, gets up, relights the thing. This time, however, instead of returning to her seat, on an impulse she sits down on a pillow facing the candle and tries to assume the lotus posture.]

MARGUERITE. I can almost get this right . . . this leg yields completely, it's the other that keeps flapping about . . . like a broken wing . . .

[SHE settles for simply crossing her legs beneath her, stares defiantly at the candle as if daring it to go out. It stays lit.]

MARGUERITE. I must be performing the right ritual . . .

[Pleased with her spiritual prowess, SHE begins to rock back and forth.]

MARGUERITE. I suppose if I tried, I could have a flair for this . . . *[She begins to chant, but only briefly.]* . . . no, that's reaching . . . I don't want to reach . . .

[SHE bows her head until it touches the floor. Holding that posture, she talks to herself.]

MARGUERITE. I believe in the mind and the will . . . the darker mysteries of the self should come easily to me . . .

[SHE lifts herself regally, like a swan coming out of a dive, then sits quite still, preening on her graceful posture. Unexpectedly, an old meter hymn erupts from her and she begins to sing.]

MARGUERITE. *[singing]*

Hold my hand while I run this race,
Hold my hand while I run this race,
Oh Lord, won't You hold my hand while I run this
    race . . .
'Cause I don't want to run this race in vain . . .

[Touched by sudden emotion, she begins to sing it louder, more vehemently.]

Guide my feet while I run this race,
Guide my feet while I run this race,
Oh Lord, won't You guide my feet . . .

[A door opens. Startled by the sound, MARGUERITE shuts up, gets quickly to her feet.

HELEN MILLS enters—a white woman in her early forties. While Marguerite's grooming is impeccable, Helen's is merely adequate. Not sloppy, but an indication of a woman for whom clothes don't count. This indifference reflects a personality that considers itself immune to the trivial. Only thoughts matter, so her careless demeanor suggests.

As SHE comes in, MARGUERITE (who barely got to her feet) stands awkwardly staring at her. HELEN goes quickly to the armchair and sits. This annoys Marguerite, who would have liked the advantage of that chair.]

HELEN. Have you been waiting long . . .

MARGUERITE. Not long . . .

HELEN. She's very good, she predicted my divorce, how many children I would have, the shape of my career . . .

[MARGUERITE nods.]

HELEN. I've been to others, they pick up certain things about my past, but she's the only one who goes deftly to the point . . . skimming across time, past present future . . . she whips across all of them without flinching. I've flinched often under her remarks, but in the long run it always does me a world of good . . .

[MARGUERITE is at a loss as to where to put herself. She reconsiders the pillow but rejects it in favor of a chair. Which chair? She settles for the one closest to the coffee table, in easy reach of a magazine.]

HELEN. Have you been to her before . . .

MARGUERITE. Once.

[SHE picks up a magazine, begins to read with feigned concentration. A moment later, HELEN takes out a notebook and pen, begins jotting down things.]

HELEN. I have so many questions. In her presence I get a bit flustered and tend to forget things . . . the children, or my husband's business. I feel badly if I go in there just for me . . .

[At some point, the candle goes out. Only MARGUERITE notices it. Exasperated, she keeps her gaze averted. But finally, unable to resist, she submits to the ritual of relighting it. HELEN watches her on the sly, pretending not to notice.]

MARGUERITE. It keeps going out.

HELEN. Oh . . .

[In a bold move, MARGUERITE sits down on the pillow, resumes her semi-lotus pose, staring at the candle belligerently.]

MARGUERITE. This is the only thing that works . . .

[HELEN nods, tries to go back to her note-taking, but is distracted.]

HELEN. *[after a while]* How did you know . . .

MARGUERITE. Know what . . .

HELEN. That if you stare at it, it won't go out . . .

[MARGUERITE shrugs.]

HELEN. Could I try it . . .

MARGUERITE. Be my guest . . .

[SHE gets up. HELEN goes and sits down in front of it, executing the full lotus posture with ease (which irritates Marguerite).]

HELEN. Now what . . .

MARGUERITE. Just stare . . .

[Helen does. The candle remains lit.]

HELEN. Should I chant . . .

MARGUERITE. It's not necessary . . .

[HELEN closes her eyes and begins to chant anyway.]

HELEN. *[eyes shut]* Is it still lit . . .

MARGUERITE. Yes.

[Helen continues to sit with her eyes closed. SILENCE. The palpable kind in which both women participate.]

HELEN. *[after a while]* I don't devote nearly enough time to the pleasures of stillness . . . *[Pleased with herself, she opens her eyes.]* Now what . . .

MARGUERITE. *[shrugging]* The point is to keep it lit . . .

[HELEN looks toward the inner door.]

HELEN. Is there someone with her . . .

MARGUERITE. I don't know . . .

HELEN. You haven't seen her . . .

[MARGUERITE shakes her head no. HELEN gets up, shakes out her legs, which feel stiff.]

HELEN. I haven't done that in a while . . .

[Aware that MARGUERITE has taken the choice seat, she makes her way to the chair nearest the coffee table, picks up a magazine, which she halfheartedly peruses.]

HELEN. Did you come for something specific . . .

MARGUERITE. What do you mean . . .

HELEN. Some people want a survey of their life, others have only one thing on their mind . . .

MARGUERITE. Which are you . . .

[*The bluntness of the question surprises Helen.*]

HELEN. We didn't exchange names.

MARGUERITE. Is that unfriendly . . .

HELEN. Helen Mills . . . I kept my first husband's name.

MARGUERITE. [*reluctantly*] Marguerite Simpson . . .

HELEN. What an elegant name. There's a character in one of my novels called Rita Simpson . . . I put that name together deliberately . . . Simpson to denote that she married into class, Rita to maintain a certain trashy air about her . . .

MARGUERITE. It's my maiden name . . .

HELEN. Both parts of which are elegant . . . I published my first book under Helen Mills. After that it was too late to change . . .

MARGUERITE. Did you want to . . .

HELEN. [*musing*] Helen Mills . . . Helen Roberts . . . as a writer I'd say they participate in the same degree of plainness . . .

MARGUERITE. My husband's name is Howard . . .

HELEN. Marguerite Howard . . . [*objecting*] A fall from grace . . .

[*They laugh.*]

HELEN. My maiden name was Curtiss . . . Helen Elizabeth Curtiss . . .

MARGUERITE. The Elizabeth adds distinction . . . debutante distinction . . . white taffeta dress, white gloves, white taste . . . *[stopping herself]* . . . I design clothes, for me a name is a dress, a hat, a scarf . . .

[SILENCE.]

HELEN. Who do you design clothes for . . .

MARGUERITE. Private women . . .

HELEN. That must be fascinating . . .

[Marguerite doesn't answer.]

HELEN. Do you sell them to stores . . .

MARGUERITE. No.

HELEN. How do people hear about you . . .

[MARGUERITE shrugs.]

HELEN. You already have a name . . .

MARGUERITE. I have enough clients, yes . . .

HELEN. How would you dress me . . .

[SHE gets up, smoothes her skirt, her hair, walks closer to Marguerite.]

HELEN. I know I lack flair . . .

MARGUERITE. What kind of novels do you write . . .

HELEN. What do you mean, what kind . . .

MARGUERITE. Serious or trashy . . .

HELEN. Serious. Though not without humor . . .

MARGUERITE. What do you write about . . .

HELEN. It's hard to summarize five books . . . *[thinking about it]* Divorce . . . identity . . .

MARGUERITE. *[slightly cutting]* Women's themes . . .

HELEN. *[feeling attacked]* You don't want to tell me how I should dress . . .

MARGUERITE. No.

HELEN. I'm beyond help . . .

MARGUERITE. You prefer it not to matter.

HELEN. What do you mean prefer . . .

MARGUERITE. You've made it a part of who you are.

HELEN. My casualness about clothes . . .

MARGUERITE. Your unwillingness to dress . . .

HELEN. I don't go around nude! *[somewhat annoyed]* Why do you take so much time with clothes . . .

MARGUERITE. It matters.

[She adjusts something on herself. Just then the inner door opens. An older WOMAN comes out. She has a gruff, intimidating manner.]

THE WOMAN. Who was first?

MARGUERITE. I was . . .

THE WOMAN. Queenie was sick last night, she's not too well now but she doesn't like to disappoint . . .

MARGUERITE. I could come back . . .

THE WOMAN. Give her time to pray . . .

MARGUERITE. If she's not any better, I'll come back . . .

[As the WOMAN turns to leave, HELEN steps forward.]

HELEN. Tell her Helen Mills sends her regards, we're like old friends . . . tell her I don't mind waiting to have an audience with the queen . . .

[The WOMAN nods, then goes back inside.]

HELEN. . . . it's true, there is something regal about her . . . Queenie the Queen . . . *[to Marguerite]* She has an African grace . . .

MARGUERITE. Meaning what . . .

HELEN. She's powerful, there's something mysterious about her, too . . .

MARGUERITE. Dark . . .

HELEN. I feel foolish sometimes in her presence, the way a child would. *[reminiscing]* The first time I came to see her, Sam . . . Mills . . . my first husband, and I were having trouble. I'd never been for a reading, I didn't know what one was, except to go hear other writers read from their work or reading from mine . . . But after the first time, I thought it's not so different, except that I'm the book . . . she's reading me. And it was comforting in a way to know that I wasn't such a secret, that someone could read me . . . *[remembering]* She gave me Queenie's name . . . this friend of mine, Celia, who's black . . . it was a pretty desperate time, I didn't see how it could hurt . . . *[reliving]* I was a nervous wreck, and Queenie is

not one to put you at ease, she has no understanding of
small talk. I made some remark about the weather . . . it
was summer, we were in the middle of a heat wave . . . I
said, 'The heat certainly adds to one's feelings of despair,'
but she didn't respond. Then I said something about this
being my first reading, but by then she'd asked for my
earring and was listening to it as if it could speak . . .
[She tries on her idea of a colored intonation to mimic Queenie.]
'Papers, honey . . .' *[shifting]*

I didn't understand what she meant . . . *[as Queenie]* 'That's
all that's left between you is papers . . .' *[shifting]* I asked
her if she was talking about my husband . . . *[as Queenie]*
'Beanstalk-looking man, frowns a lot, can't make a go of
whatever he tries . . .' *[shifting]*

'That's him exactly,' I said, 'did my earring tell you that . . .'
[as Queenie] 'Papers, honey, there ain't nothin' left between
you all but papers . . .' *[shifting]* 'Do you mean legal papers,'
I said, 'a divorce . . .' *[as Queenie]* 'That's right, honey,
papers . . .' *[She laughs with gusto.]* Of course I didn't believe
her, I'd just had my second child, for Christ's sake. I was
sure Sam and I could work things out . . . but we didn't . . .
[laughing] You know what she said about my career . . . *[as
Queenie]* 'Words are your high horse, honey, you want to
make a name for yourself with words . . .' *[giggling]* She said
the marriage would be over by the time my first book was
done . . .

   *[By this time, MARGUERITE is so annoyed she is pacing up
   and down.]*

HELEN. And of course it was, and it was a mess . . . and
there I was with one published book and two little ones . . .
[to Marguerite] What did you come for . . .

MARGUERITE. I only came once, that was several years ago . . .

HELEN. *[guessing]* A bad marriage . . .

[MARGUERITE doesn't answer.]

HELEN. It was either a bad marriage or there was a man lurking about . . .

[A bell rings from behind the inner door. HELEN turns.]

HELEN. She's about to pray, she always asks for guidance before she reads . . . *[suddenly impatient]* I hope she's better . . . I'd rather wait here forever than go home holding the same questions in my hand . . .

[SHE paces. The bell rings again, a soft cathedral-like sound that provokes Helen to prayer.]

HELEN. Hail Mary, full of grace, the Lord is with thee . . .

[SHE stops herself, turns to Marguerite.]

HELEN. I'm not Catholic, I haven't been Catholic in twenty-five years . . .

MARGUERITE. *[annoyed]* Stop handing me the story of your life as if it were a gift . . .

[The bell rings a third time. Offended, HELEN pulls away. SILENCE, inside which they both retreat. It's Marguerite who finally speaks and then more to herself it seems.]

MARGUERITE. . . . there was no man lurking about . . . no marriage of any kind, bad, good, or otherwise . . . She said there wouldn't be until late, if at all. She warned me that I might miss it altogether because I was so strict with myself and suffered like most women of the race from feelings

of unworthiness . . . *[amused]* That's how she put it . . .
the race . . . like it was an affliction . . . *[stopping]* I didn't
understand what she meant by unworthiness and I was too
young then to question her. I'd gotten my answer, that there
was no man lurking about and there wouldn't be for a long
time to come . . . if at all . . . that I was right in feeling I had
to think out a life on my own . . . somehow, out of my little
ideas . . . *[shifting]* I remember asking her what <u>direction</u>
I should take, though I didn't mean a career. But she
misunderstood and only repeated what I already knew, that
I had a flair for the way people should look and out of that I
would make an excellent livelihood . . . *[almost bitter]* Which
didn't reassure me at all, when the question was me, alone,
stretched out over so many years . . . a long blank road. I
wanted her to tell me how to bend myself so the aloneness
wouldn't hurt. But I didn't know how to say it. *[shifting]* I
doubt if she could have answered it anyway . . . prayer, she
might have said. Or insisted there were spirits around to
keep me company . . .

HELEN. Why unworthy . . .

[Startled, MARGUERITE turns.]

MARGUERITE. I'd forgotten you were here . . .

HELEN. *[offended]* One never talks out loud without wishing
for an audience . . .

[Marguerite doesn't answer.]

HELEN. I was right. You did come about a man, or to
reconcile yourself to the absence of one. He was still the
backdrop . . . a man . . .

[Marguerite remains silent.]

HELEN. And you didn't miss out, one finally came along. When . . .

MARGUERITE. Three . . . four years ago . . .

HELEN. You married him . . .

[Marguerite nods yes.]

HELEN. Why didn't you feel you deserved it . . .

MARGUERITE. Deserved what . . .

HELEN. A man . . .

MARGUERITE. [oddly] Like dessert . . .

HELEN. [a little pushy] Is it something black women feel . . .

MARGUERITE. What . . .

HELEN. Unworthy of a man . . .

MARGUERITE. [getting mad] Why are you stuck on that notion . . . [exasperated] We don't grow up expecting the same things . . .

HELEN. What does that mean . . .

MARGUERITE. [changing the subject] Why did you come . . .

HELEN. To see Queenie, you mean?

MARGUERITE. [nodding] Not a second bad marriage . . .

HELEN. [with some violence] I'm having trouble with my cervix . . . [turning away] . . . which is not to say he's not running around . . .

[SILENCE. They withdraw from each other. It's Helen who breaks the silence, speaking almost incoherently.]

HELEN. I do feel like I'm falling apart. He has only to come into me for me to want to say, 'You're in too deep.' I'm wounded but instead I hold my breath. It's not even that he's violent, he's not, he's just a man thrusting about. I think of Diana and her anxiety . . . the pages of her anxiety that I have finally gotten right, and I wish he'd stop thrusting so I could think . . . which is what he must know somewhere, that I do wish it and therefore keeps others around to thrust with . . . I haven't said to him, 'I have a wounded cervix,' it's like admitting to crow's-feet, to flabby thighs, to the fact that my flesh is shredding. Diana says to her friend when she finds out she has breast cancer, 'I like the idea of losing one, it throws into dispute any strict female notion of myself' . . . I don't know why I have her say that—was I thinking of my wounded cervix or only of Diana locating her anxiety in her body, as I locate mine in her: the fictitious Diana with her breast cancer and her attentive husband who does the dishes . . . mine does them, too, before or after he thrusts, and we talk together nicely, before or after he thrusts, and share raising the children, before or after he thrusts . . . There is no absence of communication, only the idea of myself and my wounded cervix that gets in the way . . . *[desperate]* Queenie will tell me how to breathe . . . it must be a question of not breathing correctly . . . the tissues contract when they should expand, or vice versa, it's silly, one's body is silly . . . *[to Marguerite]* . . . isn't it . . .

   [Marguerite looks at her, at a loss for words.]

HELEN. Queenie will know . . . *[mimicking Queenie]* 'Your plumbing's a little loose, honey . . .' *[giggling]* She's amazing when it comes to reading me . . .

MARGUERITE. *[fed up, mocking]* 'Honey . . . the Book of Helen is open for all to read . . .'

[Feeling attacked, HELEN retreats to one of the pillows and resumes the lotus posture. Bending her head to the floor, she takes deep yogic breaths. After a while, still not lifting her head, she speaks.]

HELEN. Is this racial spite . . .

MARGUERITE. What . . .

HELEN. Your aloofness . . .

MARGUERITE. I'm being aloof . . .

HELEN. Condescending to me . . .

MARGUERITE. I don't see it that way . . .

HELEN. As if I were a child who lacked common sense . . .

MARGUERITE. Again, I don't see it that way . . .

HELEN. We are women, both of us . . .

MARGUERITE. Which means . . .

HELEN. That's being deliberately obtuse . . .

MARGUERITE. *[mocking]* Honey, I'm a slow read . . .

[She can't help laughing, irritating Helen even more.]

HELEN. That's being difficult for no reason . . .

MARGUERITE. *[pulling away]* Then why don't we stop talking . . .

HELEN. You are, you know, all of you . . . you're difficult women . . .

MARGUERITE. *[weary]* It must be some colored thing, passed down through the genes . . . be difficult, pout, refuse the white logic of things . . .

HELEN. It's the cantankerousness that's a bore . . .

MARGUERITE. *[agreeing]* The back always arched . . .

HELEN. *[agreeing]* . . . as if you were ready to pounce . . .

[MARGUERITE does exactly that: she pounces. Helen reacts with fright.]

MARGUERITE. *[apologizing]* I couldn't resist. You expect it so vehemently. I'm supposed to be violent in the end . . .

HELEN. *[retreating]* Even Queenie's always abrupt with me . . .

MARGUERITE. *[more to herself]* We're an ill-natured breed . . . cross-grained, contentious . . .

[HELEN unfolds herself from the lotus posture, gets up, shaking out her legs.]

HELEN. That sounds like a perverse kind of praise . . . *[She looks toward the inner door.]* I hope she's better . . . her prayers aren't usually this long . . . *[to Marguerite]* What did you come for . . .

MARGUERITE. I won't be long, I've only one question to ask . . .

HELEN. Once you're in there you'll think of others, it's too tempting not to ask about everything . . . the children, past lovers, the meaning of the most trivial things. It's absurd how in her presence you think she can answer all your needs. And for weeks you hang on to everything . . .

not even what she said exactly. I often forget the details but never the atmosphere . . . the feeling of having been perceived . . .

[*She looks toward the inner door, impatient to be inside. MARGUERITE, impelled by that impatience, feels her own need quicken.*]

MARGUERITE. [*remembering*] The last time I saw her I was young . . . just out of fashion school . . . in white and navy blue. I wore long skirts, not at all fashionable then, and white silk blouses. I even had a navy-blue cape and a wide-brim navy hat . . . [*shifting*] My mother sent me to see her because I kept saying that no one would ever marry me. It was my refrain . . . 'no one will ever marry me.' And my mother partially agreed. There are more colored men in jail than free, she said, but I should go to Queenie anyway and see . . . [*shifting*] When I came back from the reading, I announced: 'Late, if ever, from now on I'd like to drop the whole thing . . .' My mother looked at me and shrugged as if it was the most matter-of-fact thing. Then, trying to spite her, though for what I'm not sure . . . for being so matter-of-fact, or for sending me to Queenie in the first place, I said defiantly . . . 'I'm going to keep on wearing pretty things . . .' and I went to the mirror to straighten my hat. When I looked up, she was standing behind me, looking pleased . . . That made me mad . . . 'It won't make a bit of difference,' I shouted, 'has it ever, that we were fashionable or well-groomed . . .'

[*The room goes silent. HELEN stares at her.*]

HELEN. [*after a while*] You mean your mother didn't sympathize with you . . .

MARGUERITE. She didn't feel sorry for me, no . . .

HELEN. *[shocked]* What did she expect you to do . . .

MARGUERITE. *[shrugging]* It was just a question of a man . . .

HELEN. *[disbelieving]* Don't tell me she wasn't upset . . . my mother would have told Queenie off . . . 'How dare you tell her that,' she'd have said, 'you owe it to her to lie so at least she can still dream . . .' *[amused]* She wouldn't have believed it anyway, I can hear her now: 'The least one can achieve is a man . . .' *[with bitter amusement]* Though she does everything to stay out of my father's way . . . gets up before dawn, eats breakfast alone, is off working in her garden by the time he eats. And when they do eat together, she reads to him from the newspaper or whatever book she's onto at the time . . . imagine someone reading out loud to you at every meal! *[shifting to an edgier note]* I wrote one book about her. I called her Eulalie, made her a southerner who'd become a well-known horticulturist . . . I kept the business about her reading to her husband at meals, except I added a cruel touch . . . I made my father deaf . . . *[shifting]* At one point, Eulalie's daughter comes to tell her she's about to divorce, and Eulalie, who's digging in her garden, turns to her and says, 'You're going to be bored all by yourself, time goes faster with a man . . .' *[amused]* That's my mother, all right . . . that's her kind of refrain. It's taken me a lifetime to decode her spiteful little aphorisms . . .

[*SHE turns to MARGUERITE, who's turned away.*]

HELEN. What did you do then . . .

MARGUERITE. When . . .

HELEN. After your mother refused to make a fuss.

[MARGUERITE shrugs.]

HELEN. Did you believe her . . .

MARGUERITE. Who . . .

HELEN. Queenie . . . they can make mistakes . . .

MARGUERITE. It wasn't just her, it was me . . .

HELEN. It's such a pessimistic thing to think. I wouldn't want to have known at, what . . . twenty-three . . . that nobody was going to marry me, not for years and years and years, if at all . . .

[She shudders.]

MARGUERITE. It settled things . . .

[The strength behind that remark unsettles Helen, makes her eager to change the subject.]

HELEN. What did you come for this time . . .

MARGUERITE. *[caught off guard]* The same question in a way, what to do about me . . .

HELEN. The marriage isn't happy . . .

MARGUERITE. It's got nothing to do with that . . .

HELEN. It came too late, you're too used to being free . . .

MARGUERITE. *[amused]* Are those the kind of emotions that go into your novels . . .

HELEN. *[insulted]* Oh for Christ's sake, the least you could do is speak . . .

MARGUERITE. *[striking back]* I don't owe you what's wrong with me . . .

[Just then the inner door opens and the WOMAN comes back out.]

THE WOMAN. She's not feeling any better. She says if one of you has an emergency, she'll see that one . . .

[They look at each other.]

HELEN. My health.

MARGUERITE. A wounded cervix comes first . . .

HELEN. Is yours urgent . . .

MARGUERITE. Measured against what . . .

HELEN. *[furious]* Stop belittling me!!

[SHE turns to the WOMAN, as if asking her to intervene.]

THE WOMAN. You'll have to decide. She's resting now, when she's ready I'll call you . . .

[The WOMAN goes back inside. An awkward silence follows in which the edginess of both women is apparent. Looking for refuge, both move toward the white armchair, colliding.]

HELEN. *[still angry]* Don't make this symbolic . . .

MARGUERITE. It's the only comfortable seat . . .

[In one swift, aggressive move, MARGUERITE lands the chair.]

HELEN. *[her dignity affronted]* This is ridiculous . . .

MARGUERITE. *[somewhat ruffled]* Only one of us could sit . . .

HELEN. I wouldn't have fought for it, that's for sure . . .

MARGUERITE. Saving yourself . . .

HELEN. For what . . .

MARGUERITE. The <u>larger</u> skirmish . . .

[That stops the exchange. HELEN steps back.]

HELEN. I'm not up to sparring over this . . .

MARGUERITE. *[playful]* We could draw straws . . .

HELEN. . . . nor reverting to childhood tactics . . .

MARGUERITE. *[more playful]* . . . pick a number, any number . . .

HELEN. *[cutting her off]* Then what . . .

MARGUERITE. *[noticing it]* The candle's out . . .

[A bell rings behind the inner door. The mood of the room shifts. MARGUERITE gets up, goes to sit down in front of the candle.]

HELEN. *[edgy]* What are you doing . . .

[MARGUERITE relights the candle. The bell rings again.]

MARGUERITE. *[staring at it]* Don't go out again. It's little things like you that matter when you live alone. That candles stay lit. That the floors shine and there are no dishes left overnight in the sink. Little things. Flowers. The smell of clean sheets. Bright colors, the rooms always neat. Little things . . .

[By now the light from the candle should dominate the room, leaving all but MARGUERITE in shadow.]

MARGUERITE. Now when I come home, nothing welcomes me; the floors don't smile, the rooms don't speak. If he's not around, I can hardly breathe . . . *[embarrassed]* I'm ashamed of me . . . who lived so long steeped in things . . . now I panic when I'm just with me. I panic . . . I can't breathe. I sit in the dark and wait for him . . . *[thinking back]* . . . the same me who used to turn on all the lights, music, run a hot bath, luxuriate in things . . . Now I sit in the dark afraid to breathe. I sit in the dark and wait for him . . . *[feeling it evaporate]* Then it goes away, like something unreal . . . a dream . . . the minute he walks in, it leaves . . .

[She sits very still, staring at the candle. Helen, out of the shadows, begins to speak.]

HELEN. *[caught up in the emotion]* I hate the idea of being alone with me . . . *[going deeper]* . . . sometimes I think my writing is like my mother's garden . . . a pretense at being alone that still isn't free . . . Early, before anyone wakes up, I retreat to my study much as she does to her plants. In my head sometimes I see both of us . . . pulling and tugging at our lives like useless weeds . . .

[SILENCE. The bell rings behind the inner door. Lights come up. The mood of the room shifts.]

HELEN. I hope that's the end of her prayers . . .

[MARGUERITE gets up slowly, feeling stiff.]

MARGUERITE. Hmph . . . I sat still too long, I've got a cramp in both feet . . .

[SHE shakes her legs loose.]

HELEN. You think she's ready to read . . .

MARGUERITE. She could be . . . at least one of us I suppose she'll see . . .

[The inner door opens and the WOMAN comes out.]

THE WOMAN. *[bluntly]* Which one . . .

[MARGUERITE steps forward.]

MARGUERITE. In a strict ordering of the thing, that should be me . . .

HELEN. But is yours an emergency . . .

[They both look to the woman, who stands there impassively.]

MARGUERITE. My appointment was first . . . I think we should leave it at that . . .

HELEN. *[raw]* I'll have to come back . . .

MARGUERITE. One of us would . . .

[Again they look to the woman for arbitration, but she stands there unmoved.]

HELEN. Is that all you want to ask her, why you're afraid to be alone . . .

[Marguerite just glares at her.]

HELEN. It's probably guilt at being happy . . . or some such thing . . . aloneness . . . *[dismissing it]* . . . who doesn't suffer from it to some degree . . .

MARGUERITE. In which case, crumbling breasts and vaginas have it all over me . . .

[In spite of herself, the woman lets out an audible giggle, which causes Helen and Marguerite to look in her direction. Marguerite smiles somewhat conspiratorially.]

HELEN. *[watching both of them]* You're not going to make this racial . . .

[The woman returns an impassive gaze.]

MARGUERITE. You mean difficult . . .

HELEN. *[hesitantly agreeing]* Yes . . .

MARGUERITE. Insinuating color into the thing . . .

HELEN. *[more firmly]* Yes . . .

MARGUERITE. Making sure I go in . . . to redeem past sins . . .

HELEN. *[forcefully]* Exactly . . . I won't have you <u>beating</u> the black drum against me . . .

MARGUERITE. *[pushing it]* Dark blood spilling out irrationally . . .

HELEN. It's you who insist on it, it's your main theme . . .

MARGUERITE. Race, always race, carried to an extreme . . .

[The WOMAN shifts her feet noisily. Both women look at her.]

HELEN. *[addressing her]* I think it's time for you to intervene . . .

MARGUERITE. *[aimlessly]* Are wounded cervixes the greater need?

HELEN. *[humiliated]* You make it sound obscene, like something I did out of <u>spite</u> against me . . .

MARGUERITE. A private female arsenal . . .

HELEN. What's that supposed to mean . . .

MARGUERITE. *[feeling crazy]* It's you who's wounded in the flesh, you tell me . . .

HELEN. *[outraged]* What in God's name gives you leeway to keep mocking me . . .

MARGUERITE. I don't see you . . . *[out of control]* . . . exist for me . . . the memory is white, it <u>provokes</u> certain things . . .

[The WOMAN shifts her feet. Still wound up, Marguerite hears herself speak.]

MARGUERITE. The lines between us are written somewhere in ink . . . you and I don't really speak . . . I'm going in . . . it doesn't matter what you think . . .

[SHE steps forward. The WOMAN opens the door.]

HELEN. *[feeling something]* . . . as if some anonymous crowd were cheering you on . . .

MARGUERITE. *[stopping]* What do you mean . . .

HELEN. *[as Queenie]* '. . . color, honey, that's all I see, ain't nothin' but color left between you and me . . .'

[Marguerite doesn't move. No one does. Lights go out.]

CURTAIN

BEGIN THE BEGUINE: A PLAY IN ONE ACT

for
RUBY and GUY

THE CHARACTERS*

A YOUNG MAN, around twenty-five.
An OLDER WOMAN, around fifty-five.

THE PLACE

A space that resembles a park.

THE TIME

The present.

[*A YOUNG MAN, around twenty-five, comes onstage dressed in black. He moves restlessly across the space with long, intense strides, a preoccupied manner, as if containing much emotion. It's important that he move gracefully and with tremendous ease.*

---

* *Both characters are black.*

HE sits down on a park bench and begins to whistle several show tunes, beginning with "Night and Day," followed by "Just One of Those Things," and growing louder and more violent as he drifts finally into "From This Moment On," at which point an OLDER WOMAN, around fifty-five, wanders onto the stage dressed in a calf-length '30s-type dress. She should be small, delicate-looking, vague of manner. She sees the young man and hesitates.]

THE WOMAN. I won't continue the fight in public.

[The YOUNG MAN stops whistling.]

THE YOUNG MAN. I didn't ask you to.

THE WOMAN. I came here to breathe, the air at home is . . .

THE YOUNG MAN. *[completing her sentence]* Cloudy.

THE WOMAN. *[defensively]* That's not my kind of word, cloudy . . .

THE YOUNG MAN. It fits. You can't see that it fits because you don't even know who you are. If you did, you'd recognize that there are clouds all over the place.

THE WOMAN. Staring at me . . .

THE YOUNG MAN. What do you mean?

THE WOMAN. I recognize that much, that they're staring at me . . .

THE YOUNG MAN. *[laughing]* No, you still got it wrong, they're not staring at you, you're <u>inside</u> the goddamn things, you are the cloud.

THE WOMAN. Now you're being offensive.

THE YOUNG MAN. Now you're playing *ma mère,* momma, mommacita, Norma, which you're not . . .

THE WOMAN. *[switching]* What's the black for . . .

THE YOUNG MAN. What are you talking about?

THE WOMAN. The black pants and jacket, up to and including the shirt.

THE YOUNG MAN. Before you came, I was whistling. Old show tunes. 'I Get a Kick Out of You,' 'Love for Sale.' That kind of stuff, Broadway Americana. I was thinking I might tap dance next.

THE WOMAN. I once played Zora Neale Hurston.

THE YOUNG MAN. I know.

THE WOMAN. I'm convinced that somewhere in this universe there's a vagabond black spirit . . .

THE YOUNG MAN. I know.

[The WOMAN turns away to cry. The YOUNG MAN watches her dispassionately.]

THE YOUNG MAN. You're a pretty woman . . . small and delicate, I miss you all the time, I have always missed you, even before I was conceived. The missing grows stronger as you grow older and I grow less sure of the memories we have in common.

THE WOMAN. *[still tearful]* This dress reminds me of Zora Neale Hurston . . .

[The YOUNG MAN gets up, takes out his harmonica, plays an old folk tune, while the WOMAN claps.]

THE WOMAN. Did I ever tell you the story about Mrs. Wind . . .

[The YOUNG MAN nods a yes but keeps playing.]

THE WOMAN. And Mrs. Water . . .

[HE nods yes again.]

THE WOMAN. Mrs. Wind and Mrs. Water . . . *[She chuckles to herself.]*

I'm just repeating Zora out loud . . .

[The YOUNG MAN plays more spiritedly, beckoning her to sing, dance, join in, which the WOMAN does, but only halfheartedly, until the mood grows despondent and his playing peters out. HE sits back down on the bench.]

THE YOUNG MAN. We're nowhere again.

THE WOMAN. *[brightening]* Which came first, the park or the trees?

THE YOUNG MAN. There are no trees.

THE WOMAN. That's shameful, too . . . a park without trees.

[She doesn't know where to put herself.]

THE YOUNG MAN. You want the bench?

[HE gets up. Shyly, SHE goes to sit down. Now he doesn't know where to put himself, so he begins to tap dance, humming softly.]

THE YOUNG MAN. This is called the 'Soft Shoe Rag.' Broadway Americana. 'Kiss the Girls Goodbye.'

[SHE sits tugging at her dress, her hair, primping.]

THE YOUNG MAN. You look fine, don't preen.

THE WOMAN. I'm at the mercy of all who love me . . .

THE YOUNG MAN. *[still tap-dancing]* We tried, as Pop would say, Lord have mercy how we tried . . .

[That makes her sad, she begins to cry again, takes out a handkerchief to stifle the sobs, then gets up faintly.]

THE WOMAN. The best thing for me to do now is perform . . .

THE YOUNG MAN. I applaud that. How can I help . . .

[HE mimes sweeping the stage, then laying out a fresh carpet for her. Then he bows, gesturing to her to take her place. SHE comes over and stands in the spot. Lights should dim, spotlighting her as if for a performance.]

THE WOMAN. When I first played Zora, I was fifty-three. She remains sleek in my memory, a feline creature but without charm. I tried to give her charm. She was molasses. I tried to sweeten her to honey. The tea stuck in my throat, I wanted a real vagabond for my dreams. She was almost it, she was almost the real thing . . .

THE YOUNG MAN. *[out of darkness]* Are we stuck on a white folk's line?

[HE begins to play the harmonica—a corny tune.]

THE WOMAN. Spotlight for two!

[It materializes. But only on the young man's face, looking anxiously at the woman, while holding the harmonica to his lips.]

THE WOMAN. You look so young . . .

THE YOUNG MAN. I try to keep myself buoyant.

THE WOMAN. Could we sing something together . . .

THE YOUNG MAN. 'All of You,' 'Anything Goes,' 'Begin the Beguine.' Take your pick.

THE WOMAN. I thought we could improvise . . .

THE YOUNG MAN. *[harshly]* There are no dust tracks on your feet.

THE WOMAN. *[sadly]* I know . . .

THE YOUNG MAN. The spotlight's waiting.

[And indeed it is, holding the woman fully, yet still holding only the young man's face.]

THE WOMAN. *[singing]*

Two little darkies lyin' in bed
One of 'em sick an' de odder mos' dead
Call fo' de doctor an' de doc done said,
'Feed dem babies some shortenin' bread'

[The young man joins in but with a different song.]

THE YOUNG MAN. *[singing]*

When they begin the beguine
It brings back the sound of music so tender

THE WOMAN. *[still singing]*

> Mammy's little baby loves shortenin', shortenin'
> Mammy's little baby loves shortenin' bread
> Mammy's little baby loves shortenin', shortenin'
> Mammy's little baby loves shortenin' bread

THE YOUNG MAN. *[still singing]*

> I'm with you once more under the stars
> And down by the shore an orchestra's playing

[And so the DUET goes, escalating in intensity, until at the end, both of them fall out laughing.]

THE WOMAN. *[laughing]* How did you come up with that . . .

THE YOUNG MAN. *[laughing]* I was about to ask you the same thing . . . it has your kind of nostalgia . . .

THE WOMAN. 'Shortenin' Bread'??

THE YOUNG MAN. *[laughing]* No, 'Begin the Beguine' . . .

THE WOMAN. Meaning . . .

THE YOUNG MAN. It wanders places I thought you might like to go.

[HE extends his arms, asking her to dance. SHE steps forward. THEY begin to dance together silently.]

THE WOMAN. Is the music still with us . . .

THE YOUNG MAN. Of course.

THE WOMAN. Is it enough that we dance . . .

THE YOUNG MAN. I don't know what you mean.

THE WOMAN. Is it enough to stop things . . .

THE MAN. *[honestly]* No.

[HE stops dancing, goes back to his bench, where he begins to whistle "I've Got You Under My Skin."]

THE WOMAN. Do you know why I drink . . .

[He doesn't answer, just keeps on whistling. She shouts over the whistling.]

THE WOMAN. Don't all mothers drink . . .

[HE keeps whistling. She drifts mockingly back into song.]

I'm comin', I'm comin',
But my head is bending low
I hear the darkies singin' yonder
Old Black Joe . . .

THE YOUNG MAN. *[stopping]* What's the point . . .

THE WOMAN. *[bowing]* My answer to Broadway Americana . . .

THE YOUNG MAN. *[annoyed]* You've got to perform.

THE WOMAN. *[defensively]* Sometimes . . .

THE YOUNG MAN. *[angry]* All the time.

[Finding the distance unbearable, the WOMAN rushes over to sit down beside the young man.]

THE WOMAN. But I can be sweet, too . . .

THE YOUNG MAN. *[gently]* You can, that you can.

THE WOMAN. And I don't miss things . . .

THE YOUNG MAN. *[amused]* No, that's true. Hardly anything gets by you.

THE WOMAN. And I remember holidays, I remember to make a fuss . . .

THE YOUNG MAN. *[enthusiastic]* They stand out as some of the finest family hours.

THE WOMAN. And you wouldn't hesitate to call it love . . .

   [He hesitates. SHE gets up, angry.]

THE WOMAN. When I was playing Zora, I called on parts of myself unwelcome in our household . . .

THE YOUNG MAN. She was one feisty dame.

THE WOMAN. I did everything I could to rid myself of my vagueness . . .

THE YOUNG MAN. You played her tart, a woman of many moods, of memories her race couldn't contain.

THE WOMAN. *[real angry]* That's not all. I tried to see myself as I might have been . . . beyond, before my color intervened . . .

THE YOUNG MAN. *[frightened]* I wouldn't know anything about that.

   [She begins to weep. He can't stand it and tries to woo her with song.]

THE YOUNG MAN.
Birds do it, bees do it, even . . .

   [She shakes her head violently no . . . He tries again.]

THE YOUNG MAN.
What is this thing called love, this crazy thing . . .

[Again, a violent no. He tries again.]

THE YOUNG MAN.

Whenever skies grow gray again
And trouble begins to brew . . .

[He begins to cry like a baby. SHE rushes over to comfort him, kneeling down in front of him.]

THE WOMAN. *[all gentleness]* Let me tell you why the waves have whitecaps . . . Now Mrs. Water used to brag something fierce about her children. 'Just look at my children,' she'd say, 'I got de biggest and de littlest in de world. All kinds of children, every color in de world and every shape . . .' But Mrs. Water didn't brag half as loud as Mrs. Wind. No, sir, Mrs. Wind was de bragginest lady there ever was. 'I got more children than anybody in the world,' she'd say, 'they flies, they walks, they swims, they sings, they talks, they cries, and they come in all de colors of de sun. T'ain't nobody got babies like mine!' Now Mrs. Water got tired of hearin' Mrs. Wind brag about her children and got so she hated 'em . . . Then one day, a whole handful of Mrs. Wind's children got thirsty and asked if they could go get themselves a drink. 'Yes, children,' said Mrs. Wind, 'you go on over there to Mrs. Water and get yourselves a nice, cool drink . . .' Well, when them children went over to Mrs. Water, she grabbed 'em, one after another, and drowned 'em . . . And when her children didn't come home, the Wind woman got worried, so she went down to the Water to ask after her babies. 'Good evening, Mrs. Water,' she said, 'I've come lookin' for my children, have you seen my children today?' 'No-o-o-o-o,' the Water lady told her, lookin' all wrapped up in herself, 'no indeed, I ain't seen none of your children . . .' But Mrs. Wind knew better. So she passed over the ocean calling out for her children, and every time she called, white feathers came up on top of the water. And that's how come we got whitecaps on the waves: it's the feathers comin' up when the Wind woman calls her babies . . . So when you see a storm blow up on the sea, that's Mrs. Wind and Mrs. Water fightin' over dem children . . .

[The young man is laughing hard by now.]

THE YOUNG MAN. So that's how come the waves have whitecaps . . .

THE WOMAN. [laughing] It's the Wind woman callin' her children . . .

[They are both laughing hard by now.]

THE YOUNG MAN. Pop always says you're a funny woman, that you've got to be one of the funniest women in the world.

THE WOMAN. [strangely desperate] Who else can I make laugh . . .

THE YOUNG MAN. [upset] Anybody, you try hard enough you can make anybody laugh.

[HE gets up, begins whistling violently "I Get a Kick Out of You."]

THE WOMAN. [desperate] You want to hear about Ole Masa and the Bear . . .

[HE shakes his head vehemently no. She persists.]

THE WOMAN. How about why Negroes are black . . .

[*Again, a vehement no. She persists, growing flirtatious.*]

THE WOMAN. What about Sue, Sal, and the Johnson Gal . . .

THE YOUNG MAN. [*viciously*] You think Zora can help you out?

[*The WOMAN reacts as if struck, turning away with a plaintive gesture.*]

THE WOMAN. I don't know <u>what</u> was on God's mind when He made colored folks . . .

[*In spite of himself, the young man can't help laughing, which annoys the woman.*]

THE WOMAN. You think it's easy to be <u>stuck</u> on this frack . . .

THE YOUNG MAN. [*shrugging*] Play Mrs. Wind to your heart's content.

THE WOMAN. [*with real pain*] My spirit's <u>broken</u> . . . all night long it cries out, it will not be still . . .

THE YOUNG MAN. [*saddened*] All my life you've been wandering and wandering.

THE WOMAN. I apologize . . .

THE YOUNG MAN. [*defensively*] I've never known you to be still.

THE WOMAN. Forgive me . . .

THE YOUNG MAN. [*trying too hard*] Even when you read me stories, tucked me in, kissed me good night, you were looking around for something.

THE WOMAN. I'm sorry . . .

[The YOUNG MAN, not knowing what else to do, drifts back to whistling "Love for Sale."]

THE WOMAN. Is that your answer . . .

THE YOUNG MAN. You gave me a taste for the broad gesture.

[HE shuffles, taps, whistles. She watches him longingly.]

THE WOMAN. I wish I could join in . . .

THE YOUNG MAN. *[suddenly pained]* All your regrets make me sad.

[HE whistles harshly and loudly to keep from crying.]

THE WOMAN. *[struggling]* 'Miss Otis Regrets' . . . 'Just One of Those Things' . . . 'Every Time We Say Goodbye' . . . *[anguished]* What if I play your favorite colored dame . . .

THE YOUNG MAN. That would be nice, it would be nice to see you strut your stuff . . .

[Holding back his tears, HE takes out his harmonica, drifts into "Begin the Beguine." SHE stands there weeping.]

CURTAIN

THE HEALING: A PLAY IN ONE ACT

for
ANNA

THE CHARACTERS

JOE, a white man in his early thirties.
ELLEN, a black woman in her late forties.

THE PLACE

A room in Joe's apartment.

THE TIME

The present.

> *[Lights come up on JOE and ELLEN. ELLEN is seated, JOE*
> *stands behind her. The room they're in is sparsely furnished. A*
> *few chairs, a low table covered with a cloth, flowers, a lit candle.*
> *Joe's hands form a sort of halo around Ellen's head. He is a*
> *white man in his early thirties, boyish-looking with an awkward,*
> *somewhat blunt manner. Yet there is about him a clarity one*
> *senses coming from within.*

ELLEN sits very still, her eyes closed. She is a black woman in her late forties. Though still good-looking, there is a heaviness about her of one often betrayed, no longer sure of anything. When she speaks, it is with brusque defiance, as if holding on to herself took all her energy.

After a few moments, Joe's hands begin to move in arc-like patterns over Ellen's body—though never touching her. What we are witnessing is a healing: the laying on of hands. The audience must have time both to absorb and feel this before anyone speaks.]

JOE. *[after a long while]* It moved.

ELLEN. Oh . . .

JOE. Could you feel it?

ELLEN. I felt something. Hot, then cool. Relief.

JOE. Good!

[HE runs his hand slowly down her back—but without touching her. His hand stops at her lower back.]

JOE. Here, too . . .

ELLEN. Yes.

[HE comes around front and bends over, placing his hand close to her chest—but again without actually touching her. Then he listens.]

ELLEN. *[self-conscious]* This part always embarrasses me.

JOE. *[still listening]* Why?

ELLEN. It's too close.

JOE. I'm trying to find the direction.

ELLEN. I'm sure I don't have one, there's not a clear impulse left in me.

JOE. *[still listening]* Sh . . .

[HE moves his hand up and down in front of her chest, slowly, carefully, for a long time.]

ELLEN. *[almost gasping]* Oh . . .

JOE. *[joyful]* There!

ELLEN. *[embarrassed]* It's as if you touched some spring . . .

[She starts to cry. HE goes and stands behind her, placing his hands once again in an arc above her head.]

JOE. Relax.

ELLEN. I'm trying.

JOE. *[gently]* You always say that.

ELLEN. I'm always trying.

[He takes a deep breath. His hands move lightly, sending out energy. She is still crying.]

ELLEN. Why . . . how . . .

JOE. It amazes me, too.

ELLEN. I don't even believe.

[HE shrugs, begins to move his hands down her arms—still without touching.]

ELLEN. You never react to that . . .

JOE. Breathe.

[She does.]

JOE. Now exhale, slowly . . .

[She does.]

JOE. Slower . . . try to empty everything.

ELLEN. That would take a tornado . . .

[He laughs. She tries to do as she's told.]

ELLEN. Last night I dreamt that it worked, that they couldn't find a thing.

[He doesn't answer, just concentrates. His fingers make pulling motions at her shoulders, as if trying to release something.]

ELLEN. Why . . . why should it work . . .

[He doesn't answer, but instead comes around front and kneels down, placing his hands on her feet. She reacts self-consciously.]

ELLEN. I don't like this part, either, it smacks of Jesus washing some poor sinner's feet.

JOE. [laughing] I have to make sure you're grounded.

ELLEN. Is that how you see me . . . a sinner . . .

JOE. [holding her feet] I'm a healer, that's all, don't read into it other things.

ELLEN. But sin must be there somewhere, sins against the body that we call disease . . .

[Joe doesn't answer, just concentrates on her feet.]

JOE. [after a while] Better . . .

ELLEN. There's a pull downward, if that's what you mean . . .

[Silence again. A strong wave seems to reach her. Unable to restrain it, she sighs, almost crying.]

JOE. Give in . . .

ELLEN. I can't . . .

JOE. For your own sake.

ELLEN. I recognize that much, that it's me who needs relief.

JOE. Let's take a break.

[HE gets up, walks offstage. We hear water running. In a few minutes, he returns, drying his hands.]

ELLEN. Why do you do that each time . . .

JOE. I have to.

ELLEN. *[softly]* Wash your hands of me . . .

JOE. *[surprised]* Is that what you think that means . . .

ELLEN. *[embarrassed]* It's a thought that comes to me.

[JOE sits down on a chair some distance from her and closes his eyes. After a while, he begins to hum softly. ELLEN gets up, goes over to her pocketbook, takes out a pack of cigarettes. She starts to light one, but then looks across at Joe and hesitates.]

ELLEN. You mind if I smoke . . .

JOE. *[firmly]* Yes.

ELLEN. It's forbidden . . .

JOE. *[amused]* You make it moral, I think of it in terms of energy.

ELLEN. What do you mean?

JOE. It interferes, blocks things.

ELLEN. Is that how you see me . . . as a piece of energy . . .

JOE. *[shrugging]* I apologize.

ELLEN. For . . .

JOE. Bypassing Ellen, the schoolteacher, wife, mother, whatever . . .

ELLEN. *[quickly]* I'm no longer married, and the energy you poke around so diligently to unleash should tell you that no child has ever come out of me . . .

[Joe doesn't respond.]

ELLEN. You knew that . . .

[Still no answer.]

ELLEN. I smell of that . . . it's got to be all over me . . .

[SHE lights her cigarette defiantly.]

JOE. *[immediately]* I have to ask you to put that out.

ELLEN. *[mocking]* It's not righteous. If pushed, you'd go so far as to call it unclean . . .

[SHE stubs it out.]

JOE. I'm ready to work.

ELLEN. *[resistant]* Not yet . . .

[SHE goes and sits in the chair farthest away from him, tries to strike up a conversation.]

ELLEN. What were you humming . . .

JOE. *[singing]*

Come by here, my Lord,
Come by here,
Come by here, my Lord . . .

ELLEN. *[interrupting]* Why that . . .

[JOE shrugs unknowingly.]

ELLEN. It's an old freedom song . . .

[HE nods agreement.]

ELLEN. <u>Slaves</u> sang it . . .

[HE nods again. She repeats the words but refuses to sing them.]

Someone's crying, Lord,
Come by here,
Someone's crying, Lord,
Come by here . . .

[Unexpectedly, this makes her cry. JOE gets up, goes and stands behind her, his hands once again forming a halo over her head. SHE closes her eyes. The healing continues. After a moment, JOE rubs his hands together, then places them directly above each of her shoulders, breathing deeply. Moments later, ELLEN shudders involuntarily.]

JOE. Where do you feel it . . .

ELLEN. Chest, heart, all around here . . . for a moment I felt ready to leap.

[HE raises his hands slightly higher, takes several deep breaths. As if a strong gust of wind had blown through her, ELLEN cries out, almost rising from her seat.]

JOE. Breathe, keep your eyes closed and try not to think . . .

[HE comes quickly around front, kneels down and takes hold of her feet. A long silence. Finally, her breathing grows more relaxed, though Joe keeps a grip on her feet.]

JOE. Better . . .

[SHE nods yes.]

JOE. You're strong.

ELLEN. What does that mean . . .

JOE. In my terms, only energy.

[They both laugh, then are silent.]

ELLEN. [embarrassed] It's as if I were in church, and the spirit got the better of me . . . [She grows even more self-conscious.] Do other black women react the same . . . shout, cry out, almost lose it . . .

JOE. Others react the same, if that's what you mean. I don't know about their color, you're the first black woman to come to me. Be still, please, close your eyes, and just breathe.

[She tries to, but unsuccessfully.]

ELLEN. I hate it when you hold on to my feet . . .

JOE. [holding tight] Right, the sinner motif.

[SHE wriggles free, turning away.]

ELLEN. [irritated] What does it mean anyway, to say you're healing me . . .

JOE. I wouldn't put it that way.

[They stare at each other. Joe is still kneeling.]

ELLEN. *[strangely]* What does it mean, actually . . . to kiss someone's feet . . .

[Suddenly embarrassed, SHE gets up.]

ELLEN. You don't even know what's wrong with me . . .

JOE. I never know.

ELLEN. Why?

JOE. It hinders things.

ELLEN. I said to you the first time . . . 'I'm sick, the doctors say' . . . and you stopped me.

[JOE nods agreement.]

ELLEN. I wanted to go on, not about my illness, but to explain me . . .

[HE stops her with a gesture, which irritates her even more.]

ELLEN. It makes me uneasy, your not knowing anything . . .

JOE. *[firmly]* I'm ready to go on . . .

ELLEN. *[pushing]* I've had two husbands and quite a few men. I'm not a whore, I teach acting to children. I used to perform, but there are too few parts for black women worth the pounding and pushing, the endless aggression you need.

JOE. *[applauding]* Bravo. Well told. Thank you.

ELLEN. *[angry, defensive]* Somewhere inside that history are the <u>reasons</u> why my body's playing tricks on me . . .

JOE. *[gently]* I'm not a psychiatrist, I don't try to make connections between things.

ELLEN. *[furious]* Can't we talk . . .

JOE. If you're not up to working, I ask you to leave.

[ELLEN, aggravated, goes to pick up her bag, stooping down in the process to retrieve her cigarettes.]

ELLEN. It changes everything to be told you're diseased . . .

[Joe doesn't answer.]

ELLEN. . . . you know it's your fault, somewhere inside you know it, that it's a <u>result</u> of things . . .

[Still, he doesn't answer.]

ELLEN. I think I came seeking forgiveness. There was in my head a biblical fantasy . . . the laying on of hands or some such thing, the feeling that it was still possible to <u>dissolve</u> things . . .

[SHE puts her cigarettes in her bag.]

ELLEN. What happens if I leave . . .

JOE. You come back whenever you feel ready.

ELLEN. What does that mean . . .

JOE. *[apologizing]* I can't play priest or shrink. I can't talk, nor take into account your need to go over things.

ELLEN. I should just sit still and allow you to play white hippie games with me . . .

[The room goes silent. It's a while before Joe speaks.]

JOE. *[thinking]* That's like a pebble thrown in to make a splash. A loud noise. <u>Bang</u>. Discomfort.

ELLEN. What do you mean . . .

JOE. Words meant to pull at invisible strings.

ELLEN. I don't get it . . .

JOE. You detoured into race to stop things.

ELLEN. And you . . .

JOE. I've said it already, I'm not here to speak on things.

ELLEN. *[taunting]* No mention of race, hippie vibes, or disease . . . *[She laughs disbelievingly.]* How long did it take you to convert this black woman into energy . . .

[*Joe doesn't answer. Instead, HE begins to pace aimlessly.*]

ELLEN. . . . or from the time I entered this room, was I never seen . . .

JOE. *[slowly, remembering]* I opened the door, saw a woman with a dark face. She looked scared, she stood there staring at me.

ELLEN. I heard your name at a meeting on alternate ways to treat disease. Why you . . . it's something. I've never asked myself. There were other healers I could have gone to see.

[*JOE, more restless, begins literally to roam the room.*]

ELLEN. You hate talk . . .

[*He doesn't answer.*]

ELLEN. Why . . .

[*Still, he doesn't answer.*]

ELLEN. You want me to leave . . .

[HE nods agreement. SHE picks up her bag, starts to go, then
on an impulse sits down in the healing chair. Pleased, JOE
makes a move toward her, ready to resume work, when she stops
him with a gesture.]

ELLEN. I just want to sit here a moment, before I leave . . .

[She sits. After a while, her eyes close. A stillness begins.
Gradually, we become aware of JOE humming softly, and a
peaceful feeling begins to pervade things. Suddenly, ELLEN
shivers involuntarily, her body begins to shake. JOE's humming,
while not rising in volume, seems to fill the room. ELLEN
responds sometimes with sounds, at other times with half-phrases
that are somewhat incoherent.]

ELLEN. Hmmmm . . . it's on me . . . [She shudders.] . . . it's
hard to give in . . . you're supposed to fight, just fight . . .
[Another wave hits her.] Oh God . . . [She holds on to herself
as if she might fall.] I keep myself tight . . . I don't move . . .
something's gone . . . I can't hold on now . . . who the hell
wants me . . . [She begins to cry.] Men—my dark body . . . my
even darker dreams . . .

[JOE's humming becomes even fuller, enveloping Ellen, the
room, opening things.]

ELLEN. Oh please . . . release me . . . release me . . . I don't
even know what that means . . . [A strong wave floods her body,
she cries out involuntarily.] Who calls out for me . . . Ellen
Harris, a black woman . . . Ellen Harris can't be seen . . .
[SHE begins to make pulling motions at her body.] These are
pieces, a dark frame that hides and covers new, these are
pieces . . . breast pieces . . . arm pieces . . . leg pieces . . .
diseased . . . dark first . . . now dark and diseased . . . what
cord do I pull to release me . . . [SHE pulls at herself violently,

then stops and a sudden spasm overtakes her.] . . . the place to be healed cries out and bleeds . . . I offer it my trembling . . . my shaking body . . . my tears . . . I offer it freedom from grief . . . when I have no idea what that means . . . *[A slow motion rocks her body.]* I, who never found anything . . . only motion . . . here to there . . . remember . . . think . . . plan and scheme . . .

[Her body shivers in distaste at all such memories. JOE's humming shifts to a more intense, more joyful pitch. ELLEN's arms begin to move loosely, like a rag doll, gesturing and swinging rhapsodically. SHE hums to herself in a kind of singsong mumble.]

ELLEN. Oh my, it's me . . . Ellen Harris . . . look at her swing . . . flesh and bones about to wilt . . . look at me . . . Ellen Harris . . . hear me sing . . . what song do I remember . . . what tune will speak . . . where's my story . . . what's there to say about me . . . *[Now she begins to sing in earnest.]*

> Someone's laughing, Lord,
> Come by here . . .
> Someone's laughing, Lord,
> Come by here . . .
> Someone's laughing, Lord,
> Come by here . . .

[She begins to cry, like a flood erupting from within. She cries, consumed by the crying, shaking violently. JOE walks quietly over to her.]

JOE. I need to take hold of your feet. *[HE kneels down, placing his hands on her feet.]* Try to breathe . . .

[SHE sucks in air, tears, more air.]

JOE. Deep breaths, then release . . .

[As she responds, the crying begins, slowly, to diminish.]

JOE. Exhale as slowly as you can . . . slower . . . good . . .

ELLEN. *[breathing heavily]* There are enough tears to wash my feet . . .

[Laughing, they both agree.]

ELLEN. Is humming one of your last-ditch maneuvers . . .

JOE. It was unplanned, if that's what you mean. How do you feel . . .

ELLEN. At sea. It's rough, the waves come fast, one right after another, they almost swallow me . . .

JOE. Is there any calm . . .

ELLEN. Yes. Some part of me knows not to move. *[Surprised by what she's just said, she chuckles.]* I don't know what I'm talking about . . .

JOE. Sit still a minute, I want to make sure you're balanced.

[HE gets up to go stand behind her, but SHE stops him.]

ELLEN. No, no more for now, I can't stand it . . . *[SHE gets up, shaking herself loose.]* I haven't thought about my father in years, but just now, in the midst of all that, I saw his face smiling at me. He's dead now, but he used to run numbers, sell insurance in an office of sorts with many back rooms. He had a desk that was so big, you could hardly see him behind it. There was a man named Ramon who stood guard at the door. It was a scene out of a film . . . Ramon, the big desk, men going back and forth secretively. It may have been why I wanted to act, I saw a lot of colored make-believe . . .

[Nervous, she turns to Joe, as if afraid he won't let her speak.] You owe me a few words . . .

JOE. *[agreeing]* Out of relief . . .

[They laugh.]

JOE. Maybe that was your father who stepped in and released all that energy.

ELLEN. And you had no part in the thing . . .

JOE. *[factually]* I hummed.

ELLEN. And me . . .

JOE. You let go of some things.

ELLEN. Hmph . . .

[They are silent a moment, when Ellen suddenly laughs.]

VI

SCREENPLAYS

A SUMMER DIARY

NOTE: All the characters are black.

FADE-IN:

INT. EMPTY HALLWAY – LATE AFTERNOON

MCU CAROLINE, holding her son. She is a striking woman in her midthirties with a soft face, haunting eyes.

> **CAROLINE**
> It's an omen, it belongs to us, I can feel it . . .

LILIANE enters frame. She is taller, around the same age but with a sharper, more abrupt manner. She looks drawn, as if in the early stages of grief.

> **LILIANE**
> Two women with two children in the same house, you're crazy . . .

CAROLINE
It's just for the summer, it's big enough, my
God, Lil, we could get lost, we won't even
have to see each other . . .

LILIANE
We'd have to share the same kitchen . . .

CAROLINE
(amused)
We'll eat at different hours . . .

LILIANE
What about Rafael . . .

CAROLINE
I've asked for a leave of absence . . .

She exits frame . . . HOLD on Liliane, who stares after
her . . .

LILIANE
Are you doing this to keep me sane?

CUT:

WS Caroline, POV Liliane. She's standing by a window at
the other end of a barren hallway.

CAROLINE
Not just you . . .

CUT:

HOLD . . .

EXT. COUNTRY HOUSE – SAME TIME

WS house. It's an old, ramshackle house, decaying but beautiful. In need of everything: a new roof, a paint job, etc. CHRISTOPHER, aged seven, comes out of the house, begins to shimmy up a tree. Two girls, SHANA and SARA, around five, open a second-story window and squeal out to him.

> SHANA
>
> Christopher, you're not supposed to climb trees . . .

He pays her no mind, keeps climbing.

> SHANA
> *(louder)*
>
> Christopher!!
> *(trying to distract him)*
> I already picked out my room, you don't even have a room . . .

By now Christopher is safely anchored on one branch, about to climb higher.

> SHANA
>
> Don't you climb any higher, I'll tell Momma on you . . .

Undaunted, he disappears out of frame. Scared, Shana disappears out of our sight to go call her mother. Sara remains looking out.

> SHANA (o.c.)
> Momma!! Christopher's up in a tree!

CUT:

MS Christopher, POV Sara. We can see his legs appearing and disappearing inside the branches . . .

INT. HALLWAY – SAME TIME

MCU Liliane standing where we left her.

> **LILIANE**
> He's just like him . . . just like him . . .

DOLLY BACK to MWS. As she moves forward, looking drawn, confused, we see Shana behind her.

> **LILIANE**
> Always looking for danger . . . Christopher . . .

CONTINUE DOLLY BACK. She reaches the porch, stops. Caroline enters frame in background.

> **LILIANE**
> Come down from there now . . .

She shields her eyes to look up.

> **LILIANE**
> I said come down, Christopher, that's high enough.

> **CHRISTOPHER (o.c.)**
> I can go straight to the top.

> **LILIANE**
> (forcefully)
> I know you can, but it's dangerous . . . Come down, now.

> **CHRISTOPHER (o.c.)**
> (reluctantly)
> All right . . .

She waits. We hear him coming down. At the last moment, he jumps, blurring across the frame with a loud squeal. Frightened, Liliane screams.

> **LILIANE**
> Christopher!!

CUT:

MWS Christopher, POV Liliane. He leaps to the ground from a branch, landing perfectly with both knees bent.

> **CHRISTOPHER**
> (*proudly*)
> That's how Dad taught me, the trick is to bend your knees . . .

He looks at his mother, suddenly stamps the ground hard . . .

> **CHRISTOPHER**
> (*violently*)
> Where is he? I want to go home . . . I want to go home . . .

He stalks off.

HOLD on Liliane and Caroline, on Sara, who is still looking out the window, on Shana, standing half hidden behind her mother.

At the bottom of the frame the title, A SUMMER DIARY, appears.

HOLD.

CUT:

EXT. A BAR – LATE AFTERNOON

MWS GILES, a tall man, around thirty-seven, looking dapper in a merchant marine uniform. He stands in the doorway lighting a cigarette.

> **CAROLINE (v.o.)**
> That's Giles, Liliane's husband who killed himself just before the summer began, yet his presence hovered over us like the most flamboyant of ghosts . . .

                                                    CUT:

Giles starts casually down the street . . .

INT. AN OFFICE – AFTERNOON

MWS RAFAEL, a polished-looking man in his late thirties, carefully dressed in a three-piece suit. A telex is running while he talks on several phones . . .

> **CAROLINE (v.o.)**
> That's Rafael, my husband, who's had many professions . . . poet, art dealer, musician, now turned investment counselor. He, too, hung over that summer, though we had agreed it would do us good to live apart . . .

                                                    CUT:

INT. HALLWAY SUMMER HOUSE

CU Liliane almost eclipsed by a tall piece of furniture she is hauling.

> LILIANE
> *(breathless)*

Tilt it . . .

We hear a dog barking . . .

> LILIANE
> *(yelling)*
> Christopher, take Simon for a walk . . .
> *(to Caroline)*
> Can you lift it . . .

> CAROLINE (o.c.)
> Drop your end . . .

Liliane does.

> LILIANE
> It wouldn't have been a bad idea to bring
> Rafael along . . .

DOLLY BACK to MWS. Caroline enters frame swinging the other end around.

> LILIANE
> Why did you tell him we didn't need him . . .

> CAROLINE
> Pride.

They laugh. Liliane shakes her head.

> LILIANE
> Ready for the steps?

We watch them maneuver the bureau with difficulty up the steps amid a clutter of boxes, suitcases, etc.

HOLD.

Main CREDITS come and go.

CUT:

INT. CHILDREN'S BEDROOM – LATE AFTERNOON

MCU Caroline, EDWARD. Bent over the crib, lifting him up. She looks tired.

> **CAROLINE**
> Hello, little one, you slept long, didn't you, you like the country, all this fresh air.

She looks out the window.

> **CAROLINE**
> Look at your sister.

CUT:

EXT. LAWN OF HOUSE – SAME TIME

MWS Shana, Sara, Christopher, POV Caroline. They're turning somersaults, cartwheels.

> **CAROLINE (o.c.)**
> Pretty soon you'll be able to do that, won't you?

We see the children stretch out like zombies.

> **LILIANE (o.c.)**
> Caroline.

CUT:

INT. CHILDREN'S BEDROOM – SAME TIME

MS Liliane, POV Caroline, standing in the doorway.

> **LILIANE**
> *(upset)*
> I don't know how to put the thing together.

> **CAROLINE (o.c.)**
> What thing?

> **LILIANE**
> My loom, Giles always put it together, I can't
> find the damn screws.

CUT:

MCU Caroline.

> **CAROLINE**
> I'll come help you, Lil.

CUT:

MCU Liliane crying.

> **SARA (o.c.)**
> Liliane.

CUT:

SIDE-ANGLE MWS Liliane, Caroline. The kids burst in
between them.

> **SARA**
> Is their daddy dead?

Caroline takes a step toward her daughter.

> **CAROLINE**
> Sara.

> **SARA**
> They keep saying their daddy's dead . . . is
> their daddy dead?

> **LILIANE**
> That's right, Sara, their daddy's dead . . .

> **SHANA and CHRISTOPHER**
> See, we told you.

They run to hold on to their mother. Sara runs to Caroline, frightened.

> **SARA**
> My daddy's not dead . . .

The children hold on tight to their mothers. No one speaks.

HOLD . . .

CUT:

INT. AN APARTMENT – NIGHT

LS dark staircase. A door opens. Liliane, wearing a coat and scarf, climbs the steps.

> **CAROLINE (v.o.)**
> Liliane says she had no real premonition about
> Giles's death, except a cloudy feeling that she
> shouldn't go to the movies that night.

Liliane stops at the top step.

DOLLY BACK and PAN as she crosses the dark hallway. In the background, a bedroom is well lit.

> **CAROLINE (v.o.)**
> She changed her mind several times but at
> the last minute decided she needed a night
> out . . . She saw his feet hanging over the
> bed and thought he'd fallen asleep watching
> television . . .

DOLLY rapidly ahead of her into MWS Giles, his eyes
open, his head twisted at a weird angle, a revolver dangling
from his left hand, blood everywhere . . .

> **LILIANE (o.c.)**
> Oh my God, my God, Giles . . .

She screams . . .

> **LILIANE**
> Giles!!

                                                            CUT:

INT. KITCHEN OF COUNTRY HOUSE – EVENING

WS everyone eating dinner. A sullen feeling in the air.

> **SHANA**
> *(after a while)*
> Do you like this house, Christopher?

> **CHRISTOPHER**
> No . . .

> **SHANA**
> Do you like it, Mom?

> **LILIANE**
> I do. It's peaceful and there's lots of space to
> play . . .

SARA
(to Caroline)
When's Daddy coming to see it, Mommie . . .

CHRISTOPHER
(to Shana)
She's a baby, she still calls her mother
Mommie . . .

SARA
I'm not a baby, don't call me a baby . . .

CHRISTOPHER
Baby, baby!!

SARA
(fiercely)
Stop it!

LILIANE
Christopher . . .

CAROLINE
Sara, leave him alone . . .

CHRISTOPHER
She's a baby, I don't like living with her . . .

He gets up to leave. Liliane pushes him down forcefully.

LILIANE
Sit down and finish your dinner . . .

He does, belligerently slamming his fists. The silence grows
even more sullen.

SHANA
(after a long while)
I like this house, it's like a dream . . .

HOLD . . .

CUT:

INT. CAROLINE'S BEDROOM – LATE AT NIGHT

MLS Caroline, POV through window. She's sitting at
her desk writing. There are still unpacked boxes and
suitcases cluttered about. The phone rings. She goes and
answers it.

CUT:

MCU Caroline, back to camera, already talking. On a shelf
in the background, a photograph of an older man.

> **CAROLINE**
> *(back to camera)*
> I knew it was you . . . sorry . . . I said I'm
> sorry . . .

PAN to MS as she stretches out on the bed.

> **CAROLINE**
> . . . it's lovely, a whole different feeling than
> the city, empty and quiet, I think I'm going to
> like it . . . no, we spent all day unpacking, Lil
> decided to give up their apartment, I think it
> was a pretty hard decision for her . . .

She rolls over, looks around the room . . .

PAN across room, POV Caroline. It has a cozy feeling,
heightened by the sense of the woods and greenery outside
peeking in.

> ### CAROLINE (o.c.)
> How are you . . . how's the job . . . you like
> it . . . I know, don't ask too many questions, it
> makes you jumpy . . . fine, she and Christopher
> have been fighting a lot but I think that'll
> settle down . . . you miss me . . .

CUT:

MCU Caroline.

> ### CAROLINE
> . . . don't answer . . .

Silence on both ends . . .

> ### CAROLINE
> I miss you . . . I guess . . . oh shit, it all sounds
> false . . . talk to you . . .

She hangs up, looking pained.

DOLLY BACK to WS as she gets up, crosses the room to
her desk, begins writing again.

> ### CAROLINE (v.o.)
> . . . it's like walking on eggshells . . . I never
> say the right thing . . . I try, but it comes out
> too earnest or prying or . . . never just right,
> never in harmony with that detached way he
> sees and does things . . . we never hit the right
> tone . . . together . . . at the same time . . .

She stops writing, stares out the window . . .

FADE-OUT:

INT. SARA'S BEDROOM – EARLY MORNING

MWS Sara waking up. She gets up, tiptoes over to her
brother's crib, peers down at him, pats him on the stomach,
then slips outside . . .

CUT:

EXT. FRONT YARD – SAME TIME

MWS Sara inside a rubber tire that hangs from a tree,
swinging . . .

PAN to MWS house, early-morning sun hitting it. We see
Christopher, half hidden behind a curtain, peering out . . .

CUT:

EXT. OPEN MARKET – EARLY AFTERNOON

MWS Liliane foreground, Caroline background, picking
out fruits and vegetables, etc. The place is somewhat
crowded. Liliane holds up some asparagus.

> **LILIANE**
> *(to Caroline)*
> Don't they look wonderful . . . we'll get some
> fish, too . . .

Caroline nods. With full baskets, they make their way to the
checkout counter. A car horn honks loudly, they both look
out . . .

CUT:

MWS station wagon, POV Liliane and Caroline. Shana
is honking the horn with her foot while hanging out the
window. Christopher is walking on the roof of the car. Sara
sits on the bumper holding Edward, who's too heavy for her
and looks as if he's about to fall.

                                              CUT:

EXT. COUNTRY LIBRARY – AFTERNOON

MLS Caroline, Shana, Sara, coming down the steps, each
of them carrying a few books. Christopher runs into frame,
tackles his sister and sends her sprawling, books and all. She
screams at him . . .

                                              CUT:

EXT. A STREAM IN THE WOODS – AFTERNOON

LS children in foreground, Liliane and Caroline in
background. The children are playing in the water.
Christopher swims out of frame. All of a sudden Liliane
rushes forward, waving her arms . . .

                                              CUT:

MLS Christopher, POV Liliane. He's climbed onto a tall
rock and is about to dive. Liliane enters frame, swims out
to meet him, forcing him to climb down. Reluctantly, he
obeys, joins his mother in the water, they swim off together,
laughing . . .

                                              CUT:

INT. LILIANE'S BEDROOM – NIGHT

MCU Liliane, POV Caroline.

                          LILIANE
              I was modeling for an art class. Whenever he
              was on leave, he used to like to take classes,
              practice his drawing . . . he came in in his

uniform looking . . . you know how he
looked . . . I went home with him that night,
stayed five days until his leave was up. It was
the same from the beginning to the end . . . all
nine years of it, like living in a closed vase . . .
him, the children, of course, but mostly
him . . . depressed a lot, then happy, then
depressed again . . . that's how we lived, inside
that rhythm that was his . . . I used to think
it just had to do with race, that he hated the
humiliation, but now I think it went further
than that, there was something in him that
found life ridiculous, a joke of some kind . . .
I don't know how to explain it, just know that
toward the end nothing made any sense to
him . . . not me . . . nor the children . . . most
of all not himself . . .

She pulls on her loom.

DOLLY BACK to MWS Caroline. She sits listening. In the
midground between the two women, a photograph of Giles.

CAROLINE
Are you relieved in some way . . . I mean with
all the depressions he lived through . . .

LILIANE
(almost violently)
No . . . he got badly depressed, yes, but when
he was happy we had such good times, then
he'd get depressed again, but just when I
thought I couldn't stand it another second, he'd
wake up full of life, start sculpting, building
things, want to go hiking or fishing with

Chris . . . he'd bring everybody back to life
with him . . . you've seen him like that . . . he
was wonderful, always laughing and lifting you
up . . .

The physical pain of his absence overwhelms her . . .

LILIANE
. . . I could handle the depressions just as long
as he rounded the circle; came back to life
again . . .

She sits very still to keep from going to pieces . . .

HOLD . . .

CUT:

INT. CAROLINE'S BEDROOM – LATER THAT
SAME NIGHT

MS Caroline, POV through window, writing at her desk.

CAROLINE (v.o.)
Once when I went to visit Lil . . . I remember
I was carrying Edward . . . Giles was asleep.
When he was depressed he slept a lot. Lil and
I sat talking while Sara and Shana and Chris
played. We were drinking tea when Giles
woke up and came to the table. We said hello,
et cetera, then Lil went off to make him some
coffee. He kept staring at the children playing.
'They're getting big' was all I could think to
say, which made him chuckle and turn and
stare at me. 'What am I doing here?' he said
after a while, almost earnestly. 'What do you
mean?' I answered. We'd known each other

a long time, I was accustomed to his moods.
'Sometimes I get the feeling,' he said quietly,
'that I'm playing house,' and he looked at the
children again. 'That's it.' He laughed in that
powerful way of his. 'I think for a long time all
I've been doing is playing house . . .'

She stops writing.

HOLD . . .

CUT:

EXT. FRONT OF HOUSE – MORNING

WS Shana and Sara in foreground, Liliane in midground,
Caroline in background. The girls are outside playing with
dolls. Liliane is hanging plants in the hallway. Caroline is
seen vaguely in the background feeding Edward.

> **SHANA**
> What's her name?

Sara holds up her doll . . .

> **SARA**
> Susie . . .

> **SHANA**
> I don't like that name . . .

> **SARA**
> What should I name her?

The phone rings. Liliane goes to answer it, exiting frame.

> **LILIANE (o.c.)**
> Hello . . . that's right . . . hold on . . .

She crosses into frame . . .

> **LILIANE**
> Caroline . . . phone . . .

Caroline comes in carrying Edward, hands him to Liliane.

> **CAROLINE**
> Hold him a second . . . who is it . . .

> **LILIANE**
> He sounded impatient, that's all I know . . .

Caroline exits frame. Liliane puts Edward down, walks him slowly over to her plants.

> **CAROLINE (o.c.)**
> Hello . . . oh . . . I haven't in a while, not
> since my son was born . . . thank you . . . oh,
> I know who you are . . . thank you . . . what's
> the play . . . could I see a script . . . I'm coming
> in on Thursday, I could pick one up . . . we'll
> talk then . . . all right . . . thank you . . .

We hear her hang up. She comes back in.

> **CAROLINE**
> You know who that was . . . Alphonso Gerrell,
> known in theater circles as the Madman . . .
> *(giggling)*
> . . . you're right about his being impatient, he
> just offered me a job . . .

> CUT:

INT. HALLWAY – SAME TIME

MS Caroline, POV behind Liliane. She comes forward, swooping Edward up . . .

> **LILIANE**
> *(back to camera)*
> Now . . . when you'd have to commute?

> **CAROLINE**
> I know . . . though most of the design work
> I'm sure I could do up here . . .

She swings Edward . . .

> **CAROLINE**
> I don't believe it . . . he kept saying 'the word
> is that you're good . . .' Me, I kept mumbling
> 'thank you, thank you . . .'

She laughs at herself . . .

> **SARA** (o.c.)
> Mommie . . .

Caroline turns around . . .

> **CAROLINE**
> Yes, Sara . . .

CUT:

EXT. FRONT YARD – SAME TIME

MWS Shana, Sara, POV Caroline. Sara is holding up her
doll . . .

> **SARA**
> Shana thinks I should call her Marta . . .

> **CAROLINE** (o.c.)
> I thought her name was Susie . . .

Caroline steps into frame.

> **SARA**
> *(to her doll)*
> You don't like Susie, do you, you'd like me to
> call you Marta . . .

> **SHANA**
> *(annoyed)*
> She can't hear, dolls can't hear . . .

> **SARA**
> *(defensively)*
> That's not true . . . is that true, Mommie . . .

CUT:

REVERSE ANGLE.

> **CAROLINE**
> *(laughing)*
> Ask Susie . . . I mean Marta . . . she should
> know if she can hear or not . . .

The girls laugh . . .

HOLD . . .

CUT:

INT. A THEATER – EARLY AFTERNOON

WS stage. ALPHONSO GERRELL, a debonair man around forty-five (flashily dressed, radiating incredible energy), is playing the piano. Leaning against it but facing away from him is a handsome woman, late thirties, dressed stylishly. She's listening to Alphonso, who's talking to three women who are clustered around him.

ALPHONSO
(to the women)

You're the chorus, yes, but you're more
than that. All her feelings are addressed to
you. You're the women of her childhood,
churchwomen . . . deaconesses and usherettes in
their white uniforms and gloves . . . old maids
who sat alone in their pew, flashy women in
derby hats who strutted down the aisle . . . all
the unfulfilled longings of the black women she
remembers are projected onto you. Try the first
number seeing yourselves that way . . .

The women begin to sing . . .

THE WOMEN
(singing)

Dance, little lady, dance,
Dance like a child of God
And bring us sweet roses from Heaven
Once, oh God, once, before we die . . .

CUT:

MWS Caroline entering the theater. She hears the women
singing, starts down the aisle . . .

CUT:

MOVING SHOT, women onstage, POV Caroline.

THE WOMEN
(singing)

Dance, little lady, dance
Be the gypsy that we've never known

Take your feet to the sky like a lady
And bring us roses, once, yes, bring us roses, once
Once, oh God, once, before we die . . .

They continue humming. TRACK and PAN to the woman
leaning against the piano.

THE WOMAN

I only have one memory of my childhood.
That's me, walking down the street one sunny
afternoon, daydreaming for the first time. Pain
surrounded me on all sides. There was nothing
happy going on. But suddenly I saw it didn't
have to be that way inside. I could dream
myself, dream how I wanted things to be. Now
when I think of my childhood, it appears before
me like one long daydream . . .

CAMERA STOPS MOVING.

HOLD . . .

THE WOMAN
(singing)
How lovely is the evening,
Is the evening, is the evening,
When the bells are sweetly ringing,
Sweetly ringing, sweetly ringing . . .

CUT:

MCU Caroline, POV stage, listening, caught up in it . . .

THE WOMAN (o.c.)
(singing)
Ding, ding, dong
Ding, ding, dong . . .

The women join her and repeat it . . .

> **ALPHONSO (o.c.)**
> Okay . . .

Caroline looks over at him . . .

                                                            CUT:

LOW-ANGLE MWS Alphonso, the woman, POV Caroline.

> **ALPHONSO**
> *(to the woman)*
> Marie, you have any problem with that
> speech . . .

> **MARIE**
> *(laughing)*
> I'm not sure I understand it but I do know it
> makes me want to cry . . .

> **ALPHONSO**
> *(nodding)*
> There's a sadness there and a longing . . . I
> don't want to probe too much at this point if
> you've got a feel for it . . .

Marie nods. As if sensing someone behind him, Alphonso
turns suddenly around, sees Caroline standing there.

> **ALPHONSO**
> Caroline Samuels . . .

> **CAROLINE (o.c.)**
> Yes . . .

He smiles, turns back to the actors . . .

                                                            CUT:

MWS Caroline, POV stage.

> ### ALPHONSO (o.c.)
> It's after twelve, we'll meet back here by
> 1:30 . . .

He comes into frame, obliterating Caroline. They walk away from the camera, moving into LS, Alphonso plying her with questions . . .

> ### ALPHONSO
> *(back to camera)*
> You drove down from the country?

> ### CAROLINE
> *(back to camera)*
> Yes, this morning . . .

> ### ALPHONSO
> *(back to camera)*
> How long a drive is it?

> ### CAROLINE
> *(back to camera)*
> Not long, a little over an hour . . .

> ### ALPHONSO
> *(back to camera)*
> You just moved?

> ### CAROLINE
> *(back to camera)*
> Yes.

> ### ALPHONSO
> *(back to camera)*
> Got tired of the city?

CAROLINE
(back to camera)

Yes . . .

They disappear out the lobby door.

HOLD . . .

CUT:

INT. A RESTAURANT – EARLY AFTERNOON

MCU Caroline.

CAROLINE

I didn't know it was a musical, I've never done
a musical . . .

ALPHONSO (o.c.)

Same problems, only people sing . . .

Caroline laughs . . .

CAROLINE

I like what I saw . . .

Alphonso changes seats, moving closer to her while at the
same time entering the frame . . .

ALPHONSO

It's about one woman's illusions . . . maybe
they're universal, we'll see . . . anyway, you
could call it a musical because it has some nine
or ten songs, but it's really serious drama. The
characters literally . . .
(acting it out)
. . . fall forward into song out of a need to say
things, express feelings that words don't reach.
There's a violence to the music, a letting go . . .

He stares at her . . .

> **CAROLINE**
> I'm eager to read the script . . .

> **ALPHONSO**
> *(switching tracks)*
> Why did you move to the country?

> **CAROLINE**
> *(thrown by the question)*
> I . . . it's good for the children . . . I have
> young children . . . the fresh air is good for
> them . . .

> **ALPHONSO**
> Does your husband like it, too?

> **CAROLINE**
> *(flustered)*
> My husband . . . no, he's still in the city . . .

He stares at her . . .

HOLD . . .

CUT:

INT. BUSY OFFICE – LATE AFTERNOON

SIDE-ANGLE LS, Rafael. In the foreground, Rafael on the
phone.

> **RAFAEL**
> What does he want me to do, spoon-feed
> him . . . Christ, man, he's talking fifty thou,
> I can't hold his hand for that . . . tell him to
> put it in CDs . . . this is fun and games, you

know that . . . soybeans . . . they might hit five
a bushel . . . that's the word right now, which
puts it at twenty-five per contract . . . of course
he could use that, anybody could use that . . .

In the background we see Caroline enter and come down
the hall . . .

> RAFAEL
>
> . . . that looks good now, too, the upside's
> about a buck sixty a pound . . . frost, the Latin
> guys say frost . . . of course he could but we'd
> do our best to get him out before then, what
> more can I say . . .

By now Caroline is standing in the doorway, watching him.
He nods.

> RAFAEL
>
> Bring him over, we'll talk . . .
> *(chuckling)*
> . . . you got a bunch of yo-yos over there,
> man . . . lunch . . . tomorrow . . .

He hangs up.

> RAFAEL
>
> I thought you'd moved to the country . . .

> CAROLINE
>
> I got offered a job, I came down to pick up the
> script . . .

> CUT:

MCU Caroline, POV Rafael.

CAROLINE

You sound jive . . .
(mimicking him)
'. . . we'll do our best to pull him out, man . . . lunch . . .'

She laughs . . .

RAFAEL (o.c.)

It's a performance, people get confused if you don't speak the language . . .

CAROLINE

I'm glad at least that you recognize that . . .

CUT:

SIDE-ANGLE MWS, both of them.

CAROLINE

How are you . . .

RAFAEL

I hate that question . . .

She raises her hand apologetically . . .

RAFAEL

How long are you down for?

CAROLINE

I'm on my way back now . . .

RAFAEL

You need anything?

CAROLINE

No . . .

> RAFAEL

Script any good?

> CAROLINE

I haven't read it yet . . .

> RAFAEL

You'll have to commute . . .

> CAROLINE

He said I could do the design work up
there . . .

> RAFAEL

Who?

> CAROLINE

The director . . .

He nods, turns toward his work . . .

CUT:

MWS Rafael, POV Caroline. He's turned away from her . . .

> CAROLINE (o.c.)

I'll stay for dinner . . .

He shakes his head no . . .

> CAROLINE (o.c.)

You look harassed . . .

> RAFAEL
> *(irritated)*

I look happy, sad, tired, busy . . . don't play
wife, please . . .

Silence.

> **CAROLINE (o.c.)**
> I keep thinking, a little time away and we'll
> find the right footing . . .

> **RAFAEL**
> Maybe you should think about other things
> while you're away . . . not me . . .

He moves toward her . . .

CUT:

MWS both of them. Caroline watches while he puts papers
in his briefcase . . .

CUT:

INT. KITCHEN OF COUNTRY HOUSE – NIGHT

MCU Liliane.

> **LILIANE**
> You're making it up . . .

She laughs . . .

> **CAROLINE (o.c.)**
> I swear! It was when he was playing at being
> a photographer . . . you should have seen his
> clientele: voodoo queens, would-be models,
> or porno stars who needed a few shots of their
> wares . . . he even had a studio, a trashy place
> I avoided as much as I could. Anyway . . . I go
> there to meet him one night . . .

CUT:

MCU Caroline, POV Liliane.

CAROLINE

I'm on my way up the steps and this belly
dancer . . . is on her way down . . . I didn't
know then that she was a belly dancer but
she looked foreign . . . thick black hair, heavy
makeup; she stops me on the steps, asks if I'm
Rafael's wife. I hesitate a minute but finally say
yes . . . 'Oh God,' she shouts, 'no woman should
own that man . . .' and she pulls out a knife . . .

CUT:

MCU Liliane, POV Caroline.

LILIANE

Stop it . . .

CAROLINE (o.c.)

I couldn't believe it . . . I go flying past her
like a bat out of hell, banging frantically on
Rafael's door . . . 'She's trying to kill me,' I
start screaming . . . 'One of your female exotics
is trying to do me in . . .' He opens the door
and runs out after her . . .

CUT:

MCU Caroline, catching her breath . . .

CAROLINE

He doesn't come back for about two hours . . .
I don't know what to do . . . who to call . . .
I swear she's killed him . . . . Finally, he walks
in with his usual ease . . . 'Where were you,'

I ask, 'why were you gone so long?' 'I had to
calm her down.' He shrugs. 'Calm her down,' I
shout, 'what do you mean you had to calm her
down, I'm the one she attacked!' 'You're not
emotional like them,' he says . . . 'these women
take things to heart . . .'

Her fist hits the table violently . . .

CAROLINE

I could kill him when he says things like that!
Like I'm not <u>funky enough</u> to feel things!

She gets more upset thinking about it . . .

CUT:

WS Liliane, Caroline. We're aware now that they're sitting
at the kitchen table drinking tea. It's late at night. The
phone rings, startling them. Liliane goes to answer it,
exiting frame . . .

LILIANE (o.c.)

Hello . . . that's all right, just a minute . . .

She comes back in . . .

LILIANE

It's Mr. Gerrell . . . he apologizes for calling so
late . . .

Caroline goes to the phone. Liliane sits back down, pours
herself more tea . . .

CAROLINE (o.c.)

Hello . . . no, I haven't finished it, I had
a busy day, I was planning to read it in

the morning . . . could we talk tomorrow
afternoon . . . I'll call you . . . all right . . .
that's all right . . .

She comes back in, stands in the doorway. They look at each
other.

FADE-OUT:

INT. HIGH SCHOOL HALLWAY IN A DREAM

WS a group of girls. A younger Caroline comes into frame
wearing glasses, a wide old-fashioned dress, and her hair
braided and pinned up. The girls whisper . . .

ONE GIRL
Here comes Miss Square-But . . .

ANOTHER GIRL
That dress looks like her grandma's, she don't
even have on a bra . . .

THIRD GIRL
Guess who she likes . . .

THE GIRLS
Who . . . who she like . . .

THIRD GIRL
Timmy Hays . . .

CUT:

MCU Caroline. MOVING SHOT. She makes her way,
embarrassed, down the hall . . .

THIRD GIRL (o.c.)
Miss Square-But's in a daze over Timothy
Hays . . .

DISSOLVE:

EXT. AN ALLEYWAY IN A DREAM

HIGH-ANGLE LS two men, POV open window. Their backs are to the camera. They are dressed in black and carry a long stretcher covered with a black cloth . . .

CUT:

LOW-ANGLE MS Caroline, POV men below. Dressed as in the high school scene, she watches the men carry the stretcher. She's crying . . .

SARA (o.c.)

Mommie . . .

CUT:

INT. CAROLINE'S BEDROOM – EARLY MORNING

MCU Caroline, crying in her sleep.

SARA (o.c.)
Mommie, why are you crying?

Caroline is pulled out of sleep, her face still wet, the sobbing not quite under control.

DOLLY BACK to MS Caroline, Sara, as Sara climbs in beside her.

SARA
Why are you crying?

CAROLINE
I guess I was crying in my sleep.

SARA

I bet you had a bad dream . . .

CAROLINE

I was dreaming about my mother . . . your
Grandmother Anderson . . .

SARA

But she's dead.

CAROLINE

I know. I'm sorry you never knew her.

SARA

You can dream about dead people?

CAROLINE
(surprised)

Yes . . .

SARA

Does Christopher dream about his daddy?

CAROLINE

I'm sure he does . . . or he will at some
point . . .

SARA

I don't like Christopher, he's a bully.

CAROLINE

He's unhappy about his dad.

SARA

He doesn't believe I have a daddy . . . can
Daddy come up today and show him?

CAROLINE

Not today, Sara, he's working, but probably over the weekend . . .

There's a knock at the door.

SHANA (o.c.)

Sara.

SARA

I'm in here.

CUT:

MWS door, POV Sara and Caroline. Shana opens it and stands in the doorway.

SHANA

You want to go finish our fort?

Sara gets off the bed, entering frame.

SARA

You should see our fort, Mommie, it's hidden from Christopher . . .

SHANA

But we need furniture . . .

CAROLINE (o.c.)

We could go to the thrift shop later on and look around . . .

That pleases the girls.

SARA

When can we go . . .

> **CAROLINE (o.c.)**
> I'd like to read this morning . . . what about
> after lunch . . .

They nod agreement . . .

> **SARA**
> Let's go see what we want . . .

They leave . . .

CUT:

MCU Caroline in a peaceful, reflective mood. She looks
around the room.

PAN: MWS room, POV Caroline. Bright sunlight peeps
through the curtains. The room feels like a garden of light
and stillness.

> **CAROLINE (v.o.)**
> When my mother died, I was ten years old . . .
> a few years older than Christopher . . . I never
> got over it, never, it can make me cry in my
> sleep . . .

PAN BACK to MCU Caroline. She's fallen asleep.

CUT:

EXT. A GARDEN IN A DREAM

MWS EDWARD ANDERSON, a tall, older man seen
several times in the photograph next to Caroline's bed. He is
clipping and pruning flowers. Caroline enters frame, dressed
as in the earlier dream sequence, holding a basket in which
Edward Anderson places the flowers . . . Off-camera we
hear a baby cry . . .

CUT:

INT. CAROLINE'S BEDROOM – LATE MORNING

MS Caroline asleep. The crying wakes her up. She gets out
of bed and goes into Edward's room. We hear her talking to
him . . .

>   **CAROLINE (o.c.)**
> We both slept late . . . your sister's the only
> early bird . . . she was up, up, and away with
> the sun . . .

CUT:

EXT. WOODS – LATE AFTERNOON

MOVING SHOT, Caroline, Liliane, walking in the
woods . . .

>   **CAROLINE**
> It's a good script . . .

>   **LILIANE**
> You said yes . . .

Caroline nods . . .

>   **CAROLINE**
> Basically it's about a woman who can't give up
> on her man . . .

Liliane laughs . . .

>   **CAROLINE**
>   *(amused)*
> But it's not done in a trite way . . .

Liliane nods . . .

> **LILIANE**
>
> How do you start to imagine the set . . .

> **CAROLINE**
>
> I get a feeling for the space . . . how it should
> be divided up . . . something like that . . . like
> with this one, I feel like everything should be
> splintered . . . in fact I keep seeing broken glass.

> **LILIANE**
> *(suddenly remembering)*
> I had a dream about you . . . in fact we were
> walking in the woods . . .

CUT:

LS Caroline, Liliane, POV through woods.

> **LILIANE (v.o.)**
>
> At first we were walking on a nice, clear path.
> Everything was spacious and open and the sun
> was shining . . . then it got thick and the path
> got harder to follow . . .

CUT:

HIGH-ANGLE LS Caroline, Liliane. They disappear along
a thin path winding upward . . .

> **LILIANE (v.o.)**
>
> . . . until it was so narrow we had to walk
> single file. Soon after that there was no path,
> just woods and bramble, and the sun was
> gone . . . I said to you, 'There's nothing ahead,
> we should turn back . . .'

CUT:

MOVING SHOT, Liliane.

> **LILIANE**
> But you insisted that if we kept going,
> we'd come to another clearing . . . I didn't
> believe you and turned back; but you kept on
> going . . .

> **CAROLINE (o.c.)**
> And was there a clearing ahead?

> **LILIANE**
> No . . . in the dream I know there isn't . . .

She looks at Caroline . . .

> **LILIANE**
> I think that's a dream about our natures . . .
> yours is forever optimistic, intent on believing
> there's something good ahead . . . mine isn't, it
> respects dead ends . . .

CUT:

MOVING SHOT, Caroline.

> **CAROLINE**
> Does that make you wise and me stupid?

> **LILIANE (o.c.)**
> I didn't say that . . .

> **CAROLINE**
> Maybe there was a clearing ahead . . .

> **LILIANE** (o.c.)
> *(coldly)*
> There was nothing . . . in the dream I'm
> positive of that . . .

CUT:

MOVING SHOT, steep path, POV two women.

> **CAROLINE** (o.c.)
> That's arrogant, Lil, how the hell can you
> know what's ahead for me . . .

> **LILIANE** (o.c.)
> In the dream I do, we're talking about the
> dream . . .

> **CAROLINE** (o.c.)
> Even in the dream, you can know it for <u>you</u>,
> you can't know it for me . . .

Liliane comes into frame, looks at her sharply . . .

> **LILIANE**
> But I do, in the dream I do . . .

Caroline comes into frame, uneasy, looks around . . .

> **CAROLINE**
> Well, you're wrong, there was a clearing
> ahead . . .

CUT:

WS lake and mountains, POV women. An absolutely
spectacular sight . . .

HOLD . . .

CUT:

INT. THE THEATER – AFTERNOON

CU Marie. She's talking to the audience as if at the
beginning of a nightclub act . . .

> **MARIE**
> Good evening, ladies and gentlemen, I've
> come here tonight to sing you some of my
> songs. Music has always been one of my main
> attractions, when all else fails, a song will say it
> all . . .
> *(amused)*
> Tonight we've arranged a medley of tunes
> about love and its disappointments . . .
> disappointments in love are a bit like
> childhood dreams . . .

> **THE PIANO PLAYER (o.c.)**
> Please . . .

DOLLY BACK to WS Marie, the PIANO PLAYER in
foreground; three women in background; on the edge of the
frame a MAN sits at a table.

> **THE PIANO PLAYER**
> Don't get maudlin, Marie . . .

The man at the table laughs. Marie looks over at him . . .
She begins to hum under her breath . . .

> **MARIE**
> *(softly)*
> How lovely is the evening,
> Is the evening, is the evening . . .

She signals to the women to join her . . .

MARIE and THE WOMEN
(singing)

When the bells are sweetly ringing,
Sweetly ringing, sweetly ringing . . .

The women begin to laugh . . .

MARIE
(laughing, too)

My mother used to sing that in the mornings,
when we'd make the beds . . .

THE WOMEN
(nodding)

Well . . .

THE PIANO PLAYER

Could we get started, please . . .

The man at the table laughs again . . .

CUT:

MCU the man. Laughing, he lifts his drink and sips . . .

CUT:

MS Caroline, Alphonso, watching from seats.

CAROLINE
(whispering)

And the man . . .

ALPHONSO
(shrugging)

Any man, her man . . . whether imagined or
real . . .

Caroline looks at him . . .

CUT:

MCU Marie in foreground, the women in background.

MARIE
. . . I'd slip into the church on the corner . . .
'Dear God in Heaven,' I'd say, 'before I
surrender to Jesus, please send me some kisses
to warm me . . .'

THE WOMEN
Well . . .

CUT:

MS the piano player in foreground, the man at the table in
background . . .

THE PIANO PLAYER
Could we short-circuit this stroll down
memory lane . . .

The man laughs . . .

MARIE (o.c.)
The house was cold . . . only my mother
sang . . .

THE WOMEN
Well . . .

They begin to sing . . .

MARIE and THE WOMEN (o.c.)
(singing)
How lovely is the evening,
Is the evening, is the evening,
When the bells are sweetly ringing,
Sweetly ringing, sweetly ringing . . .

CUT:

MS Marie in foreground, the women in background. The women continue to sing the same refrain while Marie speaks . . .

MARIE
. . . and when nobody was looking, I'd start to dance—like I was gonna be some new kind of colored lady . . . I, alone, would discover a laughing life, full of kisses that warmed me . . .

One of the women screams, begins to sing at the top of her voice . . .

ONE OF THE WOMEN
(singing)

Dance, little lady, dance,
Dance like a child of God,
And bring us sweet roses from Heaven
Once, oh God, once, before we die . . .

MARIE
(moved)
Every colored lady wants a laughing life . . .

CUT:

MCU Caroline crying . . .

DISSOLVE:

EXT. EDWARD ANDERSON'S HOUSE – LATE AFTERNOON

WS house and street. Caroline's car pulls up, she gets out.
A sign on the gate reads 'Edward Anderson, M.D.' She goes
inside . . .

CUT:

INT. EDWARD ANDERSON'S HOUSE – SAME TIME

WS a long hallway, POV Caroline. A sign on the right that
reads 'Waiting Room.' In the background, a garden. A door
opens.

CAROLINE (o.c.)

Daddy . . .

MOVING SHOT, behind Caroline, past empty waiting
room, past doctor's examining room, to garden, when
we see Edward Anderson (seen earlier in photograph near
Caroline's bed as well as in last dream sequence), busy
pruning roses.

CAROLINE (o.c.)

Hi . . .

He looks up . . . She goes forward into frame and hugs him.

CAROLINE
Finished for the day . . .

EDWARD ANDERSON
It's Wednesday . . . the sacred day,
remember . . .

                        CAROLINE
        Oh, that's right . . .

She looks around . . .

                        CAROLINE
        . . . did you put in anything new . . .

                                              CUT:

SIDE-ANGLE MWS both of them.

                    EDWARD ANDERSON
        Just those delphiniums over there . . . I'm
        hoping they take, they're not easy to grow . . .

                        CAROLINE
        . . . all my childhood I remember you here,
        planting, clearing new land . . . I'd go back and
        forth with you to the nursery . . .

                    EDWARD ANDERSON
        You had a good eye for colors, shapes . . . I
        suppose that's why you design sets . . . though I
        can't imagine a more vague profession . . .

He turns to clip one more rose . . .

                    EDWARD ANDERSON
        Can you stay for dinner . . .

She nods . . .

                                              CUT:

MOVING SHOT, behind Caroline, as she walks through
different rooms. Everything is orderly, neat. Sparely
furnished but with beautiful, simple pieces. She goes into

her old room, partially seen in the dream, and sits by the window . . .

EDWARD ANDERSON (o.c.)
Caroline . . . dinner's ready . . .

She doesn't move . . .

CUT:

INT. EDWARD ANDERSON'S KITCHEN – EARLY EVENING

MWS Edward Anderson at the stove. Caroline comes into frame from background of shot.

CAROLINE
This house is big for you alone . . .

EDWARD ANDERSON
What's that supposed to mean . . .

CAROLINE
Maybe it gets lonely . . .

He carries food over to the table . . .

EDWARD ANDERSON
Don't divert this conversation to me . . .

They both sit down . . .

CUT:

MCU Caroline, looking nervous . . .

CAROLINE
I don't know where to begin . . .

EDWARD ANDERSON (o.c.)
Start with Rafael . . .

CAROLINE
That won't go anywhere, you hate Rafael . . .

CUT:

TWO-SHOT, favoring Edward Anderson.

EDWARD ANDERSON
Then what about this house you're sharing,
where there's been a suicide . . .

CAROLINE
No . . . you've got that all mixed up, my
friend's husband committed suicide but in a
different house . . .

EDWARD ANDERSON
I see . . .

He stares long and hard at her . . .

EDWARD ANDERSON
Well, that leaves your job . . .

CAROLINE
(cutting across)
It's good for the kids to be in the country . . .
and it's a nice house . . .

He nods . . .

EDWARD ANDERSON
Is this another off-off-Broadway type of
thing . . .

CUT:

TWO-SHOT, favoring Caroline.

> **CAROLINE**
> *(nodding)*
> But it's a good play, it's about a woman trying
> to work out her feelings about love . . .

> **EDWARD ANDERSON**
> Hmph . . .

HOLD on Caroline, embarrassed . . .

CUT:

INT. LILIANE'S BEDROOM – LATE AFTERNOON

MWS Liliane busy weaving. We can hear the children
outside playing. There is the sudden intrusion of brakes
screeching to a halt, a dog yelping . . .

> **CHRISTOPHER (o.c.)**
> *(screaming)*
> Simon!!

Liliane drops everything . . .

> **LILIANE**
> Oh my God . . .

She rushes out . . .

CUT:

EXT. FRONT LAWN – SAME TIME

WS children, POV hallway, Christopher in the lead, the
girls behind him, racing . . .

CHRISTOPHER
(back to camera, screaming)
Simon! Simon!

Liliane rushes into frame, runs outside. Shana sees her.

SHANA
Mommie, something's happened to Simon . . .

Liliane rushes forward, then stops suddenly. In the background we see Christopher carrying Simon . . .

CHRISTOPHER
(crying)
Simon's dead . . . he's dead . . .

CUT:

MCU Liliane completely unnerved . . . She rushes forward out of frame . . .

CUT:

WS all of them clustered around the dead animal . . .

CUT:

INT. LIVING ROOM – NIGHT

MS Liliane, Shana, Sara, sitting by the fire, except for which the room is dark. Liliane looks over at Christopher . . .

PAN to MWS Christopher, POV Liliane. He's standing by the window looking out. Car lights approach, blinding him. We hear Sara get up . . .

SARA (o.c.)
That's Mommie . . .

We hear her open the door . . .

CUT:

EXT. FRONT PORCH OF THE HOUSE – SAME TIME

MOVING SHOT, behind Sara. She opens the door, Caroline steps forward out of darkness.

> ### SARA
> (back to camera)
> Simon's dead . . . he got run over by a car . . .

Caroline lifts Sara up . . .

> ### CAROLINE
> Oh, Sara . . . where's Lil . . .

Liliane comes out holding tight to Shana.

> ### CAROLINE
> (to Liliane)
> I'm so sorry . . .

From inside, we hear Christopher banging against the window . . .

> ### CHRISTOPHER (o.c.)
> (in a rage)
> He's dead, everybody dies . . . everybody . . .

There is the loud sound of splintering glass . . .

CUT:

MS Christopher, POV through broken window. His hand bleeding, he continues to smash it against the broken fragments. Liliane comes into frame carrying Shana. She pulls him away from the window. We watch them go up the steps . . .

CUT:

INT. HALLWAY OUTSIDE LILIANE'S BEDROOM – LATER THAT NIGHT

MOVING SHOT, behind Caroline, approaching Liliane's room.

> **CAROLINE**
> *(back to camera)*
> Lil.

She stops on the threshold . . .

CUT:

MWS Liliane's room, POV over Caroline's shoulder. We see Christopher and Shana asleep on their mother's bed. Liliane is sitting by the window. She signals Caroline, who tiptoes quietly over . . .

DOLLY FORWARD to MCU Liliane, POV over Caroline's shoulder.

> **LILIANE**
> Simon feels like the last links . . . Giles found
> him in the street, he was filthy, looked like
> he'd been mistreated . . . he and Christopher
> had to bathe him about ten times before
> you could see his coat . . . they took him
> everywhere . . . Christopher's been hanging on
> to him for dear life . . .

>   (lost)
>   . . . every time I think I'm holding on,
>   something comes along and knocks me under
>   again . . .

She leans forward violently . . .

>   **LILIANE**
>   What in God's name got into Giles to leave me
>   with all this . . .

HOLD . . .

>   CUT:

INT. HALLWAY – MORNING

LS Caroline holding Edward in foreground, Shana and Sara in background. Caroline's on the phone. Shana and Sara are coming down the steps.

>   **CAROLINE**
>   No, that's fine . . .
>   *(to Sara)*
>   . . . it's Daddy, Sara . . . he's coming up
>   tomorrow . . .

Sara runs and takes the phone. Caroline exits frame. Shana hovers in the background.

>   **SARA**
>   Daddy . . . when are you coming . . . will you
>   be here when I wake up . . . please . . . please
>   be here when I wake up . . . good . . .

She hangs up . . .

> **SARA**
> *(to Shana)*
> My daddy's coming tomorrow . . .

She calls out to her mother, running off frame . . .

> **SARA (o.c.)**
> Daddy said he'll be here when I wake up . . .

Shana stands there staring at the phone. Finally, after making sure no one is around, she picks up the receiver . . .

> **SHANA**
> Daddy . . . where are you, Daddy . . .

Perplexed, sad, she asks again . . .

> **SHANA**
> Daddy, are you there . . .

She is almost crying . . .

INT. KITCHEN – LATER IN THE DAY

MCU Liliane, leaning against the wall. She looks drawn.

> **LILIANE**
> What about his women . . .

There is no answer.

> **LILIANE**
> I didn't think that was such a sore nerve . . .

> **CAROLINE (o.c.)**
> It's not that, I was trying to think what to
> say . . .

DOLLY BACK to MWS both women. Caroline is pouring herself some tea.

LILIANE
Are they the reason you left?

CAROLINE
We've had some pretty violent scenes over
them, once I threw a knife that barely missed
his face . . .
> *(embarrassed)*

. . . he can provoke feelings in me I didn't
know were there . . .

LILIANE
Jealousy is usually pretty violent . . .

CAROLINE
I can't imagine your ever being jealous . . .

LILIANE
I wouldn't stay around long enough . . . Giles
knew that, that I would have left if there was
another woman . . .

CAROLINE
> *(only half amused)*

That makes me feel like a chump . . .

CUT:

SIDE–ANGLE both women, favoring Caroline.

CAROLINE
> *(thinking)*

Even now I wouldn't say I left because there
are other women . . . I couldn't say why I left,
except it was making me too violent . . . I
didn't like what was happening to me.

> LILIANE

So you ran away . . .

> CAROLINE
> *(irritated)*

I have a hard time maintaining my dignity
with you . . . you see things in black or
white . . . I ran away . . . I suppose you could
say that . . . I wouldn't put it that way . . . it
sounds like I couldn't face up to things . . .

She feels self-conscious . . .

CUT:

SIDE-ANGLE both women, favoring Liliane.

> LILIANE
> *(quietly)*

You're still hoping . . .

Caroline doesn't answer . . .

> LILIANE

. . . I was just thinking . . . death marks the
end of living in the future, there's nothing left
to hope for . . .

RACK FOCUS to MCU Caroline, uneasy . . .

CUT:

INT. CAROLINE'S BEDROOM – LATE AT NIGHT

MCU diary. Hands, part of Caroline's nightgown, the
photograph of her, are all composed in the frame . . . Being
written is "father," "flowers."

> **CAROLINE (v.o.)**
> In some perverse way I envy her Giles's
> death . . . the relief of it . . . if it is over
> between us, what a clean thing death
> would be . . . freeing . . . rather than all the
> shoddy stuff that comes with separation and
> divorce . . .

She stops writing . . .

FADE-OUT:

EXT. COUNTRY DRIVEWAY – DAWN

LS empty driveway. The sun is coming up, all is quiet, still.

CUT:

INT. CAROLINE'S BEDROOM – SAME TIME

SIDE-ANGLE LS Caroline asleep. Off-camera we hear
Edward awaken with fretful half-cries. It awakens Caroline,
who gets up and goes into his room, returns carrying him.
She gets back in bed, laying him down beside her, talking to
him . . . They fall back asleep . . .

CUT:

EXT. COUNTRY DRIVEWAY – SAME TIME

A car turns into the driveway, comes up the path . . .

CUT:

INT. CAROLINE'S BEDROOM – SAME TIME

SIDE-ANGLE LS Caroline. She hears the car, gets up, goes
to the window . . .

PAN and DOLLY to MLS driveway, POV behind Caroline. The car pulls up and stops in the background. She opens the door and goes out as Rafael gets out of the car.

DOLLY FORWARD to MS behind Caroline.

> **RAFAEL**
> I promised Sara I'd wake her up . . .

He looks around . . .

> **RAFAEL**
> Aren't you overdoing this rustic bit . . .

She doesn't answer . . .

> **RAFAEL**
> . . . where's Sara's room . . .

> **CAROLINE**
> *(back to camera)*
> Come on . . .

PAN and DOLLY BACK to MWS both of them. She turns, he follows her, sees Edward.

> **RAFAEL**
> He's asleep . . .

He bends over to look at him . . .

> **RAFAEL**
> *(whispering)*
> How you doing, little fella . . . he's getting big . . .

Rafael touches him gently. Caroline moves forward toward Sara's room, Rafael following behind her . . .

DOLLY FORWARD. They go into Sara's room. She's still asleep. Rafael goes over to her bed. Caroline hovers in foreground of shot.

> **RAFAEL**
> Sara . . . Sara . . . it's Daddy, Sara . . .

She wakes up . . .

> **SARA**
> Daddy . . . you woke me up . . .

She hugs him . . . sees her mother in the doorway . . .

> **SARA**
> I dreamt he didn't come and Christopher made fun of me . . .

> **RAFAEL**
> I told you I'd be here when you woke up . . .

HOLD . . .

CUT:

EXT. A STREAM IN THE WOODS – AFTERNOON

WS Rafael, children, in the water, playing. Christopher climbs on top of the same high rock, like before.

> **CHRISTOPHER**
> Rafael . . . watch me dive . . .

> **LILIANE (o.c.)**
> Chris, that's too high . . .

> **RAFAEL**
> (turning to her)
> It's okay, I'll watch him . . .

He dives, surfaces . . .

> **RAFAEL**
> I'll race you to that rock.

They go fast out of sight . . .

CUT:

SIDE-ANGLE MWS Caroline and Liliane, foreground;
Rafael and Christopher, background . . . Christopher surfaces
first . . .

> **CHRISTOPHER**
> Did you let me beat you . . . did you . . .

He walks back toward the women.

> **RAFAEL**
> *(laughing)*
> You're fast . . . and I'm out of practice . . .

They both come over to the women.

> **RAFAEL**
> *(to Liliane)*
> He's a good athlete . . . like Giles . . .

Liliane nods, goes on braiding the edges of a woven coat.
Rafael touches it . . .

> **RAFAEL**
> That's fabulous, Lil, is it for a client . . .

> **LILIANE**
> No, this one I'm making for myself . . .

RAFAEL

You don't do them on spec . . .

LILIANE

I can't afford to . . .

RAFAEL

You could if you had a shop that handled
them . . . the work's fantastic . . . how long
does it take you to make one?

LILIANE

It depends . . . two weeks, maybe longer if
they're lined like this one, or there's some
special finishing work . . .

RAFAEL

Do you have one I could show . . . there's
a friend of mine who just opened a boutique
and he's looking to sell unusual stuff . . .

LILIANE

I have a couple back at the house you could
show him . . .

RAFAEL

I'll take them with me . . .

LILIANE

Thanks, Rafael, I . . .

CHRISTOPHER (o.c.)
(interrupting)
Hey, Rafael . . . let me show you something.

He exits frame . . .

> **CAROLINE**
> *(to Liliane)*
> You might get rich, lady, the last of the great
> hustlers just took you under his wing . . .

They laugh . . .

CUT:

EXT. BACK OF HOUSE – MIDDLE OF THE AFTERNOON

MCU Christopher, swinging . . .

> **CHRISTOPHER**
> Hey, Rafael, you want to see where I buried
> my dog . . .

> **RAFAEL (o.c.)**
> Sure . . .

PAN and DOLLY BACK to MWS as he jumps off the
swing. Christopher in foreground, Shana, Sara, Rafael in
background. Rafael is putting a roof on their fort.

> **CHRISTOPHER**
> Come on . . .

They all troop down into the woods . . .

CUT:

INT. KITCHEN – LATE AFTERNOON

MWS Rafael in foreground, children outside in
background.

RAFAEL
(back to camera)

His name was Winston, I buried him just
like Chris . . . but I wouldn't tell anybody
where . . . I used to sneak out and leave things
for him . . . bones, old shoes . . . but the thing
that made me happiest is that no one else knew
where he was buried . . .

CAROLINE (o.c.)

That's true to form . . .

Rafael turns around . . .

RAFAEL

What does that mean . . .

CAROLINE (o.c.)

That you still have a need to keep things
secret . . .

She comes to the edge of the frame . . .

RAFAEL
(half amused)

That's probably your most annoying trait . . .
your perception . . .

He walks away. In the background, Christopher, suddenly
angry, throws down a piece of wood, stomps his foot
violently, and stalks off. The girls look after him . . .

SHANA
(screaming after him)

I hate it when you get mad like that . . . for no
reason . . .

HOLD . . .

CUT:

INT. LIVING ROOM – EARLY EVENING

MCU Rafael.

> **RAFAEL**
> I gotta be going . . .

He lifts Sara into frame . . .

> **SARA**
> Why aren't you spending the night . . .

> **RAFAEL**
> I can't, baby, too much work . . .

> **SARA**
> *(suddenly hysterical)*
> I want you to spend the night, why aren't you
> spending the night . . .

She begins to cry uncontrollably, Caroline moves forward into frame.

> **CAROLINE**
> Daddy'll be back soon, Sara . . .

The child's crying is out of control. Rafael touches her hair, kisses her quickly, and is gone . . .

HOLD . . . on Sara in Caroline's arms crying . . .

CUT:

EXT. FRONT PORCH – LATE AT NIGHT

MS Caroline, Liliane, sitting on the steps. The house is quiet, the kids asleep.

LILIANE

It was a nice day . . . Christopher enjoyed having Rafael around . . . I did, too . . . it's nice, the sound of a man . . .

CUT:

HOLD . . .

INT. THE THEATER – EARLY AFTERNOON

MCU Marie onstage, singing her heart out . . .

MARIE
(singing)

It might be that in the morning
When we woke to find a moistness in the air
That that was all the time we had for loving . . .
It might be that in the early glow of dawn
When all the world felt soft and green
That that was all the time we had for loving

Then time went quickly by to light upon
   another
And all we had was just one misty rose-filled
   morning
With all the passion teasing through the time
   between us
It might be that that's the only time we're
   given . . .

Just one second inside a flower
One split second inside a star

A flash of light inside a rainbow
It might be that that's the only time between
    us, between us . . .

It might be that in the morning when we
    woke to find a moistness in the air
That that was all the time we had for
    loving . . .

As she finishes, she bows her head, emotionally
exhausted . . .

                                              CUT:

SIDE-ANGLE MS Caroline in the wings, moved, while she
measures a flat . . .

                                              CUT:

WS stage, POV Caroline. The man at the table applauds
suddenly and loudly, shouting, "Bravo! Bravo!" The three
women look at him, so does the piano player. Marie turns
toward him.

                    MARIE
                    (softly)
        What are you doing here . . .

                    THE MAN
        I came to hear you sing . . .

                    MARIE
        Why . . .

                    THE MAN
                    (shrugging)
        For old time's sake . . .

The piano player dips discreetly into a little melody as if to separate himself from the conversation . . .

> **MARIE**
> *(to the piano player)*
> Don't add any sentimental touches . . .

The piano player shrugs . . .

> **THE MAN**
> Would you like to dance . . .

He gets up . . .

> CUT:

MS Marie, POV man.

> **MARIE**
> You never liked to dance with me . . .

He comes into frame . . .

> **THE MAN**
> That's true, it made you so happy it annoyed me.

He takes her hand . . .

MOVING SHOT, as they dance . . .

> **MARIE**
> We'd go to parties, I'd pretend I was having
> a good time, try not to notice all the women
> who passed through your arms . . . then we'd
> go home . . . where at least I felt you belonged
> only to me . . .

THE MAN

You'd wake up in a panic if I wasn't by your side . . .

MARIE

You liked that apartment . . .

THE MAN
(agreeing)
I liked that apartment . . .

MARIE

Not for long . . .

THE MAN
(sadly)
For longer than I expected or admitted . . .

They stop dancing. Marie exits frame . . .

HOLD on MCU the man.

MARIE (o.c.)

One day you went away, when you came back everything was different . . .

THE MAN

From here on the story gets harder to tell. Scenes take place in other rooms, in other cities . . .

MARIE (o.c.)

Women came along I knew too much about . . .

THE MAN
(trying for laughter)
We could stop here . . .

CUT:

MCU Caroline, listening intently . . .

CUT:

MS Alphonso, sitting in the front row listening and taking notes . . .

> **MARIE (o.c.)**
> No, name names instead . . . recall faces . . .
> who was the woman who almost killed me . . .

> **THE MAN (o.c.)**
> The one who sat in her car all night . . .

> **MARIE (o.c.)**
> No, she was harmless, there was one with a
> squeaky voice . . . big eyes . . .

CUT:

MS Marie, POV behind man.

> **THE MAN**
> *(back to camera)*
> I don't recall . . .

> **MARIE**
> What do you mean you don't recall . . . she
> kept coming back, this one . . . with her
> squeaky voice and bright eyes . . .

She looks at him hard . . .

> **THE MAN**
> Did she have a long neck . . .

MARIE

I leave that to you . . .

She giggles suddenly . . .

MARIE

Once, in a fit of rage, I worked up an imitation
of your women . . . always leaving me on the
sidelines . . .

She draws away . . .

DOLLY BACK to LS Marie, POV behind man. She
begins to sing and dance in a deliberately seductive
way . . .

MARIE
(singing)

I'm soft and wide
With the eyes of a child
And I open from the inside
Like a windup doll

Ooh, let me tease you
You're hard, let me please you

Take it slow
Soft and sweet
Find the spring
I open on the inside . . .

Ooh, let me tease you
You're hard, let me please you

I'm soft and wide
With the eyes of a child

And I tremble inside when
You move me

Take it slow
Soft and sweet
Find the spring
I open on the inside

Ooh, let me tease you
You're hard, let me please you

I'm soft and wide
With the eyes of a child
Stretch me like fire
Till I cry . . .

Ooh, let me tease you
You're hard, let me please you
Ooh ooh . . .

As the song ends, Alphonso enters the frame.

ALPHONSO
(back to camera)
Nice . . . now when Pepsi gets here, he'll
choreograph that number for you and the
women . . .

He signals to the women to come closer . . .

ALPHONSO
Caroline . . . the women will need a platform
of some kind for this dance . . . something that
can disappear, I suppose, or be made integral,
that's up to you . . .

He turns to the man . . .

ALPHONSO
Dick, have you figured out for yourself why
you left her . . .

CUT:

SIDE-ANGLE MS Dick, Alphonso. Dick stands there
looking sheepish.

DICK
Well, the closest I've gotten so far is that he
likes being an asshole . . .

The two men crack up . . .

CUT:

EXT. STREET OUTSIDE THEATER – NIGHT

SIDE-ANGLE MS Alphonso, Caroline.

ALPHONSO
Not even a drink . . .

Caroline shakes her head no . . .

ALPHONSO
The first sketches are wonderful . . .

CAROLINE
I'm glad you're pleased . . .

ALPHONSO
(with sudden abruptness)
Good night . . .

He walks off, leaving her standing there, surprised by his
abruptness. After a moment, she starts off in the opposite
direction, exiting frame . . .

CUT:

INT. CAROLINE'S BEDROOM – LATE AT NIGHT

MS sketching board, POV over Caroline's shoulder. Rough lines are sketched, defining the space. A small piece of glass is gently broken onto the board and the fragments glued, then painted different colors . . .

> **CAROLINE (v.o.)**
> She is a woman who has almost no clarity about herself, only the memory of once being happy for a moment . . . like fragments of a photograph . . . or broken glass . . .

She breaks another piece of colored glass, scatters it across the board.

> **CAROLINE (v.o.)**
> I want to break all the fragments myself, feel them splinter in my fingers, glue and paint them in place, like a personal collage I was pulling out of my stomach . . .

LOW-ANGLE MCU Caroline, bent over the work, crying, sweating, as if driven by some strong, internal need . . .

CUT:

EXT. A STREET IN CAROLINE'S MEMORY IN A DREAM

TRACKING SHOT, Caroline dressed similarly as in the other dream, braids, etc., walking quickly as if trying to catch up with someone . . .

CUT:

MOVING SHOT behind YOUNG MAN, POV Caroline.
We gain on him, moving in closer until it feels we are
right on top of him. He wears a high school club jacket,
walks with a brisk, cool stride, when all of a sudden there
is laughter, a chorus of female voices giggling shrilly. The
young man turns around . . .

CAMERA STOPS . . .

CUT:

MCU Caroline, POV young man. She stops,
embarrassed . . .

CUT:

WS Caroline, young man in foreground; three girls in
background. The girls are standing with their hands on their
hips, laughing.

> **ONE GIRL**
> Look at her . . . ridin' herd on the boy . . .

> **ANOTHER GIRL**
> Old Miss Square-But herself . . .

Laughter.

> **THIRD GIRL**
> Ridin' <u>herd</u> on the boy, about to mow him
> down with her square-but-lookin' self . . .

Caroline, who is facing the young man, looks about to
die . . .

CUT:

MCU Caroline frozen in her tracks . . .

CUT:

MS young man, POV Caroline. He looks at her.
Embarrassed, he turns up his collar, tries to make a cool
exit . . .

CUT:

INT. CAROLINE'S BEDROOM IN A DREAM

MS Caroline dressed as in the preceding scene, sitting at her
desk doing homework. On a scratchy phonograph we hear
Patti Page singing "Tennessee Waltz." Caroline sings along
fervently . . .

> **CAROLINE**
> *(singing)*

> I was dancing with my darling
> To the Tennessee Waltz
> When an old friend I
> happened to see . . .

She giggles . . . begins to write . . .

> **CAROLINE**
> *(writing out loud)*

> Timothy Hays has got me in a daze
> Oh, how happy I'll be
> The first day I see
> That Timothy Hays has noticed me . . .

> **EDWARD ANDERSON (o.c.)**
> Caroline . . .

Caroline turns around abruptly . . .

DOLLY BACK to WS Caroline in foreground, Edward Anderson in background.

> **EDWARD ANDERSON**
> It's time for your bath, then I'll braid your hair . . .

> **CAROLINE**
> Yes, sir . . .

She covers what she's writing until he closes the door . . .

CUT:

INT. CAROLINE'S BEDROOM – DAWN

MLS Caroline, getting out of bed. She carries her sketches over to a drafting table, goes to the window, and looks out.

PAN to LS window. The sky is a deep flamingo . . .

CUT:

MCU Caroline, looking out the window, pensive. After a while she turns away . . .

CUT:

MOVING SHOT, behind Caroline. She goes into the children's room, hovers momentarily over them (asleep), moves on into the living room. All is quiet, a faint crimson light illuminates everything. She stops in front of a photograph of Giles and Liliane.

> **CAROLINE (v.o.)**
> Giles was my first lover. I was twenty-two, just
> out of college and working in summer stock.
> He had just gotten his seaman's papers and
> was waiting for a ship. We met in a restaurant
> down near Fisherman's Wharf . . .

CUT:

EXT. HILLY STREET – LATE EVENING

LS Caroline, Giles, walking up a steep hill such as one
might find in San Francisco or Boston. Finally they turn
and go up the steps of an old brownstone . . .

> **CAROLINE (v.o.)**
> At the time, he lived in a boardinghouse for
> sailors that didn't allow women . . .

CUT:

MLS behind Caroline and Giles. They go inside the
brownstone, quietly tiptoeing. As they clear the glass door,
Giles lifts her over his shoulder and starts up the steps . . .

CUT:

INT. ATTIC ROOM – SAME NIGHT

LS door. It opens. Giles comes in still carrying her over his
shoulder. He turns on a light, revealing an old-fashioned brass
bed, a small desk with papers, an easel, books, a typewriter.
Clothes are scattered about. The room is small, personal,
masculine feeling. He puts her down on the bed . . .

CUT:

MCU Caroline, POV Giles standing over her. She is much younger, still quite innocent-looking. He kneels down beside her, filling the frame . . .

DISSOLVE:

LOW-ANGLE MS Caroline, Giles, asleep. Sunlight streams through the window. Caroline wakes up first, leans over, and begins kissing him until he wakes up, pulls her to him . . .

> **CAROLINE (v.o.)**
> I remember waking up and kissing him again and again. He opened his eyes, smiled, recited the beginnings of a poem I can no longer remember . . .

HOLD: the two of them laughing, hugging . . .

FADE-OUT:

INT. FOYER OF AN APARTMENT BUILDING – EARLY AFTERNOON

TRACKING SHOT, behind Giles.

> **CAROLINE (v.o.)**
> One weekend he came to see me on leave . . .

He goes through the foyer, up a short flight of steps, rings the bell. Caroline opens the door wearing a white dress . . .

> **CAROLINE (v.o.)**
> I looked lovely that day . . . I don't know why . . . there are days when that happens, when you seem to radiate life . . .

CUT:

MCU Giles, POV Caroline. His eyes are dark, intense, almost in awe of her . . .

CUT:

EXT. WHARF – LATE AFTERNOON

MOVING SHOT, Giles, Caroline. She is in the foreground, he follows behind at a distance . . .

> **CAROLINE (v.o.)**
> We went for a walk, he started walking quite
> far behind me, pretending he was following
> me . . .

DISSOLVE:

EXT. A PARK – LATE AFTERNOON

MWS Caroline, sitting alone on a bench, a perplexed look on her face. She looks sideways . . .

PAN to MWS Giles, staring at her. After a while, he approaches her.

> **CAROLINE (v.o.)**
> In the park, he made me pretend I was alone,
> then he came up to me as if he were trying to
> pick me up . . .

DISSOLVE:

INT. A BAR – LATE AT NIGHT

SIDE-ANGLE LS Caroline, Giles. She sits on a barstool in foreground of shot. We see Giles in the background at the other end of the bar . . .

CUT:

MS Giles. He looks angry, frustrated. Suddenly he crushes
the glass between his fingers, cutting himself. Just as
quickly, he exits the frame . . .

CUT:

SIDE-ANGLE LS Caroline in foreground, Giles in
background. She watches him leave, gets up and runs out
after him.

> **CAROLINE (v.o.)**
> We were in a bar when he got angry, it was the
> fourth time he pretended to pick me up, when
> suddenly he got angry and stalked out . . .

CUT:

EXT. STREET OUTSIDE BAR – SAME TIME

MOVING SHOT, Caroline in foreground, Giles in
background. She walks fast to try to catch up with him.
Suddenly he turns and shouts something out to her . . .

> **CAROLINE (v.o.)**
> I didn't know what was the matter. I followed
> him outside, but when he saw me, he screamed
> at me . . . 'I've been trying all day to fall back
> in love with you,' he shouted . . . 'but I can't
> do it, I can't do it . . . and you look so fucking
> beautiful . . .'

CUT:

MCU Giles, wrought up and out of control. He looks at her
one last time, then walks rapidly out of sight . . .

CUT:

INT. THE THEATER – AFTERNOON

MWS the piano player, Dick, singing together . . .

THE PIANO PLAYER and DICK
(singing)
> I dream my women,
> I dream them, baby
> I dream my women
> I dream them, baby . . .

Alphonso enters frame . . .

ALPHONSO
(to Dick)
> A simple tap dance will do . . .

He acts it out while the piano player continues to sing . . .

THE PIANO PLAYER
(singing)
> Make them come out of thin air
> Pull them out of hats and that's how they
>   appear . . .

Alphonso signals Marie and the three women, who enter frame . . .

ALPHONSO
> When he choreographs this, you'll be
> the dream women, you'll be dressed for
> fantasyland . . .

The piano player continues to sing . . .

THE PIANO PLAYER

They're dream women, fantasy women
Who I make to be there

It's just some little thing
That releases a spring inside me . . .

Now it may be the turn of the wrist
Or the way an ankle twists
Or the shape of the nose
Or the fit of the clothes
After all, it's sometimes hard to recall
What I saw . . .

But at the moment I dream it
It's all there is or so it seems

And I think that I've found it
And can deny the past
And start living life from that moment on
But it never lasts . . .

Now it may be a thin wispy voice
Or lips so full and moist
Or a high-sitting ass
That I couldn't let pass

After all, it's sometimes hard to recall
What I saw . . .

'Cause I dream my women
I dream them, baby
I dream my women,
I dream them, baby . . .

Dick has joined in the singing at some point, and as the song
finishes, the two men slap five.

DICK
(to the piano player)
Oh, man, I feel like I could blow around
forever . . .

They laugh . . .

DOLLY BACK and PAN to MWS Marie and the women.
Their pose is deliberately pouty and provocative . . .

MARIE
(to the women)
We give them their best lines . . .

THE WOMEN
Well . . .

MARIE
A whole string of fast one-liners they can
throw our way . . .

THE WOMEN
Well . . .

MARIE
Then we start acting the fool . . .

She begins to sing . . .

MARIE
(singing)
Baby, please don't go . . .

THE WOMEN
(singing)
Baby, please don't go . . .

MARIE
(singing)

. . . pout, smile, tell tales out of school . . .

THE WOMEN
(singing)

Baby, please don't go . . .

MARIE
(singing)

. . . as if LOVE were the main event,
The one skirmish we better win hands
   down . . .

THE WOMEN
(singing)
BABY, PLEASE DON'T GO . . .

MARIE
(her voice rising)

Come out on the other side,
Absolved by love, absolved by love . . .
(screaming)
BABY, PLEASE DON'T GO . . .
BABY, PLEASE DON'T GO . . .

CUT:

MCU Caroline in the wings, laughing and crying
uncontrollably . . .

FADE-OUT:

INT. HALLWAY OF COUNTRY HOUSE – LATE
AFTERNOON

MS Liliane on the phone.

> **LILIANE**
> Rafael called . . . the man wants to sell my
> coats, Caroline . . . we're to meet sometime
> next week . . .

CUT:

INT. PHONE BOOTH IN THE THEATER – SAME TIME

MS Caroline.

> **CAROLINE**
> That's wonderful, Lil . . . you deserve it, you
> should make a fortune. How're the kids . . . I'll
> call back if I'm going to be real late . . .

She hangs up, then dials another number.

> **CAROLINE**
> Rafael Samuels . . . his . . . Caroline
> Samuels . . . Hi . . . I just talked to Liliane,
> she's excited, that was nice of you . . .

CUT:

INT. RAFAEL'S OFFICE – SAME TIME

SIDE-ANGLE MWS Rafael, reading the telex while he
talks . . .

> **RAFAEL**
> . . . are you giving out points for good
> behavior . . .

CUT:

INT. PHONE BOOTH IN THE THEATER – SAME
TIME

MCU Caroline.

> ### CAROLINE
> I'm not giving out points for anything, it was
> nice of you, she could use the money and the
> attention . . . fine, they enjoyed you . . .
> *(shyly)*
> You want to have dinner tonight . . .

CUT:

INT. RAFAEL'S OFFICE – SAME TIME

MS Rafael.

> ### RAFAEL
> I thought we were separated . . .

CUT:

INT. PHONE BOOTH IN THEATER – SAME TIME

MCU Caroline. She doesn't answer.

> ### RAFAEL (o.c.)
> Well, are we . . .

> ### CAROLINE
> *(after a while)*
> I guess you're right . . .

She hangs up, stays there . . .

CUT:

INT. THEATER – EARLY EVENING

MWS Alphonso, POV behind Caroline, onstage alone while she sits in the front row watching him. He mimes a clumsy, lumbering man with a heavy gait . . .

> **ALPHONSO**
> 'Hey, Alphie,' he says, 'how you doin',' and grabs my hand, throws his arms around me like a teddy bear . . .

He comes closer to the edge of the stage.

> **ALPHONSO**
> . . . so there's him and two sisters who each have four or five babies apiece . . . then my mom who stares out the window all day and waits for my calls . . .
> *(miming)*
> '. . . is that you, Alphie,' she says . . . 'are you famous yet, Alphie . . . will you let me know when you're famous . . .'

He paces . . .

> **ALPHONSO**
> . . . I never know what to say . . . I've formed my own company, done two Broadway shows . . . but am I famous . . . and in whose eyes . . .
> *(shifting abruptly)*
> Come to my house for dinner . . .

CUT:

HIGH-ANGLE MS Caroline, POV Alphonso.

> CAROLINE
> *(hesitant)*

All right . . .

He jumps off the stage, filling the frame . . .

> CUT:

INT. ALPHONSO'S APARTMENT – LATER IN THE EVENING

SIDE-ANGLE MLS Alphonso, Caroline, seated at a table in a modern apartment that is full of windows overlooking the New York skyline. A wide, empty room, barely furnished, except for a solid, rectangular table at which they sit. Alphonso is in the midst of a story, which he tells energetically with mime and gesture.

> CAROLINE
> *(after a while)*

Were you ever married . . .

> ALPHONSO

Twice. The second time is almost over . . .

A buzzer rings, he goes to answer it.

> ALPHONSO

Yes . . . now? . . . okay . . .

He turns to Caroline.

> ALPHONSO

. . . you're about to meet her . . .

> CAROLINE

Who?

ALPHONSO

My second wife . . . she has to pick up some of her things, she's downstairs in the lobby . . .

CUT:

MS Caroline.

CAROLINE

I think I should leave . . .

ALPHONSO (o.c.)

No, please stay, for my sake . . .

CUT:

MS Alphonso, POV Caroline. He looks edgy, his composure is gone.

ALPHONSO

She's an unusual woman . . .

The bell rings. He exits frame . . .

CUT:

LS Alphonso, POV Caroline. He opens the door, a woman enters wearing glasses, sees Caroline . . .

HIS WIFE

I could have done this some other time . . .

ALPHONSO

No, no . . .

He gestures toward Caroline . . .

ALPHONSO
Caroline Samuels, she's doing the set . . .
Caroline, this is Vera . . .

VERA comes forward into MS and nods. She's beautifully
dressed with a swift, extremely disarming manner.

VERA
I left too many things here . . .

She exits frame . . .

CUT:

MOVING SHOT, Alphonso, Vera, POV Caroline.
Alphonso follows behind his wife as she picks up things and
stuffs them in her shopping bag. He behaves like a petulant
child.

ALPHONSO
Don't take anything I bought you . . .

VERA
Then you want the clothes off my back . . .

He snatches something out of her hand . . .

ALPHONSO
I gave you that, you can't go around wearing
my impression of you . . .

Vera looks over at Caroline.

VERA
Ain't this the cat's meow . . .

CUT:

MS Caroline, POV Vera, watching, astounded by both of them . . .

CUT:

MOVING SHOT, Vera, Alphonso, POV Caroline.

ALPHONSO
You never thought about clothes until you met me . . .

VERA
And now I should go out naked as a lamb . . .

DOLLY FORWARD: Vera steps forward at the same time into MCU.

VERA
(to Caroline)
. . . there's no furniture in this place, you notice that . . . that's because we never left this table, we've been sitting at this table for three years! Dissecting every sentiment known to man . . . love, pity, death . . . I hardly had time to pee!

Alphonso enters background of frame, pacing awkwardly . . .

VERA
. . . he's got a wonderful mind, it will dazzle the hell out of you for about three years . . . three years of his enthusiastic energy and you'll drop dead from exhaustion . . .

She walks away, laughing . . .

CUT:

LS Alphonso in foreground, Caroline in midground, Vera
in background . . . Vera gathers her shopping bags, starts
toward the door.

VERA
You wore me out, you hear me . . . I'm a
friggin' basket case!

And she's gone, slamming the door behind her. Caroline
and Alphonso remain where they are.

ALPHONSO
(quietly)
I hear she's living with a musician . . .

CUT:

LOW SIDE-ANGLE MWS Alphonso's bed later that night.
Alphonso stirs, sits up. We become aware of Caroline lying
beside him.

ALPHONSO
You want dinner . . .

CAROLINE
What time is it?

ALPHONSO
Around eleven . . . I could make us some
spaghetti with clam sauce, and cold white
wine . . .

CAROLINE
I better get home . . .

> ALPHONSO
> *(ignoring that)*
> Then we could go for a walk . . .

Caroline gets up.

> ALPHONSO
> Don't go . . .

CUT:

MS Caroline, POV Alphonso. She starts putting on her clothes . . .

> ALPHONSO (o.c.)
> You're a nice lady, you know that . . . When you're back in the country will you be sorry you slept with me . . .

She looks at him . . .

CUT:

MS Alphonso, POV Caroline, staring at her . . .

CUT:

EXT. DRIVEWAY OF COUNTRY HOUSE – LATE AT NIGHT

LS Caroline's car, POV house. It comes into MS. Stops. She gets out and comes inside.

CUT:

INT. CAROLINE'S BATHROOM – SAME TIME

MS bathtub, water running. Steam. Her body crosses frame and slips into the bathtub . . . .

                       CUT:

MCU her skin, gently rubbed . . .

                       CUT:

INT. CHILDREN'S BEDROOM – SAME TIME

MS Sara. Caroline leans into frame and kisses her . . .

                       CUT:

INT. CAROLINE'S BEDROOM – SAME TIME

MS bed, unmade. Her body crosses frame, slips into bed . . .

           CAROLINE (v.o.)
      Does it come down finally to my incredible
      need for the warmth of sex . . .

Her body settles into a comfortable position.

HOLD . . .

                   FADE-OUT:

INT. STAGE OF THEATER – LATE AFTERNOON

WS Caroline, TWO TECHNICIANS. She's directing the
hanging of several panels.

                       CUT:

             CAROLINE
      It has to hang on a diagonal, can you twist it
      more . . .

She goes around to the back and climbs up on a ladder . . .

MWS Caroline, panels, adjusting them . . .

> **CAROLINE**
> *(to technician)*
> Could you bring in the two platforms . . .

>   CUT:

REVERSE ANGLE, behind Caroline.

> **CAROLINE**
> *(to the lighting man)*
> It has to hit them obliquely so that everything
> feels jagged . . .

She climbs down from the ladder, moves around to the front
to look . . .

>   CUT:

MS panels, POV Caroline, reflected through light . . .

>   CUT:

MCU Caroline.

> **CAROLINE**
> *(to the lighting man)*
> We'll correct it during the tech . . .

She exits frame . . .

>   CUT:

WS behind Caroline, Alphonso in background. She's
walking toward the wings, Alphonso is coming toward her
holding a sketch . . .

ALPHONSO
I'm worried about the environment around
Dick . . .

CAROLINE
I'm suggesting a nightclub . . . tables, the slight
feeling of a bar . . . but it's his space only . . .

ALPHONSO
That's what I'm talking about, it's too stern . . .

They stop . . .

CUT:

SIDE-ANGLE MS both of them.

ALPHONSO
. . . it doesn't allow him much room to
move . . .

CAROLINE
But I've deliberately boxed him in. All he
likes, as he puts it, is 'casual shit' . . . drinking,
smoking, women . . . which the nightclub
atmosphere expresses . . .

ALPHONSO
But why box him in . . .

CAROLINE
(indignant)
You think a lot of casual shit gets somebody
very far . . .

They look at each other and laugh . . .

HOLD . . .

CUT:

EXT. FRONT YARD OF COUNTRY HOUSE – EARLY AFTERNOON

MS Sara, POV car pulling up. She's standing on the porch.

> **SARA**
> Mommie, Grandpa's here . . .

The car stops . . .

CUT:

MLS Caroline, Liliane, POV Sara, getting out of the car, carrying groceries.

> **CAROLINE**
> *(thrown)*
> Grandpa . . .

Sara runs into frame . . .

> **SARA**
> He's changing Edward's diaper . . . it
> smelled . . .

Caroline walks toward the house . . .

INT. CHILDREN'S BEDROOM – SAME TIME

MWS behind Edward Anderson, bent over the crib changing his grandson's diaper.

> **CAROLINE (o.c.)**
> Daddy . . .

He turns around, lifting Edward out of the crib.

EDWARD ANDERSON
He was a bit loaded down . . .

Caroline comes into frame and hugs him.

CAROLINE
I didn't expect you but I'm glad . . . what a
nice surprise . . .

Sara runs in . . .

SARA
Come outside, Grandpa, I want you to push
me on the swing . . .

CAROLINE
You have to meet Liliane . . .

CUT:

EXT. FRONT YARD OF HOUSE – LATER IN THE
AFTERNOON

MWS Edward Anderson, Shana, Sara. He's pushing Shana
on the swing, while Sara waits her turn impatiently.

SARA
It's my turn . . .

SHANA
He only pushed me three times . . .

SARA
But he's my grandfather . . .

EDWARD ANDERSON
Well, for today I'll be Shana's grandfather,
too . . .

> ### SHANA
> Then push me higher, much higher, if you're
> my grandfather . . .

She giggles gleefully . . .

CUT:

INT. HALLWAY OF HOUSE – SAME TIME

LS Caroline, crossing from kitchen with a picnic basket,
tablecloth, etc.

CUT:

EXT. LAWN OF HOUSE – LATER IN THE
AFTERNOON

MS Christopher, upside down, standing on his head.

> ### CHRISTOPHER
> My dad taught me that . . .

He flips over . . .

DOLLY BACK to MWS Edward Anderson, Christopher.

> ### EDWARD ANDERSON
> That's very good, I could do a pretty sharp
> cartwheel when I was your age, nobody could
> keep up with me for long . . .

> ### CHRISTOPHER
> They're simple . . .

He executes a few beauties. Edward Anderson applauds.

DOLLY BACK to WS that includes Caroline, Liliane, a
picnic lunch spread in front of them.

EDWARD ANDERSON
(to Liliane)
He could be an acrobat . . . I hope not, for
your sake, but he's got wonderful control . . .

LILIANE
He'll do something that's dangerous, I'm afraid
it's in his blood.

Edward Anderson looks at her . . .

EDWARD ANDERSON
. . . and you'll take too much responsibility for
whatever he becomes . . .

He looks at his daughter . . .

EDWARD ANDERSON
Hmph . . .

CUT:

MS Caroline, POV Edward Anderson.

CAROLINE
It's nice here, isn't it . . .

CUT:

MS Edward Anderson, POV in between both women. He
nods . . .

EDWARD ANDERSON
Yes, it is . . . two women alone in the
woods . . . but maybe a little too modern for
me . . .

He looks at them . . .

                                SHANA (o.c.)

     Grandpa . . .

Shana and Sara come rushing in. Shana climbs on his
shoulders, Liliane tries to shoo her down, but Edward
Anderson insists it's all right. Sara, a bit jealous, climbs on
his lap . . .

DOLLY BACK to EWS all of them . . .

                                                    CUT:

EXT. SIDEWALK THRIFT SHOP – EARLY
AFTERNOON

TRACKING SHOT, Alphonso, Caroline, walking on
opposite sides of a long table heaped with furs, dresses,
shawls, dishes, etc. Alphonso throws her an elegant-looking
wrap . . .

                              ALPHONSO

     Try it on . . .

                              CAROLINE

     What would I do with it . . .

                              ALPHONSO

     Wear it to the opening . . .

                              CAROLINE

     It's too elegant . . .

CAMERA STOPS. She tries it on . . .

                              ALPHONSO

     It looks great, how much . . .

                              CAROLINE

     Five dollars . . .

> **ALPHONSO**
> It's yours if you'll wear it to the opening . . .

> **CAROLINE**
> With what?

> **ALPHONSO**
> Well, now we'll look for a dress . . .

He grins . . .

CUT:

EXT. OUTDOOR CAFÉ – LATE AFTERNOON

SIDE-ANGLE MS Alphonso, Caroline, sitting at a table, drinking . . .

> **ALPHONSO**
> It looks great, a bit eccentric but in
> character . . .

> **CAROLINE**
> Me . . . eccentric?

He looks at her . . .

> **ALPHONSO**
> . . . no . . . old-fashioned . . . the things that
> happen to modern women are happening to
> you, you just don't like to believe it . . .

> **CAROLINE**
> That makes me stupid . . .

He touches her . . .

> **ALPHONSO**
> . . . no . . . just old-fashioned . . . unwilling to
> give up on a happy ending . . .

CUT:

INT. STAGE OF THEATER IN A DREAM

MWS Caroline in an old-fashioned dress, standing in the spotlight as if singing to an audience. She sings in a tiny, fey voice . . .

CAROLINE
(singing)
I got no space at all to believe in
But a tiny little hole in my shoe
Which I wear threadbare, down to the cold,
   damp ground
And don't ever allow to be seen

I dance to hold on to my footsteps
Echoing behind me as I move
Like a blind lady groping backward
Toward something that she's scared to lose . . .

The space I believe in is tiny
Like a crack in the wall by the door
And I go to it often
And stumble and falter
And scream when I fall to the floor

I dance to hold on to my footsteps
Echoing behind me as I move
Like a blind lady groping backward
Toward something that she's scared to lose . . .

The space I believe in is me
Lying in the shadow of a dream
The footsteps I walk to are circles I talk to
To hold on to the beauty I see.

I got no space at all to believe in
But a tiny little hole in my shoe
Which I wear threadbare down to the cold,
      damp ground
And don't ever allow to be seen . . .

At the end, she curtsies . . .

CUT:

INT. LILIANE'S ROOM – LATE AFTERNOON

LS Liliane. She's weaving. Caroline comes in wearing the dress and wrap Alphonso bought her.

> **CAROLINE**
> *(happy)*
> What do you think . . .

> **LILIANE**
> It looks like you . . .

> **CAROLINE**
> Does it make me look eccentric . . .

> **LILIANE**
> You're too straightforward to look eccentric . . .

> **CAROLINE**
> He's fun . . .

> **LILIANE**
> I can tell . . .

> **CAROLINE**
> . . . but also crazier than a loon . . .

> **LILIANE**
> It probably doesn't matter, anything to put
> distance between you and Rafael . . .

> **CAROLINE**
> You mean any man would do . . .

She feels suddenly annoyed, glares at Liliane, when
Christopher's voice cuts across . . .

> **CHRISTOPHER (o.c.)**
> I can't find my racing cars . . .

> **LILIANE**
> They've got to be in your room, did you look
> in your desk . . .

> **CHRISTOPHER (o.c.)**
> I looked everywhere . . .

Liliane gets up . . .

> **LILIANE**
> I'll help you find them . . .

She exits frame. Caroline crosses to the mirror . . .

CUT:

MWS Caroline, POV mirror, pleased with her outfit . . .

CUT:

> **CHRISTOPHER (o.c.)**
> I looked there, I looked everywhere . . .

> **LILIANE (o.c.)**
> Everywhere but the right place, they're under
> your bed . . .

CHRISTOPHER (o.c.)
How did you know that . . .

LILIANE (o.c.)
I didn't, I could just think better because I wasn't angry . . .

She comes back looking annoyed . . .

LILIANE
Giles used to do that when he lost something . . .

CAROLINE
You mean have a fit and drive you crazy . . .

MS Liliane, standing in the doorway . . .

LILIANE
. . . once he was looking for a tool he needed, I was busy weaving and wouldn't stop to help him . . . he got so furious he lifted my loom in the air and sent it crashing . . .

CAROLINE (o.c.)
What did you do . . .

LILIANE
Left . . . went for a long walk, he was gone when I got back . . . didn't come home until the next day . . . with a new loom, the one I have now . . .

She smiles . . .

DOLLY BACK to MWS both women, as she crosses the room, resumes her weaving . . .

CAROLINE

. . . you weren't still mad . . .

LILIANE
(shrugging)

That was him . . . he went to extremes . . .

CAROLINE

That's a bit romantic . . . Giles wreaking
havoc . . . you bathing in his needs . . .

The room grows silent . . .

LILIANE
(coldly)

He took me along until the end, is that what
bothers you . . .

CAROLINE

. . . as opposed to what . . . Rafael riding any
old wave in sight . . .

Caroline turns toward her, angry . . .

CUT:

MS Caroline, POV Liliane.

CAROLINE

I don't think it's that simple . . . he jumped
ship, that leaves you free to make it anything
you want . . .

CUT:

MCU Liliane, POV Caroline, pulled up short . . .

CUT:

INT. A HALL OR CHURCH – EVENING

LS platform. A crowded hall. A SPEAKER at the podium.
To his left, Edward Anderson.

> **THE SPEAKER**
> . . . and it is our privilege this evening to pay
> homage to a man who has given relentless
> service to this community. Two new clinics
> now exist because of his efforts, his almost
> single-minded devotion on behalf of the health
> and care of our people . . .

Caroline comes into frame, slips down the aisle and takes a
seat . . .

> **THE SPEAKER**
> . . . he *continues* to see, day in and day out, far
> more patients than any one doctor should . . .

CUT:

MWS Caroline amid a group of folk, listening.

> **THE SPEAKER (o.c.)**
> . . . he has given active service to our
> Frontiersmen Organization, served on
> committees and on the boards of organizations
> too numerous to mention. He just recently
> came back from Washington as part of a panel
> to advise the president on current health
> issues and concerns. It is with great pride and
> gratitude that we honor tonight Dr. Edward
> B. Anderson . . .

Loud applause . . .

CUT:

MWS Edward Anderson, POV Caroline, walking over to the podium . . . ·

CUT:

INT. A CAR – LATE AT NIGHT

SIDE-ANGLE TWO-SHOT, favoring Caroline.

> **EDWARD ANDERSON**
> How did you know about this . . .

> **CAROLINE**
> They sent an invitation to the apartment, Rafael called me . . .

> **EDWARD ANDERSON**
> Why did you come . . .

She shrugs . . .

> **CAROLINE**
> . . . you've done a lot of things, I don't remember your being that busy when I was growing up, you always seemed to be around . . .

He doesn't answer . . .

> **CAROLINE**
> How did you do it . . .

> **EDWARD ANDERSON**
> Do what . . .

> **CAROLINE**
> Raise me and do all those things . . .

He doesn't answer . . .

CUT:

REVERSE ANGLE, favoring Edward.

CAROLINE
I knew nothing about the clinics, nor the
president's committee . . .

EDWARD ANDERSON
I don't take pride in doing what was expected
of me . . .

CAROLINE
You're not even pleased . . .

EDWARD ANDERSON
Hmph . . .

Silence . . .

CAROLINE
. . . you don't like living that much, do you,
Daddy . . .

No answer. They drive in silence for a while . . .

EDWARD ANDERSON
Who could like a life that imposed so
much . . .

He touches his skin inadvertently, catches himself doing it
and grunts . . .

INT. CAROLINE'S OLD BEDROOM – LATE AT NIGHT

MS Caroline, sitting at her desk, wearing a nightgown and
writing . . .

CAROLINE (v.o.)
. . . it's been a long time since I spent a
night here, I feel cut off, peacefully amputated
from my own confusion . . . I take shelter
in my father's sternness . . . it feels clean,
upright . . .

There's a knock at the door . . .

CAROLINE
Yes . . .

DOLLY BACK to MWS room. Edward Anderson stands in
the doorway . . .

EDWARD ANDERSON
I came to tell you good night . . .

CAROLINE
(teasing)
I thought you'd come in to braid my hair,
you used to braid it so tight I can still feel the
pain . . .

FOCUS ON Edward Anderson. There are tears in his
eyes . . .

CUT:

INT. HALLWAY OF COUNTRY HOUSE IN A
DREAM

MOVING SHOT, Liliane walking toward us in a white
gown, looking distraught . . .

DOLLY BACK as she opens Caroline's door . . .

> **LILIANE**
>
> . . . he's here . . . he's been walking through
> the house . . .

CUT:

LS Liliane, POV behind Caroline's bed . . . Caroline sits
up . . .

> **LILIANE**
>
> . . . lifting the children and carrying them
> around . . . I could touch him . . . he's not
> dead . . . he's all over the place . . .

She breaks down, begins to cry uncontrollably. Caroline
rushes out of bed, goes to put her arms around her . . .

DISSOLVE:

EXT. EDWARD ANDERSON'S GARDEN IN A DREAM

MWS Edward Anderson wearing a tuxedo, bent over,
digging in the ground . . .

CUT:

MS the ground being turned over, hands scooping out a
planting space. The photograph of Caroline's mother, seen
earlier, is placed in the hole, flowers are heaped on top of it,
flowers and more flowers . . .

CUT:

INT. PHONE BOOTH OF THEATER – EARLY AFTERNOON

MS Caroline talking . . .

CAROLINE

. . . it was lovely, I'm glad I went . . . tell Sara I miss her and I'll be home early. I can cook, I'll pick up some fish . . . oh, and I had a dream about you . . . I'll tell you when I get home . . .

She hangs up . . .

PAN to WS as she walks down the aisle of the theater toward the stage. In the background we see Alphonso onstage with Marie.

ALPHONSO

No, the key to that line is her taking hold of the darkness . . . the memory of his charm is a throwaway . . .

EXT. FRONT LAWN OF COUNTRY HOUSE – LATE AFTERNOON

WS children, Caroline. They squeal as she gets out of the car.

SARA

Look at Edward, Mommie, he can walk to you . . .

Shana and Sara guide him over to her . . .

CAROLINE

That's wonderful . . .

She scoops him up, goes into the house . . .

CAROLINE

Lil . . .

CUT:

INT. KITCHEN OF COUNTRY HOUSE – SAME TIME

MOVING SHOT, behind Caroline.

> ### CAROLINE
> Lil . . .

We see Liliane standing at the stove.

> ### LILIANE
> I'm in here . . .

> ### CAROLINE
> . . . you're not supposed to be near the
> kitchen, it's my turn, in fact my turn is long
> overdue . . .

By now we are in MS Liliane, POV behind Caroline.

CAMERA STOPS. Liliane turns toward Caroline, her face
looks ravaged . . .

> ### LILIANE
> . . . nobody's supposed to bring me any more
> bad news, but they do . . . I pick up the phone
> and it's more bad news . . . your father's dead,
> Caroline . . . he had a heart attack about two
> hours after you left . . . apparently he didn't
> linger, he died right there in his office . . .

> ### CAROLINE (o.c.)
> I just saw him . . .

She comes into frame.

> ### CAROLINE
> . . . was just there, we had such a good
> time . . .

They grab hold of each other . . .

> ### CAROLINE
> . . . I just saw him . . . I just saw him . . .

She muffles a scream, holding tight to Liliane . . .

HOLD . . .

CUT:

INT. BEDROOM OF EDWARD ANDERSON'S HOUSE – EVENING

LS Edward Anderson, stretched out on the bed, hands folded. Caroline comes in and kneels beside him . . .

HOLD . . .

CUT:

MCU Caroline kneeling, talking to him . . .

> ### CAROLINE
> Why now, Daddy . . . why did you walk away from me now . . .

In background of shot, Liliane enters the room with Rafael. He comes up to her, puts his hand on her shoulder . . .

HOLD . . .

CUT:

INT. KITCHEN OF EDWARD ANDERSON'S HOUSE – LATER THAT NIGHT

SIDE-ANGLE WS Liliane, Rafael, seated at the table . . .

LILIANE

There isn't to be a funeral . . . he left
instructions . . . cremation, ashes placed in the
backyard at Caroline's discretion . . .

DISSOLVE:

EXT. EDWARD ANDERSON'S GARDEN – EARLY
EVENING

MS ground, Caroline's hands scooping out dirt as if for
planting. An urn is placed in the hole, then covered over.
The hands begin to plant flowers on top and around it . . .

CUT:

WS Caroline kneeling, planting. Off-camera, Marie's voice
singing . . .

How lovely is the evening,
Is the evening, is the evening
When the bells are sweetly ringing
Sweetly ringing, sweetly ringing . . .

Bells toll as if from a nearby church . . .

HOLD . . .

DISSOLVE:

INT. THE THEATER IN A DREAM

MWS Edward Anderson in the spotlight. Wearing his
tuxedo. Seated at the piano as if singing to an audience in
that old-fashioned half-talking way . . .

EDWARD ANDERSON
(singing)

It's time that kills a tune that is starting to
    grow
A sweet little buzz in your ear
And it's time that takes a note out of hiding
With all the longing it excited still thriving

I'm searching for a new melody
For a tune that I can sing to
Any little beat will do
Just as long as it's something to cling to

'Cause finally you see
When the melody starts to go dry
Hitch on to the thunder inside you
To the heart that is never denied you
Listen close and you may decide
That you have discovered a whole new
    song . . .

Growing sad, talking now more than singing . . .

EDWARD ANDERSON

But now time has stopped rehearsing the music
And left me silent, and mute as a stone now
Time has turned her back on the rhythm and
    the
Melody's as dry as a bone . . .

I'm searching for a new melody
I'm searching for a new melody
Melody . . .

DISSOLVE:

INT. CAROLINE'S BEDROOM – JUST BEFORE DAWN

MCU Caroline, crying in her sleep . . .

DOLLY BACK and PAN slightly to include Sara asleep beside her mother. She wakes up and wipes her mother's eyes . . .

HOLD . . .

FADE-OUT:

EXT. HALLWAY – LATE MORNING

MWS Christopher, coming down the steps.

> **CHRISTOPHER**
> (*furious*)
> I can't find it!

> **LILIANE (o.c.)**
> You didn't look hard, Chris, go back and look for it . . .

> **CHRISTOPHER**
> I already looked!

He goes out, slamming the door. Caroline comes into the hall from the kitchen, yelling up . . .

> **CAROLINE**
> Lil . . . there are two tech rehearsals, I'm afraid I'll be real late . . . where are the girls . . .

> **LILIANE (o.c.)**
> Down at the stream washing their dolls . . .

> CAROLINE
> *(laughing)*
> Edward should sleep until around two . . .

> LILIANE (o.c.)
> Don't worry about it . . .

> CAROLINE
> Tell Sara I'll call her before she goes to bed . . .

> LILIANE
> Good luck . . .

> CAROLINE
> Thanks . . .

She exits frame . . .

CUT:

INT. THE THEATER – LATE AT NIGHT

WS stage, everybody. Alphonso, wired up . . .

> ALPHONSO
> Marie . . . that's your final position for the last
> number . . . the women take their first curtain
> call from the platform . . . Dick . . . you stand
> up right at your table . . . the same holds true
> for you, Al . . . you never leave the piano, even
> if the gods bless us with several calls . . .

Everyone laughs. Alphonso turns to Caroline, who is seated
in the front row . . .

> ALPHONSO
> Anything you want to adjust . . .

CAROLINE
(back to camera)
. . . nothing that concerns the actors . . .

He signals a wrap. People begin to disperse. He comes down off the stage to Caroline . . .

CUT:

SIDE-ANGLE MWS Alphonso, Caroline.

ALPHONSO
You want to spend the night . . .

She shakes her head no . . .

CUT:

INT. LONG HALLWAY OUTSIDE RAFAEL'S
APARTMENT – LATE AT NIGHT

SIDE-ANGLE MWS Caroline, coming down the hall and knocking on his door . . .

RAFAEL (o.c.)
Who's there . . .

CAROLINE
It's me . . .

He comes to the door . . .

CAROLINE
I suppose I still have a key somewhere . . . but that would be indiscreet . . .

RAFAEL
It's late . . .

> **CAROLINE**
> I know, can I spend the night . . .

> **RAFAEL**
> Is something wrong . . .

> **CAROLINE**
> No, I just felt we should talk . . .

She moves to go in, he stops her . . .

CUT:

MS Caroline, POV Rafael, the reason for his reluctance dawning on her. In a sudden fury, she pushes past him . . .

CUT:

INT. RAFAEL'S APARTMENT – SAME TIME

MLS two women, sitting on the couch smoking, drinking. Caroline runs into frame and stops . . .

MS Caroline staring. Rafael comes into frame.

> **RAFAEL**
> Why don't we talk in the hall . . .

He tries to move her toward the door.

> **CAROLINE**
> No . . .

> **RAFAEL**
> Come on, Caroline.

> CAROLINE
> *(losing control)*
> No, I said . . . why don't we talk right here,
> your little Miss Square-But of a wife and
> your . . .

He pushes her forcefully toward the door . . .

CUT:

INT. HALLWAY OUTSIDE APARTMENT – SAME TIME

MWS door. Caroline is pushed forward into frame, followed by Rafael . . .

> CAROLINE
> Send them home, I want to talk to you . . .
> every time I try and talk to you there's a chick
> chick here and a chick chick there . . .

> RAFAEL
> Stop . . .

He pulls the door shut behind him . . .

> CAROLINE
> Send them home . . .

> RAFAEL
> No . . .

CUT:

MCU Caroline, POV over his shoulder.

> CAROLINE
> Why . . .

                              RAFAEL (o.c.)
         I don't want to . . .

                                                              CUT:

MS Rafael, behind Caroline.

                                RAFAEL
         I want to go back in there and drink and enjoy
         myself . . .

                               CAROLINE
                               (shivering)
         . . . it's cold the way you see things . . . why do
         I keep hoping you'll let me come in from the
         cold . . .

She stands there shaking . . . He looks at her, then goes back
inside . . .

HOLD . . .

                                                              CUT:

EXT. SIDEWALK PHONE BOOTH – LATE AT NIGHT

MS Caroline, looking scared, talking quickly . . .

                               CAROLINE
         A few blocks away . . . are you sure . . .

She hangs up . . .

                                                              CUT:

NOTE: This scene is to be shot silent, with only mime and
gestures. The only sound will be Caroline's V.O.

INT. ALPHONSO'S APARTMENT – SAME TIME

MS WOMAN, a homely woman, but who exhibits great vitality. She mime-sings a jazz riff, her face contorted while she scats up and down, moving her body . . . The doorbell rings . . .

PAN DOWN and ACROSS to WS Alphonso, standing there listening and drinking. The bell rings again. Finally, he hears it and goes to answer it . . .

CUT:

HIGH-ANGLE LS Alphonso and Caroline, POV woman. He greets her. They walk toward the woman . . .

> **CAROLINE (v.o.)**
> When I arrived, a woman was standing on the table singing . . .

CUT:

WS woman, POV Caroline. She continues her performance, as if delighted to have more of an audience.

> **CAROLINE (v.o.)**
> Alphonso introduced her as his first wife, who was now studying to be a professional singer. She'd invited herself over that evening because she wanted to know if she was any good . . .

CUT:

MS Alphonso, responding appreciatively, nodding enthusiastically . . .

CUT:

INT. THEATER – EVENING

MWS Marie in foreground, the women in background.
They're all in costume, makeup, etc., against a backdrop of
Caroline's set. It's the end of the show, the last conversation
between Marie and the women before she sings her final
number . . .

> MARIE
> *(to the women)*
> You get left with a funny hand . . .

> ONE WOMAN
> *(gently)*

Well . . .

> MARIE
> The aces have all been played, the queens smile
> benignly at you, there are no kings left in the
> deck . . .

> ANOTHER WOMAN
> *(laughing)*

Well . . .

> MARIE
> *(growing amused)*
> Fortune tellers say to you that love is just
> around the corner, mystics look in your eyes
> and see the face of God . . .

She turns away abruptly, twisting her body as if in pain . . .

> MARIE
> *(softly)*
> . . . but you ain't having none of it . . .

THE WOMEN

Well, well . . .

She drifts forward into song, pouring out her heart . . .

MARIE
(singing)
I wish you were real, Mr. J
A real live man that I could stay with
When the nights are long and cold . . .

I wish you were real, Mr. J
A real live man that I could play with
On a nice bright sunny day . . .

DOLLY SLOWLY FORWARD to MCU Marie.

I wish I didn't have to work to love you
Store up every crumb you throw my way
Save them, keep them, hoard them
For a rainy day . . .

I wish you were real, Mr. J
A man with time to say 'I love you'
You don't have to run away . . .

I wish you were real, Mr. J
A man who'd let me lie beside him
On any kind of day

I wish that love came free and easy for us
Didn't make me grab for silly straws
Save them, keep them, hoard them for
A rainy day . . .

I wish you were real, Mr. J
I wish you were real, Mr. J . . .

Loud, thunderous applause . . .

HOLD . . .

FADE-OUT:

INT. KITCHEN OF COUNTRY HOUSE – DAWN

SIDE-ANGLE MS Caroline, dressed in the outfit Alphonso picked out for her, reading the newspaper.

> **CAROLINE**
> '. . . in black theater the work will probably be remembered as a milestone in the exploration of new themes . . . Caroline Samuels's fragile set manages to convey a sense of life at its most brittle, a feeling of things closing in and reaching a dead end. It even seems to suggest that the only possible solution is from within . . . no mean accomplishment for a set designer . . .'

She laughs . . .

> **LILIANE (o.c.)**
> Bravo!

She enters frame, also elegantly dressed . . .

> **LILIANE**
> . . . it's the first critic I ever agreed with . . . you deserve every word, really . . .

> **CAROLINE**
> Thanks for staying up with me . . .

Liliane turns toward the window . . .

LILIANE

It gives me a chance to see the sun rise . . .

CUT:

MS Liliane, watching . . . crimson light hitting her face . . .

LILIANE
(abstracted)

. . . I like to watch life, its colors, the shape and
meaning of things . . . I see very well . . . and
to see is almost enough for me . . . maybe that's
why it worked with Giles . . . maybe only a
passive woman could hang in that long . . .

She looks at Caroline . . .

CUT:

MS Caroline, sun rising behind her. She smiles at
Liliane . . .

CAROLINE

That's funny . . . I don't think I see at all . . .
I think life goes by me like a dream, and I am
always hoping it will be a good dream . . .

HOLD . . .

FADE-OUT:

END CREDITS COME UP.

LOSING GROUND

INTRODUCTION

The screenplay for *Losing Ground* was labeled "Shooting Script" by Kathleen Collins. It is also identified, in her hand, as the "Directing Copy (Summer 1981)" that she used during the shoot. Her changes in dialogue (emphases, additions, deletions), camera placement, and movement, as well as scene cuts, are written—sometimes scribbled—in and are often illegible.

In reproducing the screenplay I have tried to stay as true to the original typescript as possible, while at the same time indicating major changes, such as the elimination of entire scenes, with the use of brackets. As with most films, the final cut—even when the filmmaker is in total control—differs from the shooting script. It is fascinating to conjecture about the changes made during the editing process, such as the rearrangement of scenes. The best authority for what happened on location is Ronald K. Gray, cinematographer and coproducer of *Losing Ground*.

In an October 1989 interview, Gray recalled scene by scene the metamorphosis of Collins's script ("essentially literature") into a film. Changes were not always made for artistic reasons. Some were necessary adaptations to restrictions of location, money, weather, time, performers. Collins preferred working with professional actors; she felt more comfortable with them. She and the actor and director Bill Gunn differed on this issue. He liked the challenge of eliciting a performance from someone who had never been before a camera. Collins, on the other hand, delighted in directing Gunn, a consummate professional, whom she could trust with her character Victor, as she did Seret Scott with Sara and Duane Jones with Duke. And it is clear, by comparing the finished film with the script, that she allowed—sometimes reluctantly—both freedom and improvisation in the dialogue and in the "stage" business.

Collins and Gray started making *Losing Ground* with about $25,000 (AFI and NEA grants) and twenty-two production people—blacks, Puerto Ricans, Chinese, Polish—the core of the crew were students of Collins's. Then they emptied their bank accounts. Post-production costs were picked up by ARD, a West German television network. They submitted the script without notes for consideration of a prescreen agreement; suddenly they were notified that ARD representatives were coming to view the work because the network was interested in the script. It was their last hope. Gray put together a rough cut of about thirty minutes in ten days; then when the ARD representatives arrived, he and Collins showed them the rough cut and the raw, unedited dailies. The money would be forthcoming upon completion of the rough cut, but the ARD people were returning to Germany in a week. Within seven days,

Gray prepared a rough cut of one hour, which was approved: they got the money.

The film cost approximately $125,000. The agreement with ARD was for exclusive TV rights in Germany and Austria for two to three years. Distribution, however, was a problem. According to Gray, art houses wouldn't take the film because they didn't know what audience it would attract. Even in Europe (in Amiens, France, for example), the audience—at least some—didn't respond positively because there was no ghetto in the film, no "poor suffering black folk."

Characterized by Collins as a comedy drama about a young woman who takes herself too seriously, *Losing Ground* was the first feature film by an independent African American woman filmmaker. Her protagonist is a professor of philosophy who tries to examine "ecstasy" from a purely rational perspective, while her artist-husband finds it much more interesting to *pursue* ecstasy. A rare breed, Sara is immersed in the philosophy of Western civilization, but ironically the limitations of her life are illuminated by her involvement in black folk culture. She "becomes" Frankie in a student film (within the film) based on the folk song "Frankie and Johnny."

Music is an important part of any imaginative work by Collins—she even decided to make a musical drama out of her screenplay on Bessie Coleman, the remarkable black woman flyer. Music for *Losing Ground* was composed by Michael Minard to Collins's lyrics.

—Phyllis Rauch Klotman

Seret Scott in a scene from the Collins/Gray production
Losing Ground, directed by Kathleen Collins. *Courtesy of
Nina Collins and Milestone Films.*

LOSING GROUND

1 INT. COLLEGE CLASSROOM – LATE
AFTERNOON

[1] SLIGHT HIGH-ANGLE LS, TELEPHOTO, SARA,
POV behind students. We are in a large college lecture
hall. Sara, a black woman in her mid- to late thirties, is
delivering a lecture.

SARA

. . . in Sartre the question of absurdity has clear
historical antecedents: for one, a violent need
to explain war . . . Camus, Sartre, the whole
existential movement is a consequence, or
perhaps a better way to put it, a reaction to the
consequences, of war . . .

CUT:

[1A] LOW-ANGLE MWS row of students, POV Sara.
Several black male students, wearing glasses, sit listening
attentively or taking notes.

TILT DOWN and PULL BACK to row after row of black
male students, all wearing glasses, all looking exceptionally
scholarly, all giving strict attention to the lecturer . . .

SARA (o.c.)

. . . 'the natural order' . . . if there is such a
thing . . . has been violated. Chaos exists. Not
as a mental possibility—in the way that, say,
Descartes might experience it—but as
a physical and emotional fact. War is chaos,
and war was the existentialist's primary
reality . . .

As we tilt down to the front row, we now see there is one
male student who is white and one female student who
is white. As the odd couple in the group, they are seated
beside each other, somewhat crouched down in their seats.

HOLD . . .

CUT:

[2] SIDE-ANGLE MS Sara. She is a stunning woman. Creole features and color. Lively eyes, playful yet intense energy . . .

> **SARA**
> . . . how to explain it in all its terrifying horror except by acknowledging that no explanations satisfy, that human existence must be a priori without rhyme, without reason . . . in the face of sustained horror the argument for an absurd universe becomes the only rational argument.

She pauses to reflect . . .

CUT:

[3] MS YOUNG MAN, listening, his dark, powerful eyes devouring the teacher . . .

> **SARA (o.c.)**
> There are precedents of course for this kind of thinking . . . in Nietzsche, for example, in the logical positivists' hypothetical suspension of causal connection . . . but let's see how you handle all that in your term papers . . . I'm talked out, you're free to leave unless there are questions . . .

> **A STUDENT (o.c.)**
> Are we expected to include a discussion of the Fall in our papers, Professor Rogers . . .

PAN to student.

> **SARA (o.c.)**
> Absolutely, and at least one of Sartre's plays,
> either *No Exit* or *The Flies* . . .

> **ANOTHER STUDENT (o.c.)**
> I had a question about that, Professor . . .

PAN to student.

> **ANOTHER STUDENT**
> . . . where are they supposed to be in *No Exit*?

Sara laughs . . .

CUT:

[4] SIDE-ANGLE MWS Sara, classroom.

> **SARA**
> Well, they're in a room with no windows or
> mirrors. The door is locked, and they must
> endure each other's company without relief or
> privacy . . .

> **ANOTHER STUDENT**
> And Sartre defines this as Hell.

> **SARA**
> *(laughing)*
> It seems a plausible definition to me . . .

The students laugh, begin to leave. Our young man moves
swiftly from his seat to Sara . . .

DOLLY FORWARD to MS Sara, young man.

> **YOUNG MAN**
> I got hold of the book on Genet . . .

SARA
(enthusiastically)
Good! It's the finest analysis of being an
outsider I've ever read, and it applies as much
to race as it does to homosexuality . . .

Students pass through the frame as they exit . . .

YOUNG MAN
(excited)
He talks about exclusion in such clear terms,
he makes you see . . . really see and feel how a
society can impose group definitions that the
individual is powerless against . . .

Sara nods in agreement.

CUT:

[5] MCU young man, POV Sara.

SARA (o.c.)
(agreeing)
. . . it's a wonderful book, he touches every
feeling, every mental attitude connected with
exclusion . . .

The young man stares at her with deep respect.

CUT:

[6] MCU Sara, POV young man. She is a little embarrassed
by his intensity.

SARA
I'm glad you found it, there are books that can
make a difference in a life, I think that's one of
them . . .

YOUNG MAN (o.c.)

Next week is our last class . . .

SARA

That's right, you've been a good group.

She begins to gather her papers, looking away.

SARA

. . . I've enjoyed this class tremendously . . .

CUT:

[7] MCU young man, POV Sara. He leans forward . . .

YOUNG MAN

You're just terrific . . . always so alive and terrific . . .

SARA (o.c.)

Thank you . . . and I wish you all the best with your exams . . .

YOUNG MAN
(desperate)

. . . and your husband appreciates you . . .

CUT:

[8] MCU Sara, POV young man. She is shuffling papers, her back to the camera. She turns around.

SARA

. . . my husband . . .

YOUNG MAN (o.c.)

I bet he appreciates you tremendously, you're so full of life . . .

She nods her head, one step away from bursting into laughter . . .

SARA
(overly gracious)
Thank you, that's very sweet, I'll remember to tell him . . .

She turns to pick up her papers . . .

CUT:

[9] MLS young man, POV behind Sara. He stands there a moment while she continues to gather her papers.

YOUNG MAN
(almost violently)
I'll see you next semester in Critical Approaches . . .

He stalks out before she can answer him.

CUT:

[10] MCU Sara, looking after him with a bemused smile . . .

DISSOLVE:

2 INT. LOFT APARTMENT – EARLY EVENING

[11] HIGH-ANGLE MLS Sara, POV Victor. She comes in the door carrying a briefcase.

SARA
Victor . . .

                    VICTOR (o.c.)
I'm in here . . .

She comes slowly forward to the edge of the doorway . . .

                       SARA
                      (wary)
What's the insane moment for today . . .

VICTOR laughs.

                                        CUT:

[12] LOW-ANGLE MLS Victor, POV Sara. He is standing
on a ladder in the middle of the floor painting the upper
half of a huge canvas. He is surrounded by paints, canvases,
stretchers. Finished paintings and sketches hang on the
walls. Drawings clutter a huge drafting table. He is a
handsome man in his midforties with Sara's same Creole
looks. He smiles at her with boyish glee.

                      VICTOR
Would you go look in the refrigerator . . .

                       SARA
                      (wary)
All right . . .

We hear her go toward the kitchen, open the
refrigerator . . .

                       SARA
                      (wary)
Now what . . .

                      VICTOR
. . . just bring the whole tray . . .

She crosses into frame, back to camera, carrying something.
She stops at the bottom of the ladder.

> VICTOR
>
> Come on, bring it up . . .

> SARA
> *(back to camera)*
> You mean you want me to climb up . . .

> VICTOR
> *(excited)*
> This is a ceremony . . .

> SARA
> *(starting up)*
> Can't we have it on land . . .

CUT:

[13] HIGH-ANGLE MS Sara, POV over Victor's shoulder.
She climbs cautiously up the ladder carrying a tray on which
there is a bottle of champagne and two champagne glasses.
It's a wobbly climb.

> SARA
>
> What are we celebrating . . .

She almost falls backward. He reaches out to steady her . . .

> SARA
>
> Victor, I'm gonna land on my . . .

> VICTOR
>
> Ass . . . say it . . . give me the tray, 'ass' is the
> perfect word, that's exactly what you'd land
> on . . .

He takes the tray. Sara is relieved—

> **SARA**
> What are we celebrating?

He leans forward, kisses her.

> **VICTOR**
> Ten years of living with me, and she still can't
> say the word 'ass' . . .

Sara's face softens.

CUT:

[14] MS Victor, POV behind Sara. He is opening the
champagne, grows suddenly genuinely excited like a little
boy . . .

> **VICTOR**
> They're buying *Landscapes in Blue,* Sara, for
> their permanent collection . . .

> **SARA**
> *(back to camera)*
> The museum . . . oh, Victor . . .

He is beside himself, pops the cork violently, splattering
Sara.

> **VICTOR**
> I'm a genuine success . . .

He pours champagne here, there, everywhere . . .

> **VICTOR**
> . . . your husband is a genuine Negro
> success . . .

He comes down a step to hand her a glass of champagne. The ladder teeters precariously. They stand stock-still to steady it. Victor grins silently . . .

DISSOLVE:

3 INT. BEDROOM OF LOFT APARTMENT – LATE AT NIGHT

[15] MWS Sara in her nightgown, sitting cross-legged on the bed correcting term papers. The bed is strewn with papers. At the same time she is talking with Victor, who is in his studio.

> **VICTOR (o.c.)**
> Two more weeks . . .

> **SARA**
> *(nodding, reading)*
> Huh-uh . . .

> **VICTOR (o.c.)**
> What if we looked for a summer house . . .

> **SARA**
> Where?

> **VICTOR (o.c.)**
> You remember that place upstate with all the Puerto Rican ladies living in old Victorian houses . . .

He comes into frame.

> **VICTOR**
> *(back to camera)*
> I dream about that place . . .

                        SARA
                    (looking up)
You would, it's like a painting . . .

                       VICTOR
                   (back to camera)
. . . maybe rent a house for a month . . .

                        SARA
I need to be near a library.

                       VICTOR
                   (back to camera)
They've got libraries . . . those ladies read all
the time . . .

She smiles, shakes her head . . .

                                        CUT:

[16] MWS Victor, POV Sara. He is standing near the
doorway wearing a painter's cap, looking boyish and funny.

                       VICTOR
   I think I'll pass myself off as a house painter,
   go from door to door, offering my services . . .

He switches into rapid Spanish, acts out the whole scene,
laughing outrageously, dancing to some internal Latin beat
that carries him out of the room . . .

                                        CUT:

[17] LS Victor as he dances forward into his studio, picks up
a paintbrush, begins to make bold, flamboyant strokes on a
piece of sketch paper hung against the wall.

HOLD . . .

CUT:

[18] LS Sara, correcting papers with aggravated concentration.

HOLD . . .

FADE-OUT:

4 INT. SARA'S OFFICE AT THE COLLEGE – LATE AFTERNOON

[19] MWS Sara, a student. It's a medieval-looking room: high ceilings, stained-glass windows. Sara is reviewing the exam paper of a young black woman.

> **SARA**
> But on what basis did you come to this conclusion?

> **YOUNG WOMAN**
> All the data seemed to point in that direction . . .

> **SARA**
> But that's the trap . . . it's a purely speculative conclusion . . . *argumentum ad hominem* they call it. Any logician would stand you on your head . . .

The young woman laughs.

> **YOUNG WOMAN**
> Does that mean I fail?

> **SARA**
> Logically?

They both laugh.

> **SARA**
>
> No, your term paper takes you out of
> danger . . .

> **YOUNG WOMAN**
> *(relieved)*
> I like philosophy, but I don't like logic . . .

> **SARA**
>
> A lot of students don't; unfortunately it's one of
> the required courses . . .

> **YOUNG WOMAN**
>
> Are you teaching Critical Approaches?

> **SARA**
> *(nodding yes)*
> . . . and an advanced course in logical
> positivism, which I suggest you avoid.

They both laugh. The young woman gets up, shaking Sara's
hand.

> **YOUNG WOMAN**
>
> I still enjoyed the course. It's mostly you, I
> guess . . .

> CUT:

[20] MCU young woman, POV Sara.

> **YOUNG WOMAN**
> *(shyly)*
> . . . you're so bright, and lively, a real
> inspiration . . .

CUT:

[21] MCU Sara, POV young woman.

> **SARA**
> *(nodding too much)*
> Thank you . . .

> **YOUNG WOMAN (o.c.)**
> And lucky . . . with a husband and all . . .

> **SARA**
> *(surprised again)*
> . . . a husband . . . what . . .

She is about to ask her something but the young woman leaves quickly . . .

CUT:

[22] MWS Sara, looking after her.

> **SARA**
> What's this thing they've got about my having
> a husband . . .

She starts to record grades when a young black man enters the room whistling, wearing a monocle. He is dressed with the slight flair of a would-be movie director. He tips his monocle at her.

> **YOUNG MAN**
> Got you in close-up, Professor . . .

CUT:

[23] MCU young man, POV Sara. He is looking through his monocle . . .

YOUNG MAN
You look just like Pearl McCormack in *Scar of Shame,* Philadelphia Colored Players, 1927 . . .

CUT:

[24] MCU Sara, POV young man. She is laughing.

SARA
I've always wanted to know why, as a film major, you take so many of my classes . . .

YOUNG MAN (o.c.)
You could be a movie star, Professor . . .

CUT:

[25] MS young man, POV Sara. He is looking through the monocle walking backward into LS.

YOUNG MAN
. . . this would be a great long shot from here . . .

He peeks out at her.

YOUNG MAN
Any chance you would act in my senior project, Professor . . .

Sara bursts out laughing, he slips back behind the monocle . . .

CUT:

[26] MLS Sara, POV through monocle. She has the slight medieval air of a Negro nun in a cloister . . .

HOLD . . .

CUT:

5 EXT. STREET

[27] LOW-ANGLE LS, Victor's car in background. He gets out of the car, on a block with old, somewhat dilapidated Victorian houses that still have a trace of their former elegance. Puerto Rican women lean out the windows and talk to each other; several women are clustered together on front porches. He comes toward the camera . . .

CUT:

[28] TRACKING SHOT, Victor walking, watching, listening. Women walk by. The scene has a colorful, dancelike quality. Victor turns around often as someone interesting passes by . . .

CUT:

[29] TRACKING SHOT, POV Victor, past the women on the front porches . . .

CUT:

[30] MWS Victor, leaning against a tree, sketching . . .

CUT:

[31] MONTAGE: scenes as if they were paintings composed in Victor's head.

CUT:

[32] HIGH-ANGLE WS village, like one final painting with its smokestacks, Victorian houses, abandoned railroad

station. A strange, displaced feeling of cultures meeting and superimposing themselves on each other . . .

CUT:

6 EXT. ANOTHER STREET IN THE VILLAGE – LATE AFTERNOON [marked omit by Collins in the shooting script]

[33] MWS real estate office. Through the window we see Victor sitting with a broker discussing houses.

HOLD . . .

CUT:

7 INT. SARA AND VICTOR'S LOFT – LATE AFTERNOON

[34] Profile MCU Sara in foreground, entrance door in background. She is talking on the phone.

> **SARA**
> . . . I'm sure he wouldn't mind some kind of celebration, just the three of us . . . I don't think that's a good idea . . .

We hear the door click. Sara looks toward it. Victor comes in.

> **SARA**
> . . . he hates parties, Momma . . .

She waves to him.

> **SARA**
> No, it's finished . . . I turned in my grades today . . .

She follows Victor with her eyes.

PAN to LS Victor, POV Sara, as he goes into his studio, tears sketches out of the pad he is carrying, begins to hang them on the wall.

> **SARA (o.c.)**
> We could come on Friday, probably, I'll
> ask . . .

CUT:

[35] MS Victor, staring intently at one particular sketch, his face quite animated. Sara comes into frame in the background.

> **SARA**
> Momma wants to celebrate with us . . .

Victor doesn't answer . . .

CUT:

[36] MS Sara, staring at the sketches . . .

> **SARA**
> You did these today . . . in Riverview?

> **VICTOR (o.c.)**
> Yes.

> **SARA**
> Did you look at any houses?

> **VICTOR (o.c.)**
> Two. You want to drive up on Sunday?

She nods her head yes . . .

SARA
What's the matter . . .

CUT:

[37] MWS Victor, POV Sara. He turns around, shaking his
head . . .

VICTOR
I feel a little light-headed, like I've
been walking around in a dream . . . it's
unbelievable that place, like a brand-new
universe to paint . . . come here . . .

She enters frame, paces with him as he looks at sketches,
tears some others from his pad.

PAN to follow them . . .

VICTOR
I could do a whole series, shift direction . . .
break new ground, today was like a release . . .

He stops, hangs up one more sketch . . .

VICTOR
Here's what one of the houses looked like . . .

CUT:

[38] MCU sketch of house.

VICTOR (o.c.)
It's in the woods, behind the village, about a
fifteen-minute walk . . .

SARA (o.c.)
It's pretty. Any libraries around . . .

VICTOR (o.c.)
There's a sort of small lending library in the
village, but the odds are pretty good that they
don't carry Kant and Hegel . . .

He chuckles.

CUT:

[39] MCU Victor.

VICTOR
(dismissing the subject)
Drive down to New York once or twice a
week . . .

He becomes immersed in looking at one sketch.

CUT:

[40] MCU Sara. She is angry, turns and exits frame . . .

CUT:

[41] MLS Sara. She crosses the studio, disappears into the
bedroom . . .

CUT:

8 INT. BEDROOM OF LOFT APARTMENT – EARLY
EVENING

[42] MLS Sara, changing her clothes . . .

VICTOR (o.c., yelling in)
You want to eat out . . .

> ### SARA
> *(yelling back)*
> We could . . . I'll need to save my strength for
> all that driving back and forth . . .
> *(mimicking him)*
> 'Drive down to New York once or twice a
> week . . .'
> *(yelling louder)*
> . . . if I did something artistic, like write
> or act . . . would that get me a little more
> consideration?

CUT:

[43] MS Victor, standing in the doorway . . .

> ### VICTOR
> *(grinning)*
> . . . if you were any good . . .

CUT:

[44] MLS Sara, POV Victor.

> ### SARA
> *(upset)*
> Nothing I do leads to ecstasy . . .

Victor enters the frame, holds out his arms.

> ### SARA
> *(ignoring the innuendo)*
> You stay in a trance, you ever notice that, a
> kind of ecstatic private trance, it's like living
> with some musician who sits around all day
> blowing his horn . . .

Victor goes and sits on the bed.

> **VICTOR**
> What's the matter, Hegel and the boys let you
> down . . .

DOLLY SLIGHTLY FORWARD toward Sara but keeping them both in frame . . .

> **SARA**
> I could be another Dorothy Dandridge . . .

CUT:

Sara (Seret Scott) and Victor (Bill Gunn) in *Losing Ground*. *Courtesy of Nina Collins and Milestone Films.*

[45] MCU Victor, a look of utter surprise on his face . . .

> **SARA (o.c.)**
> Come to grips with a certain fullness . . .

He can't even imagine what to say . . .

CUT:

[46] MCU Sara.

> **SARA**
> I am so reasonable . . .

She takes off her glasses . . .

CUT:

[47] MLS Sara, Victor. Neither has moved. Sara begins to pace. Slowly. Thoughtfully.

> **VICTOR**
> You think this might have something to do
> with your mother . . .

> **SARA**
> My mother . . .

> **VICTOR**
> Well, she's an actress . . .

> **SARA**
> That was just an example . . .

> **VICTOR**
> I see . . .

They are silent awhile . . .

> **VICTOR**
> You still want to go out for dinner . . . put the
> mulatto crisis on hold . . .

That cracks him up.

> **VICTOR**
> *(laughing)*
> I was thinking about your mother . . . that bit
> she does on the light-skinned Negro . . .

> **SARA**
> What's all this ethnic humor got to do with
> anything . . .

> **VICTOR**
> *(loudly)*
> I am fucking starving, I've had two espressos
> the whole day . . .

They stare at each other.

HOLD . . .

> FADE-OUT:

9 EXT. UNIVERSITY LIBRARY – LATE MORNING

[48] MLS Sara, walking across campus, carrying her
briefcase.

PAN with her as she goes up the library steps, disappears
inside.

> DISSOLVE:

10 INT. LIBRARY CATALOG ROOM – LATE
MORNING

[49] MLS Sara. She pulls out a catalog drawer, begins going
through, taking notes.

PAN to a stranger watching her. He is an exceptionally tall,
good-looking black man in his early forties, unusually dressed

with a black top hat, eccentric but elegant clothes. Sara passes across the frame on her way to the librarian's desk.

PAN with her to desk . . .

DISSOLVE:

11 INT. READING ROOM OF LIBRARY – EARLY AFTERNOON

[50] Profile MCU Sara. She is reading with such intensity that the words seem to spill forth . . .

> **SARA (v.o., reading)**
> '. . . it does not come then exactly from
> without. Each of us belongs as much to society
> as to himself. Yet our consciousness, delving
> downward, reveals to us, the deeper we go,
> an ever more original personality, capable
> of private ecstatic experience that is often
> undefinable in words. To call it ecstasy forces
> us to borrow from the theologians, who have
> used the word in terms of man's immediate
> connectedness and/or apprehension of the
> Divine; ecstasy in this sense . . .'

> **MAN'S VOICE (o.c.)**
> What on earth are you reading . . .

The man's voice seems to reach Sara as if through a fog. She is pulled out of her reading as if by a shock . . .

CUT:

[51] MS man, POV Sara. He is the same stranger who was watching her in the catalog room.

> **MAN**
> *(amazed)*
> I have rarely seen anyone read with such
> intense concentration . . .

                                                    CUT:

[52] MS Sara, POV man. She is still somewhat disoriented.

> **MAN (o.c.)**
> Why are you reading with such
> concentration . . .

Sara smiles.

> **SARA**
> I'm doing research for a paper on ecstatic
> experience . . .

> **MAN (o.c.)**
> From a theological perspective?

> **SARA**
> *(surprised)*
> No . . . though I'm using religious ecstasy as a
> point of departure . . .

> **MAN (o.c.)**
> Whose? Saint Thomas Aquinas with his
> rational repression of the experience . . .

                                                    CUT:

[53] MS man, POV Sara.

> **MAN**
> Saint Teresa? There's a splendid woman
> whose whole life was defined by ecstatic

experience . . . or we can go back a little
further . . . to the deviant Gnostics, who are
really pre-Christian in their thinking . . .
man in more intuitive harmony with the
divine, et cetera, et cetera, a definite psychic
orientation . . .

[54] MS Sara, POV man, staring at him . . .

MAN (o.c.)
What's the thesis of your paper?

SARA
(drawn in)
. . . that the religious boundaries around
ecstasy are too narrow, that if, as the Christians
define it, ecstasy is an immediate apprehension
of the divine, then the divine is energy . . .
amorphous energy . . . artists, for example,
have frequent ecstatic experiences . . .

The man begins to applaud.

CUT:

[55] MS man, POV Sara, applauding . . .

MAN
A lucid approach, but definitely pre-Christian.
Christianity has had a devastating effect on
man as an intuitive creature . . .

He is amused . . .

SARA (o.c.)
Who are you . . .

CUT:

[56] SIDE-ANGLE MWS Sara, the man.

> **MAN**
> In which life . . .

Sara looks at him strangely.

CUT:

[57] MCU man, POV Sara.

> **MAN**
> *(bluntly)*
> In this life I'm an out-of-work actor who once
> studied for the ministry, in other lives . . .

CUT:

[58] SIDE-ANGLE MWS Sara, the man.

> **MAN**
> . . . so the psychics tell me, I've been an Italian
> count, an English lord, even a Confederate
> soldier. Apparently this is my first incarnation
> as a Negro . . .

That makes him laugh.

CUT:

[59] MCU man, POV Sara.

> **MAN**
> *(laughing)*
> I must have built up a lot of karmic debt . . .

He smiles at her . . .

CUT:

[60] EXTREME SIDE-ANGLE LS Sara, the man, still talking . . .

HOLD . . .

CUT:

12 EXT. PHONE BOOTH ON CAMPUS – ALMOST EVENING

[61] LS Sara, rushing toward the phone booth, coming into MS as she does. She dials quickly.

> **SARA**
> Victor . . . I'm late, I got talking to this
> wonderful man, and I lost track of time . . .
> I could meet you at Momma's, that would
> probably be easier, all right . . .

She hangs up, exits frame . . .

CUT:

13 INT. DINING ROOM OF SARA'S MOTHER'S APARTMENT – EVENING

[62] MS Sara's mother. LEILA is a good-looking woman, still quite young-looking for her age, and with definite dramatic flair. Her way of speaking is somewhat uncanny, disconnected, but full of humor. She holds up her glass.

LEILA

To my son–in–law . . . that's what happens
when you have children, they beget husbands
and paintings and soon we're talking about
galleries and museums and the whole world
becomes larger than life . . .

DOLLY BACK and PAN to MWS Sara and Victor, sitting
opposite each other. They sip their champagne.

LEILA

I always knew you would try hard not to be a
failure . . .

Victor starts to laugh . . .

VICTOR
(amused)
You've been concerned about that . . .

DOLLY BACK to include Leila.

LEILA
(abstractedly)
I've thought about it . . . not with any blame, I
wouldn't blame you for being a failure . . . I'm
not white . . . and racial excuses are the best,
I could always tell my friends that you were
talented but unseen . . .

VICTOR
(laughing)
That would be very generous of you . . .

SARA
How's the play going, Momma . . .

LEILA

It's one of those family dramas. I play someone's mother, someone else plays my husband . . . I stand before God as the family's guiding light, a beacon of strength and humility . . . It is a thoroughly colored play . . . we dance, we sing, there is even a character who runs track . . .

Victor is almost doubled over with laughter.

VICTOR

What do you dream of doing, Leila . . .

LEILA

I'm not a snob, you know . . . I'm not longing to do *Macbeth* . . . but I'd love to play a real sixty-year-old Negro lady who thinks more about men than God . . .

She looks at Sara . . .

LEILA

That's what you should do, stop writing all those dissertations and write a play about your mother . . .

DOLLY FORWARD to MCU Sara.

SARA
(laughing)
It would be too eccentric, Momma, no one would believe it was about a real person . . .

She smiles abstractedly at her mother . . .

> **LEILA**
> You've got that vague look you get when
> you're tired . . .

> **SARA**
> *(nodding)*
> I have two papers to finish, and I'm not
> through the research on either one . . .

> **LEILA (o.c.)**
> Still building your castles . . .

Sara laughs . . .

DOLLY BACK to include Sara and Victor, Leila soft in the
background.

> **SARA**
> *(to Victor)*
> When I was little and wouldn't play with
> anyone, Momma used to say . . . 'She's busy
> building castles reaching up, up, up to some
> quiet private sky . . .'

She looks at her mother . . .

DOLLY BACK, bringing all three of them gently in
focus . . .

HOLD . . .

CUT:

14 INT. CAR – LATE MORNING

[63] MLS behind Victor and Sara. Victor is driving. Sara is
leaned way back, fast asleep. Victor touches her.

>   **VICTOR**
> We're almost there . . .

She lifts her head slowly . . .

>   **VICTOR**
> Look at the view from here . . .

PAN to view.

>   **SARA (o.c.)**
> I was dreaming we were moving into this
> castle that was at the top of a huge mountain, it
> was so high up it was smothered in fog . . .

PAN back behind them.

>   **VICTOR**
> That's a dream straight out of last night's
> dinner . . .

He begins to turn a corner . . .

                                              CUT:

15 EXT. DESCENT INTO VILLAGE – LATE MORNING

[64] LS car going downhill and disappearing into the village . . .

16 EXT. DRIVEWAY OF COUNTRY HOUSE – EARLY AFTERNOON

[65] LS behind car. It goes up the driveway and stops. Sara, Victor, and a real estate agent get out. The real estate agent is talking continuously; we can hear only snatches of what she's saying . . .

REAL ESTATE AGENT

. . . it's furnished . . . it belongs to a writer who's
gone to Australia for the summer . . . I'm sorry,
but he didn't do much straightening up . . .

They disappear inside . . .

CUT:

17 INT. DOWNSTAIRS OF COUNTRY HOUSE – EARLY AFTERNOON

[66] LS Sara, back to camera. She is looking out the
window. We are in a large, spacious room furnished in
an old-fashioned country style with solid antique pieces,
paintings, odds and ends. The windows are bare and look
out on the woods.

VICTOR (o.c.)

Sara . . .

SARA

I'm down here . . .

VICTOR (o.c.)

Come upstairs, there's an unbelievable studio,
it's like a dream . . .

She crosses the room, disappears around the corner . . .

CUT:

18 INT. UPSTAIRS OF COUNTRY HOUSE – EARLY AFTERNOON

[67] MS Victor. He is standing at a huge window looking
out on quite lovely woods. Light also comes down from a
skylight over his head. We hear Sara enter the room.

VICTOR
(hearing her)

It's pastoral . . .

SARA
(coming into frame)

What do you mean . . .

DOLLY BACK to LS both of them. The full scope of the room with its extraordinary light is now visible. Victor turns around.

VICTOR

It's got nothing to do with concrete and granite . . . they're abstractions, this is soft, specific . . . things belong one place and nowhere else . . .

He looks toward the window.

VICTOR

There are perfect still-lifes out there . . . I wouldn't change a thing . . .

Sara comes forward, crosses to the window.

SARA

It's a nice house, it would be the first time we ever lived in a house . . .

VICTOR
(suddenly)

You look terrific there . . . all healthy and correct . . . where's the damn real estate agent, tell her we'll take the place, I'll paint you by that window, that'll be my first project . . .

He goes off looking for her, exiting frame.

HOLD on Sara . . .

> **VICTOR (o.c., yelling from afar)**
> Sara! Come down here this minute . . . you
> won't believe this . . .

He is laughing. Sara exits frame . . .

HOLD . . .

CUT:

18A INT. BARBERSHOP ROOM – LATE MORNING
[marked omit by Collins in shooting script]

[67A] MWS Sara, POV Victor. She is coming through a door.
As she looks around and sees Victor, she begins to laugh . . .

> **VICTOR (o.c.)**
> . . . one's own private barber shop . . .
> *(laughing)*
> . . . that's not money, that's wealth, with a
> capital *W* . . .

Sara, laughing, goes and sits in the other chair. They sit
looking at each other through the mirrors . . .

HOLD . . .

FADE-OUT:

19 INT. PAINTER'S STUDIO – LATE AFTERNOON

[68] LS Victor, CARLOS. We are in a small atelier that is
cluttered and somewhat dark. Most of the light comes from
one deep window at the end of the room. Carlos is around

Victor's age. He has the bearded unkempt look one associates
with painters and a kind of brusque, moody manner that goes
with it. The two men are drinking wine, talking. It will be
clear from the conversation that they have known each other
a long time and that all they ever talk about is painting.

> **VICTOR**
> It is a purist's approach, you deny or repress—
> repress might be closer to the truth, any
> narrative impulse.

> **CARLOS**
> I don't deny it, it never occurs to me . . .

> **VICTOR**
> Well, it's starting to occur to me . . .

> **CARLOS**
> *(amused)*
> Why . . . you feel like telling stories . . .

DOLLY IMPERCEPTIBLY FORWARD to MLS.

> **VICTOR**
> You're amazing, you know . . . you really
> just paint . . . like a child, no literary guile
> anywhere . . .

He looks at his friend.

> **VICTOR**
> I think I envy that a little, even at its most
> abstract I still have landscape references . . .

> **CARLOS**
> *(laughing)*
> So you admit that . . .

VICTOR
(nodding)
Theatrical imagery in the underpainting . . .
that's where I try and hide it . . .

DOLLY IMPERCEPTIBLY FORWARD to MCU Carlos.

CARLOS
There's nothing wrong with telling
stories . . . Guston went back to it in the
end, Hartigan . . . Johns does it brilliantly
sometimes . . . lots of painters reach a dead end
with form . . .

He smiles at his friend.

CUT:

[69] MCU Victor, POV Carlos.

VICTOR
Wait till you see this place . . . it'll have you
doing still-lifes . . .

Carlos laughs . . .

CARLOS (o.c.)
We didn't even drink to the acquisition . . . I love that
painting, man . . .

CUT:

[70] LS both men. Carlos is holding up the bottle, laughing.
He pours wine in both their glasses. The light in the room
seems to fade . . .

CUT:

20 INT. SARA AND VICTOR'S LOFT – EVENING

[71] LS Sara in background, Victor in foreground. They are packing. Sara is taking clothes out of a closet and folding them in piles. Victor is packing his paints in a box. They are talking at the same time . . .

> VICTOR
>
> I realized today that in many ways I've made Carlos my mentor . . .

> SARA
>
> You defer to him . . .

> VICTOR
>
> No, it's not exactly that, it's that his work is really pure, and I've tried to emulate that purity, but it's not me . . .

> SARA
> *(stopping)*
> What is this, you sell a painting you love, and now you deny its validity . . .

He thinks about that . . .

> VICTOR
>
> No . . . I just never recognized how much influence he's had on me, and that it's over . . .

A pile of clothes and boxes come tumbling down . . .

> SARA
>
> Oh Lord . . .

Victor rushes over to help her . . .

CUT:

[72] MS Sara, Victor, down on the floor, sorting out all the fallen things . . .

> **SARA**
>
> What's over . . .

> **VICTOR**
>
> You have this amazing knack for holding on to the thread of a conversation . . .

> **SARA**
> *(ignoring that)*
>
> What's over . . .

> **VICTOR**
>
> My efforts at purity . . .

They look at each other.

HOLD . . .

CUT:

21 EXT. VILLAGE STREET – EARLY AFTERNOON

[73] LS street, POV inside car over Victor's shoulder. Coming down the hill into town, then down along the main street. It's a bright day, and the street is filled with people. Music is blaring from different shops and apartments. The car comes to a stop.

CUT:

[74] MLS Victor. He gets out of the car, crosses to an art supply store, and goes inside.

DOLLY FORWARD to MLS storefront, next to art supply store. A salsa band is playing/rehearsing, people are dancing.

HOLD . . .

Victor crosses into frame carrying supplies, stops to watch
what's going on . . .

CUT:

22 INT. STOREFRONT – EARLY AFTERNOON

[75] LS band in background, people dancing in foreground,
POV Victor. There is one young woman whose dancing
stands out; there is fast, angry humor in the way she moves.
She teases the other dancers, sets off a playful exchange
of insults and compliments, all in Spanish. Then she sees
Victor. Assuming he's Spanish, she yells something to
him . . .

CUT:

[76] MLS Victor, POV young woman. He tries to answer in
Spanish, falters . . .

> **VICTOR**
> *(faltering)*
> Oh shit . . . this is like losing an erection in
> midstream . . .

He tries for a certain macho Latin stance, tilts his beret at a
different angle . . .

> **VICTOR**
> *(to himself)*
> A cigarette would help . . .

He exits frame, dancing like the boldest of Latin lovers . . .

CUT:

[77] REVERSE ANGLE. He moves forward, takes her hand. They start to dance . . .

HOLD . . .

                                              CUT:

23 EXT. VILLAGE LÍBRARY – EARLY AFTERNOON

[78] LS Sara, from behind. She goes up the steps of the local library and disappears inside . . .

                                              CUT:

24 INT. VILLAGE LIBRARY – EARLY AFTERNOON

[79] SIDE-ANGLE MS LIBRARIAN. Sara comes into frame, crosses to the librarian's desk, who looks up . . .

> **SARA**
> Excuse me . . . I'm spending the summer here, and I'd like to be able to order some books through the library loan system . . .

> **LIBRARIAN**
> Novels . . .

> **SARA**
> No, research books . . .

> **LIBRARIAN**
> On what subjects . . .

> **SARA**
> Ecstatic experience . . .

> LIBRARIAN
> *(flustered)*

I see . . .

DOLLY BACK to WS.

> LIBRARIAN
> *(handing Sara a card)*
> Just fill this out . . .

Sara begins to fill it out . . .

CUT:

25 INT. UPSTAIRS STUDIO OF COUNTRY HOUSE – LATE AFTERNOON

[80] MLS Sara in background, Victor at drafting table in foreground. Sara is at the window modeling for him while he sketches. They are talking . . .

> VICTOR
> . . . too representational . . .

> SARA
> What do you mean . . .

> VICTOR
> I've shied away from it as too easy . . .

> SARA
> You mean to paint people or things is a cop-out . . .

He laughs.

VICTOR

I've never put it that way, I just felt abstract
work was purer . . . in a painterly sense . . .
it stuck to simple truths . . . color, form,
space . . .

SARA
(deliberately obtuse)
And people and things were dishonest . . .

Victor gets up and moves across the room to a different angle.

TRACK across behind him . . .

VICTOR

What is this honesty, cop-out business . . .
you nailing me to the cross as a coward and a
cheat . . .

She laughs.

SARA

It hurts to laugh when you can't move . . .

VICTOR

The light is incredible from here . . .

He moves in a little closer.

TRACK in behind him . . .

VICTOR
(almost to himself)
You think about light differently when dealing
with people . . .

SARA

What . . .

VICTOR

You have a good face . . .

SARA

That's not what you said . . .

VICTOR

You do that all the time, say 'what . . .' and
you've heard every word . . .

SARA
(ignoring that)

What about my face . . .

Victor chuckles, moves in just slightly closer.

TRACK in behind him.

VICTOR

Cold, analytical . . .

SARA

Can I stand still and hit you at the same
time . . .

VICTOR

How about noble . . . one of those words
your mother hates . . . 'she had a distinct
colored face, broadly chiseled but with noble
features . . .'

SARA

Ain't that a blip . . .

Victor bursts out laughing.

VICTOR

Where did that come from . . .

SARA
(laughing)
I don't know . . . I've always wanted to say that
at a faculty meeting, all of a sudden turn to
somebody pompous like Warren or Levine and
say, 'Aint that a blip . . .'

VICTOR
(laughing)
That is totally unlike you . . .

He moves in closer to her.

TRACK in behind him to MCU Sara, POV over his
shoulder. She turns to look out the window.

VICTOR
Are you pretty, or is it just the light . . .

She turns to look at him.

SARA
You want a murder the first week in this
house . . .

CUT:

[81] MCU Victor, POV over Sara's shoulder. He is grinning
in the most boyish, prankish manner . . .

CUT:

[82] MCU Sara, watching him warily . . .

DISSOLVE:

26 INT. BEDROOM OF COUNTRY HOUSE – LATE
AT NIGHT

[83] LOW SIDE-ANGLE MS Sara, Victor. They are in bed. Sara is curled up, resting against his side, the feeling between them of spent lovemaking.

> **VICTOR**
> *(after a while)*
> There's a place in the Bible where they talk about woman fashioned from the rib of man . . .

Sara looks up at him.

> **VICTOR**
> That's how you sleep . . .
> *(pointing)*
> . . . right against my rib cage . . .

> **SARA**
> And that makes you feel exceptionally creative, like you fashioned me . . .

> **VICTOR**
> I notice it . . .

He laughs, she curls back up against him, he touches her hair . . .

HOLD . . .

CUT:

27 EXT. STREET IN VILLAGE – EARLY AFTERNOON

[84] SIDE-ANGLE WS Victor, walking along. He passes several stores, including the art supply store, then the storefront where the salsa band was playing. It's deserted. He

keeps walking. A woman's voice yells out loudly in Spanish. He looks up . . .

CUT:

[85] LOW-ANGLE MWS young woman, POV Victor. She is leaning out an apartment window that is above a store.

> **VICTOR (o.c., yelling across)**
> I was looking for you. I wanted to know if I could paint you . . .

> **YOUNG WOMAN**
> You want to paint me . . .

She lapses into Spanish, giggling, calls to her mother. An older woman leans her head out the window . . .

CUT:

[86] MS Victor, POV women.

> **VICTOR**
> *(to himself)*
> Oh Lord, next it'll be the father . . .
> *(yelling across)*
> What's your name?

CUT:

[87] MS two women, POV Victor.

> **YOUNG WOMAN**
> Celia . . . *me llamo Celia* . . . why do you want to paint me?

CUT:

[88] MS Victor, POV Celia.

> **VICTOR**
> *(to himself)*
> This is the closest I ever felt to a dirty old man . . .
> *(yelling)*
> I'm from New York, I've taken a studio up here for the summer to do some paintings about the village . . .

Off-camera we hear her talking to her mother in Spanish. Victor starts mumbling to himself in broken imitative Spanish.

HOLD . . .

CUT:

28 EXT. REAR OF SUMMER HOUSE – AFTERNOON

[89] LS Victor, Celia, coming up the path to the house. She is dressed in a wild, wonderful way. They are talking, but we can't hear them well. When they get to the back door, he disappears inside the house.

HOLD on Celia looking around . . . as Victor comes out the door carrying his paraphernalia . . .

CUT:

[90] MCU Celia, POV over Victor's shoulder. This is the first time we've seen her up close. She has a wonderful face—young, sassy, innocent, wild . . .

VICTOR (o.c.)

There's a place over there in the woods where
I'd like to work . . .

He moves into frame . . .

CUT:

29 EXT. THE WOODS – LATE AFTERNOON

[91] EXTREME LS Victor, Celia. He is painting her. She
is posed in some careful balance to the woods surrounding
her. The shot itself has the feel and look of a painting . . .

CUT:

[92] LS Celia in background, canvas on easel in foreground,
Victor on periphery of shot . . .

We see the painting of her being rapidly brushed in.

HOLD . . .

CUT:

[93] MCU Celia, POV Victor. She is obedient, still, her eyes
fixed on him . . .

HOLD . . .

CUT:

[94] LS Celia, POV behind Victor. He puts his brush down.

VICTOR
(back to camera)

Let's take a break . . .

He gets up, they start toward each other.

TRACK behind Victor as he walks toward her. She almost dances toward him, shaking out her muscles, loosening the stiffness from standing still so long . . .

> **VICTOR**
> *(back to camera)*
> It's hard work . . .

> **CELIA**
> You said it, man . . . my limbs are like
> frozen, and the sun is going down too fast for
> comfort . . .

She stops, stretches, shakes herself out. He stops.

TRACKING STOPS.

> [marked omit by Collins in shooting script:]

> **CELIA**
> I feel like a butterfly . . .
> *(she looks behind her)*
> I sit there so still, man, somebody could trap
> me in their net . . .

She turns and smiles at him . . .

HOLD . . .

> CUT:

30 INT. UPSTAIRS STUDIO OF HOUSE – LATE AFTERNOON

[95] LS empty studio. The light is changing outside, and the room has a pleasant late-afternoon feeling. Off-camera we hear a car pull up, the door slam, someone come inside.

>   **SARA** (o.c.)
>   Victor . . .

There is no answer, then Sara's footsteps are heard on the stairs.

>   **SARA** (o.c.)
>   Victor . . .

She comes into frame carrying some books, looks around, then goes back downstairs, exiting frame. The phone rings. She answers it.

>   **SARA** (o.c.)
>   Hello . . . who . . . yes . . . how did you . . . I
>   see . . . you're kidding, I couldn't do that . . .
>   that's ridiculous, George, that's carrying it too
>   far . . .

>   CUT:

31 INT. LIVING ROOM OF HOUSE – LATE AFTERNOON

[96] LS Sara in foreground, Victor and Celia walking toward the house in background.

>   **SARA**
>   *(still talking)*
>   I'm not an actress . . .

She hears voices, looks around, sees Victor and a woman coming toward the house.

>   **SARA**
>   *(still talking)*
>   I couldn't do it . . . that's all the more reason to

use a professional, it's your thesis . . . using me
might be considered poor research . . .

She laughs. He obviously doesn't.

> **SARA**
> Well, I know that's a dry analogy.

Victor and Celia pass out of frame as the door opens . . .

> **VICTOR (o.c.)**
> Sara . . .

> **SARA**
> *(answering)*
> I'm in here . . .
> *(to George)*
> I have to say no, George, I'd be awful, and
> you'd be embarrassed and wouldn't know how
> to say it . . . all right . . .

She hangs up, turns around . . .

[97] MLS Victor, Celia, POV Sara, standing in the doorway,
grinning like twin Cheshire cats. Victor steps forward.

> **VICTOR**
> This is Celia Cruz . . . I mean Celia Ruiz . . .
> *(apologetically)*
> I was thinking about the singer . . . who's
> fabulous by the way . . .

> **CELIA**
> *(to Sara)*
> We've been in the woods, he's been painting
> me, man . . .

She walks toward Sara, exiting frame . . .

CUT:

[98] MS Sara, Celia back to camera, POV Victor. Celia goes forward to shake Sara's hand.

CELIA

Pleased to meet you . . . what's your name?

SARA

Sara . . . I'm pleased, too, to meet you . . .

VICTOR (o.c.)

What about some tea ᵧ . .

Celia turns, both women look at him . . .

CELIA

I don't drink tea . . . espresso . . . café mocha, Coca-Cola, 7 Up . . . no alcohol, I don't drink alcohol . . .

Silence . . . glances going here and there . . .

SARA
(finally)
What about iced coffee . . .

She starts toward the kitchen . . .

HOLD . . . on Celia . . .

DISSOLVE:

32 EXT. PATIO OF SUMMER HOUSE – LATE AFTERNOON

[99] MS Celia. She is chattering away . . .

PAN to MS Victor, chattering back . . .

PAN to MS Sara, smiling, nodding, making an occasional remark . . .

The whole scene is shot silent, making a complete circular pan of their faces . . .

                                                            CUT:

[100] WS three of them. They are sitting at a round table drinking and talking.

HOLD . . .

                                                            CUT:

33 INT. KITCHEN OF SUMMER HOUSE

[101] Profile MCU Sara. She is at the stove cooking.

                        SARA
            She's not Negro . . . she's Puerto Rican . . .

                    VICTOR (o.c.)
            Puerto Rican, Negro . . . what's that got to do
            with anything . . .

                        SARA
            I'm just telling you what she is . . .

Sara moves sideways to reach a cooking utensil . . .

                    VICTOR (o.c.)
            You got something against Puerto Ricans . . .

                        SARA
            I don't know any Puerto Ricans . . .

                VICTOR (o.c., factually)
            They're an island people . . . of Spanish,
            Indian, and African ancestry . . .

She turns to him.

> **SARA**
>
> What is this . . . Puerto Rican History
> Week . . .

She moves forward carrying a casserole.

DOLLY BACK behind Victor. He is setting the table.

> **VICTOR**
>
> I think they're more mellow than we . . . is it
> we Negroes or us Negroes . . .

Sara puts down the casserole.

> **SARA**
>
> Us . . . more mellow than us . . .

DOLLY SIDEWAYS to MWS both of them, as they sit
down . . .

> **VICTOR**
> *(factually)*
> Traditionally the relationship between Negroes
> and Puerto Ricans has been fraught with
> uneasiness . . .

> **SARA**
>
> Is that right . . .

> **VICTOR**
>
> Third World thinking has, of course,
> readjusted some of that, I suspect . . .

> **SARA**
> *(nodding)*
> I see . . .

He hands her the casserole. She begins to serve herself . . .

HOLD . . .

CUT:

34 INT. SMALL STUDY IN SUMMER HOUSE – LATE MORNING

[102] LS Sara at the desk, typing. The study has a quiet, cool feeling, reinforced by soft shadows. Like in the library, Sara is lost in her work.

DOLLY SLOWLY FORWARD as we begin to hear her on V.O.

> **SARA (v.o., writing)**
> . . . From the perspective of comparative psychiatry, Louis Mars's research on Haitian voodoo is instructive. He analyzes, from both a physiological and psychological standpoint, a subject who is 'possessed' by one of the gods. In this experience the subject is 'mounted' by the god in question . . . i.e., his behavior changes radically as he begins to assume the personality of the god in question. Similar experiences are described by those who have studied Greek and Roman Dionysian rites and African rites of passage, but the striking note for our purposes is that during the actual experience the 'possessed one' is unconscious. He falls into a trance. Afterward he scarcely remembers what happened to him. Yet a sensation of physical well-being, of mental alertness, sometimes clairvoyance, even of deep

private fulfillment generally accompanies the
return to consciousness. The ecstatic moment
is, so to speak, after the fact . . .

By now we are in MCU Sara. She looks up from her typing,
reflects a moment, then starts again . . .

HOLD . . .

CUT:

35 EXT. WOODS – LATE MORNING [marked omit by
Collins in shooting script]

[103] HIGH-ANGLE MLS Victor, POV tree, crossing the
woods toward the tree, carrying his sketch pad.

TILT DOWN as he begins to climb it.

TILT UP and PAN as he settles in one of the branches,
arranges his sketch pad on his lap, begins drawing.

PAN to woods, POV Victor: a precise composition, just like
a painting . . .

HOLD . . .

CUT:

36 EXT. SMALL STREET IN VILLAGE – LATE
AFTERNOON [marked omit by Collins in shooting script]

[104] LS Sara, walking along. The street is dark, somewhat
quiet; gypsy women sit in the doorways . . .

CUT:

[105] SIDE-ANGLE LS Sara. She walks past several
storefronts where gypsy women sit in the windows

playing with cards or lighting candles, advertising their skill as fortune tellers. She goes past several storefronts, turns around, and seems, arbitrarily, to choose one. She disappears inside . . .

CUT:

37 INT. GYPSY STOREFRONT – LATE AFTERNOON

[106] Profile MCU Sara.

> ### SARA
> When you read someone . . . for instance, now, looking at me . . . what happens inside you . . .

PAN to profile MCU gypsy woman.

> ### WOMAN
> I don't understand . . .

PAN back to Sara.

> ### SARA
> Can you see my future . . .

Pause.

> ### WOMAN (o.c.)
> I see that you're very intelligent, and secretive . . .

Sara looks frustrated . . .

> ### SARA
> Anyone could say that, my face tells you that . . .

PAN back to woman.

> **WOMAN**
> I don't understand . . .

> **SARA (o.c.)**
> I'd like to understand what it feels like to see
> something that hasn't yet happened . . .

> **WOMAN**
> *(smiling)*
> I see you . . . with a tall, dark man with a top
> hat, and they're taking your picture . . .

She snaps an imaginary camera . . .

PAN back to Sara. She is frustrated, looks disbelievingly at
the woman.

HOLD . . .

DISSOLVE:

38 EXT. VILLAGE CHURCH – LATE AFTERNOON

[107] MLS behind Sara. She is standing on the church steps,
hesitant . . .

CUT:

[108] SIDE-ANGLE MCU Sara.

> **SARA**
> *(to herself)*
> This is ridiculous . . . what am I looking
> for . . .

She turns away, exiting frame . . .

CUT:

39 INT. LIVING ROOM – LATE EVENING

[109] MLS Sara, Victor. They've built a fire. Victor is in the middle of the room, stretching a canvas and attaching it to the frame. Sara is reading, watching the fire.

> **SARA**
> *(after a while)*
> I'm not a gypsy or a priestess . . .

Victor looks up.

> **SARA**
> *(using her hands)*
> I want magic . . . real magic . . .

She laughs . . .

> CUT:

[110] LOW-ANGLE MS Sara, POV behind Victor.

> **SARA**
> All of a sudden, things start to happen . . .

She snaps her fingers, as if trying to invoke some undefined power in herself. She laughs . . .

HOLD . . .

> FADE-OUT:

FADE-IN:

40 INT. UPSTAIRS STUDIO – MID-AFTERNOON

[111] MWS a large unfinished painting on the wall. It is of Celia, in the woods.

HOLD . . . salsa music comes from a tinny-sounding radio.

PAN to MWS Celia, sitting cross-legged on the floor near the window, looking out . . .

PAN to MWS Victor, sketching her from across the room . . .

> **VICTOR**
> You getting tired?

She doesn't answer. He looks at her . . .

PAN back to MWS Celia . . .

> **VICTOR (o.c., louder)**
> You getting tired . . .

She doesn't move or turn her head.

> **CELIA**
> Not tired, man . . . paralyzed . . . I will never move again, you hear me . . .

Victor bursts out laughing; she turns, starts laughing, too . . .

> CUT:

41 EXT. GARDEN OF SUMMER HOUSE – MID-AFTERNOON

[112] HIGH-ANGLE MS Sara, kneeling on the ground, digging and planting. Her face is dirty, she has on a funny railroad cap, she works at terrific speed. All of a sudden the laughter and the music from the studio seem to drift down to her. She looks up, scratches her face, leaving more dirt on it . . .

HOLD . . .

CUT:

42 EXT. TERRACE OF UNIVERSITY BUILDING – AFTERNOON

[113] WS camera crew. The same "film buff" student, GEORGE, seen earlier, is talking to his cinematographer, holding up a storyboard. There are two or three other "techies" milling around . . .

> **GEORGE**
> Now they cross camera left, sit down on the wall, you pan and hold on their shadow . . .

> **CINEMATOGRAPHER**
> That's deep man, truly deep . . .

They chuckle proudly . . .

> **GEORGE**
> *(excited)*
> Then you dolly back to wide shot . . .
> *(nudging him)*
> . . . catch that subtle mise-en-scène . . .

The cinematographer laughs.

> **CINEMATOGRAPHER**
> I'm with you, I'm with you . . .

They both turn to follow the shot through, when Sara comes into frame on the periphery of the shot. George spots her immediately, breaks into a run . . .

> **GEORGE**
> *(shouting, running)*
> Professor Rogers . . .

CUT:

[114] SIDE-ANGLE MS Sara. George rushes into frame . . .

> **GEORGE**
> I don't believe it, oh man, did you get the
> script . . .

Sara nods . . .

> **GEORGE**
> *(proudly)*
> It's a takeoff on the theme of the tragic
> mulatto . . .

Sara nods with complete incomprehension . . .

> **GEORGE**
> *(beside himself)*
> Oh man, you came . . . you actually came . . .
> this is going to be magical!

He practically dances with excitement.

CUT:

[115] MS George, POV behind Sara, smiling at her . . .

> **GEORGE**
> I'll bring you a chair . . . what about some
> coffee . . . I just have to finish with my
> cameraman . . .

He runs off. She turns around, facing the camera, suddenly
sees something . . .

CUT:

[116] LS man, POV Sara. A tall man, back to camera, wearing a top hat, moves down a long shadowy corridor. When he gets to the end, he turns around and starts back up. There is something majestic and powerful in the way he moves. As he starts back up . . .

CUT:

[117] MLS Sara, POV man. George runs up bringing her a chair. She sits down. He runs off. She turns around again, looking for the man . . .

CUT:

[118] LS corridor, POV Sara. The man is nowhere in sight . . .

CUT:

[119] MCU Sara, bewildered. A shadow crosses the frame . . .

MAN'S VOICE
> Why, for God's sake . . . and you haven't even got a book in your hand . . .

GEORGE (o.c.)
Professor . . .

She turns, the shadow turns . . .

CUT:

[120] MWS behind Sara, the man, George in background. George runs forward.

GEORGE

You've met . . .

CUT:

[121] SLIGHT LOW-ANGLE MWS Sara, the man, POV George. He is the same man she met in the library. They stare at each other. George enters frame, back to camera.

GEORGE
(back to camera)

This is my uncle, Professor . . . Professor Rogers, Duke Richards . . . he's Sidney Poitier and Calvin Lockhart rolled into one, he's a pro, Professor . . . I conned him into this . . .

CUT:

[122] REVERSE ANGLE.

GEORGE

You two play a vaudeville team in a silent comedy . . . you come to this terrace to rehearse your routines . . .

(turning around)

Hey, Vicky . . .

(turning back)

They're letting us use the dressing rooms in the theater department. Vicky's made all the costumes . . .

He runs off to get her, calling her name. Sara and Duke look at each other . . .

DUKE

I told you I was out of work . . . now what the hell is your excuse . . .

They both laugh . . .

DISSOLVE:

43 INT. LOBBY OF THEATER – AFTERNOON

[123] MWS George, Sara, and Duke on periphery, back to camera. They are sitting on the steps in an empty lobby. George is explaining the plot.

> **GEORGE**
> . . . you live in an old rooming house, and there isn't much space or light, so on good days you come to the terrace to rehearse, it's there that . . .
> *(he looks at Duke)*
> . . . you meet another woman who tries to compete with . . .
> *(he looks at Sara)*
> . . . you as Duke's partner. She's always there trying to get his attention . . .

[124] MCU Sara, POV George.

> **GEORGE (o.c.)**
> Then one day you have a fight, he goes off to the terrace to rehearse by himself, then you start to feel badly and rush out to meet him, but when you get there he's rehearsing with this other woman . . .

PAN to MCU Duke.

> **GEORGE (o.c.)**
> And in a fit of rage you kill him . . . that's the plot . . .

CUT:

[125] MWS George, Sara, and Duke on periphery—same as 123.

GEORGE
. . . it's a kind of archetypal interpretation of the "Frankie and Johnny" myth . . .

He beams proudly

HOLD . . .

CUT:

44 INT. HALLWAY OF SUMMER HOUSE – EARLY EVENING

[126] MLS phone ringing. Victor comes in carrying a beer and answers it.

VICTOR
Hello . . . where are you . . . you're what . . .

CUT:

45 EXT. PHONE BOOTH ON STREET – EARLY EVENING

[127] Profile MS Sara on the phone.

SARA
It's about five days shooting . . .

CUT:

44A SAME AS 44

[128] MS Victor.

> **VICTOR**
>
> You went into the library . . . what's this acting
> bit, when did you decide that . . .

CUT:

45A SAME AS 45

[129] MS Sara.

> **SARA**
> *(nodding)*
> I just thought it might be . . . fun . . .

CUT:

44B SAME AS 44

[130] MCU Victor.

> **VICTOR**
>
> You're mad . . .

CUT:

45B SAME AS 45

[131] MCU Sara.

> **SARA**
> *(laughing)*
> Is that mad like in crazy or mad furious . . .
> I'm staying at Momma's . . . it's too long
> a drive, we start shooting early in the
> morning . . . I'll call you later . . .

She hangs up, comes out of the booth.

PAN as she starts down the street.

DISSOLVE:

46 INT. SARA'S MOTHER'S APARTMENT – EVENING

[132] LS Sara, Leila, POV inside living room. They are drinking coffee at the dining room table. The living room and dining room are cluttered with antiques and memorabilia. Dinner is over. One has the feeling of a conversation that has been going on for quite a while.

> #### SARA
> *(making circles on the table)*
> It's not a question of if, it's a question of when . . . there have always been women . . .

> #### LEILA
> And the very idea, what does that do to you . . .

> #### SARA
> What do you mean, the very idea . . .

> #### LEILA
> *(illustrating it)*
> That he lifts himself up, then puts himself down inside someone else . . .

Sara starts to laugh uncontrollably . . .

> #### SARA
> You grow more and more outrageous every day . . .

> #### LEILA
> Some women get stuck on that picture, and it drives them crazy . . .

SARA

It's graphic enough . . . I remember once,
when I was about twelve, overhearing a
conversation between you and Wells, and you
kept saying . . . 'take it out, please' . . . and
he kept saying no, he would not, unless you
agreed to such and such . . . and I kept trying
to figure out what you were begging him to
take out . . . was it his stamp collection, the
garbage . . .

They are both laughing almost uncontrollably . . .

DOLLY GENTLY FORWARD . . .

SARA
(after a while)
The actual sex doesn't bother me, Victor has
sex all the time . . . with a new color, a room,
the way the light falls across a building . . .
all that private ecstasy . . . so detached and
free . . .

She shakes her head with wonder . . .

LEILA
(gently)
You envy that . . .

SARA
(nodding)
Why can't I just go . . . lose control . . . fling
myself about or something . . .

LEILA
(laughing)

When I'm acting really well it's like that . . .
I'm gone . . . I lift a finger, turn my head,
smile, hold back a line, let another one fall
with perfect timing . . . I'm in complete
control, yet gone . . . the gods have me, or
Satan . . . somebody does . . . Wells was jealous
of that, once after a show I couldn't seem
to come back, I was perspiring and in kind
of a trance . . . he walked out, never came
backstage again . . .

SARA

I remember you like that . . . you'd come in to
kiss me good night, your eyes were so bright
I used to think you'd been to Heaven and just
came back to tell me good night . . .

They are quiet awhile.

SARA
(after a while)

The only thing I've ever known like that is
sometimes in the middle of writing a paper
my mind suddenly takes this tremendous leap
into a new interpretation of the material . . . I
know I'm right, I know I can prove it . . . my
head starts dancing like crazy . . .

She laughs sadly.

SARA

But that is so cold and so dry, Momma . . .
how did someone like you produce a child
who thinks so very very much . . .

She looks at her mother.

HOLD . . .

CUT:

47 EXT. TERRACE OF UNIVERSITY – LATE MORNING

[133] MLS Sara. She is in costume, like an early vaudeville performer. She is prancing deftly along the parapet wall. Duke enters in top hat and tuxedo. A mime routine follows to the music of "Frankie and Johnny." In the midst of their routine, Duke suddenly turns his head . . .

CUT:

[134] MLS other woman, POV Sara and Duke. She, too, is dressed like a vaudeville performer. She is imitating Sara's every step, making flirtatious gestures at Duke . . .

CUT:

[135] Extreme WS Duke, Sara, other woman. Sara runs through a routine. The minute she finishes the other woman imitates her, making every effort to outshine her performance . . .

CUT:

[136] MCU Sara, watching the other woman. She looks down at Duke . . .

CUT:

[137] MCU Duke, POV Sara. He turns away from looking at the other woman, looks up at her, and smiles.

CUT:

[138] MLS other woman, working hard for attention.

CUT:

[139] MLS Duke, Sara. He takes her hand, she jumps down from the parapet, they walk off across the terrace . . .

HOLD . . .

CUT:

48 EXT. VILLAGE, DOWN BY THE RIVER – LATE AFTERNOON [marked "dropped" by Collins in shooting script]

[140] MWS musician, Puerto Rican, playing the quatro and singing.

PULL BACK: Celia, sitting in the grass, listening to him.

PULL BACK: Lovely-looking older Puerto Rican woman, leaning languidly against a tree, listening to him.

PULL BACK: Victor at his easel, painting the scene.

PULL BACK: Extreme WS, the whole scene, like a painting outside a painting.

HOLD . . .

DISSOLVE:

49 INT. KITCHEN OF SUMMER HOUSE – EVENING

[141] LOW SIDE-ANGLE WS Celia in foreground, Victor in background. Celia is sitting at the table grinding coffee

to go in an espresso pot. Victor is in the background putting
pastries on a tray. They have just finished dinner.

> **VICTOR (o.c.)**
> How come you people don't like dessert?

> **CELIA**
> What . . .

> **VICTOR**
> All you eat for dessert is flan . . . you're just
> like the Chinese . . . the basic food is full of
> variety, the desserts are paltry . . . sherbet, fresh
> pineapple, the old standby fortune cookie . . .

He comes over with a tray of pastries . . .

> **VICTOR**
> The Italians understand the word 'dessert' . . .
> *(pointing)*
> . . . cannolis, napoleons, spumonis, tortonis . . .

> **CELIA**
> They have funny-sounding names, man . . .

> **VICTOR**
> Why do you always say 'man' . . .

> **CELIA**
> It's like a beat . . . the words go da, da, da . . .
> then they need a beat at the end . . . man . . .
> that's very American . . .

They laugh. She hands him the ground coffee.

> **CELIA**
> Here, make the espresso . . .

He goes over to do so . . .

                    VICTOR
          How long have you been here . . .

                    CELIA
          Two years . . . first in New York City, which
          smells bad and is ugly, then up here . . . I'm
          trying now to become an airline hostess so I
          can fly back and forth to Puerto Rico free . . .

                    VICTOR
          You miss it . . .

Celia nods.

                    VICTOR
                (not hearing anything)
          What . . .

                    CELIA
                (nodding)
          I nod my head yes . . . you can't hear that, hard
          as I was nodding . . .

They both laugh. He comes back to the table and sits down,
looking hard at her . . .

HOLD . . .

                                                    CUT:

50 INT. UPSTAIRS STUDIO – NIGHT

[142] LS two shadows dancing. Salsa music playing.

                CELIA (o.c., softly)
          It's three beats . . . one, two, and one . . . one,
          two, and one . . .

DOLLY BACK and PAN gently to LS Victor and Celia dancing. The room is dark, lit only by the full moon.

>   **CELIA**
>   *(softly)*
>   You slow down, man . . . one, two, and
>   one . . . one, two, and one . . .

HOLD . . .

FADE-OUT:

51 EXT. TERRACE OF UNIVERSITY –
AFTERNOON

[143] Profile MCU Duke.

>   **DUKE**
>   How's the final treatise on ecstasy coming . . .

>   **SARA (o.c.)**
>   I've finished the first draft . . .

PAN DOWN and PULL BACK to MS both of them. They are in costume. Sara is sitting, Duke is standing next to her looking out. It appears to be a break in the shooting. We hear George yelling at someone.

>   **GEORGE (o.c.)**
>   Vicky . . . where the hell is Vicky . . .

>   **SARA**
>   How is George your nephew . . .

>   **DUKE**
>   His mother is my sister . . .

> ### SARA
> *(nodding)*
>
> I see . . .

George comes running into frame . . .

> ### GEORGE
>
> I'd like to try and do the tennis scene,
> Professor . . .

> ### DUKE
> *(to Sara)*
>
> Can't he call you something else besides
> 'professor' . . .

> ### SARA
> *(to Duke)*
>
> He could call me Sara . . .

> ### DUKE
> *(laughing)*
>
> And Sara begat Rebekah, who begat Ruth . . .
> you would have some goddamn biblical
> name . . .

> CUT:

[144] MS George; Sara, Duke on periphery. They're still
laughing, George is trying to get a word in edgewise . . .

> ### GEORGE
>
> This is an imaginary tennis scene, ladies and
> sirs . . . you've come up with this funny new
> routine . . . we've got about an hour before we
> lose the light, so I'll skip the explanations, let's
> just shoot the sucker . . .

> (turning around)

Vicky . . .

He moves away into LS.

GEORGE
> (back to camera)

They have to change into these tennis
costumes . . .

DISSOLVE:

52 EXT. DIFFERENT PART OF TERRACE – LATE
AFTERNOON [marked "been replaced" by Collins in
shooting script]

[145] SIDE-ANGLE WS Sara, Duke, film crew. Miming a
game of tennis, their movements choreographed to heighten
the comic effect. The cinematographer is shooting the scene.
George is watching it carefully. There are others milling
around watching or taking care of equipment.

CUT:

[146] MCU Sara. As she returns an imaginary ball the shot
slides into slow motion. She looks pleased, happy, when all
of a sudden she notices something out of the corner of her
eye. Her face grows uneasy . . .

CUT:

[146A] MWS other woman, POV Sara. In a rather dark,
shadowy corner she, too, plays out an imaginary game of
tennis, miming Sara's every gesture . . .

CUT:

[147] MS Duke, POV Sara. He catches the imaginary ball in his top hat, then propels it into the air with the hat and returns it with an imaginary racket . . .

CUT:

[148] SIDE-ANGLE WS Sara, Duke, film crew.

GEORGE
(yelling)
Cut . . . cut . . . we've lost the light . . .

The shot seems to be eclipsed by shadows . . .

FADE-OUT:

53 INT. KITCHEN OF SARA'S MOTHER'S APARTMENT – EVENING

[149] TWO-SHOT, Sara, Leila; favoring Sara.

SARA
(laughing)
I don't try to understand a thing, I just do what I'm told . . .

DOLLY BACK: Sara is standing next to her mother, who is cooking. She is drinking a glass of wine; the phone rings.

SARA
That's Victor . . . I'm not here . . . yes, I am . . .

Leila looks at her as she goes to answer it, exiting frame . . .

LEILA (o.c.)
Hello . . . I'm fine . . . same awful lines . . . no, she's here . . . Sara . . .

Sara puts down her wine, crosses with her mother, who comes back in and goes on with her cooking . . .

HOLD . . . on Leila.

> **SARA (o.c.)**
> Hi . . . fine . . . I don't know, I just do what
> I'm told . . . I play a tragic mulatto . . .

Leila turns around quizzically for a second . . .

CUT:

53A INT. UPSTAIRS STUDIO OF SUMMER HOUSE – LATE EVENING

[149A] MLS Victor on the phone, surrounded by his work.

> **VICTOR**
> *(laughing)*
> Then you're doomed, baby . . . impure blood
> runs in your veins . . .

He paces, as if not quite sure how to say what he wants . . .

> **VICTOR**
> *(aiming for casualness)*
> You planning to come home sometime . . .
> you get a day off, don't you . . . okay, see you
> then . . .

He hangs up, improvises an attitude . . .

HOLD . . .

CUT:

54 EXT. TERRACE OF UNIVERSITY – EARLY AFTERNOON

[150] MOVING SHOT, Sara and Duke in costume.

TRACK BACK as they come toward the camera, making a complete square around the entire terrace.

> **DUKE**
> Are we supposed to talk . . .

> **SARA**
> I don't know . . .

> **DUKE**
> What's the purpose of the scene . . .

> **SARA**
> Something about the relationship between the characters, the space, and the light . . .

> **DUKE**
> Is this what they call an avant-garde movie . . .

> **SARA**
> It might be . . .

> **DUKE**
> How the hell did you ever get hooked into doing this . . .

> **SARA**
> I wanted to . . .

> **DUKE**
> Why . . .

> **SARA**
> It's not abstract . . .

> **DUKE**
> What does that mean . . .

SARA

Everything I do is abstract . . .

DUKE
(understanding)

Papers on ecstasy, that sort of thing . . .

SARA
(nodding)

Yes . . .

DUKE

Do you have a husband?

SARA

Yes . . .

DUKE

Is he abstract . . .

SARA
(laughing)

He used to be an abstract painter, now he
only wants to paint people . . . places . . .
recognizable things . . .

DUKE

He's approaching middle age.

SARA

He's already there . . .

DUKE

No children . . .

Sara shakes her head no . . .

DUKE

Too concrete . . .

She looks at him . . .

SARA
(realizing it)

Maybe . . . I could never imagine it . . .

She almost stops . . .

GEORGE (o.c., yelling)

Keep moving, this sucker is brilliant!

DUKE
(sighing apologetically)

He's just a nephew . . .

SARA

According to the faculty he's very talented . . .

DUKE

He makes me feel old . . . doing this film
makes me feel old . . . when I was his age there
was no such creature called a Negro movie
director . . .

SARA
(laughing)

Would you have been better off as a
minister . . .

DUKE

An annual salary, a built-in audience, the
chance to theologize at will . . .

He shrugs his shoulders.

> **SARA**
> I can't see it . . . are there women . . .

> **GEORGE (o.c., yelling)**
> Now lift her on that parapet, Duke, make
> it a clean sweeping gesture . . . dolly in,
> Ricardo . . .

Duke lifts her gracefully. Camera dollies in . . .

> **DUKE**
> *(while doing so)*
> I have a misanthropic personality, I like to
> read, think, account to no one for my time or
> whereabouts . . .

> **GEORGE (o.c., yelling)**
> I'm sorry I didn't prepare you for this, but
> could you kiss . . . really kiss . . .

They do as they're told.

> **GEORGE (o.c., yelling)**
> Hold it, don't stop . . . dolly in to close-up,
> Ricardo . . .

Camera dollies in . . .

HOLD . . .

CUT:

55 INT. UPSTAIRS STUDIO OF SUMMER HOUSE – LATE AFTERNOON

[151] MLS Carlos, Victor POV through open window. Victor is pacing. Carlos is looking at the paintings and sketches that hang on the wall. Latin music is coming from downstairs.

> **VICTOR**
>
> I'm telling you . . . I feel like I'm about
> twenty-five . . . the most simple specific things
> about painting are finally clear to me . . .

> **CARLOS**
> *(looking at the work)*
>
> It's your rhythm . . .

> **VICTOR**
>
> You can see it . . .

Carlos turns and smiles.

> **CARLOS**
>
> I see it . . . it's lovely . . . theatrical, too, but in
> a genuinely playful way . . .

Victor becomes more animated, pleased at Carlos's
approval . . .

> **VICTOR**
> *(laughing)*
>
> I was always trying to be your kind of
> child . . . abstract, pure . . . I'm not. I'm a pure
> son-of-a-bitch . . . deceptive, vulgar, full of
> dirty tricks . . .

He comes over to the window, moving into MS.

> **VICTOR**
>
> Only stories satisfy a crude mind . . .

He looks out . . .

> **VICTOR**
>
> See the way that bridge is almost eclipsed by
> those willow trees . . .

Carlos comes into frame, looks out, shakes his head . . .

CARLOS
(laughing)
I have no interest in duplicating nature,
man . . . everything I want to paint is up
here . . .

He touches his temple. Off-camera we hear footsteps down
below. They both look down . . .

CUT:

56 EXT. BACK OF SUMMER HOUSE – LATE AFTERNOON

[152] HIGH–ANGLE LS Celia, POV Victor and Carlos. She
is coming across to the house, looking like the least abstract
yet loveliest of paintings. She stops near the door.

HOLD . . .

CUT:

57 INT. DINING ROOM OF SUMMER HOUSE – EVENING

[153] WS Carlos, Victor, Celia, at the dinner table. Carlos
and Celia are chattering away in Spanish. Victor is pouring
wine, carving chicken, serving food. He throws in a Spanish
word every few seconds as a jealous punctuation of their
remarks.

VICTOR
(to Celia)
His father's Spanish . . . his mother is a pure
well-bred American Negro . . .

CELIA
(not understanding)

What . . .

VICTOR

And his father left home when he was six . . .

CARLOS
(laughing)

Four, man . . .
(to Celia)
. . . this is the beginning of one of his jealous
tirades . . .

Victor tries to imitate them talking in Spanish. Celia and
Carlos break out laughing . . .

CARLOS
(laughing)

Victor was raised by a possessive mother who
felt he should never be left out of anything . . .

Off-camera we hear a car pull up, a door slam, then
footsteps. Victor gets up . . .

VICTOR

That must be Sara . . .

SARA (o.c.)

Victor . . .

She comes to the doorway, followed by Duke . . .

CUT:

[154] MCU Victor, POV doorway, turning around. A really
strange expression takes over his face.

> ### SARA (o.c.)
> Hi . . .

> ### VICTOR
> *(nodding)*
> Hello hello . . .

CUT:

[155] WS whole group. Sara, seeing Carlos, leaves the doorway and runs over to hug him . . .

> ### SARA
> Carlos . . . what a long time it's been . . .

> ### CARLOS
> It's good to see you, Sara . . .

> ### SARA
> *(she nods to Celia)*
> Celia . . . this is a real party . . . this is Duke Richards, everybody, we're working in the movie together . . .

She designates everyone . . .

> ### SARA
> Duke, this is Carlos, an old family friend, and that's Celia, a new family friend, and that's Victor . . .

Duke nods to everyone, everyone nods to Duke . . .

> ### SARA
> *(looking at the table)*
> Let me get two more place settings. Sit down, Duke . . .

Victor shows him a seat . . .

CUT:

[156] MS Carlos, Duke sitting down opposite him.

> ### CARLOS
> *(to Duke)*
> Did you play in a movie called *Tenth Street Exteriors* . . .

PAN to MS Duke.

> ### DUKE
> That's right . . .

> ### CARLOS (o.c.)
> I remember you well, man, you were wonderful in that . . .

> ### DUKE
> Thank you very much . . .

Sara crosses behind him, putting down a plate and silverware, then crosses to a seat . . .

CUT:

[157] MWS Sara, Duke, Carlos, Celia, POV Victor. Sara sitting down.

> ### SARA
> *(with exaggerated joviality)*
> We can have a real party . . .

She smiles at everyone . . .

HOLD . . .

DISSOLVE:

58 INT. LIVING ROOM OF SUMMER HOUSE – LATE AT NIGHT

[158] SIDE-ANGLE WS Celia, Carlos, dancing, laughing, wildly and with pleasure. Duke and Sara are in the background, dancing in a more gentle fashion. Victor crosses into frame, dancing by himself but in obvious pursuit of attention.

VICTOR
(goading Carlos)
Hey hey hey . . . the silent purist has a touch of lechery in his bones . . .

Carlos looks at him suspiciously but keeps on dancing. Victor begins to dance beside them for a while, then dances away, grabbing Sara onto the center of the floor, pushing Celia and Carlos almost out of frame. They dance uneasily together . . .

VICTOR
I always forget you can't dance . . . the basic rhythm escapes you.

He walks away from her, grabs Celia from Carlos.

CELIA
Hey, man.

CARLOS
This is uncalled for, man, what kind of behavior is this . . .

VICTOR
(laughing)
I resent your Latin ancestry, I'd like to express
that resentment openly . . .

CELIA
(pulling back)
Leave me out of it, man . . .
She distances herself, starts to dance by herself.

CELIA
(dancing all the time)
You come to a party, man, people dance, they
fool around, none of this bullshit about who
can dance with who what when and where,
that's not dancing . . . that's no party, man . . .

Duke breaks out laughing . . .

DUKE
(laughing)
That's very well put . . .

VICTOR
(turning to him)
What do you think this is . . . a
performance . . . a little cinematic moment . . .

CARLOS
Hey, my man . . .

VICTOR
Hey, man, my man. I mean, man, what's with
you, man . . . what's the scene about, my man,
my man . . .

DUKE
This is getting ridiculous, man . . .

Celia laughs out loud . . .

CUT:

[159] MWS Celia, POV everybody.

CELIA
That's very good, that's like dancing . . . man,
man, man . . . you say that enough times you
can't stop, you just go 'I don't know, man' . . .
and 'this is how it goes, man,' and 'I don't even
know what's happening, man' . . .

Duke laughs out loud . . .

CUT:

[160] MWS Duke, POV everybody.

DUKE
That's really well put and very true, there is
a cold but funny humor there . . . about the
rhythm of speech and how it defines the truth
far more deeply than the words we attempt to
say . . .

VICTOR (o.c.)
What the fuck is he talking about . . .

CUT:

[161] MWS Victor, Sara on periphery of frame.

VICTOR
(to Sara)
Leave it to you to stumble into some goddamn academic actor . . . what do you two do on-screen . . . read from Plato's *Republic* . . .

The room grows silent . . .

CUT:

[162] WS everybody looking at Victor, who, feeling his power, begins to execute some private, irreverent dance . . .

HOLD . . .

DISSOLVE:

59 EXT. POND OR LAKE NEAR SUMMER HOUSE – NIGHT

[163] LOW-ANGLE MLS Victor, in silhouette, nude.

VICTOR
I gotta do this quickly, or I'll freeze my ass off . . .

He races forward.

PAN to follow him, as he dives into the water.

VICTOR
(surfacing)
God, it's cold . . .

Off-camera the others laugh . . .

PAN and DOLLY BACK to Sara, Carlos, Duke, Celia, sitting around a fire, laughing . . .

CARLOS
(getting up)
This is too irresistible . . . takes me back to
the summers I spent with my father in Puerto
Rico . . .

He begins to undress, starts speaking in Spanish to Celia
about Puerto Rico. They both laugh. She gets up, starts to
run forward . . .

CELIA
I go in, but just like I am . . .

PAN as she runs forward, followed by Carlos in his
underwear. She goes right in with all her clothes. He follows
behind her, laughing and chattering away . . .

PAN back to MS Sara and Duke.

SARA
(shivering, laughing)
I hate water . . . I feel like I'm drowning in the
bathtub . . .

Duke laughs. They watch . . .

CUT:

[164] MWS Carlos, Victor, Celia, POV Duke and Sara,
fooling around in the water. After a while Celia runs out,
stands on the shore shivering . . .

SARA (o.c.)
I'll get you some clothes . . .

She crosses into frame, runs off down the beach. Victor
sneaks up behind Celia, lifts her over his shoulder, dives
back in the water with her . . .

CUT:

[165] MWS Duke, watching. All of a sudden he laughs, begins to slip off his shirt.

DUKE
(laughing to himself)
It's true . . . it is irresistible . . .

He runs out of frame, we hear him dive forward into the water, laughing . . .

[166] MLS Sara, POV water, coming across the field carrying some clothes . . .

CUT:

[167] MWS Victor, Celia, Duke, and Carlos on periphery, POV Sara. Celia struggles playfully out of the water. Victor takes her by the hand to help her. They go toward the fire. Victor begins to unzip a sleeping bag.

VICTOR
You should get in here until Sara comes back . . .

She slips down inside the sleeping bag, shivering. Victor, on a sudden impulse, starts climbing in beside her . . .

CELIA
What are you doing . . .

He is halfway inside the bag by now, they start rolling around—Victor laughing, Celia getting angry . . .

CELIA
Why you think this is a funny moment, this is no funny moment . . .

CUT:

[168] LOW-ANGLE MS Celia, Victor, rolling almost directly into the camera.

TILT UP to MCU Sara, as she lowers herself down, almost on top of them, and throws her robe over Victor's face . . .

> **SARA**
> You don't go around taking that thing out in front of me . . .

CUT:

[169] SIDE-ANGLE MS three of them. Sara is pulling the sleeping bag down from both of them . . .

> **SARA**
> (furious)
> That's uncalled for, for you to fling all your little private ecstasies in my face . . .

Celia rolls out of frame . . .

> **VICTOR**
> (yelling)
> You're not teaching a class, don't talk to me like you were delivering a lecture . . .

DOLLY FORWARD to MCU Sara, Victor.

> **SARA**
> (forcing herself)
> Don't fuck around then . . . don't take that giant dick of yours out and fling it willy-nilly here and there like it was artistic . . . pointing it at trees, and lakes, and women . . . like it was some artsy-craftsy paintbrush . . .

(beside herself)
I got nothing to take out, goddamn it . . .
that's what's uneven, that I got nothing to take
out!

They stare at each other . . .

CUT:

[170] WS everybody. Sara turns and walks away, Duke
remains in the water looking after her, Celia starts off across
the field, Carlos runs over, begins walking beside her, Victor
remains where he is . . .

HOLD . . .

CUT:

[171] LS Sara, walking back across the field.

HOLD . . .

FADE-OUT:

60 EXT. PHONE BOOTH NEAR UNIVERSITY – LATE MORNING

[172] MCU Sara on the phone, talking already . . .

SARA
(upset, but laughing)
I'm on shaky ground . . .

CUT:

61 INT. SARA'S MOTHER'S APARTMENT – LATE MORNING

[173] MCU Leila.

> **LEILA**
> That's not the kind of feeling you'd like . . .

CUT:

60A SAME AS 60

[174] MCU Sara.

> **SARA**
> Order . . . that's what Victor loves about me,
> that there's no chaos anywhere . . .

CUT:

61A SAME AS 61

[175] MCU Leila.

> **LEILA**
> *(gently moved)*
> It's a quality in you that even I admit to
> counting on . . .

She waits . . .

CUT:

60B SAME AS 60

[176] MS Sara.

> **SARA**
> Then maybe I should marry some nice
> conservative man, have children . . .

CUT:

61B SAME AS 61

[177] MCU Leila. She doesn't say a word, has no idea, in fact, what to say . . .

CUT:

60C SAME AS 60

[178] MLS Sara.

SARA
(confused)

Momma . . .

HOLD . . .

DISSOLVE:

62 EXT. TERRACE OF UNIVERSITY – EARLY AFTERNOON

[179] MCU Sara—TRAVELING SHOT. She is in makeup and costume, walking toward the camera.

DOLLY BACK as she moves forward with a kind of light eagerness. Off-camera George is directing her performance . . .

GEORGE (o.c.)

. . . you don't sense anything's wrong, you've just come to apologize, you've even got a great idea for a new routine, when all of a sudden you see them . . .

Sara stops, her expression changes . . .

CUT:

63 EXT. STREET NEAR UNIVERSITY – EARLY AFTERNOON

[180] LS Victor's car. It pulls into a space and parks. Victor gets out, walks across into one of the buildings . . .

CUT:

64 EXT. TERRACE OF UNIVERSITY – EARLY AFTERNOON

[181] LS Duke, other woman, George, POV behind student cinematographer. Duke and the other woman are practicing a routine. George is directing their performance.

>   **GEORGE**
> . . . lift her up, Johnnie, same sweeping gesture
> you used with Frankie, her seduction has paid
> off . . .

Sara enters frame . . .

CUT:

[182] LS Victor, POV film crew. He emerges onto the terrace, looks around, crosses toward the film set . . .

CUT:

[183] MS Sara.

>   **GEORGE (o.c.)**
> Okay, Frankie . . . raise the gun . . .

She raises the gun slowly . . .

>   **GEORGE (o.c.)**
> Take your time, and when it feels right, blow
> him away . . .

Sara fires . . .

CUT:

[184] MS Victor in shock . . .

CUT:

[185] MLS Duke, other woman, POV Sara. The other woman falls out of frame, Duke falls forward in slow mime-like fashion.

HOLD . . .

CUT:

[186] MCU Sara. Like a consummate performer, her face is now distraught, wet with grief . . .

HOLD . . .

CUT:

[187] MS Victor, other persons on periphery, still shocked, but added to that is surprise at her performance . . .

HOLD . . .

CUT:

[188] HIGH-ANGLE WS, whole scene. No one moves . . .

HOLD . . .

THE END

CAST CREDITS

Sara	Seret Scott
Victor	Bill Gunn
Duke	Duane Jones
Mother	Billie Allen
George	Gary Bolling
Carlos	Norberto Kerner
Celia	Maritza Rivera
Male student in class	Zachary Minar
Other students in class	Anthony McGowan, Darryl Reilly, Joe Garcia
Man on radio	Clarence Branch Jr.
Female student in office	Maureen Grady
Real estate agent	Deborah Tirelli
Librarian	Marjorie Spring
Celia's mother	Hilda Vargas
Gypsy	Rose Zito
Student cameraman	Joseph B. Vasquez
Nelly Bly	Michelle Mais
Students in class	David Bryan, Aaron Burks, Gerald Burks, Antonio deCabellero-Marrero, Joseph Chan, Al Fletchman, Reginald S. Gant, Ray Ray Gonzales, Milton Emanuel Greer, Gregory Govan, Maben Hugues, Joe Hunt, Julius Johnson, Chauncey Jones, Percell Knight, Marc G. Manigault Jr., Patrick Mathieu, Cornell McGrue, Rodney Nugent, Russell K. Parker, Janus Adams Roach, Stephen M. Rooks, Robert Smith, Karma Omowale Stanley, Rodney Thompson, Andre

	J. Washington, Cedric J. Washington, Len Winfield
Village women	June Corey, Maureen Kocot, Nellie Nieves, Alvia Wardlaw
Girl in library	Stella Hughes
Man on porch	Mike Prestipino
Student crew	Radar Long III, Andre Martin

PRODUCTION CREDITS

Written and directed by Kathleen Collins
Coproduced by Kathleen Collins and Ronald K. Gray
Editing: Ronald K. Gray and Kathleen Collins
Choreography: Pepsi Bethel
Music: Michael D. Minard
  "Love Does Her Thing," Music and Lyrics by Michael
    D. Minard, Sung by Frankie Diaz
  "Sabor a Conga" by Los Patines

FIRST WEEK'S CREW

Production Manager	Cheryl Hill
Unit Managers	Audreen Ballard, David Ticotin
Director's Assistant	Janus Adams Roach
Costumes	Lamont Foreman
Dresser	Rodney Nugent
Camera Assistant	Margot Peters
Head Gaffer	Vincente Galindez
Gaffers	Joseph Chan, Joseph Zulkowsky, Leonard Rodriguez
Continuity/Stills	Lou Draper
Sound	Shi Sun
Props/Set Dresser	Radar Long III

Production Assistants	Kim Gaskins, Lonzo Green, Anthony McGowan, Joseph B. Vasquez, Francisco Villar, Rebecca Williams
Production Secretary	Kathe Sandler

LAST THREE WEEKS

Production Coordinator	Radar Long III
Sound	Shi Sun, Radar Long III, Billie Jackson
Camera Assistants	Kathleen Collins, Adrian Best
Gaffers	Gary Bolling, Radar Long III, Joseph Zulkowsky
Production Assistant	Anthony McGowan
Victor's Paintings	Robert E. Kane, George Norris
Carlos's Paintings	Jack Witten
Installations	Jorge Rodriguez, Charles Abramson
Musicians	John Ballestros, James Byars, Chris Berg, Jack DiPietro, James McLoryd, Michael Minard, Jim West, Daniel Wilensky

Running time: 86 minutes; 16mm; color.

TELL THE WORLD THIS BOOK WAS

GOOD   BAD   SO-SO

A NOTE ABOUT THE AUTHOR

Writer, director, teacher, independent filmmaker Kathleen Conwell Collins Prettyman was born on March 18, 1942, in Jersey City, New Jersey. She attended Skidmore College (B.A. in Philosophy and Religion) and later did graduate work in France, where she studied French literature and cinema (M.A., Ph.D., Middlebury Graduate School of French). She worked from 1967 to 1974 as a film editor for NET (*American Dream Machine, Black Journal, The 51st State*), USIA, the BBC, Craven Films, Bill Jersey Productions, John Carter Associates, William Greaves Productions, and the New Lafayette Theatre. From 1974 until her death in 1988 she served on the faculty of the Theatre Arts Department, City College, New York, where she taught courses in directing for film, scriptwriting, editing, theory and aesthetics of cinema, and 8mm and 16mm camera techniques.

In 1971, before she started teaching at City College, she completed a film script (*Women, Sisters, and Friends*) and tried to raise the funds to produce it. But no one wanted to give a black woman the money to direct and produce a film. It was her students, particularly Ronald Gray, who later urged her to take up the cause again. With $5,000 from friends and lab credit, she and Gray undertook the making of *The Cruz Brothers and Miss Malloy* (1980), which Collins adapted from a Henry Roth novel. Over the next two years she wrote and directed *Losing Ground,* which was completed by 1982.

Making two films, one feature length, and teaching were

not all that occupied Collins during the two decades before her death. Writing was the central focus of her creative life: she completed six plays, all of which were produced or published; four screenplays; numerous short stories; and a novel. Her reputation as an extraordinarily gifted artist-teacher grew with each new work and each new student.

Collins's sensibility was unique. She never apologized for or explained why she made a film about three Puerto Rican brothers and an old Irish woman, from a work by a Jewish author, *The Cruze Brothers* from *The Cruze Chronicle: A Novel of Adventure and Close Calls*; nor did she feel it worthwhile to discuss the fact that ghetto poverty was absent from *Losing Ground*. Until she read the works of Lorraine Hansberry, to which she was introduced by her good friend, filmmaker Haile Gerima, she never felt connected to another artist. In an interview with David Nicholson (1986), she explained what Hansberry meant to her: "A lot of her preoccupations are my preoccupations. She had a really incredible sense of life that fascinates me; anything in life was accessible for her to write about, instead of feeling the black experience was the only experience she could write about. And it was that breadth of vision that I have always sensed was ultimately my vision" (*Black Film Review*).

A NOTE ABOUT THE EDITOR

Nina Lorez Collins is the executor of her mother's literary estate. She is a graduate of Barnard College, earned a master's degree from Columbia in the field of narrative medicine, has a professional background in book publishing, and is the author of *What Would Virginia Woolf Do?: And Other Questions I Ask Myself as I Attempt to Age Without Apology.*